OldEarth

NEB ENCOUNTER

By A. K. Frailey

Hardcover Edition

Cover design: A.K. Frailey and James Hrkach
Photo credit of head: Галина Саква

ISBN of Hardcover: 979-8-9861803-8-0

The Writings of A. K. Frailey

Books for the Mind and Spirit

https://akfrailey.com/

Contact

akfrailey@yahoo.com

Historical Science Fiction Novels

OldEarth ARAM Encounter

OldEarth Ishtar Encounter

OldEarth Neb Encounter

OldEarth Georgios Encounter

OldEarth Melchior Encounter

Science Fiction Novels

Homestead

Last of Her Kind

Newearth Justine Awakens

Newearth A Hero's Crime

Short Stories

It Might Have Been—
And Other Short Stories 2nd Edition

One Day at a Time and Other Stories

Encounter Science Fiction
Short Stories & Novella 2nd Edition

Inspirational Non-Fiction

My Road Goes Ever On—Spiritual Being, Human Journey 2nd Edition

My Road Goes Ever On—A Timeless Journey

The Road Goes Ever On—A Christian Journey Through The Lord of the Rings

Children's Book

The Adventures of Tally-Ho

Poetry

Hope's Embrace & Other Poems 2nd Edition

**Audible Versions Now Available.
Check book details on Amazon
for current listings.**

CHAPTER ONE

—GRASSLANDS—

FOR THOSE WHO COME AFTER

Gizah stepped outside her home into the glaring sun, balancing a food tray, two bowls, and a carafe of wine in her arms. A long yellow dress with wide, fringed sleeves draped her pregnant figure as she stopped before a wooden table built onto the exterior wall. Laying the tray laden with boiled fish, bread, and fruit next to the carafe, she tilted her head and smiled at her handiwork. A shout in the distance turned her gaze.

Her husband worked alongside five other men in the north field, a band holding back his long black hair and sweat gleaming across his shoulders. Amin hunched over the golden wheat and cut the stalks with a swift, steady hand. He called to another man and wiped his brow. Laughter erupted from the group.

Gizah grinned as a picture of her father Aram filled her mind. Aram and Amin were so alike, strong men who ruled their clans with skill and wisdom—yet so bewildered by their own souls. An ache swelled somewhere deep inside. She clasped her chest and shook her head to drive away the sense of loss. Aram had been a gentle father and a wise friend, and though years had passed since his death, still she longed for his presence.

Glorious sunshine cascaded over the undulating grasslands of their village, and a warm breeze stirred the distant line of river trees. Insects buzzed in late summer activity, and birds chirped and cooed their end-of-the-season songs.

Inhaling a cleansing breath, Gizah blinked away old

memories and tried to rejoice in the glorious setting. She rubbed her rounded belly and smiled at her husband, but a memory rose and shadowed her mood. Her lips moved in silent rhythm as she repeated the names she and Amin had discussed the night before: Neb, Enosh, Kenan, Madai…

She frowned. As distantly related clan members, she and her husband shared a long history, yet she knew little of their actual family ties. Last night, they had discussed baby names, and Amin had grown restless, abrupt even, his mood darkening with every reference to his family history.

She shaded her eyes and followed Amin's muscled arms as he cut great swaths of grain. She bit her lip.

Though the clan had often recited their lineage from long past into present day in tales, poems, sagas, and recitations, Amin would not relate his lineage to her. In taciturn moodiness, he had curled up on their pallet and fallen into a disturbed sleep. When he began thrashing and crying aloud, she awoke, afraid that invaders were at the door. Once she realized that Amin was dreaming, she shook him, but the nightmare continued. In fright, she splashed water on his face.

After spluttering his indignity, Amin calmed down, but the terrifying images returned even before his wide-awake eyes. He sat wide-eyed and shivering, babbling about horrors she could little comprehend.

As she listened, Gizah had grown afraid. What was this heritage that threatened to invade their present world? Who were these figures from long ago that formed so much dark legend?

Gizah sighed and turned from her recent memories to her home. Then she considered the tray at her fingertips. The midday meal lay ready, and her expanding stomach rumbled. She looked up and caught Amin's eye.

He smiled and waved.

Gizah waved back.

With a call and a gesture to his men, Amin started home.

Gizah poured a measure of wine into the bowls, clasped her hands, and waited.

Amin trudged to the house and flopped down on a wooden bench shaded by a thatched overhang. "I'm as weary as a rabbit after a long chase."

Gizah grinned and wiped a stray lock of hair from his face. "Well, it's your own fault. Unlike the rabbit, you could've stayed abed a bit longer."

Averting his gaze, Amin tore off a plump hunk of fish and stacked it on a piece of bread. "Not after last night. I couldn't sleep." He bit into the fish and bread and gripped the wine bowl with the other hand.

A snort escaped, but Gizah held a laugh in check. "You'll choke eating so fast. Slow down."

Chewing with dramatic emphasis, Amin stared at his wife as if in challenge. After a loud gulping swallow, he slurped the last of the wine and swiped a dribble on his chin with the back of his hand.

Leaning on the table, Gizah grinned and shook her head. "You're such a child."

Amin nodded through a shrug and continued to eat. He glanced up. "Aren't you hungry?"

Gazing across the field, Gizah absently tore off a piece of bread and pinched a morsel of fish. She chewed her bite-sized pieces meditatively, her gaze unfocused. After a dainty sip, she slipped onto the bench.

Amin leaned against the wattle and daub wall, closing his eyes.

She poked him in the shoulder. "Wake up. We need to talk."

With a groan, Amin waved her away, his eyes still closed.

"Amin!"

His eyes opened with forced effort. He blew air between his teeth. “You wanted me to rest.”

“This morning I wanted you to rest. Now I want you to talk.”

Amin straightened with a groan.

A twist in her middle sent anxiety shooting through Gizah’s body. “You need to explain what happened. What…or who…sent you into nightmares?”

Amin slid off the bench and paced away. “I don’t know. I’ve only heard snatches of our family history.” He glanced at his wife. “Did Aram tell you anything?”

Gizah shook her head. “A little, but he didn’t like to talk about the past.”

Amin sighed and returned to his seat clapping his hands on his thighs. “Those names have a terrible history…a curse. We can’t pass them on to our children.”

“A curse?” Gizah stared ahead, her shoulders slumping as weariness enveloped her. “We need to know. We must ask—”

“We can’t! Neb nearly drove my father mad. I can’t ask him to revisit a past that could have destroyed him. Besides, he’s old—”

Rising, Gizah stared at her husband. “Our child won’t live haunted by fear! We must face our past if we ever hope for a future.” She rubbed her belly. “Besides, our ancestors don’t decide our destiny. In his love for you, Ishtar crossed barren deserts and jumped through fire. I’m sure he’ll share his family history to bring us peace.” She shrugged. “I would.”

Taking Gizah’s hand, Amin caressed her fingers. “Of that, I have no doubt.”

~~~
~~~

Ishtar sat in the shade outside his home and relished a soft evening breeze. Clouds scraped over the mountains in the west, but he didn't mind. The harvest was nearly in, and the long-awaited rain would refresh the depleted rivers and ponds.

A stone's throw away, Amin and Gizah approached with sober faces. He smiled indulgently and feasted his eyes on Gizah's expanding middle. A familiar thrill raced over his skin. *Amin will make a wonderful father…and I'll be a grand—* He swallowed the joyful thought as Amin stopped before him, grim-faced.

"Father."

Ishtar stood and beckoned them inside.

As the couple sat on pallets in the corner of the room, Ishtar placed twigs on a smoldering fire in the hearth. He fanned the flames, which brightened the room. After pouring wine into small bowls and placing them before the couple, he brought out a tray heaped with nuts, figs, and dates.

Gizah accepted the fruit with graciousness, but Amin waved the offering away. "Father, we've been talking..."

Amused though perplexed, Ishtar settled cross-legged across from them, chewing languidly on a fig. He leaned back and grinned. "I would hope so."

Gizah laid her hand on Amin's knee. "Amin has been having nightmares."

Ishtar's smile vanished as he straightened. "About what?"

Amin climbed to his feet with a grunt and paced across the room, breaking through swirling smoke. "I can hardly explain. We were discussing names for the baby…and I mentioned those I knew from our history: Neb, of course, though we'd never choose that one. Serug, Athaliah, Madai, Kenan, Enosh—"

Ishtar leaped to his feet, his heart pounding, and nausea

rising from a cauldron in his middle. “You don’t know those people—who they were or what they did.”

Amin swallowed and stared hard at his father. Their gazes locked. “That’s the problem. We don’t know. Not enough.”

Gizah rose and clasped her husband’s hand. “But we should. How can we keep our family traditions alive and remember those worthy of renown if we don’t know who they were and what heroic deeds they accomplished?”

Loath to revisit the past, Ishtar grimaced. “Not all our ancestors were heroic. Some were devilish.” Flashes of memory tore through his mind. Gritting his teeth, he willed himself to remember Matalah’s gentle face, the innocent flock of sheep he tended in the distant hills, and the face of his beloved, departed son. “I don’t know if I can—” He broke off and stepped to the doorway, gulping the cool evening air.

Gizah stepped near and rested her hand on his shoulder. “For the sake of our child—and those who come after—tell us about your great-grandfather, Neb the Great. Do as you have done many times before; tell us a story, but this time, tell us our true heritage. Weave what you learned from others and your own insight. Let Neb’s life be your guide.”

Clasping her hand, Ishtar turned and met Gizah’s imploring eyes. Though their clansmen had never considered her beautiful because of her misshapen hand and slight stoop, Ishtar saw beauty that soared far beyond the earthly realm. He remembered Pele, the slave girl who had saved his entire clan with her daring courage. He glanced at his son, a boy now grown to manhood, who deserved to know his real heritage, no matter how bitter that truth might be.

Ishtar nodded.

CHAPTER TWO

—WOODLANDS—

DESTINED FOR GREATNESS

(THREE GENERATIONS EARLIER)

Neb knew that he was destined for greatness. The first son of a first son who was also a first son. When he was born, his mother, Meshullemeth, declared that he would rule far and wide and great would be his name. She repeated this prophetic declaration to him on more than one occasion and then proceeded to raise Neb as a ruthless despot who would let nothing get in the way of his all-consuming desire to rule everything—and everyone.

Standing with his hands clenched on his hips, Neb stared at a shivering servant bowing before him on the floor of his tent. He scowled in disgust. Even at the tender age of eight, he knew when he had been defied. He puffed his cheeks in raging indignation.

The servant, a mere boy himself wearing only a scanty tunic, trembled in clear expectation of the accustomed blows that Neb was known to hurl against anyone guilty of a clumsy mistake or a thoughtless word.

Neb glared at his mother who stood to the side. "I want him thrown off a cliff or speared through the chest!"

Meshullemeth glanced from the servant to her son, one eyebrow lifted, accenting her long face and sharp features. She pursed her lips. "Seems a waste…he's young enough to be useful for years to come."

"I don't care!" Neb stomped to the wall of his tent and dragged his spear forward. With blind fury propelling his every move, he grabbed the hapless slave, and shoved him through the open doorway. "Get out there where I can line you up properly."

Meshullemeth followed, clucking her tongue.

His head down, the slave dragged himself across the compound until Neb called a halt.

Neb shoved the boy against the wide girth of an ancient tree. "Stand still!"

The servant wailed as he watched Neb take a giant step backward, his gaze fixed, aiming the spear. "Please! Master, it wasn't my fault. I didn't know—"

Gray-haired and slump-shouldered, Hezeki dressed in a fine robe and soft leggings trotted near, his face reddening with each step. "Neb? What are you doing?"

Scowling, Neb faced his father. "I'm going to kill this worthless—"

Meshullemeth's eyes darted from husband to son, her lips pursed.

With surprising agility, Hezeki swooped forward and plucked the spear from his son's grasp. "Foolish boy! An infant, indeed, if you think you can kill an innocent slave—"

Spit flew as Neb's wrath exploded. "Innocent? He broke my best knife!"

Hezeki glanced at the trembling slave whose eyes implored mercy. Hezeki turned to his son and pointed the spear at Neb's chest. "You must learn patience and understanding. Anyone can make a mistake. Even you!" Without another word, the old man beckoned the teary-eyed slave forward. "Go home and get the mid-day meal ready."

The day's entertainment over, Meshullemeth shrugged and, with a sly wink at her son, meandered away.

Hezeki cleared his throat. "I won't speak of this again. You can kill anything in the forest, hunt to your heart's desire, but you must never kill a human being except in uttermost need."

Neb turned his piercing black eyes from the retreating slave to his mother's back and then shifted his gaze to his father. His spine stiff and his teeth clenched, he muttered under his breath, "Uttermost need."

~~~

Neb grew like a sapling, wiry and strong like his father, never as thick or robust as his mother. When Meshullemeth gave birth to two strapping boys three years apart and eventually to a beautiful daughter, he paid them little mind. As long as his mother's attention stayed focused on him, he was satisfied.

On a bright day in the southern hills with no hint of a breeze, Neb, grown to his full stature, went into the wild to seek game for his family. Other hunters in the clan could do the job as well, but rumors spread near and wide that a bear of enormous size roamed the hills to the south.

Long desiring a noteworthy prize to bring home to his people, Neb wandered the woods, scanned tree trunks for claw marks, and searched the ground for scats, crushed stems, or bits of victims scattered among the ferns and saplings. When he came upon promising signs, he slowed his steps through the undergrowth.

Late in the day, as sweat dripped down the side of his face, he stopped at the sound of rustling in the distance. He scanned the forest and saw the brown humping form of a great she-bear. It padded slowly, stopping and snuffling through the bracken with a small form shadowing her left side. Neb smiled. Mother bears with cubs were hard to kill. Finally, a feat worthy of his skill.

Keeping his scent downwind, he stealthily followed, and when he came upon the mother from the right side, he
~~~

readied his spear. In his mind, he could hear his father's voice. "Never attack a dangerous animal alone. Always keep a clear path to escape." Neb chuckled at the memory. The bear, not he, would long for escape.

With an upturned nose, the bear stopped and sniffed the air. Suddenly, she swiveled around and rose on her back legs to her full height, a low growl emanating from her chest. Her black eyes glittered in alarm and fury.

Neb's heart exalted. "Frightened? Ah! Fight as you wish, but I'll spill your blood and take your cub for my own." He approached steadily, lifting his spear, and balancing his weight with each step. After bracing himself and leaning back, he gave a mighty grunt and threw, using every bit of his muscled strength.

The spear arced through the air and then…fell short…landing softly, ignobly, in the ferns.

The bear's growl deepened and grew louder.

In all his years of certain kills and absolute demands, Neb had never been so defied. He had willed his spear into the heart of the beast, and yet it had landed harmlessly before the animal like a pathetic offering. He stood transfixed.

Pure instinct incarnate, the mother bear charged, her muscles rippling. Her thrusting shoulders and grunts throbbed to the rhythm of her fury.

Shock quickly gave way to self-preservation. Neb turned and ran for his life. Branches and thorns tore his skin, nettles pricked his feet, sweat poured down his back, but Neb pressed on, running beyond his strength, even though he feared his heart would burst with the effort. By the time he dropped to the ground in exhaustion, the bear had given up and returned to her young.

Well after dusk, Neb dragged his weary body into his village. Seeing his ripped, bloody clothes and multiple wounds, word quickly spread that a bear had bested Neb.

He slipped into his tent and collapsed on his pallet.

Meshullemeth scurried to his aid, brandishing wet cloths and strong brew. "My poor boy! How could this happen?"

Neb pushed her away. "Leave me alone, woman. I'm resting." He curled on his side and offered his back along with his scorn.

With a huff not unlike the disgruntled bear, Meshullemeth turned away.

Neb closed his eyes, but burning shame scoured his cheeks and intensified the stings across his body.

Heavy footsteps padded near.

Neb squeezed his eyes tighter to shut out the intrusion.

His father spoke into the darkness, undoubtedly with his mother wringing her hands beside him.

"Stupid child, you could've been killed. What made you attack such an opponent, alone, against all wisdom? A mother bear is often beyond the skill of even experienced hunters."

Ignoring the pain searing his skin, Neb turned and rose to his feet. He glared at his father. "I will challenge her again. I'll kill her and take the cub. She will fear me in the end."

In the darkness, Hezeki chuckled. "And who will undertake to support you in such a challenge? Not I or any of my men. We have more sense. There are many fine animals that may be had at half the risk. We are not so desperate for food as you seem to think."

Neb's gaze fixed on his father. "It's not her flesh I wish to consume but her life."

Hezeki snorted. "You, of all my children, are the most senseless. Enosh and Kenan would never attempt such a thing. Even Eva, a little girl, knows better."

Meshullemeth stood by, watching the exchange between father and son, her eyes narrowed.

With a wave of dismissal, Neb grabbed his pillow and closed his eyes, shutting out his parents.

Grunting in disgust, Hezeki left. His distant voice soon mingled with anxious villagers who shouted questions, asking about Neb's condition, but Hezeki did not answer.

Meshullemeth laid her hand upon her son's head and stroked his hair. "You need more than your father or I can give you. A power we do not possess."

Turning, Neb opened his eyes, and for a moment, he stared at his mother feeling like an infant needing comfort. But the glittering fury of the she-bear blackened out every other thought. He clenched his hands. "Truly, you cannot give me what I need."

Exhaling a long sigh, Meshullemeth rose and stepped away. "I will find someone who can."

His mother's footsteps padded out the door, and at long last, Neb let exhaustion have its way with him…

In the dark of night, a howl rose with the wind. Neb stirred.

A hulking bear rose before him, large and menacing, opening her mouth in a bellowing roar.

Neb turned to run, but he tripped and fell backward. Suddenly, a frenzy of hate enveloped him. He sprang to his feet and faced the wild animal that towered over him. Gripping his spear, his gaze met hers.

The great hulking beast growled in human speech. "Honor me, and I will spare you."

In response, Neb braced himself and thrust with every bit of his strength. This time, his spear struck true.

CHAPTER THREE

—WOODLANDS—

PERFECT VENGEANCE

(TEN YEARS LATER)

Enosh watched his younger brother, Kenan, with fascinated interest. His little brother had been practicing with a man-sized spear for months now, and though still growing, he had mastered it with respectable skill. His unusual height gave him an advantage, for he could aim at a distant goal and leverage his weight for greater strength. Enosh grinned at the thought of his little brother intimidating even seasoned warriors.

Leaning against a tree, Enosh rubbed his bearded jaw as he observed the determined care his brother took of his stance and the power behind each throw. Clearly, in his preoccupation with staying out of Neb's way, he had missed the developing potential of his little brother.

As he glanced around the quiet village, Enosh sighed. Life was hard in the southern hills of late. The past few years had seen little rain, and animals were scarce. Raiders constantly threatened, and illness plagued young and old alike.

Hezeki strode by with his gaze down, his shoulders stooped, and his steps slow and unsteady. One leg had swelled alarmingly of late, shifting his normal stride to a halting limp.

On impulse, Enosh ran forward and intercepted him.

Hezeki peered up, blinking. After a startled grunt, a smile broke over his face. "Oh, Enosh. It's you. I thought—" He shook his head. "Never mind. You need something?"

Enosh glanced at his brother lining up another throw. "I've been watching Kenan. He's grown strong and able. I thought perhaps I'd begin to train him in earnest." He met his father's gaze and wavered. "That is, if you don't mind. I know he's still young—"

Hezeki squinted in the strong light as he pointed at his youngest son. "Not at all. He's a worthy boy and should be trained. I've neglected him for the cares of the village." He tugged Enosh aside. "You see well enough that I'm growing old, and Neb should rule after me, but—" He bit his lip and peered into the distance. "He's grown too secretive and impossible to control."

Enosh winced and clenched his jaw against a stinging retort.

Hezeki's eyes narrowed, a sly glint twinkled. "But you—you and your brother—as allies could challenge Neb."

Foreboding boiled in Enosh's middle. "We're hardly in a position… And besides, you're still our leader."

Distracted, Hezeki fixed his attention on the horizon. "Neb runs off to gods-know-where and returns cockier and more determined than ever. He wants leadership…soon. Mark my words; he'll try something. He hardly listens to me now." He glanced at his leg and winced. "His mother prowls like a hungry cat—"

A shout caught their attention as a gathering of clansmen lined up to match Kenan's throws. One man hung a bright rag on a tree branch on the other side of the compound. It fluttered in a soft breeze like a bird caught in a snare.

Man after man threw their spears at the target, some nearly hitting it, others flushing as their spears fell short of the mark.

Hezeki laughed and pointed as a fifth man cursed his ill luck. "Couldn't hit a boulder that one, never was a good shot."

Enosh peered at his brother, standing patiently aside as the older men vied for the glory of a perfect throw. He called out and limped closer. "Let Kenan try!"

Kenan's eyes widened, but as he fixed his gaze on his father, he stepped in place.

Hezeki crossed his arms and thrust out his chest, a studied frown replacing his grin.

Kenan arched his shoulders, steadied his footing, fixed his gaze on the cloth, positioned his spear, and threw.

The shaft flew across the compound, tore into the cloth, and pinned it to the ground.

A shout rose from the watching villagers. Women and children clapped their hands and cheered.

Hezeki shuffled forward; a smile spread wide across his face. "Well done, son!" He patted Kenan on the shoulder and pointed to Enosh. "Your bother has offered to attend to your training, and I agree. With you two at my side, I'll never fear the approach of an enemy."

Nodding at respectful murmurs of agreement, Hezeki turned and limped into the village, his gaze now meeting the approving stares of clansmen.

Enosh followed Kenan as the boy retrieved his spear. "I hope you don't mind. I probably should've asked you if you wanted—"

Kenan clasped his spear and snorted. "Of course, I want your help. Need it, more like. I may have aim and strength, but I don't know much about battle or handling an opponent." He yanked the rag away and wiped down the spear point. "Father once mentioned a contest inviting the clans all around. You think I'd be allowed to participate?"

"Don't see why not. After all, there's not a man here who could best you without serious effort, and few put forth the thought and time you have. You'll impress many."

Kenan pursed his lips. "I am not interested in

impressing anyone…" His gaze dropped to the ground. "There's one man I'll never please. My very existence irritates him."

Enosh wrinkled his nose, disgust rising. "Don't let him—"

"No, little brother, don't let *anyone* bother you." Neb stepped around Enosh; a sneer disfiguring his otherwise perfectly balanced features.

Enosh smothered a curse, his face flushing.

Neb pointed at Kenan's spear. "I hear you amazed the clan with your skill and prowess. Let me see." He gestured to indicate a knothole in a distant tree. "Hit that, if you can." A snarl crept across his face. "We'll both try."

Enosh rubbed his mouth to keep from uttering an oath.

Kenan lifted his spear and hesitated, his gaze skipping over Neb to Enosh. "I doubt any man alive can throw that distance."

A smaller knothole, closer but still a respectable target, caught Enosh's eye. He lifted an eyebrow and glanced aside.

Without changing his expression, Kenan nodded. He lined up next to Neb and fixed his gaze on Neb's target. They both lifted their spears and steadied their arms. Neb threw, but his spear fell short, hitting the tree at the base.

In a flash, Kenan threw at the second knothole, hitting it dead center.

Enosh laughed and clapped with thunderous delight.

A responding grin spread wide across Kenan's face.

Neb scowled and retrieved his spear.

Enosh faced his older brother. "Your throw was certainly the farthest, and your aim was good, but I admire Kenan's choice. Far more reasonable to aim for something he could actually hit."

Neb stared at Enosh, turning his back on Kenan. "You like to make sport of me, but a man can't always pick an easy target. A time will come when the impossible must be made possible for your own survival. Don't forget, I am the eldest, and when I give an order, it'll be worth your life to obey it."

Kenan rested his spear on the ground, his knuckles whitening and anxiety lining his eyes.

Enosh shrugged Neb's taunt away as he glanced at his father's figure in the distance. "You may be the eldest son, but you may not be the leader. Many will not follow you. Don't speak of what a life is worth for you care for no man." He laid his hand on Kenan's shoulder, and the two strode away.

~~~

Neb clenched his hands and watched his brothers retreat into the village. The memory of a towering bear flashed before his eyes. The mammoth beast had defeated him the first time, but only because he had not been properly prepared. Months later, he tracked her down and thrust a spear into her chest, though he never found the cub. In his vengeance, he burned the animal carcass so that its spirit could never return to earth. He exiled it, powerless, into the spirit world where it could use neither tooth nor claw again. He savored his vengeance for years.

He would do the same with his brothers—exile their spirits into the world beyond where they would have no power over him. He glanced aside, fixing his gaze on his father's bent back. Disgust rose like bile in his throat.

With a grunt, he turned and headed toward the woods.

A call stopped him in his tracks. He glanced over his shoulder.

Hezeki, with sneering eyes, beckoned his eldest forward.
~~~

Neb clenched his jaw. His father's feeble power still held him—but not for much longer.

CHAPTER FOUR

—WOODLANDS—

FACE YOUR DESTINY

Meshullemeth watched, fascinated, as a gnarled, old woman chanted incantations into the black night.

Men stood in a circle, their eyes glittering while women hovered, shushing their children, and clutching them close.

A dank, earthy smell permeated the air. An owl shrieked.

The crone hunched and cavorted around a blazing fire, her voice dropping into guttural speech, then rising into a screech.

Meshullemeth glanced at an old man, who sat slumped and scowling, cross-legged in the shadows. He had promised that he could contact the forces of nature, only to discredit himself by admitting that the other world was beyond his power to control. Meshullemeth frowned. What had the idiot thought? That she wanted an idle chat with the spirits?

Crackling sparks flew into the air. The old woman's lilting chant halted, and a familiar yet horrible drone rose from the old hag's mouth.

A wraith demanded attention.

Chills ran along Meshullemeth's arms as she sucked in a deep breath. For Neb. She would do anything. She shuddered as the old crone's eyes fixed on her.

Anything?

A cavernous voice echoed into the night. "Certain, you must be, to seek my aid."

Meshullemeth swallowed a lump rising in her throat. She glanced at her son.

With his arms crossed over his muscled chest, Neb stood against an ancient tree, his body shadowed by the black wood.

The voice beckoned, cajoling. "Come forth, Seeker. Face your destiny."

Unfolding his arms, Neb stepped into the light. He squared his shoulders and glared through unwavering eyes.

"What would you have?"

"Power."

"To what end?"

"To rule all that I will."

"And in return?"

"Whatever you wish."

A gloating chuckle turned into screeching madness and fled into the night sky.

The old woman collapsed.

Neb retreated into the shadows.

Disorientated as the crowd dissolved, left only with a slumped figure on the ground, Meshullemeth frowned. She had arranged for the two greatest forces in her world to meet and come to agreement, but she had understood none of their conversation.

She realized with a start that only her son would know what had happened because the old woman never remembered what had occurred once she came out of her spells.

Exhaling a long cleansing breath, Meshullemeth felt a heavy burden fall from her shoulders. Neb would now be assisted by something greater than his mother. She glanced aside.

Neb stood motionless, his gaze fixed on the flames.

Meshullemeth rose and winced at the familiar ache in her feet. Clutching the sorcerer's shoulder, she shook the old hag. "Wake up. It's over. You can go home now."

The slouched figure crumpled like a discarded rag.

Her heart clenched in terror. Meshullemeth crouched low and peered into the wide-open eyes.

They did not waver.

Meshullemeth waved her hands before the crone's face.

Nothing.

A sick foreboding clawed at her insides. "Neb! Come quickly. She's sick, struck dumb, or—"

With marching steps, Neb paced across the compound. Using his foot, he nudged the old woman.

Her body rolled to one side, her flabby arms falling askew, her head tilting at an unnatural angle.

"She's no use now."

Burning nausea caught in Meshullemeth's throat.

Neb waved to two men standing around the fire. "Carry her to her hut and leave her there. She'll wake up eventually."

Meshullemeth tottered forward and clutched her son's arm. "You have what you need, thanks to me." She winced as two men clumsily shifted the woman's body and hauled her away. "You'll remember that, won't you?"

An owl hooted in the distance, and a cat yowled at an unseen threat.

Neb peered down at his mother, his chin a sharp outline against the flickering light. Without another word, he turned and stepped into the darkness.

Meshullemeth shivered and wrapped her arms around her frozen body.

Chapter Five

-Planet Sectine-

Every Intimate Detail

Zuri, wearing his sleek bio-ware armor but without the headgear or heavy boots, meandered along the Sectine City main street with his blond hair fanning over his shoulders and his sandaled feet darkened with their first real tan. He stared at his datapad and stepped aside as a runner padded in his direction.

The jogging Uanyi—a slim youth just over a meter tall with a soft, rubbery exoskeleton, a slim breathing mask fitted over enormous mandibles, and wide eyes bulging from a faintly green face—grinned like an idiot and laughed out loud. He peered over his shoulder and shouted, "Hey, Mechanical Man…you lose some of your parts?"

Ark, a water-born Crestonian, potbellied and wearing his usual white terrestrial bio-suit, loped beside Zuri with his four tentacles swaying at his side. He scowled at the youth, his bulbous eyes growing ever wider, though still not as spectacular as natural Uanyi orbs. He wiggled one tentacle like a snake ready to pounce.

The youth sped away.

After snorting a storm of bubbles through his breathing helm, Ark turned his attention to the Ingot and frowned. "We don't want to be conspicuous, remember?" He grasped Zuri's arm and led him into a busy intersection where a uniformed Uanyi traffic guard waved them across the street with a stoic I'll-be-doing-this-forever expression.

His fingers flying, Zuri tapped another message and scowled. He halted in the middle of the street.

The guard blinked his huge eyes. His chest expanded as if preparing for a serious challenge to his pedestrian authority.

Croaking, Ark tugged Zuri safely across the busy intersection. "What? Trying to get us killed?"

Zuri's attention stayed glued to his datapad. He tapped a third message. He waited and tapped again. Alarm zipped through his synapsis. "She cut me off right in the middle of—" He peered at Ark's frowning face. "Something must've happened…or she's—"

Ark shook his head. "You're obsessed with that Bhuaci. Forget about that shapeshifter and focus on our mission. Think about Teal, Sterling, and all the humanoids who are counting on us—"

With a shake, Zuri pocketed his datapad and chewed his lip, irritation replacing his alarm. "First of all, Kelesta isn't just a Bhuaci shapeshifter, second, Teal is meeting with Queen Tcesni right now, and third, humanity doesn't even know—"

A scream turned their attention.

One of the Sectine buildings appeared to melt; a cascade of dirt and rubble slid to one side like a giant collapsing anthill.

Zuri and Ark raced to the edge of the street and hovered on the periphery as a crowd gathered. The crossing guard scuttled forward and blew a piercing whistle. Sirens across the city responded.

The jogging youth appeared on Zuri's left, his eyes bigger than ever, and clutched the Ingot's shoulder. "Did you see what happened?"

Zuri shook his head. "It just fell apart…your buildings aren't reinforced like—"

"No!" The youth shoved Zuri aside. "It was sabotage, idiot." He stared from Ark to Zuri. "I'd think with your superior bio-ware, you'd see better, but it's obvious you're blind." He stomped away.

Ark swayed on his stiffly booted feet, glaring from the departing Uanyi to his friend. "We're supposed to manage a treaty with these people, but they can't even keep their buildings upright or their tempers in check."

Zuri shrugged. "I always said they were inferior. I don't even know why Sterling wants them as allies. Now the Bhuaci—"

"Stop! If I have to hear one more word about the glorious world of Bhuacs, I'll—"

From the damaged building, medics carried the bodies of a woman and child on stretchers, both partially crushed and clearly dead. The crowd surged forward, exhaling a collective groan.

"You know, I'm still wearing most of my protective bio-ware."

Ark nodded, his somber gaze fixed on the scene. "You want to help?"

His shoulders slumping, Zuri shook his head. "I'd just get in the way." He clasped his hands over his chest. "My heart is pounding like a turbine…" He winced. "I'm going to be sick."

Ark glanced at a spiral building on the top of a high, gray plateau. "Your emotions are getting the better of you. Extremely dangerous, my friend." He gripped Zuri's arm. "We'd better head to Invicta Hall and find out what kind of deal Teal is making—before he gets us into trouble."

A fog settled over Zuri's mind as he lurched forward. "Don't be ridiculous. Teal is sensible. Luxonian and all. *He'll* never be caught off guard."

~~~

Teal swallowed and licked his dry lips. *Oh, God.* In a thirty-year-old muscular male human form, dressed in a
~~~

sleeveless tan shirt, dark blue pants, and black shoes, Teal faced the most exotic, insectoid creature he had ever met in his life. He wiped his brow and scowled at the accumulated sweat. Formally crossing his arms and bowing, he showed proper Uanyi obeisance. "Your Majesty. I was supposed to meet with representative Jasmine, I believe."

On a jewel-studded throne, Tcesni sat with a straight back. Her eyelids lifted a couple of millimeters over her verdant green, almond-shaped eyes. Wearing a multicolored, nearly translucent dress, her form appeared to shimmer in air rippling in the desert heat. An orange glow enveloped her. With a flick of her long-fingered hand, she beckoned. "Jasmine no longer serves the imperial throne. Come closer, Luxonian. I have always wanted to meet one of your kind."

Clearing his throat, Teal started forward.

The closer he came, the more intense her orange silhouette grew.

She lifted her palm, halting his momentum. "Not too close." A tiny smile tugged at the corner of her ruby lips. She slipped off her throne, stretched to her full height—a good meter taller than the average Uanyi—and straightened her high-ridged shoulders.

Forcing his gaze away from the six rounded breasts straining the fabric of her dress on her mid-section, Teal clenched his jaw. *No one told me—*

Tcesni chuckled as she sashayed forward. She stepped around her guest and directed her steps to a wall dispensary. "You thought we were Earth insects, maybe? Laid eggs on a branch somewhere?"

"I've studied your—"

Pulling a tube from the wall, Tcesni offered it to Teal. "Come, take a refreshment. It's a sweet scent. A kind of chewy air…or breathable liquid. Sure to give your exhausted body a much-needed lift."

Accepting the tube, Teal's fingers touched Tcesni's. He flinched.

Tcesni grinned as she placed a second tube to her lips. "Don't be afraid. I allow as much closeness as I want. It's you who must be careful." She took a long drag on the tube, her cheeks caving inward with the effort. Closing her eyes, she suspended her breath.

Teal followed her example but with his eyes open.

Exhaling in a long, sensuous stream, the Uanyi queen opened her eyes and grinned. "I knew you'd keep yours open. Never one to let your guard slip."

The most intoxicating thrill sped through Teal's entire body. His mind expanded as his vision sharpened. Every sense sizzled with brilliant lucidity. He dropped the tube and swayed to a luxurious couch set in a cozy pattern with three other chairs under a dazzling skylight.

Settling on the largest chair padded with plump pillows in a stunning array of colors, Tcesni crossed her legs and laced her fingers over her thorax. She leaned back and sighed. "So tell me…what did you study? Our body structures? Cultural habits? Mating procedures?"

As a sudden nausea swept over him, Teal leaped to his feet. He glanced around, his euphoria devolving into a frantic need to vomit.

Tcesni flicked an elongated finger to a side room. "Over there. But be quick."

Retching his nearly empty stomach into a metallic sink, Teal heaved repeatedly. Then he sighed and washed his face under water streaming from a wall faucet. Sidestepping the water flowing onto the floor and into a central drain, he shuddered and padded to the sitting room. He stood before the queen. "A test?"

Tcesni shrugged. "Not really. No one ever passes. I'm not sure why I bother."

Clenching his jaw to hold down the vestiges of bile, Teal plunked down on the chair opposite. He looked at her through blinking eyes. "I don't understand. I came here with the best of intentions…and you poison me?"

A lilting laugh. Very amused.

Teal fought the desire to turn into a prehistoric bird of prey and devour the insect-woman.

Controlling her giddiness, Tcesni swept a slender chalky white stick off the table and bit off the end. She chewed languidly. "Listen, Luxonian. I know exactly why you're here. You want allies against the Cresta incursions stealing your quaint little playground on Earth."

"It's more than that!" Teal rose unsteadily and paced to a dirt-packed wall with scooped-out shelves. Examples of primitive natural art and exotic plant specimens lined the edge like items for sale at market. He turned and faced the queen of Sectine. "Earth is important…not because we want to own it but to protect it. I have seen with my own eyes the power of a man named Ishtar to turn from a cruel heritage and choose his own destiny. Humans are developing rapidly, and at some point, they might be in a posi—"

"Spare me!" Having nibbled the stick to a nub, Tcesni flicked it aside. She rose, and once again, her rounded breasts bulged.

Teal looked away.

Scampering forward, the Uanyi Queen plucked his arm and tugged him close. "Look at me, Luxonian. I'm insectoid and mammalian. Nothing you've ever encountered before. I give birth to live young…though there are a few remnants who—" She shivered. "I can feed six at a time, but I lose half within the first three cycles."

Teal pulled away. "You don't have to—"

"If you want our help, you should know every intimate detail." Wrapping her arms around Teal's waist, she focused her gaze on his, her eyes widening, her lips parting, and her sharp incisors sparkling.

With a yelp, Teal broke free.

CHAPTER SIX

—WOODLANDS—

NEB MUST RULE

Hezeki tossed and turned, his blanket wrapped around his middle. Finally, in fretful exhaustion, he sat up, threw the blanket aside, and wiped his sweaty brow. Darkness covered the stifling room. Meshullemeth, a bulky lump, slept not a handbreadth away.

Heaving a long sigh, he dragged his fingers through his hair. Images chased each other before his eyes: Neb shoving Kenan to the ground and standing over the boy with his belligerent smirk.

Hezeki could still feel the rush of heat flush his face as he tried to intervene.

Neb's smirk vanished at his approach and reformed into a scowl. He had pointed to the embarrassed youth. "He's grown insolent. *Someone* must teach him manners."

Fearing that his teeth might break under pressure, Hezeki had unclenched his jaw and muttered, "You couldn't teach a dog manners!"

As the next image rammed through his mind, Hezeki squeezed his eyes shut. Once he reached Kenan, he had bent low to assist the boy, but Neb had swiped his foot under him, unbalancing him.

Hezeki rubbed his swollen leg. He could still feel the burning pain where his skin broke against the rocky ground. Pits and dark spots grew each day as it continued to swell to disfiguring size.

Clansmen had rushed to his aide, muttering their fears. "Neb challenges Hezeki!"

Neb's voice had lifted above the tumult as he yanked

Kenan to his feet. “Show more respect, brother. Danger approaches, and only those found worthy will join me as I go into battle.”

Hezeki had climbed to his feet, spitting fury at his eldest son. His mind had whirled as if he were seeing an apparition from another world.

Enosh had stepped forward and stood at his side.

Encouraged by his second son’s loyalty, Hezeki had lifted his arm and voiced his opinion. “By the gods above, Neb, respect is earned. Not grasped at as a spoiled child grabs at a honeycomb. You’re a usurper, an unnatural heir, a—”

Neb had merely raised the flat of his hand, peered at the frightened crowd, and carried his voice over his father’s. “Prepare your weapons! An enemy approaches! I have seen him, and he is fierce.” In a mighty flourish, Neb had swept toward his tent.

Standing with his two young sons in confused amazement, Hezeki, disabled and in pain, could do nothing.

With shuffled steps and disconcerted frowns, the clansmen returned to their duties, their gazes shifting away from their leader.

Even Kenan grunted and looked aside.

Refusing to acknowledge the pain in his leg and the ache in his heart, Hezeki stood trembling. “Strike the leader, and the clan will scatter.”

Enosh had merely spluttered. “He’s mad! And dangerous. What will you do, Father?”

Hezeki’s response echoed in his mind. “Your mother will follow Neb, but you two must decide for yourselves. Neb is right; a terror has come upon us, but it was of our own making.”

Clapping his hands over his face as if to block any further revelations, Hezeki dropped back onto his bed, stared out the window, and prayed for the release of a deep sleep…or a quick death.

The clouds parted. A sliver of the moon and a patch of stars shone through, but grief seared his heart.

Hezeki glanced at the lump of his snoring wife. "I should've stopped him long ago."

~~~

Enosh and Kenan packed their bags in silence. After tying the cord in a tight knot, Enosh traipsed outside. He crossed the compound, entered his parent's house, tiptoed to the far corner, and lifted his sleeping sister from her pallet. Her long black hair cascaded over his arm. He carried her back to his dwelling.

As he entered, Kenan's eyes widened.

Enosh shook his head. "She will be safer with us. I don't know what Neb is planning, but I'll not trust him with this defenseless child." He placed the girl on his own pallet and drew a cover over her. When she stirred, he murmured softly. "Sleep, Eva. You'll rest with us tonight."

Kenan dropped his voice to a whisper. "How many men will come with us?"

"Maybe half the clan, if we're lucky. Few men like Neb, but they see his youth and strength, and father is growing frail. His prophecies of doom will make many side with him who might otherwise have followed Hezeki. It was a clever move on Neb's part to suggest we might be attacked."

"So, it's just a story?"

"If there is an attack, he has something to do with it."

Kenan's eyes rounded with shock. "He wouldn't attack his own clan!"
~~~

Standing in the doorway, Enosh slapped the doorpost. "Neb must rule, even if he destroys his clan to do it."

With a shake of his head, Kenan returned to his packing.

Eva turned onto her side; her sleep only briefly disturbed.

Enosh stared at the star-strewn sky and wondered if he would ever sleep again.

CHAPTER SEVEN

—WOODLANDS—

WHAT EVERY MAN MUST

Hezeki pictured his brother at their last meeting. A large man with a thick beard, eyes that could pierce silent thoughts, and muscles a bear might envy. He struggled up a steep incline, grabbing branches and exposed roots to keep from slipping backwards. His leg, despite being swollen and disfigured, still allowed him to move freely. Once he reached the plateau, he glanced around. A glory of dark green pines to the left, grasslands to the right, and mountains in the distance. But no people. No neighbors, friends, or enemies anywhere.

Despite the cuts and welts on his hands and the pain in his leg, Hezeki grinned as he rubbed his arms to keep warm. "Ashkenazi was never a man to welcome strangers. Or family members for that matter. More comfortable in the wild, he left home without a word many long years ago."

Clansmen fanned out in an array behind them, hefting heavy packs on their shoulders, grim-faced but patiently enduring.

Enosh reached for a handhold. "So, how do you know he's here?"

Hezeki braced his feet as best he could and pulled Enosh the last treacherous step.

Kenan and Eva traipsed along the winding incline along with the others.

"I heard news of his…peculiar lifestyle. Word spreads. Even in his isolation, folk speak of his marvelous strength." Hezeki shrugged, his gaze following his younger son as the boy held Eva's hand, assisting her over a boulder. "A man like Ashkenazi can never truly leave the world behind, because the world will never leave him behind."

Enosh exhaled a long breath, his glance sweeping the perimeter. "What does he do in the wilderness, all by himself?"

"What every man must. He survives. Though…" Hezeki rubbed his bearded chin. "Ashkenazi has a taste for unusual pastimes."

Enosh frowned, shifting his eyes from Hezeki's leg.

"Nothing gruesome. He just likes to…" Hezeki peered at the sky, a blush of embarrassment working up his face. "Paint pictures on cave walls." He toed a small rock and tipped it over the edge of the cliff. "Our father was not enchanted with such doings. And when disturbed, he was not gentle in expressing his opinion."

With a snort, Enosh traipsed to where Kenan led Eva to the cliff edge. He stretched out a helping hand.

Eva clasped it while Kenan shoved her upward from behind. She scrabbled with her feet and finally flopped down on the plateau with a sigh.

Kenan followed and sat next to his sister.

Three vultures circled high overhead, and the sun continued its descent, tinting the sky with pink edges.

Enosh propped his hands on his hips. "Though I know well enough that blood relatives do not always make good relations, doesn't your brother care about you? Wouldn't he assist us if he knew of our need?"

"It is hard to know what Ashkenazi would do. Likely he'd prefer that we fight our own battles—from a distance. He might come to our aid if we were being slaughtered, but what then?"

"Where else can we go?"

Surveying the valley, Hezeki paused in thought.

"There's a clan not three day's march from here. They're in a valley between two foothills to the northwest. A pine forest stands there, and they take shelter from the woods. I once traveled into the territory, and they were very hospitable. They know of Ashkenazi as he used to live not far away. They said that he prefers caves but will make use of any protection when it suits his fancy."

"So we'll meet with this clan and ask—"

"We won't ask for anything. Just being in their territory will make Neb pause. He'll think we've made an alliance. We could live in obscurity, and then move to any land we choose."

With a smile, Enosh nudged his younger brother. "Time to get moving again, lazybones."

Eva grimaced as she sat up. "I don't understand why we had to leave home in the first place. Mother didn't want me to go."

"Mother thinks that anyone who displeases Neb is guilty of treachery. Besides, she had plans for you, little sister." Clenching his jaw, Enosh crouched beside Eva. "You'd little enjoy the match she had planned for you. Believe me; we're doing you a favor taking you away."

Eva stood and slapped the dust from her dress. "Into the wilderness?"

"Better the wilderness than slavery."

"Mother said you aren't her son anymore. And Neb will find us and curse us."

Hezeki shuffled between his son and daughter. He looked the girl in the eye. "Your brothers have made their choice, and yours too, whether you like it or not. Neb wants leadership at any cost. Too much of the clan sides with him to stay safely at home. His father, weak as I am, and his brothers are expendable. Do not be so vain to think that you would be exempt if you disagreed with him."

Kenan laid his hands on Eva's shoulders and peered

into her eyes. “Would you rather be with him or us?”

Eva swallowed and glanced at her father. “Lead on.”

Hezeki straightened his aching back, gripped the staff Enosh held out to him and limped forward.

CHAPTER EIGHT

—WILDERNESS—

BEYOND HER SIGHT

Eva trudged along silently behind her elder brothers, while some of her father's faithful men marched silently behind her. Hezeki had met his men in the woods at an appointed time, each taking a separate route to confuse Neb and delay any attempt to catch up with them.

Winter winds blew, and the sky was heavy with gray clouds. Large white flakes drifted before her eyes. She brushed stray tears away as anger brought a flush of heat to her cheeks. She did not wish to grieve so much, yet she couldn't help it. A heavy weight pressed on her chest with each step.

Guilt tugged her heart at leaving her family and people behind. Her mind filled with fury that Neb had made this journey necessary. Why could he not wait until his father had died of whatever ailed him before ascending as leader? What was the advantage of rushing the natural course? She wiped her futile tears away again.

Eva patted the bulging sack slung over her shoulder, grateful that she'd been able to help with the harvest and knew how to pack grains safely. The hide she had tanned herself, and she carried a couple of clay bowls and cups wrapped in her spare dress.

After tracking northward and taking rests in the thick winter forests, they arrived in worn grasslands. In the distance, a forest covered rounded hills and led up into white-capped mountains. Eva's heart stirred. Something about this vast expanse and the huge mountainous ranges spoke of a power so great and wondrous that joy surged through her. She stared, glorying in the rosy skyline as the sun blinked behind the mountains.

Enosh nudged her forward.

~~~

Eva pulled her cloak tight around her body. The weather grew colder as they ranged northward, and the sky turned white with falling snow. The few naked trees that grew upon the edges of streams shivered their foreboding branches in the evening light. She drank in the beauty with her whole being.

Once again, Enosh drew close, disturbing her concentration.

"Eva? You all right?"

"Of course." She dropped her gaze to her muddy boots.

"Come then. We will lay our blankets under that copse of trees by the creek. There's shelter from the wind to keep us through the night. Plenty of kindling, so we'll make a fire. You can wrap up in your blanket. You won't freeze; don't worry."

Eva hid a smile. The cold did not touch her. Her clothing was well made, and she wore layers. The thrill of the magnificent scenery had warmed her blood. "I'm all right. I can walk a little faster if you want."

Enosh nodded and ran ahead, stepping once more into his father's footsteps.

Kenan fell back and plodded beside his little sister.

"Are you sure you're all right? You must feel strange, so far from home."

Eva bowed her head. "Are you not far from home as well?"

Kenan squared his shoulders. "I've been on hunting trips. I know what it is to travel and sleep out in the weather, but this is new for you." He bumped her shoulder playfully.
~~~

Eva stared at the snowy ground. A trail of footprints melted the whiteness into oozing mud. She glanced over her shoulder. A ragged, muddy mess contrasted sadly against the unbroken snow before her. She sighed. "I was sad at leaving, and I'm sorry Mother is angry, but it's all Neb's fault." She peered at her brother. "Perhaps Mother will join us when she realizes what Neb is like."

Kenan shrugged his pack high over his shoulder. "Mother made her choice, but I fear she'll never know peace as long as Neb rules." Dropping silent, they marched side by side as darkness settled into night.

A wolf howled, and distant wolves answered.

Eva stopped, her heart hammering against her chest.

Kenan wrapped his arm around her and led her forward. "They're far away and won't bother a group like us." He leaned in and dropped his voice. "You're safe now. You're lucky we got you away in time, for Neb wanted to—"

Hezeki called, "Kenan, come here, son!"

Kenan smiled at his sister and ran ahead.

Hezeki pulled his son into a confiding huddle as they continued their march toward the trees.

Eva watched them and then glanced at Enosh, who peered back at her. She dropped her gaze and trudged on in silence.

The mountains faded into the black night, and cold enveloped her heart. Hezeki's men trailed behind in weary silence. It seemed a small group to be making a fresh start in the world. Her brother's words echoed in her mind. What would Neb have done if she had stayed? A shiver ran down her spine.

Suddenly her body ached from weariness. When the sun rose the next day, would it shine clear and bright, or would frozen clouds still hinder the light and warmth?

As they meandered into the grove of trees, she lifted her eyes. The clouds had moved off, and uncountable stars twinkled in the night sky. Peace swelled in her chest. Surely, if the beauty of daylight could be replaced by the glory of the night, then there was a reason to hope, for clouds only hid the sky, and trees only blocked her view. Beauty existed beyond her sight.

After her brothers arranged her blanket before a crackling fire, she curled up with the stars to comfort her.

CHAPTER NINE

—WILDERNESS—

A NOBLE ENDEAVOR

Ashkenazi knelt on the soft ground and lifted his hand before the frightened deer.

The animal's eyes widened, its nose twitching, and stared at the hand. Blood oozed from a gash down her back leg.

Humming softly, Ashkenazi leaned forward. Gently, he stroked the soft fur behind her left ear. "Easy. I won't hurt you." Scuffling closer, he managed to lift the fragile doe. He carried her over the rough terrain to his cave entrance. He laid her down on a soft bed of grass he had made for himself and retreated to a bag slumped against the west wall. After a moment, he returned to the fawn and spread a thick layer of berries under her nose.

After sniffing the berries, she snatched at the food and chewed in rhythmic motions, her gaze rising sporadically as if to keep an eye on her benefactor.

Ashkenazi grinned. "There's more where that came from." He poured water from a jug into a bowl and placed it before her.

She leaned in and lapped at the water, knocking the container aside.

Holding the bowl steady with one hand, Ashkenazi stroked her head with the other. "You'll live. If you can eat and drink in my company, you'll get better very soon." He wagged a finger in admonishment. "But no running about until that leg heals." He snorted. "Stupid hunter. Clearly an amateur."

He stood and stretched as he peered out the entrance

and considered the sun falling near the horizon. "No more work. Time for a little visit." He grinned as he sauntered down the incline and rounded the embankment. On the far side, he gazed over a valley and watched the calm activities of a small clan preparing for supper.

Smoke rose from a communal fire set in the central compound. A gathering of women leaned over a large pot. Smoke from smaller fires drifted from homes, spiraling into the dusky sky, mingling with clouds of sparrows, which flew into the distance.

As he jogged down the hillside, women and children turned, their eyes wide with startled fear, but as recognition set in, grins formed. A horde of children cried out and scampered in his direction, their hands reaching. Dust rose from their feet as they pelted across the village and surrounded him.

Ashkenazi laughed. Joy surged through his chest and his whole body, thrilled with the pleasure of being among friends.

One woman called and waved a finger. "Adah wants you. Her boy's been sick again, and she doesn't have the herbs for the tea you made last time."

With a nod, Ashkenazi turned toward a simple hut. He dipped his head as he stepped into the dim interior.

An intake of breath on his left focused his attention, and a hand slipped into his. "Finally! I was worried you wouldn't come."

"I was distracted…another patient needed my attention." Bending low, Ashkenazi squeezed his large frame into a small shelf space used as a bed where a small boy lay panting. The child's breath rasped as his chest labored for air.

The mother stood by, wringing her hands. "He was fine until yesterday, then all of the sudden, he started wheezing and collapsed in a heap. His father carried him here, and

I've watched over him, but nothing settles the cough."

Ashkenazi shook his head. "It's not a cough or sickness." Frowning in puzzlement, he felt the boy's pale, dry skin and patted his hand. "You were playing hard. Running?"

The child panted through a nod, his eyes wide and frightened.

The mother caressed his cheek. "When he's well, he's the fastest boy in the village."

Ashkenazi patted the boy's arm and retreated from the small space. He strode to the door. "His body works too hard when he gets excited. He needs to calm down. Do you have strong wine?"

The mother bit her lip. "I tried to give him some last night, but he didn't want it."

"It needs to be strong…very strong."

"But he's only a boy—"

"I could give him herbs for a soothing tea, but I think the wine would work better."

A large man strode through the doorway, blocking the last rays of light. "Give the child the wine, Adah. Ashkenazi knows what he's doing."

Ashkenazi grinned. "Not always. But the wine will help. If nothing else" —he glanced from the wife to her husband— "Hillel can drink it, and you'll enjoy a peaceful night."

Hillel laughed and pounded Ashkenazi on the back. "Come out and have supper with us." He stood aside and let the older man pass into the twilight.

Leading the way to the center of the village, Hillel pointed to a young woman. "Get our guest some of our best wine."

The woman scurried away, and Ashkenazi perched on the edge of a log set near the fire.

Hillel stood beside him and stared at the flickering

flames. "I'm glad you've come. I was about to go find you."

The woman returned and placed a bowl with a brimful of dark liquid into Ashkenazi's hands.

He nodded his thanks, took a long drink, and enjoyed the warmth seeping through his body. "The boy is in no serious danger."

"Not about the boy." Hillel peered down and met Ashkenazi's gaze. "Trouble is coming. A Southern Hills clan has divided, and the remnant is heading this way. They may want your assistance, but we know how you value your privacy—"

Ashkenazi held up his hand. "You're kind to warn me, but I'm just an old man, and there is little anyone can want from me but perhaps a few herbs." He gestured toward Hillel's robust frame. "However, they might desire your strong arms in their next battle. Perhaps you should stay out of sight."

Hillel frowned. "If they want a fight, we'll give them one, but word has it that they are only a small group, not battle-ready."

"How do you know they want battle?"

"Either they come to conquer, or they come to keep from being conquered. Something brought them here."

Ashkenazi exhaled a long breath and turned his gaze to the skies.

~~~

Hezeki stood leaning heavily on his strong leg on the crest of the hill. He peered at the sleeping village in the early morning sunlight. His sons, daughter, and his faithful men ranged in a meandering line behind him. Should he
~~~

wait until full day when the clan began their everyday business or surprise them before they had a chance to gather their weapons?

Enosh strode forward and stopped at his side, his hands on his hips. "Shouldn't we go down now?"

Hezeki bit his lip and stared at the communal fire below.

A large bundle wrapped in a thick blanket rolled to the side, and like a bear waking from sleep, unfolded itself and revealed the face and form of a large man. He stood and stretched, unaware of his audience.

A thrill surged through Hezeki. "Ashkenazi!"

Enosh's eyes widened. He glanced from his father to the man now standing in the center of the village. "That's your brother?"

"At one time, my only friend."

As if sensing their presence, Ashkenazi looked up. He squared his shoulders.

Enosh made to start forward, but Hezeki gripped his arm. "No, let him come up. He may not want us so close to his friends."

"He's your brother!"

Hezeki put his finger to his lips.

Kenan and Eva ranged in closer and watched as Ashkenazi strode across the village and began the ascent up the hill, his shoulder muscles rippling in the morning light, his short tunic swaying with every movement.

Once Ashkenazi reached the brow of the hill, he stood before Hezeki and stared, his eyes grave and his whole demeanor somber. "My brother?"

His heart hammering, Hezeki wiped his sweaty hands on his tunic and nodded. He cleared his throat. "Ashkenazi, it's good to see you again."

With barely a flicker at Hezeki's leg, Ashkenazi nodded. "It's been a long time."

Hezeki dared a brief smile. "I didn't think you would be so easy to find. For many years, I have longed to know that you're well."

"I have often thought of you." Ashkenazi relaxed his shoulders and glanced from his brother to the two young men and the girl standing near. "But I knew that one day you'd come to annoy me." He grinned.

Kenan exhaled a long breath, and Eva smiled.

Enosh maintained a sober expression, glancing from his father to his uncle.

Hezeki lifted his arms, and the brothers embraced.

As he pulled away, Ashkenazi pointed toward the cliff. "Follow me to my home. I must hear all the news. Is your wife well?"

Hezeki hobbled at his brother's side, attempting to match Ashkenazi's great stride. "She is alive."

Ashkenazi shook his head. "I warned you about her…remember?"

Hezeki sighed.

~~~

Ashkenazi nodded at his brother as the family group sat down to bowls of mead and broken loves of dark bread. "Who do you run from now? It can't be Father, for he's long dead. So is it your wife or another son?"

Hezeki bowed his head as if he searched the dust for an explanation. He looked up and met his brother's stare. "Both. But how did you know?"

Ashkenazi waved the question aside. His pointed stare and then shifting his gaze away from Hezeki's leg proclaimed his refusal to discuss the obvious problem. "Never mind. News travels faster than weary travelers."
~~~

Hezeki forced a light tone and gestured to the assembly. "Here are my two faithful sons and my beautiful daughter to become acquainted with their wise uncle."

Ashkenazi washed down a bite of bread with a long draught of mead. Once satiated, he focused his full gaze on his brother's children. He beckoned them forward.

Enosh and Kenan stepped forward and knelt before him in respect.

Ashkenazi smiled, glancing aside to his brother. "They are younger than we were when we migrated away from the Great Clan but not by much. Do you remember how eager I was?" As if old grief tugged at his insides, he winced. He waved it aside. "Let me guess who is more eager."

With a renewed smile, Ashkenazi stood and gripped the shoulders of each young man. "By the sun above, I see a matchless eagerness in both your faces. That is well, for survival is never easy, and life is precarious when dealing with ambitious men."

Enosh jerked back.

Kenan nodded in assent. "In truth! If it had been our wills, we'd have stayed among our own clansmen, but Neb forced us out into the world. We're determined to find a new home and live in peace and prosperity."

Ashkenazi let his hands fall to his sides. He turned away. "A noble endeavor—one I've spent my life trying to accomplish—but one must be willing to sacrifice much prosperity to live in peace."

He gestured to the cave entrance. "You and your family can stay with me awhile, and your men can find shelter and hunt in the hills." His gaze rested on Hezeki, sadness filling him. "But soon you'll have to find a new home. I can do nothing for what ails you, and I've grown used to my solitary life. I have no wish to change my ways."

~~~

Hezeki considered the bright stars in the vast darkness. Then he conferred with his strongest warrior, Thubal, and told him to let the men rest for a few days while he and his sons scouted out the land.

As he watched them traipse into the hills, pain clenched his body into a tight knot while agony squeezed his heart. Their faithfulness had cost them much, and he was sorry for their grief, leaving loved ones behind though no one had been forced to go.

Some would retrieve family later, while others would probably never see their families again. With care and hard work, they might put their lives back together again.

If only Neb would leave them alone.
~~~

Chapter Ten

-IANA-

Inter-Alliance-Neutrality–Agreement

Ark eyed Tcesni with unabashed skepticism. Inside the well-camouflaged ship, IANA, circling Earth, he lounged on a heavily upholstered swivel chair and stretched his aching legs.

Zuri, luckless fellow, sat in the front row of the assembly hall and had to endure a much stiffer seat, right before the glaring eyes of Sterling and the Insect Queen.

Ark smothered a chuckle. Yes. Insect Queen. His pet name for the repugnant—

"Are you even listening?"

Ark swiveled his gaze to Teal's blue eyes as the Luxonian bent over him, effectively blocking the entire assembly from view. "Have your eyes always been so dark? I thought they were lighter…brighter somehow."

Teal's jawline tightened. Propping a firm hand on Ark's chair, he leaned in close. "We're not here to do portraits of each other. We're here to get this damned agreement—"

Sterling tinkled a bell and grinned at Tcesni, who towered above him without a hint of humor on her elongated face.

Teal straightened with a smothered sigh.

Ark's stomach dropped to his boots, his eyes widening. "He brought the bells? I thought that was an only-on-Lux kind of torture." He wiggled around Teal and smacked Zuri's shoulder. "Couldn't you have swiped the stupid bells?"

Zuri swiveled and stared through bloodshot eyes. "He sleeps with them beside his bed. I'd never dare get that close."

"What? So he can ring for room service?"

Teal tapped Ark's breather helm.

A very personal move. Invasive actually. Ark felt his temperature rising. He reared back. "Please! I'm not some common—"

Sterling clapped his hands like a teacher on-the-brink-of-killing-every-last-one-of-his-students, sing-songing the class to order, his tone too bright for his expression. "We're ready to begiiiin."

The door at the back of the oval, pale-yellow assembly room swished open, and a line of representatives traipsed forward. Three Luxonians, three Ingots, three Uanyi, three Cresta, and one lone Bhuac—who had insisted on her interplanetary rights—entered the room. Though she could not partake of full representation, she could take formal notes and report back to the Regent of Song upon her return to Helm. Though some eyes had rolled at the "Neediness of some people!" no one had bothered to argue.

Tcesni's narrow lips turned in a sly grin as she watched the chubby, red-cheeked Bhuac tuck her cute white skirt under her adorable little figure and take her seat in the front row. The queen leaned over and nudged Sterling. "She'd make a delicious snack, don't you think?"

Wincing, Sterling dragged his fingers down the side of his face.

Teal traipsed up the seven steps to the platform and glanced from Sterling to Tcesni. "Everyone is assembled. We're ready?"

Ark rubbed his thick neck, desperately wanting to scream—*What do you think the torturous bell is for?*

Zuri glanced in his direction as if he had read the Cresta's thoughts.

That's rather alarming. Ark wondered if he made himself so obvious on a regular basis.

Teal tapped a wall console and a large image shimmered on the back wall. Sterling stepped to the right, and Tcesni stepped to the left. A formal greeting in each representative's language began the brief introduction to the Intra-Alliance-Neutrality-Agreement (IANA), which also appeared on each representative's personal datapad. A short bio of each representative soared across the screen. Finally, a brilliant picture of planet Earth filled the viewing space. Today's subject: the formal treaty between interested parties to pledge open and honest communication while furthering studies on the third planet from…

Ark yawned.

~~~

Zuri grabbed Teal's arm as he started for the door. "I need to speak with you."

Teal waited until the last of the representatives exited the assembly hall then turned his full attention to the Ingot. "About the treaty?"

Zuri shook his head.

Exhaling a long breath, Teal limped toward the last row of seats and plunked down. "Good. I was afraid you'd have some kind of Ingot issue, and we'd have to bring it up at the next—"

"With that paranoid Bhuac jumping to her feet in protest every few minutes, and the Crestas sending constant messages back and forth, and your Insect Queen grinning like an assassin bug at everyone…" Zuri straightened his shoulders. "Actually, I thought you managed the whole thing with gracious decorum."

Teal practically squeaked. "Really?"
~~~

Zuri nodded. “Certainly. Now, can we talk about my problem?”

Waving a languid hand, Teal leaned back, clearly trying to get comfortable. “Why not?”

Zuri scanned his datapad and paced. “I’ve tried reaching Kelesta repeatedly, but she isn’t answering—”

A smothered groan. “You aren’t going to tell me about your latest romance gone wrong—”

“Shut up and listen!”

Teal scowled.

“There’s a report from a passing trader that there’s been an attack on Helm, and the entire population is panicking. Something about a chain reaction… I’m not sure what he meant. I’m trying to get details, but the messages keep getting corrupted. It’s as if someone is trying to interfere, so no one knows the full extent—” Zuri clenched his jaw and stiffened, trying to control his emotions.

With near paternal gentleness, Teal stood and pressed Zuri’s arm. “I’m sorry. I’ve been obsessed with…well…I haven’t been paying attention as I should. She must’ve poisoned me or something.” He stared at the door a moment and then shook his head, as if trying to free himself of an unwelcome thought. “You’re right. We need to look into this.”

Zuri frowned. “Are you all right?”

Teal nodded and glanced at the doorway. “Of course. I just need to get some fresh air…or sunshine. Maybe some food.”

“You’re Luxonian. You need food?”

“I sure as hell need something.” A buzz rose from his datapad. Teal scanned the surface and blinked. “She’s waiting for me. I’m late.”

“Who? For what?”

“Dinner. Tcesni has something special prepared.” Teal swallowed. “Come with me?”

"I'm invited?"

The door swished open, and Ark sauntered in. "Thought I'd find you two..." His scanty eyebrows wiggled. "Whispering together."

Teal rubbed his forehead. "Do *you* know what's happening on Helm?"

"No reports have come my way. Besides, Bhuacs have never been considered all that interesting. Too malleable."

With an unaccustomed flush, Zuri snorted. "You're just jealous since Crestonians can't change form."

Ark waved a languid tentacle. "Their research techniques are infantile" —he waved another tentacle— "and they don't produce weapons of any kind." He folded his tentacles over his middle like a judge passing sentence. "Foolish to the extreme."

Stepping between the two, Teal held up a hand. "Someone may have attacked Helm, and Zuri can't get any clear idea of what's going on with Kelesta."

Zuri tapped his tentacles together, lowered his brows, and looked very much like a professor considering the mysteries of the universe. "Could be our mutual rival. They like to experiment by decimating a part of a planet. If the inhabiting race survives, they just might be worthy of notice." His gaze slid to Teal. "Or your Uanyi Queen may have decided she didn't like the little Bhuac's attitude and has given them something to think about."

"She wouldn't do that."

"Oh, no? I think she's quite capable of any measure of treachery." Ark eyed Teal closely. "And if your brain were working properly, so would you."

Zuri stuffed his datapad into his pocket, set his face, and started forward. "It's about time I had a chat with that...insectoid."

Teal jumped ahead and grabbed Zuri's arm. "Don't even think about it. You'd be dead before you asked your first question."

Ark sidled up and grinned at Teal. “So, you do see the danger then?”

“I see her power. You have no idea.”

“Does she by chance bite or spin webs?”

Zuri pulled free from Teal’s grip. “Who cares? The Uanyi treaty that Sterling wanted is set, and everyone can go home. But I’ve got to find out what’s happened on Helm.” He stopped and peered from Ark to Teal. “And…I’d rather not go alone.”

Teal closed his eyes.

Ark grinned.

CHAPTER ELEVEN

—NEB'S VILLAGE—

INTO THE BLAZING SUN

Neb strode through the bustling village with his head up and shoulders thrust back. He relished the sensation of ownership. *His* village. *His* clan. The winter sun beat down on his bare arms, warming them against a cool breeze. He sneered at a man sitting outside his dwelling, sharpening a long knife. His layered clothing and hunched shoulders spoke of a body suffering from inclement weather.

Neb halted before the man. "Cold, Elion?"

The man peered up, one eyebrow lifted in derision until recognition rippled over his face. He straightened. His sharpening stone fell on the ground with a thud. "Oh, Neb…"

"Your mother still sick?"

Elion swallowed and pointed to his hut. "Delia has been looking after her. She's better. But now Tisza's father is ill."

Neb chewed his lip. A fever had run through the village after a sudden warm spell, but with the cooler temperatures, most villagers appeared to be recovering. He shrugged. The weak and the old died as nature decreed.

Two ragged children raced out the doorway, brushing between Neb and their father as they passed.

Scowling, Neb stopped them with a sharp command. "Stop! Give my mother a message."

The younger boy cowed, ducked his dark head, and peered at Neb through hooded eyes.

The taller boy clenched his jaw and met Neb's gaze. "Yes?"

"Tell her to prepare my things for travel. I'm going over the mountain tomorrow."

The children's mouths dropped open.

"I want supper before sundown." He waved at them. "Go! I have no time to waste."

Elion watched his sons race away. With a puckered frown, he faced Neb. "Why over the mountain?"

A fresh gust of wind rippled over the short grass, and Neb's gaze turned inward. "Stories tell of a glorious city on the other side, where the people eat sumptuous food, wear beautiful clothes, and craft tools beyond imagining. Even their temples dare to touch the sky." He nodded at the mountains and grinned. "I'll see that for myself." He shifted his eyes. "You'd like to see it, too, wouldn't you?"

Elion tilted his head, a smile playing on his lips. "Perhaps." A cloud swept overhead, and he dropped his gaze. "Though I hear enchantments rule such lands. Gods walk hidden among the people, and living slaves are buried with their masters. The Other World demands much."

"So I've heard, too." Neb nudged Elion in the arm. "But I've also heard that they have beautiful women. The temple brides are alluring beyond compare."

Elion snorted. "No good to me. Delia would never allow another woman. Beauty would be no protection against a jealous wife."

Neb sneered as disgust rose to his throat. "You're hardly a man for such an adventure." Without another word, he turned away.

With a shrug, Elion reentered his dwelling.

After crossing over the threshold into a large thatch and grass dwelling, Neb glanced at the pack lying on his pallet and sniffed the air. Satisfied with the bundle and the stew pot boiling over the hearth, he crossed his arms and faced his mother. "I'll meet with Uz before I go."

Meshullemeth stepped around a stack of baskets, her

hands on her hips and her lips in a pout. “First, you send word for me to pack your bag without any explanation and expect dinner at a moment’s notice, and now you want to visit that vile old man.” Her eyes narrowed. “Why?”

“He knows more than your old crone. Besides, Cozbi has the smell of death on her.”

Meshullemeth wrinkled her nose and batted Neb’s assessment away. “Cozbi has served us well, but Uz is—”

“When Cozbi last called the spirits forth, I could see into her mind. Treachery lay within the hag. She’s not long for this world.”

Her eyes widening, Meshullemeth hurried forward. “What do you mean?”

“She stinks of death. I’ll have her sent out of the clan.”

Setting her jaw, Meshullemeth poked her son’s chest, a scowl building. “You think to do away with her because she knows where your power comes from. But do not forget, my son, I arranged for the two greatest powers on earth to meet. It was I who—”

“Watch yourself.” Neb grabbed a bowl off a shelf and thrust it at her. “I’ll eat now and meet Uz in the morning. After that, I’ll travel into the mountains.” He peered into her shocked eyes. “While I’m away, you’ll protect my interests.”

With a snort, Meshullemeth turned away. “And if I do not?”

A flush of fury flooded Neb’s body. He grabbed her arm and forced her to face him. He pointed to the empty pallet on the floor where Hezeki used to lie. “Where’s your protection, woman?”

~~~
~~~

Neb strode across the village at daybreak, entered a simple grass hut, and shook a sleeping figure.

A gray-haired man roused from a deep sleep growled, "Leave me be awhile, woman. I'll eat—"

Neb grabbed a pitcher of water off a shelf and poured the contents over the man's head. "Get up, Hul. We have things to attend to."

Spluttering, Hul shook his head, sending a spray of water across the room. He sat up.

"Take the old sorceress and set her in the woods tonight after dark. Give word that no one is to give her shelter or assistance. By the morning, she'll no longer be a threat to us."

Hul's eyes widened as he rasped out his horror. "Is she a threat now?"

"With such a diseased body and dark mind, Cozbi must be sent out or killed directly. I chose mercy, but if you think it'd be best to kill her outright, then do so."

Voices called to each other as the villagers awoke to the new day.

Hul rose and stumped forward. "I've never killed except in battle. I can't murder a defenseless old woman."

Neb considered Hul, a sour taste in his mouth. "It's not difficult. Come, I'll teach you. Gather Riphath, Torgama, Kittam, and Puti and meet me at her dwelling." With a shake of his head at Hul's frozen stare, he turned and strode away.

Neb paced across the village, impatience warring with curiosity. Exhilaration ran through his body at the thought that he could finally do as he saw fit without interference from either his mother or his father.

When they were assembled inside, Cozbi sent darting scowls between Neb and the other men.

Neb crossed his arms over his chest and blocked the doorway. "Speak to the spirits, Old Woman."

Cozbi gaped, saliva clinging to the edges of her mouth. Her ragged gray hair jutted in soiled disarray around her face and fell in limp strips over her shoulders. "Now? In the daylight?" She tried to peer around Neb to the doorway. "Where is Meshullemeth? She always—"

His disgust rising like bile at her noxious stink, Neb stomped forward. "She is nothing to you anymore."

Startled, Cozbi skipped out of Neb's reach and hastily reached into a skin bag hanging on the wall. "I'll need my—"

"Get on with it."

Hul glanced from Neb to the other men, his face as stiff as stone.

Puti, a thin, disheveled man, leaned against the wall and crossed his arms, his gaze scraping the ceiling in an attitude of boredom. Torgama and Kittam, muscled warriors, stood guard on either side of Neb and wrinkled their noses.

Cozbi swallowed a draught from a small vial, tossed a wide shawl over her head, and began rocking back and forth, her voice falling into a rhythmic moan.

As Cozbi fell under the power of the trance, Neb turned his gaze from the old woman to each of the other men in the room.

Hull shifted from foot to foot, his face pale; he shivered like a frightened dog.

Puti smirked, crinkles of derision crowded around his eyes.

Torgama set his jaw and widened his stance like a man expecting battle.

Kittam pursed his lips, his gaze wandering.

With a shriek, Cozbi fell to the ground and sniveled a plea for help. "Something's wrong. They're hurting me! They—"

A jolt ran through Neb. He ripped the blanket off her

pallet, tossed it over her head, and wrapped it tightly around her skull, twisting as he went.

Cozbi's feeble strength was nothing compared to Neb's youth and vigor.

Hul swallowed convulsively. "She's just a defenseless—"

Neb's heart pounded in exhilaration as he dragged her outside.

The woman fell into a limp heap.

With a grunt, Neb thrust her body in the woods. He faced Hul. "She was a conniving wench. Even the spirits abandoned her." He wiped his hands and faced his men with an attitude of perfect composure. "Now, let's meet Uz."

—UZ'S VILLAGE—

Uz, though shrunken with age, still had a head of thick black hair and a vigorous will. He cared little for the thoughts of other men. His mind centered almost exclusively on the delicious food his granddaughter delivered to his dwelling at regular intervals. He enjoyed lounging on a soft couch near his doorway so that any who sought him might find him readily accessible, and he might comment on the passing world.

He had cheated death so many times; invincibility had become a way of life. As a youth, he had hunted wild game in reckless abandon, yet he always returned home unscathed. This was not always true for his companions, but the hunting accidents had never been his fault. It was no concern of his if other men were unlucky. Him alone, the gods had graciously favored.

Years ago, he had traveled with a company of men across the woodlands, over the foothills, into the mountains, and through the great pass into a new land—a place the like he had never seen before and would never see again.

The City of Prosperity still haunted his dreams.

His traveling companions had been foresighted enough to bring trade items from the woodlands, and though their items were not considered valuable, a passing entourage of nobility took notice of them. They chose Uz above all the others to come to the Palace of the King to tell the stories of his people.

When he arrived, he had stood frozen, staring in awe at the magnificent temple still under construction.

Uz could not believe that the inhabitants were mere mortals like himself. Their clothing rivaled the most beautifully arrayed birds. Their homes rivaled the most cunning eagle's nest. They spoke rapidly with fluttering hands and ate sumptuous feasts.

He soon understood that the only souls that mattered were those who had the skill to become full of an unnamed power. One day, he saw a snake poised to attack an old man, and in instinct, he intervened, killing the viper and saving the man.

In gratitude, a bronze-skinned elder had rested his gnarled hands upon Uz's forehead and had chanted a barrage of garbled words. A guard soon informed Uz that he was forevermore invincible while on the hunt.

And so it had proven true.

Even while traveling the long road home—and through all the years that had lapsed—no matter how daring his actions, he never experienced a serious injury.

He was old now, but he still relished the hunt, though only in story. He could no longer track and kill his prey, but he retold his adventures to any willing listener.

Neb was such a listener, and in time, Uz saw a resemblance between himself and the youthful clan leader who had returned time and time again. Though he could never control the mysterious power that enchanted his life, he spoke as if he could.

As he watched Neb draw near, satisfaction spread like spiced wine through Uz's body. He enjoyed an audience almost as much as a well-cooked meal.

Neb bowed low. "How is my wise mentor today?"

Uz laughed, glee bubbling like a spring brook. "What brings you, my tireless child? Do you wish to hear, yet again, about the great wonders given to me?"

A hawk soared overhead and cawed in challenge as it neared a large nest atop a tree. Another hawk soared forward, darting and screeching in fury to defend its own.

Standing tall, Neb's shadow fell across the old man. He lifted his gaze to the battle above even as he spoke to the man at his feet. "I believe the time has come for your gift to be passed onto the rightful heir so that my people will grow as great as those in The City of Prosperity."

The old man cackled, his confidence rising to the challenge like a hunter facing his quarry. "Ha! There can be no rival to the great city! I should know. I have seen it with my own eyes. Besides, my long life was a gift given to me for a good deed, and no one gave me leave to pass it on to another." An unexpected thought sent a chill over his arms. He glanced at the sky. Not a hint of a cloud. He frowned. "Besides, what would happen to me if I gave it away?"

Neb smiled with the barest hint of cunning behind his eyes. "You would be twice blessed." He crouched low and peered into the Uz's eyes. "Tell me, what happened to the one who gave you the gift? Did he not grow in power? How do you think he grew so strong? He used his gift. Think of how strong you might yet become if you bestow some of your grace on me."

A knot of uncertainty tightened in Uz's middle, but

Neb's mesmerizing stare shattered his composure. "It could be so... Perhaps, I'm wearing my memories thin." He paused, perplexed. "But I am not sure of the words. I can remember all else, but the words escape me."

Neb knelt and took the old man's hands and placed them on his head. "It does not matter. Those who bestow the gifts will understand your intent…and my need."

The knot tightened, sending shoots of pain into his chest. "I remember. I was asked a question. It seemed a little matter at the time. Without hesitation, I agreed. You must do the same."

Neb scowled. "What question?"

"Will you worship me?"

"Worship you?"

"Those were the words, and I agreed. Do you agree?"

Neb peered over the old man's head to a smoldering heap of low burning coals in the center of the village. He nodded.

"Say the words."

Neb's voice seemed to vibrate through his whole body. "I will worship you."

Exhaustion seeped into Uz's bones, dragging him to earth. "You meant it; I could tell." He wiped his sweating brow and longed for sleep. "You may go. My memories have grown old. I'll rest now."

Neb let the old man's hand drop from his fingers. He rose and strode toward the village center.

A few heads rose, and a nursing mother clutched her child as she watched him pass. Every voice stilled as Neb unflinchingly walked across the burning coals and continued undisturbed toward the mountains.

Uz fell backward onto the soft pillows that had supported his aging frame. With waning strength, he attempted to clutch the air. Panic clawed his innards. "Where did Neb go?"

His granddaughter rushed to his side and grabbed his flailing hands. She hugged him.

Blind terror seized Uz, and he cried out like a child ripped from his mother's breast. "He stole my blessing!"

As life seeped from his body, Uz slumped forward, and watched a shadow of himself stride into the blazing sun.

CHAPTER TWELVE

—VILLAGE OF SETH—

ALWAYS APPEAR COMPOSED

Seth considered his visitors with unease. He glanced from the approaching entourage to his friend, Accad, on his right, tall and heavy with piercing brown eyes, and on his left, Accad's younger brother, Jubal, who though of only medium height, carried a hidden strength both in body and mind. The two stood like guards, watching the visitors with interest.

Ashkenazi, with Hezeki and his family arrayed at his side, stopped before Seth. They bowed their heads as befitted beseeching visitors before a stalwart clan leader.

Ashkenazi cleared his throat. "My friend, I wish to introduce my brother, Hezeki, and his family. They have come in need of counsel and direction. Though new to your role, your most excellent father taught you well, so I am certain of your generous reception."

Seth suppressed a smile, an ironic grin playing on his lips. After so great a father, no son, loyal or otherwise, could properly fulfill the leadership role. He sucked in a lungful of air. *Still...*

His gaze wandered across the assembly, tripping over the old man's enlarged leg, flittering around the two young men, and landing on the beautiful girl. His heartbeat quickened, his attention lingering.

In benevolence, Ashkenazi spread his hands wide and stepped back. "It would be best if they spoke for themselves."

With a nod, Hezeki hobbled into his brother's place. "First, I wish to thank you, Seth, for allowing us to stay here in our time of need. We are not fleeing from an enemy as you might suppose. Our clan was safe when we left, as I brought prosperity to my people. But because of a lingering illness, my success was not enough for my eldest son. It's an old story, though one you may not be familiar with as it involves treachery and deceit from within."

Hezeki paused and took a deep breath as if he needed all his strength to explain further. "My wife raised my firstborn to believe that he was first in all matters. As sometimes happens, we did not agree on important decisions, and all too soon, my son grew to disdain my opinion and presence. He even disregarded the rights of his brothers. Forced to flee, we seek refuge in the larger world. We're too few to fight for our rights, so we'd rather live in secret, at least for a while…" Hezeki's words stumbled to a halt as a blush spread over his cheeks.

Seth rubbed his chin and nodded as he had seen his own father do to good effect. An ache pulsed behind his eyes. Hezeki bewildered him. How could a leader leave his people? Who was this son who dared to supplant the rightful leader, his father, no matter the size of his leg?

His gaze returned to the girl as she watched him through piercing dark eyes. Could she see into his mind?

Composure—his father had often said—instilled confidence. *Always appear composed.* Seth leaned forward, frowned, and clasped his hands. "I'm disturbed by your predicament, Hezeki, but I will give your problem thought. I don't understand why you did not simply assert your authority and demand obedience from your son. Your authority rests in here." He pounded his fist against his chest, averting his eyes from the misshapen leg. "My father would say that those who do not stop evil when it approaches will be haunted by its footsteps."

Seth stood.

Hezeki hobbled back.

"Be that as it may, your decision has been made. I know

of no land open for the taking, for in truth, there is always someone willing to challenge newcomers. But I will think on the matter… In the meantime, you are free to mingle with my people and find shelter here."

Seth called a clutch of women to his side and spoke in an undertone. "Prepare a meal for all." He gestured toward the center of the village where a large communal fire burned. The women smiled and nodded.

Seth turned once more to his guests. "I've arranged a dinner in your honor. Ashkenazi has done much good, and we're always looking for ways to repay his kindness. Please eat with us. Forget your troubles for tonight and share stories and laughter with us."

Hezeki relaxed as he glanced at his sons and grinned.

Enosh nodded, smiling in relief. "Thank you. We wish to form a clan like yours—where kindness rules and strangers are welcome."

"I only do as my father would have done. He was my friend, my leader, and my guide. I honored him in life with my loyalty and obedience. I honor him in death the same way."

Enosh bit his lip while Kenan dropped his gaze.

Hezeki blinked back tears.

Ashkenazi's booming voice interrupted the silence, as if breaking a somber spell. "Where are all the children?" He glanced around. "If there are any sick, let me tend to them now, for I must leave tomorrow. Otherwise, the animals under my care will wonder where I've gone, and they'll come looking for me."

Laughter filled the air, lifting the tension.

Seth motioned Hezeki toward the center of the village, and his sons fell in line behind Accad and Jubal. Though his heart still felt heavy, a surge of gladness swept over him. His first real trial, and he had managed well. Even the girl appeared pleased.

He stepped aside and watched the villagers mingling with the newcomers. The girl stood alone, still watching him through luminous eyes.

Seth beckoned Jubal and whispered in his ear, “Keep an eye on that girl. She knows more than all the rest.”

Jubal’s eyes narrowed as he stared at the girl.

Seth waved the men forward, leading them to a family feast.

~~~

Eva observed her father, brothers, and clansmen chatting with the villagers as shadows lengthened on the rough terrain. As the food was prepared, unaccountable surprise and wonderment filled her. She had sensed Seth’s wariness but also his kind spirit. He was nothing like Neb, who treated everyone with arrogant determination. She considered the two leaders in sober speculation. Which one would prove the most enduring?
~~~

CHAPTER THIRTEEN

—NEB'S VILLAGE—

JUST BETWEEN US

Neb walked along the bank of a meandering river south of his village. A cool breeze rippled the fabric of his shirt. Dark gray clouds saturated the skyline, muting the natural colors around him. He stopped and stared at the racing current, motionless as the rocks sunk deep in the muddy depth.

Lifting his head, he scanned the village. With a shout, Neb called two of his men, Hul and Puti.

With his disheveled red hair, blue eyes, and a sharp tongue, Puti kept most villagers at a wary distance. He hustled forward with a loping stride.

Hul's broad body shuffled close behind.

Watching his men closely, Neb crossed his arms over his chest. "I have a message for my father and brothers. We'll follow their tracks and find them—wherever they may be."

Hull chewed his lip.

Puti stared through expressionless eyes.

Neb lifted his chin. "You have a concern, Hul? Speak."

Hul shifted his weight. "I was sorry to see your father leave the clan, but as for your brothers, their absence is probably for the best. Do you think it wise to follow them? Clearly, they have made up their minds. You're the leader now. No one questions that."

As if Hul had not spoken, Neb uncrossed his arms and started forward. "We'll leave early tomorrow. Torgama and Kittam will be in charge. Riphath can cook and attend to my personal needs. The two of you will do the hunting, tracking, and scouting. I know where my father and brothers were heading. However, it'll be a long journey, and there are many dangers along the way, so be well prepared and follow my directions exactly."

Hul frowned, nodded his acceptance, and strode away.

Puti nodded also, but his eyes followed Hul's back as he marched out of earshot. The two men watched the slump-shouldered figure retreat inside his dwelling. Puti's raspy voice broke the silence. "There's a man who does not rejoice in his duty."

"I've noticed."

Puti's eyes slid sideways. He peered indirectly at his leader. "Some men long for the past, while others yearn for the future."

Neb stared directly ahead, clenching his jaw, his anger rising.

"I face each day as it comes. Regrets and dreams are for other men." Puti offered a slight bow and strode away.

A tug of admiration toppled Neb's anger and turned his attention to his next duty…

Torgama and Kittam stood together. They were strong, muscled warriors who looked like they had been breaking rocks or heads from their infancy. They watched Neb approach with matched caution.

Neb strode forward and pointed toward the mountains. "I'm going on a journey. You two will maintain order here in my stead."

Torgama grinned and rubbed his jaw.

Kittam licked his lips.

Though he hadn't expected opposition, he had expected questions, but neither man seemed inclined to propose any. Neb shrugged. Just as well. He had no details to offer. As an afterthought, he merely pointed to a distant hut.

"Mother will do as you say."

The two men fixed their gazes on Neb; he could feel their surprise. A chuckle bubbled from his chest. His mother would've been surprised, too, had she heard.

With nothing else to impart, Neb sauntered toward the last dwelling on the east side of the village.

Riphath, a small and tidy man, known for his efficiency, stood outside his home, apparently giving instructions to his wife.

As Neb approached, the wife patted her husband's arm and backed inside her home.

Riphath eyed Neb and bowed servilely. "Yes, Neb, I've heard the news from your mother. I'll be ready to leave early. I could even be ready by this evening if you like."

Neb waved his hand in generosity. "No need. The four of us traveling at good speed will catch up with my father easily. Do you know the north hill lands? My father used to speak of a brother who lived in that region."

"I've gone on many expeditions, but I believe that Hul has traveled more than anyone. He used to spend a great deal of time with your father. Perhaps he knows something?"

Neb stroked his chin, a quiver of uncertainty marring his sanguine nature. "I am taking Hul with us. But while we travel, I want you to pay close attention to things that others do not usually notice." He leaned in. "If you see anything the least suspicious…"

Riphath nodded, his expression slipping from impassive to interested.

After a few more curt instructions, Neb walked back to his hut and considered the weapons he would take.

The room stood open with his skin bags hanging on pegs in neat rows, and his weapons placed carefully on a wooden shelf.

The familiar sound of padding feet and a bulky shadow

in the doorway plucked Neb's nerves, tensing his whole body.

Meshullemeth arrived full of her own importance. She waved grandly, her voice shaking with emotion. "Neb, I must speak with you. I've thought about your plan, and-"

Neb slid his favorite obsidian knife into his bag. "Mother, I'm busy. I have a great deal to settle before I leave."

A snake slinking across the room, Meshullemeth wiggled closer and grinned, one hand squeezing her son's arm. "Perhaps I can be of assistance."

Neb peered through the dwindling light. "What do you know about my father's brother, Ashkenazi? I've heard that he is greatly renowned for his healing powers."

Meshullemeth waved Neb's words away with a flick of her finger. "None of your father's family was renowned. They were a lazy, loosely allied gathering. Your father hardly spoke of them."

A hot flush worked up Neb's face. He stepped nearer. "What did he say?"

Meshullemeth squinted in the failing light. "What does it matter? He lives away in the hills, and your father has not seen him for ages." Suddenly her face froze, a glimmer of understanding lighting her eyes. "Who cares if they went to find a long-lost relative? They're no threat to us."

Neb returned to his bag and tucked in small items. He could hear his mother breathing in agitated gusts, fanning her face with her hand.

After a moment of heavy silence, he faced her. "I'm merely curious. Now tell me, where in the hills does he live?"

Meshullemeth tilted her head. "I don't know, but I could guess. It's said that a clan of long history lives there, and a man of good fortune travels those lands. I wondered if the man they spoke of was your father's brother, but when I mentioned it to Hezeki, he would not discuss the matter."

Neb continued to move about the small room, stashing objects into his bag. He kept his face averted and spoke with indifference. "If my travels lead me in that direction, I may want to stop and meet my uncle and speak of family matters."

Neb's mother pursed her lips. "Look for the clan I mentioned rather than search for your uncle or your father. After all, a settled clan is easier to find than travelers or a solitary man."

Surprise at her intuitive sense made Neb pause. "Do you know anything about this clan?"

Meshullemeth smiled. "I know their name, but I have one request before I tell you."

Neb's chin rose as he fastened his eyes on his mother's face. "What?"

Strolling idly around the small room, Meshullemeth caressed small objects as she passed. "Someone should be appointed leader in your absence. Of course, as your mother, I am the most knowledgeable and reliable person in the village. So, before you leave, let your men know that they are to answer to—"

Neb slammed his fist on the table. He tore his words like meat off a bone. "I've already made arrangements for my absence. Torgama and Kittam will rule in my place until I return."

Meshullemeth's eyes blazed, her face darkening. "Torgama and his imbecilic friend Kittam? Those two are not fit to lead a hunting party. They are boorish with little imagination. They have no manners and less skill—"

Neb's hand rose to strike. "I do not care for your evaluations! I know what I'm doing. When I come back, I want my people to rejoice in my return. Warriors are not soft-spoken or gentle. They must keep everyone safely together. Warriors are not nice."

"But I'm more suited to rule!"

"A woman will not rule my clan."

Meshullemeth's fury broke loose. "Why not? I was a woman when I bore you, a woman when I raised you. I made you what you are today."

Neb turned away, dismissing her with a wave. "You think too well of yourself." He returned to his packing.

~~~

Meshullemeth swept her large body out the door and stalked through the village, rage nearly blinding her. Her son was not going to dismiss her and leave two stupid oafs in charge. Torgama and Kittam disgusted her. She paused a moment to collect her thoughts.

Hul stood outside his dwelling.

She grinned and started forward.

Hul met her gaze and seemed to read her mind. He motioned away from his home.

They walked out of the village and stopped at the bank of the stream. Hull clasped his hands like a penitent child. "I'm sorry to make you walk so far, but it's a fair evening, and—"

Meshullemeth patted Hul's arm. "Yes, the evening is beautiful—especially for those about to embark on a journey."

Hul jerked back. "I've made arrangements so that I can assist Neb." He paused and chewed his lip. "What do you want?"

Meshullemeth smiled. "It occurs to me that my son is still young, and he'll need the assistance of an older and wiser man. I'm relieved that you'll be attending to him. But I do have one request."
~~~

Children screamed playfully in the background.

Hul frowned. "Anything."

"Report to me everything that happens while you are away. I want to know where you go, whom you meet with, and what events take place from first to last. Can you do this for me, Hul? You were my husband's favorite, so I know I can trust you."

Hul swallowed and blinked at the blushing horizon. With a sigh, he looked Meshullemeth in the eye. "I will do as you ask. But keep this conversation between the two of us."

Meshullemeth grinned, innocent compliance pouring from her soul. "Of course, just between the two of us." She patted Hul's arm and sauntered away, fresh plans dancing in her mind.

~~~

Torgama, sitting under the shade of an old tree on the bank of the river, waited for the two figures to recede. He stood and rubbed his stiff neck. But the momentary discomfort was replaced by a sense of coming pleasure. His whisper could barely be heard above the noise of the stream. "Just between the three of us."
~~~

CHAPTER FOURTEEN

—VILLAGE OF SETH—

WHAT EVIL YOU FACE

Eva strolled through the quiet village of Seth and watched the inhabitants as they went about their daily duties—men repairing thatched roofs and sharpening tools, women preparing meals, sifting wheat, and caring for babies. Everyone seemed occupied, but there was no hurry. An air of peace prevailed among these people, the like of which she'd never experienced before.

Seth wandered through the village, chatting with men and women as if he had never known a day's worry in his life. Only a slight frown when he glanced her way hinted at dark thoughts.

Struck by his gentle manner, so different from Neb's commanding presence, she shadowed him. When he stopped to visit a sick, old woman, confusion tied a knot on her brow.

Though an old woman might be important to her immediate family, she could not understand the village leader's tender concern. She padded to a neighbor who stood by, watching as Seth entered the old woman's dwelling.

The neighbor smiled as she shook out her rugs in the morning sunshine.

Eva peered at the woman, hesitation tightening her voice. "Is Seth's grandmother seriously ill?"

Wrinkles of amusement sped over the woman's face. "That's not Seth's grandmother. His father's parents died long ago, and his mother's parents passed on in the epidemic a few seasons back. Though we are all related in some measure, he has no special claim on her."

"Then why does he visit her? Does she have power over him?"

The neighbor's eyebrows rose as she tilted her head, staring fixedly at Eva. "What do you mean? Seth is a good man, and he cares for us all. She's ill and will probably pass soon. He wants to make sure she is comfortable and happy in her last hours."

The knot of confusion tightened Eva's stomach. "But if she's about to die, what use can he have for her?"

The woman dropped the rug before her door and faced Eva, her hands on her hips. "How strange you are! Does your father not say goodbye to those who are about to die?"

"Perhaps if he had a reason to. Sometimes those approaching death need to explain how to divide up their things or settle old disputes, but the dying have no need of counsel. They have no future and nothing to consider beyond the next moment. Our clan doesn't worry the dying with thoughtless visits when all they can possibly want is peace without discord."

With a grunt, the woman snatched two pillows from a bench and began to smack them together, sending billows of dust into the air. "My people do not think dying is so simple a matter. Don't you consider where their spirits go?"

"They go into the grave. Where else can they go?"

"Most extraordinary!" The woman tossed the pillows inside and beckoned Eva nearer. "Come, child, and sit with me a moment."

Reluctance slowed Eva's steps. Visions teased her thoughts: her mother standing by while the wizened hag brewed charms and curses, and spoke in a dreadful voice to dark power. Prickles broke over her arms. She stopped and swallowed her fear. "I'm content to stand."

"Very well, do as you please. But step a little closer. This is a delicate conversation, not meant for everyone's ears."

Eva took two steps forward and waited as her curiosity sparked. "Why? What do you fear?"

The woman glanced around before returning her gaze to Eva's face. "I do not fear what I am about to say, but I do fear those who would scoff and cause trouble." She nodded significantly at a hut across the way. "You see, child, our world is ruled by a single God who created all things. The first Seth was a follower of the One…a descendant of Noah. But there are those who turn away and follow after other things not so wholesome."

Violent thoughts raced through Eva's mind. Many spirits she understood, but who was this God Seth followed? Who did Neb follow? Most importantly, who was stronger? She licked her lips. "But what does that have to do with the old woman?" She gestured to the hut Seth was now leaving.

"Well, when a person—like that old woman—dies, her soul goes to join God. Seth wishes to send his greeting so that when his turn comes, God will not think him a stranger."

Her mind whirling with these strange thoughts, Eva struggled to disentangle them from past conceptions. If those who believe in God go to Him, then where did those who did not believe in Him go? What had happened to her mother's old sorceress? What happened at death? She rubbed her head where an ache pounded in her temple. "I only know of spirits, for we had an old woman who called on the unseen powers to do the bidding of the living. They did nothing for the dead."

The woman jerked to her feet, her hand rising to her throat as if in fear of being choked. "Oh, child, you live in darkness. Spirits spark terror and corruption. Only God is good. But I think we have talked enough. You must ask your father. Surely he knows of these things."

Eva shook her head. "We are escaping my brother, Neb, who rules through spirit powers. If my father had known your God, perhaps he would've stayed at home."

The woman shook her head, sorrow filling her eyes. "If you do not know God, you'll never find peace." She turned to her doorway.

Seth had stopped to chat with another villager, and now he moved on toward the woods.

With a quick nod, Eva excused herself and crept slowly after Seth, keeping far enough back to remain unnoticed.

Seth walked some distance into the brambly woods with his eyes sweeping the ground.

Finally, after Eva had walked further than she really wanted to, Seth sat down on a fallen tree trunk. His back to her, she crept behind him, stepping slow and cautiously. She stopped beside a nearby tree and listened attentively. An odd sound sent chills down her spine. She leaned forward.

Seth sat with his head in his hands, sobbing.

A lump swelled in her throat. Before Eva realized what she was doing, she stepped forward, but a loud rustling stopped her in her tracks.

Two young men bounded through the woods. The larger one, Jubal, with thick black hair and brown eyes, spied Seth and shouted a greeting.

Eva retreated behind the tree.

"Hello, Seth! We've been looking for you! Come let us—" Jubal came to a quick halt in front of his friend. "What's wrong?"

The second young man, Accad, smaller and with reddish hair, marched sedately forward, his voice dropping low. "Seth is upset, can't you see?"

"I see as well as the next man, but my eyes only work

at close distance, and I wasn't close when I started talking."

Accad folded his arms and glared at his brother.

Jubal plunked down beside Seth and nudged him with his shoulder. "So, what is it? Has someone dared to insult my leader and friend? If so, name the—"

Accad fluttered his hands. "Let him speak!"

A flush crept up Seth's neck. He rubbed his face. "I'm a fool."

Eva covered her face as a blush heated her cheeks. Could a leader call himself a fool in front of his men and live?

Jubal patted him on the back. "That's all right."

Eva's eyes widened.

Accad silently mouthed, "Shut up!" He turned to Seth. "Talk quickly before he starts up again."

A gentle breeze stirred the leaves overhead.

Seth stood. "When I went to visit my old friend, I realized that she would be on the other side soon, and I wished I could go with her. I don't feel equal to the trouble that Hezeki's family brings. Neb will not be content to let them escape in peace. When he finds that we have given them shelter, he'll take his anger out on us."

Jubal faced Seth, his hands clenched. "You're fretting over nothing! This Neb, son of Hezeki, doesn't know where they've gone. Even if he should find out, he can have no grievance with us. We've done nothing wrong."

Eva suppressed a weary sigh.

Accad rose to his feet, doubt in his eyes. "Some men don't need a reason to make war. They enjoy battle and conquering others. There is nothing quite as satisfying to some men as killing innocent villagers to impress the clan."

Accad scowled at Seth. "You think Neb is that kind of man? Hezeki is not. We have known Ashkenazi for many long years, and he has always been our friend and support.

Could his own flesh and blood be so evil?"

Eva nodded.

Seth eyes swept through the woods. He lifted his hand in silent warning. "I don't know Neb, but I have reason to fear him. Did you not notice his sister? She was taken from her own mother for her protection. Something is terribly wrong when the mother is a danger to her own children."

Her heart twisting, Eva stared at the moss clinging to the branch before her.

Taking Seth's silent warning, Jubal cocked his head, stood, and circled around the trees in the near vicinity.

As he drew near, Eva's heart raced. She straightened and lifted her voice. "You don't know what evil you face if you think my mother is the source of our danger."

Jubal beckoned her closer, but she walked straight to Seth. "I've never seen a man cry, and I've been told things today about your people that confuse me. Still, I see you have something we lack." She glanced at the brothers. "Seth is right: Neb is dangerous, and he might come looking for us. He is rarely content. We must leave your village soon. I don't believe he wants to make war with everyone. At least, not yet." She paused and frowned as she considered a new thought. "Even though you cried like a child, I believe you are stronger than Neb. It is we who are at risk of either being destroyed by him or becoming like him."

Exhausted beyond measure, Eva turned and strode away.

~~~

Accad watched the strange girl disappear into the tangled woods. The two brothers turned toward Seth,
~~~

whose gaze stayed fixed on her passing.

Jubal threw up his hands. “I’ve never heard a child speak so. What do we have that her people lack except a leader who knows how to cry?”

Accad shook his head in warning. “She’s right. Trouble lies ahead. She fits with her whole family. They must be from an extraordinary line. Ashkenazi lives alone in the wild, healing yet never completely healed. Hezeki is a man of grief. Neb has a mind for conquest. Now this child speaks like an old woman who has seen too much.”

Seth followed Eva’s path back to the village. He seemed to be speaking to the trees. “I fear that what we have to offer Hezeki may be very different from what Hezeki offers us.”

Accad leaned toward his brother and dropped his voice low. “We’d better hope that whatever we have is stronger than whatever they bring.”

Chapter Fifteen

-Planet Helm-

A Bloody Statement

Zuri crouched low and waited for the signal. His knee bounced rhythmically, but his heart pounded erratically. Helm was nothing like he remembered. Debris covered the once pristine streets. Kelesta's hometown had been reduced to rubble. A perimeter of raging fires created an orange glow on the horizon, and black smoke ringed the dusky sky. "Come on, answer me, damnit!"

Nothing. Dead silence.

Ark scooted forward and wrapped a tentacle around Zuri's shoulder. He pulled Zuri back toward an unbroken wall. "Sit down and calm yourself. You'll overwhelm your system if you keep this up, and then I'll have to make Teal turn into something with gigantic muscles to carry you back to the ship. You know how cumbersome you can be."

Zuri hated to admit that he did feel lightheaded and wondered if perhaps his whole return-to-nature spree might have a downside. "I'm fine. I just want to find Kelesta and get out of here. Half the planet has been decimated. Who could've done this? And why?"

Ark plunked down on his well-padded behind and yanked off a boot. His three toes, red and swollen, gave off an unpleasant odor.

Zuri covered his mouth. "Put that back on. Don't I have enough to deal with?"

"I can hardly walk another step. The heat and dry air are killing me." Ark peered around. "And not a drop of water in sight. Amazing, everyone didn't evaporate in this inferno."

A bleep turned Zuri's attention. "It's Kelesta…or at least her signal. She's around here…someplace." He held out his hand. "Come on! Let's go."

"Help me with my boot first. I can't very well hop on one foot."

Anxiety tightening his innards like pinchers at the landing dock, Zuri bent over and did the needful, holding his breath against the awful stink. "You really need to see a podiatrist." He rose and swung his datapad in a 360-rotation, peering at the signal. He swung back forty degrees and pointed. "This way."

Ark jutted a tentacle forward with heroic resignation. "Lead the way, oh besotted one."

~~~

Teal muted his figure to blend in with the shadows as he stood beside an ancient tree blasted in two. The heart of it exposed, the rough wood grain ran in amber waves from the branches to the roots. A large, broken limb created a leafy niche where he could look out through a veil of green, while those standing on the other side would likely assume they were alone.

Two Uanyi Service Patrols in their smart green uniforms relaxed in easy repose, one rested his plump foot on the blasted tree trunk, while the other folded his arms over his ample thorax.

Teal frowned. He had never seen an overweight citizen of Sectine before. He had imagined it was not in their nature to get fat. But these two proved his theory wrong, or at least proved he'd not been fully informed. Trying to imagine Tcesni with hefty curves, he winced at the mental image. The patrols' conversation jerked his attention back
~~~

to reality.

Plump Foot chuckled. "Got to hand it to the queen. She has more brains than the last one. Course, she's as power-hungry as all get-out. Amazing, in this day and age, we can't do any better. I mean, look at the Crestas. If they don't like their leader, they just exterminate him."

His compatriot scowled. "A new queen might hatch and take her out, but that's not our place to say."

"Yeah. First rule. Always remember your place. How is it that queens ascend to the Celestial Delights while workers like us end up in Death's Stagnant Pool? Bet the Crestas have a better system. More logical."

With a quick shoulder shrug, the thick waisted Uanyi begged to differ. "Crestonians don't have it so good. Muddy water and sterile laboratories and all that. But you just wait. Some have new ideas back home. I did a tour at Capital City Chrysalis, and I'll admit, I was impressed. Those young, educated sorts have brilliant plans for the planet."

Plump Foot apparently fell into despair at the idea, his tone rising to a whine. "Yeah, so what? We've always got young'uns with fresh ideas and exciting plans, but as long as the same old traditions rule, we'll never break free. Look at the Queen. Think she'll ever agree to share power with the workers? Or let anyone interfere in the nursery? Not her!"

Ample Gut bent forward and dropped his tone. "Don't get so discouraged. You know, we were sent here to investigate this disaster—find out who did it. I think she's worried that someone is after her throne. Someone who might just send *her* to Death's Stagnant Pool."

Teal's muscles went rigid; he cocked his head.

Plump Foot slid off the tree trunk, sounding like stone scraped over rock.

"Who?"

"Oh, I have my suspicions." Ample Gut peered around

and then tugged on a leafy branch. A knowing grin spread across his face. "One of those Ingots is here pretending to be frantic with worry. He's been asking about a Bhuaci named Kelesta."

"So?"

If a frown could scold, Ample Gut's expression slapped his compatriot across the face. "Think, would you? An Ingot in love with a Bhuac? A mechanical man and a Bhuaci sentimentalist? Really. Use the brain your ma gave you."

Apparently deciding that he wanted to rise to the honors list, Plump Foot took a mammoth mental leap. "So…Ingots are experimenting on the weakest race around so they can challenge Tcesni?"

Ample Gut slid a graceful finger under his belt, loosening it, a sigh escaping at the effort. "Could be."

A loud bang cracked the still air, and the two patrols straightened and focused their attention. Ample Gut marched forward with his partner close behind.

Teal waited, letting the two disappear into the milling throng by the dilapidated building that had crumbled on one side. Dust billowed into the sky, and yells rose over wailing sirens.

As everyone turned to the collapsing building, Teal parted the hanging fronds and stepped away from the tree trunk. He watched the crowd, depression falling like a heavy weight on his shoulders. He lifted his datapad and scanned the area. Then he tapped a code and stared at the screen.

Ark's face materialized before him.

Teal frowned. "I signaled Zuri."

Ark's normally jovial expression darkened, his jowls drooped and his lips turned down. "He's rather busy at the moment. I took the liberty of answering."

Frustration stewed in Teal's gut. He clenched his hand

and almost crushed the datapad. "You'll be benevolent enough to explain that."

"We found Kelesta."

Ice flowed over Teal's body. He had often heard the term, but for the first time, he understood what it meant. "Is she—?"

"Not yet."

"But soon?"

"Very likely." Ark shook his massive head, his purple jowls swaying like empty wineskins. "Apparently, she was in a building that collapsed. Zuri's gone in to get her. He thinks there is still a chance."

"Is he wearing his armor?"

"Love is his armor."

Teal closed his eyes.

~~~

Zuri supported his head in his hands as he sat on the edge of the seat next to a stark hospital bed. Fire seemed to flicker through his innards. Never had he felt this weak before. He couldn't move or say a word when Ark and Teal entered the room.

Ark peered at Teal and waved him forward with a low murmur. "I don't know what to say to the besotted fool."

Teal laid a hand on Zuri's shoulder. "There is still hope."

Tears sprang to Zuri's eyes. Confusion mixed with embarrassment washed over him. "That's something Kelesta might say."

"She always looked on the bright side."

Zuri reached out and caressed Kelesta's cheek. "She did…" He stood, swallowed hard, and stepped away from the bed. "But why she decided to connect with me is more
~~~

than I can explain. She should've stuck with one of her own kind. Someone who wouldn't—"

Teal frowned. "I've always held to the belief that inter-alien relationships are hard enough without adding romance. But that hardly means I'm one to chastise you. But still, you're both renegades of sorts. Reaching beyond the boundaries of your—"

Zuri swiveled on his heel, the fire in his body exploding, seething from every corpuscle. "It was an *Ingot* bomb that destroyed the building…that almost killed Kelesta. My own people did this!"

Ark waddled forward at a cumbersome trot, a perplexed frown drawing his eyebrows together. "Ingots blew up half this planet? Why?"

Zuri bit his lip and dropped onto a chair by the wall. "We were never meant to become a warlike people, but we've developed to the point where no one can attack us with impunity." He waved to the bio armor still attached to his torso. "Hence my biological accouterments."

Teal glanced from Kelesta's limp form to Zuri's slumped figure. "But why attack Helm? It's not as if they are a threat to Ingilium."

Ark waved a tentacle. "Ah... But, as Zuri can attest, there have been recent uprisings by numerous Ingoti Old-World groups wanting to return to their honest origins. They see danger in their technological developments and sporadic incursions into the universe. Isolationists at heart, they want a simpler life, stripped of all modern accessories."

Teal's glance swiveled from Ark to Zuri. "And the connection to Helm?"

Zuri clasped his hands, his head bowed. "Our leadership, definitely not in favor of Old-World ways, wants to make a point. A bloody statement. Without our modern developments, we will be just as weak—just as vulnerable—as Bhuacs."

Teal swallowed against a scowl deepening the lines on his face. "You would attack an innocent—"

Zuri sprang to his feet. "Not me! This has nothing to do with me. I heard rumors…but I never thought they'd carry it out." He turned away, a sob heaving from his burning chest. "I can't live with my own kind anymore. Not knowing…what beasts we've become." He turned and glanced at Teal, pressure aching behind his eyes. "I hate Ingilium—my own people! We think we're better than Bhuacs because we can destroy them? Because we are less vulnerable? Oh, God!"

Ark gripped Zuri's arm, supporting his friend, glancing aside at Teal. "I'll stay. You'd better go back to Earth and find out how Ishtar handles becoming a grandfather. If you remember…"

Teal nodded. He stepped up to Zuri and placed his hands on his shoulders. "You're not the only one shamed by your own people. There is a reason Luxonians must debate even the least decision in council for long cycles. We're afraid of ourselves." He strode to Kelesta's bed. With a gentle sweep of his hand, he caressed her forehead. His voice dropped to a low whisper. "Rest for now, daughter of Helm. We'll need your strength soon enough."

A tear slid down Zuri's cheek. Only Ark's firm grip on his shoulder kept him from falling.

CHAPTER SIXTEEN

—VILLAGE OF SETH—

MATCH YOUR DEEDS

Enosh ground a brittle leaf through his dry fingers. The crunching turned into silence as he watched the separate particles fall to the earth. Another new day. Time was running out.

Neb would surely follow soon.

They had camped in the northwest, not far from the daily bustle of the small village. Enosh stepped inside a simple tent and studied his father's sleeping form. His heart squeezed painfully. No matter where they went or how hard they tried to escape their fate, Neb would have to be faced and defeated. But Hezeki could never accomplish the deed. He would not fight in open battle against his firstborn son. He could never win.

A sigh escaped Enosh's lips before he realized it.

Hezeki stirred. He looked up, fear rippling over his face.

Enosh took a step forward and lifted his hand in reassurance. "No, Father, nothing has happened. Not yet, anyway."

Hezeki struggled to sit up and rubbed his face. "Not yet?"

"I think it's time to leave this village. There's a great river to the east—across the grasslands. We ought to settle near there. I don't know much about the land or the people yet, but we'll learn as we travel, and it'll be good to move on. Don't you think?"

Hezeki nodded slowly; his eyes fixed on Enosh's face. Then he dropped his gaze and clasped his hands, rubbing his fingers together like a fretful child. His shoulders drooped, and his whole frame seemed to shrink.

Enosh waited, bewildered, anxiety rising like a storm in his chest.

Finally, Hezeki rose and staggered to the corner. He dug through his bag and pulled out a skin bag. Gulping, he took a long drink and then wiped his dripping mouth with the back of his hand. He peered at his son. “Enosh, you must lead our people into the new lands yourself. The great river is attractive, but that will bring trouble. Many clans will claim the lands along its banks. Go south instead, deeper into the grasslands. Travel along the hills east and leave no trail behind. Neb will never imagine that you headed south. Stay out of the mountains, for they can be treacherous.”

A burning cauldron fired Enosh’s insides. “But I don’t understand. Won’t you lead us?”

“The men must become accustomed to you as their leader. I was afraid to do this earlier because I worried that you were too young, but after meeting Seth, I’m convinced that you are as much a man as he and can do all that I ask of you.”

A woman called to her child in the distance, and Enosh gazed out the doorway, his heart aching.

“I will follow my brother’s example and live out my last days in peace.” Hezeki gripped Enosh’s arm and stared into his eyes. “Will you let me go?”

Sorrow and loss filled Enosh. “But where will you live?”

Hezeki waved into the distance. “Out there. Somewhere. Not far.”

Enosh pulled away and stepped out into the bright sunshine. He stared at the morning glow on the horizon. “What about Neb? Will you be safe?”

Hezeki stood under the open flap and crossed his arms over his chest. “As safe as anywhere. After a year has passed and you have made the beginning of a village, come back, and tell me about it. Then I'll consider joining you. But you must get away first." He peered at his son's back. "Do you understand?"

Enosh nodded. His father was not telling him everything. Pressure mounted behind his eyes. He turned and met his father's gaze one last time before he stepped outside.

Enosh strode into Kenan's tent and put the matter before him.

Eva walked in during their discussion and raised her eyebrows at Enosh's report.

Neither his brother nor his sister argued the point. Their silent response weighed heavily on Enosh. Before he stepped back outside, he glanced from one to the other. "You know as well as any that Neb will not leave us in peace. We must move on as soon as possible."

The flap swooshed heavily into place as Enosh left to gather his men. With few words, he placed the new plan before them, and again, he was met with silence. He searched the gaze of his most trusted friends and advisors, but no one offered a word of argument or comfort. When he directed them to make the necessary preparations for departure, he returned to his brother and sister.

The three siblings assembled their things, rolled up their tent, and after a hasty meal and a refreshing drink, they hefted their goods and went in search of their father.

Hezeki sat on a stump outside his dwelling, gesturing for his children to draw closer. His tone remained light and conciliatory. "I'll join my brother for a time. We have many years to catch up on. Don't worry about me; for an old man, I can take care of myself. If I need anything, the people of Seth are generous and will assist me." He focused on Enosh. "See that you guide the men well and travel in safety."

Kenan glanced from his father to Enosh, chewing his lip.

Enosh squared his shoulders.

Eva peered at her father and then at her two brothers. Her eyes narrowed. "Why are you doing this, Father? You are still a better man than Neb." Her face flushed, and her eyes blazed in anger.

Kenan stiffened, and Enosh exhaled a ragged breath.

Hezeki forced a grim smile. "I'm doing what I must for your safety, daughter."

The girl's voice turned hard. "For us? Not for yourself? Neb will follow us, and where will we be, then?"

Unable to fight another battle, Enosh pressed the girl's shoulder with a firm hand. "We don't know what Neb will do. But father does have a right to peace in his last days. Neb shall not take that from him."

With cold, blue eyes, Eva stared at her father for the last time. "I will say goodbye then, Father. We'll leave now and disturb you no further."

The old man's voice dropped to a plaintive sigh. "Don't leave in anger." His gaze swept the ground. "I've been weak for too long. Now I must accomplish an impossible task."

Eva's voice softened though her scowl deepened. "And what is that, Father?"

"I must tame a wild beast." He stroked her hair and then dropped his hand to his side. "Now, go. Find a new home."

Eva blinked back tears.

Kenan embraced his father in a strong hug.

Enosh swallowed a lump in his throat and patted his father's shoulder. How he would accomplish his goals, he did not know, but he must try. "I'll take good care of them."

The three turned away.

Hezeki's voice rose, wavering in the afternoon stillness. He called after them, "Remember, children, your true home is inside you."

Kenan and Eva shuffled forward.

Enosh glanced back once, staring at his father's slight figure, his leg thrust out, his back hunched against a glaring sky.

~~~

Neb peered at the village of Seth in the shadow of protecting trees, drinking in the view of a peaceful clan as they went about their daily duties.

There were no hurried movements, though surely they must've been aware of his approach.

The sun had risen well past its zenith, making straight for its nightly retreat. The warm, humid air hummed with the sound of busy insects.

A weak and yielding people, he judged them to be. He had caught one of Seth's hunters and discovered both the location of his father in the village and also the cave of his uncle.

Ashkenazi was so easy to find that it was almost a disappointment. Neb felt no kinship with the big-hearted, gentle soul. When he had presented himself to his uncle, Ashkenazi had simply stared and said nothing in words, though his eyes spoke as they swept up and down Neb in obvious disgust.

Anger boiled through Neb. "You are neither welcoming nor courteous, Uncle."

Ashkenazi merely shrugged and turned to his cave.

Startled by the large man's indifference, Neb stalked behind, pounding his spear into the ground at each step. "Is my father well?"

Ashkenazi continued inside and poured water from a pitcher into a bowl. He splashed his face and wiped the
~~~

cooling drips away with the back of his arm.

Neb's face grew hot. He stood at the mouth of the cave and flexed his muscled arms. "I would have you tell me of my father, Hezeki!"

Ashkenazi faced Neb, his eyes blazing red and furious. "You are no son of Hezeki. Son of a demon is more likely, but not Hezeki!"

A sudden calm descended on Neb. His decision was easy. He gestured to his men.

Puti stepped forward. He lifted his spears and fixed his gaze on Ashkenazi.

Neb dropped his voice to a calm whisper. "When a son comes looking for his father, he does not expect to be met with angry insolence. Especially from his own uncle."

It only took one silent look from Neb, and Puti ended the confrontation.

Ashkenazi groaned as he fell. With a look of twisted pain, he reached out. "Your end will match your deeds, brother's son."

With a shake of his head, Neb looked upon the dying figure. "I hope so." With a quick thrust, he ended Ashkenazi's suffering. Then he stepped out into the sunshine.

Puti, in an unusual moment of self-direction, pressed his hand to Ashkenazi's bloody chest then placed the bright red handprint upon the wall painting of a doe with gentle eyes.

Neb looked back and snorted.

CHAPTER SEVENTEEN

—VILLAGE OF SETH—

ALL THE TEARS OF YESTERDAY

Hezeki saw Seth standing alone the next morning, his shoulders squared and his jaw set in a firm line, and he knew he had waited too long. His skin prickled, and his shoulders slumped as he lifted his hand to his eyes, trying to keep the brightness of the new day from blinding him.

Seth turned. Their eyes locked.

Hezeki hobbled near the young leader, in pain, and feeling very much alone.

"Have they left, then?"

"Yes, very early. I told them to head north into the mountains. They can find shelter and plenty of hiding places among the caves." He forced a smile but feared it appeared more of a grimace. "I know I've said alarming things about my eldest son, but surely he is only one man, and your warriors are more than a match for him and his few companions."

Seth stared at the bleeding horizon.

"It's possible that he just wants to know where we plan on settling, and then he'll return home." Hezeki shuffled forward, so the two men stood shoulder to shoulder, staring ahead as if in agreement.

A breeze meandered through the village.

Seth glanced aside at Hezeki and nodded, though doubt lingered behind his eyes. "Our men have seen little battle in recent years. We only train warriors because it has become a custom handed down from father to son, and it's considered a point of honor to be able to fight well."

"A worthy skill for every man."

"I doubt true bloodlust still runs in their veins."

The slight breeze stilled into a dead calm.

A chill ran over Hezeki.

"I hope you will convince your son that there's nothing of interest for him here. The sooner he moves on, the better." Seth hesitated, though his gaze stayed fixed. "I'm concerned that he may have some unwholesome desire to see his brothers."

Hezeki paused as if to think the matter over, but a swift runner cut his musings short.

The slender youth bowed before Seth, panting with his exertion. "A group of armed men are but a half day's march from here." His eyes flickered to Hezeki. "I believe he is your son, the one called Neb."

Seth tipped his head in acceptance, turned, and marched toward his home without a word.

A cold sweat broke over Hezeki's forehead. He looked to the ground, tears mounting behind his eyes. His firstborn son, a dread beyond words even to himself.

A child's shriek lifted his gaze. A mother caught her toddler in her arms, roundly scolding him for what misbehavior, Hezeki did not know. He looked to the north then shifted his gaze to the south. "Escape, my children. Escape while you may." Then he faced the rising sun and lifted his chin in defiance.

~~~

Neb stared at the cowering figures. They were trying so hard to appear brave and warrior-like. He saw a few who, with training, might make useful servants, but the vast majority appeared weak and nervous. Disgust rose like gall into his throat. Merely walking into their midst frightened them.
~~~

He strode to the center of the village. There, his father stood with a young man at his side. At first, he imagined it must be Enosh, but to his surprise, it was a young man slightly older than Enosh, taller and slimmer. He wore the ceremonial robes of the leader. Neb felt a smile curl around his lips. Could this baby face be the leader? How had he assumed his role?

Neb stopped in front of his father and stared at him for a long, cold moment.

Hezeki's uneasiness pulsated through the air. His eyes flickered from Neb to the man at his side.

Without a word of greeting, Neb turned and addressed himself to the young man. "You're the leader here?"

"Yes, my name is Seth. I am—"

Neb waved Seth's next words away in a bored but commanding gesture. "I know all about you. I have learned much in my travels. Do you realize who stands beside you?"

With furrowed brows, Seth glanced at Hezeki, clearly taken aback. "Yes, of course, here is your father and leader, Hezeki. Surely you—"

Again Neb raised his hand. "I see you are not aware of the full truth." He glanced around, appraising the possibilities. "Let's go someplace comfortable."

Neb gestured to his warriors to fan out throughout the village. "My men will make themselves at home, so do not concern yourself with them." He fixed on the largest, most central abode. "Is that your lodging?"

Seth's men watched in tense silence. The villagers appeared frozen in place. Even the children stopped their games and stood with wide eyes, curious, waiting.

Accad and Jubal held their weapons at their sides, still and waiting.

Seth waved Neb forward, and with hurried steps, led the way.

Relaxed and already certain of his authority, Neb followed, allowing his eyes to roam freely over the lodgings and the inhabitants. He allowed his gaze to rest on a few likely figures, several robust men and a couple of comely women.

A vulture circled overhead, sizing up the scene.

Neb grinned.

When they arrived, Seth motioned Neb inside.

Hezeki hesitated and dragged himself meekly behind.

Without ceremony or leave, Neb strode to the best pallet arrayed with pillows and colorful rugs. He sat down and gestured for the others to sit before him.

"Come, I expect no more than common cordiality while I am here. Please, sit and be comfortable." He tipped his head to the warriors guarding the door. "They can send for refreshments. I've been journeying for many days. A hot spiced drink would do me good."

Seth's body stiffened, reflecting the incongruity of a guest telling him what to do in his own house. Confusion flushed his face. With his hands clenched, he called a man to his side and whispered in his ear. Then he turned to Neb and sat down on a simple pallet, one usually offered to guests. Seth clasped his hands in his lap and stared directly at Neb—in challenge or in mere curiosity?

Swelling with pride at his latest achievement, Neb lifted his voice to reach the men circled around the doorway. "I have come into your midst, Seth, to warn you of a great danger. I have followed this man" —he gestured toward his father with a dismissal—"because he is a traitor to his own people and must pay the price that all traitors pay. He undoubtedly told you a story of how I am an evil, over-reaching son who forced him to run for his life. I'm sure that my brothers and the weak-minded followers they brought with them convinced you of his lies. But I am here to warn you. They've come here to destroy your people."

Hezeki struggled to his feet, wincing in pain. His hand trembled like a man ready to strike. "How dare you accuse me of such crimes when it was you who treated me and your brothers with abhorrent disdain? You forced—"

Neb stood and approached, stopping a few inches from his father's face. Disgust rose as the stink of his father's deformed swollen leg assaulted him, a curse beyond redemption. He spoke slowly, enunciating each word with great care. "You left your people unprotected. When the attack came, as I foretold it would, we were prepared, and we defeated the enemy. I have come here to see that justice is done. I'm surprised you are not cowering in some cave like your brother."

At the mention of Ashkenazi, Seth rose and stepped between Neb and Hezeki. "This is not the place for your accusations. If you have complaints against your father and you want to address them in this village, then you must abide by the traditions of this clan. I will hear both sides in the evening, when the sun has set, and tempers have cooled. For the time being, I want you two to stay away from each other and—"

Cold fury rose in Neb at Seth's impudence. A baby trying to act as arbitrator of Neb's dominion? He brushed Seth aside as he might an insect that had dared to land on his arm. "I have not asked for your assistance. I do not need your counsel. This matter is already judged, and I have decided a fit punishment. I will see my two brothers and dispose of the disloyal members of my clan who followed my unworthy father into your midst."

Hezeki's shoulders slumped, his resolve appearing to melt.

Seth stared at Hezeki's submission, and his lips tightened into a hard line. "I'm the leader of this clan, and if you attempt any violence against me or any man under my protection, then you'll have to fight me and every man here, down to the last warrior. I doubt you are prepared for the battle I am willing to wage!"

Neb's eyes narrowed. A glimmer of respect kindled in his mind. Ashkenazi had not faced death so valiantly. Neb studied Seth and desired to test him to see the proof of his words. In the end, he would win, and Hezeki and his brothers would die at the time of his choosing, but there was no rush. He sat back down and gestured for Hezeki to leave.

Hezeki looked to Seth, but Seth nodded his agreement.

Limping through the door, Hezeki dragged his useless foot.

Neb returned to his seat and leaned back expansively. He gestured for Seth to do the same. "Apparently, I have a man in my midst, and this pleases me very much. You have no idea how lonely the world becomes with so few strong men. I do not see the need to destroy you or your people unless it is absolutely necessary. After all, I came here with a just complaint."

Neb stretched and stifled a yawn. He looked about. "But right now, I'm hungry and weary. I'll rest, and tonight we can gather everyone so that full justice will be done before all."

Seth remained stiff, his hands tightly clasped in his lap.

Neb grinned. "I assume Enosh and Kenan are hiding someplace. Please let them know that they can run, but they cannot hide. It'll be much better if they simply face me. After all, I may be in a mood for clemency. They are my brothers, after all." Neb leaned back and closed his eyes. "I will rest until the food is brought. You may go."

~~~

Seth hardly knew how he managed to get to his feet.
~~~

The situation had spun out of his control so quickly; his breath seemed lost along with his rightful position. He stalked out, saying nothing. All the tears of yesterday had dried, all the sorrow burned away. Rage ruled now.

CHAPTER EIGHTEEN

—VILLAGE OF SETH—

CULMINATION OF CRIMES

Neb admired Seth's home. Though a simple thatched hut with a central doorway much like that of all common dwellings, he appreciated the addition of two extra rooms in the back, private areas, probably for women and children to work or rest while the men of the village discussed matters of significance.

One room contained a small door built into the east wall, undoubtedly for the purpose of a secret escape if need or desire arose. If it were his home, it would be clearly understood that when the back door was used, no one was to follow or ask questions.

After perusing each room, Neb stepped to the doorway and studied the hushed village. The homes were arranged in an oval pattern around a central fire pit. A small crowd hovered around a large stew pot, likely used in communal feasts. His stomach rumbled.

Returning to the central room, he noticed two beautifully embroidered cloaks, obviously intended for ceremonial occasions, hanging upon ornate pegs on the right wall. Caressing the cloth between his fingers, he delighted in the soft texture and admired the vibrant colored threads.

Squinting in the dim light, Neb studied the pictures sewn into the cloth: a multitude of animals entering a great structure while enormous raindrops fell from a stormy sky.

Where had these backward people learned to produce such picturesque robes? He glanced at his own worn leggings and stained tunic and scowled.

Puti ambled through the door. He crossed his arms and waited in silence, though his eyes strayed to the fine cloth that Neb rubbed between his fingers.

Neb let the cloth drop into graceful folds against the wall. Impatience filled him. "Come closer and speak low."

Puti strolled forward, his deliberate stare and slow movements only adding to Neb's annoyance.

Puti spoke in a husky whisper and pointed as if they could both see through the wall. "Hezeki is in the dwelling behind this one on the left. Baskets hang from the posts and rafters. Must be weavers. He and Seth are taking council with the village elders and a few warriors—if you can call them that." Puti peered into Neb's eyes with a meaningful sneer.

Neb controlled a desire to slap Puti. He contented himself with flexing his hands and giving a sharp nod. Considering the situation, he stepped to the wall, peered out a slim crack, and stared at the dwelling that Puti had described. Chuckling at the irony of fate, he imagined the distance from the back door to the next dwelling.

Neb returned his gaze to his servant, who waited in narrow-eyed silence. His annoyance at Puti vanished like mist under a hot sun. "Tell Riphath that I want him to help with tonight's meal. He will invite Seth's hunters to go with him to get meat. Also, inform Seth that he should invite my brothers to this evening's feast."

Neb clasped his hands and closed his eyes as he perfected his plan. When satisfied, he opened his eyes and focused on Puti. "While everyone is busy making preparations, go to the furthest end of the compound and set one of the dwellings on fire. Then quickly join the hunters in a round-about path so it will look like you came from a different direction."

He paused and tapped his fingers together, his gaze

turning inward again. "But before you leave, send Hul to me."

Trained well, Puti simply nodded and stepped out the door.

Neb followed, calling after him, "Good hunting!"

Villagers lifted their heads and stared at Neb.

Puti merely bowed and started on his away again.

The sun dropped near the horizon, and the mountains' shadows lengthened. Brilliant daytime colors faded to shades of gray.

Neb strode to the back room and watched through a crack until Seth and his men left the weaver's dwelling. He tapped his fingers rhythmically on the post.

Finally, Hezeki lurched to the doorway and glanced around with nervous, darting eyes. Chewing his bottom lip, he stumbled back inside the weaver's house and closed the door.

Hul called Neb's name from the front room.

With exhilaration hastening his steps, Neb grinned at Hul when they met.

Hul frowned and dropped his gaze.

Neb patted the man's arm as if to give him courage. "I have a job for you, Hul. Inform Hezeki that after tonight's feast, he will join his brother and stay with him forever—in peace if he can find it. After you give the message, join Puti's hunting party to help prepare for the feast."

Hul's shoulders relaxed, and a relieved smile played on his lips. "Of course, this is good news. Hezeki will certainly comply with your wishes."

With a snort, Neb dismissed Hul with a wave. After Hul had left, Neb retreated to the back door and watched the assigned conversation. When Hezeki retreated into the weaver's dwelling once again, Hul marched off toward the center of the village, his head up and his gaze focused.

Neb planted himself in the doorway, propped his hands

on his hips, and surveyed the villagers busy about their work. He met sidelong glances with a silent nod.

The sun fell behind the horizon. Dusk arrived in full armor.

Panicked shouts rose from the southern section of the village.

Neb stepped back and slipped on the ceremonial robe. In the twilight, as everyone's attention focused on the flames leaping in the south, he dashed the few paces into the weaver's dwelling and opened the door.

Hezeki, his eyes wide, staggered backward.

Neb barred the way outside. "Don't worry, old man. Your work is done." He pushed his father back into the dark dwelling.

Hezeki glared at his son and tried to shove past.

Neb squared his shoulders, flexing his muscles.

Hezeki spat his words, "So, you've come to say farewell before I join my brother?"

His heart pounding, a broad smile spread over Neb's face. "Yes, indeed. That is so."

Hezeki shook his head. "Why pretend filial concern now when you've never shown any before? We have nothing to say to each other. Leave me, and I will set out at once to meet Ashkenazi."

"Ah, but you have one last duty to perform for me."

Hezeki appeared momentarily amazed. "What could you possibly want now? You have everything!" Then with a low chuckle, he nodded, leaning on the wall for support. "Or do you have a request from your mother? There's no limit to her advice or ambition!"

Neb's eyes narrowed, and his breathing evened as coolness settled over his skin. "I decide how I will live." He paused and his grin disappeared. "It is time for you to go beyond the reach of all living men. Rid me of your disgusting weakness forever." He slipped his knife from his belt then pointed from his father's leg to his chest.

Hezeki blinked and raised his chin, his chest thrust out in a daring attitude of utter contempt. "It is a curse to kill your father."

"Then it will be my greatest curse!" Neb raised his arm and plunged the knife downward.

Parrying the blow with his shoulder, Hezeki stumbled for the door. He didn't make it to the threshold.

Neb's agility quickly overpowered his father. He wrapped his arm around his father's neck and stabbed him in the back.

With a grunt and a slow groan, Hezeki fell to the ground.

One precise stab to the heart completed Neb's plan. He stood and stared at his father's sightless eyes.

An owl screeched in the night, and men's voices drew near.

Shaking himself free of a moment's trance, Neb dragged his father's body to the bed, flopped him on top, closed the sightless eyes, and turned the old man's head to the side. Then he tossed a blanket over his body and peered out the doorway.

Night covered the land. The men's voices passed toward the center of the village.

Neb bustled back to Seth's dwelling and disrobed. Bloodstains now marred the fine material, but Neb only shrugged at the ruination of the glorious robe. He stretched through a yawn and plopped down on the comfortable pallet. With a sigh, amazed at how easy he had achieved his end, he lay down and fell asleep.

~~~

Jubal crept noiselessly under cover of dark to Seth's
~~~

dwelling. The time for action had come. They must drive the enemy away quickly. The only solution was to kill Neb before he suspected any serious opposition.

Jubal stopped outside the door and glanced around. He should consult with Seth, but he feared his friend's hesitancy. Jubal chewed his lip and thought of his older brother, Accad. He shook his head. Time was of the essence, and the planning needed to coordinate two men would cause serious delay. Surely, Neb planned some treachery under the cover of tonight's grand feast.

Crouching low with deliberate caution, he opened the door and peered inside. Everything remained quiet. Creeping forward, he passed over the threshold and entered the dwelling.

Flames played in a small hearth set against the wall, highlighting the room in a dim, flickering glow.

A wolf howled in the distance, sending a shiver over Jubal's arms. He froze.

Directly in front of him, Neb lay still as a stone but staring at the ceiling with wide-open eyes. He did not move or even seem to breathe, but a scowl plainly showed that he was awake. He clenched a knife in his hand.

Jubal held his breath and waited. His best hope lay in a sudden attack, but stark fear bound him. The critical moment passed.

Neb spoke in a monotone, calm and composed. "I see Seth has a friend."

The opportunity lost, Jubal straightened, thrust back his shoulders, and planted his feet wide, prepared for anything. "Many."

Neb rose in one fluid action, stepped forward, and met Jubal's gaze. "He'll need friends. Loyalty is not always found in brave men. Most men are either brave and independent or loyal but timid. Being both brave and loyal, you and I will be friends."

Completely flummoxed by this reasoning, Jubal felt his face flush. "The loyalty you so value bars our alliance. You've shown yourself to be brutal to your brothers and disloyal to your father. How could I ever trust you as a friend?"

A smile crept across Neb's face. "You have wit, too! Better and better." He leaned in, peered deep into Jubal's eyes, and then placed his hand on the young man's shoulder in a fatherly gesture. "You'll find that I'm a different man from the stories told about me. Surely you do not judge a man without hearing from his own lips the proof of his innocence. Or does truth have no place in your society?"

An icy chill spread over Jubal's body as reason warred with his emotions. "You may speak for all the good it'll do you. But honest words must be backed by honest actions, or they are phantoms at best and deceiving treachery at worst. I'll never again trust a man who has once lied to me. Speak now if you dare."

A bubbling laugh burst from Neb. "I like you. I really do. My brothers are not half so clever. If they had been, things would've been different, believe me."

Neb gestured for Jubal to sit across from him. They settled on mats, and Neb leaned against a soft pillow. "I'll tell you my story, and you must judge for yourself the truth of it—if *you* dare. For judgment is a tricky thing. It requires conviction, and conviction demands action—even loyalty."

His jaw aching in tension, Jubal merely glared at Neb.

Crossing his legs and clasping his hands in his lap, Neb settled for a comfortable pose. "My father, though a caring man, never had the presence of mind to raise me as a leader. Because of his weakness, I realized it was my duty to be strong for the sake of the clan. My brothers resented my efforts to grow beyond my father. If we had been raised as equals, we would've been equals in weakness. And" —Neb paused and nodded at the doorway as if to indicate Seth's entire village—"in times of trial, the weak die. My father and brothers are terrified. They ran away in secrecy as if in fear for their lives, so I must conclude that they have convinced themselves that I am the enemy. It is apparent they have told everyone they met the same lie." His eyes narrowed as he locked his gaze on Jubal. "Am I wrong?"

Confusion engulfed Jubal as uncertainty tangled his thoughts.

Neb grinned and clapped his hands like a child winning a game. "I see the truth in your face." Neb pulled at his collar and exposed his neck. "Do now what you had planned to do earlier—if you dare."

Running his fingers through his hair, Jubal dropped his gaze to the dirt floor.

"As I thought, you are a reasonable man. Kinder than my own kin."

Shouts rang outside as women called the men and children to the feast.

Jubal stood. "I'm not sure what to think, but this I will say, I'll not judge a man again until I hear the full story from both sides. You've had that much influence on me."

Neb clapped Jubal on the shoulder. "You're cautious. A healthy attitude." He started toward the door, leading Jubal. "How about this? Tonight, when the moon is at its zenith, bring forth my father, and we will discuss this matter in full. I want you to see that though he is weak, useless, and unjust, and even though he lied about me, I will spare him. He can live out his remaining years with his brother, who I hear lives not far from here. Let them keep each other company in their declining years. As for my brothers, I will let them live in peace wherever they may find it. I just want them to stay far from me so as not to taint the very air I breathe with foolish prattle. I'll rule my clan in justice. They are safe for now, but they must not attempt to cause rebellion and discontent among my men. I think I'm perfectly justified in making that request."

His stomach clenched tight, Jubal nodded. "I see no fault with that. I'll tell Seth; I see no harm in allowing you to meet your brothers." Jubal exhaled slowly and started for the door. As he faced the clammy night air, he frowned at patches of the star-studded sky and wondered why he felt more burdened now than when he arrived ready to kill Neb.

~~~

Neb strolled across the room, poured a measure of amber liquid into a carved cup, tasted it, and smiled. He lifted the cup in a salute. "Man of Seth, you and I will meet again, and our conversation will be of a very different sort."

~~~

Seth clenched his hands. Frustration clawed at his insides.

Slivers of the full moon glimmered through gathering clouds.

Jubal, Accad, and many of his men stood in the circle around a roaring fire in front of Seth's dwelling.

Heavy moisture stifled the night air.

Three boars roasted over glowing coals in a trench pit while women carried bread, hot drinks, and delicious delicacies to outdoor tables. Tall drinking vessels stood on each end of the tables. Spiced fish piled onto platters tickled noses with their salty tang.

Jubal shifted from foot to foot as he waited by his brother. He glanced aside.

Accad turned and scowled. "What's wrong with you? You're as jumpy as a netted squirrel.

Jubal tapped his thigh spasmodically. "Nothing. I'm just waiting for this night to be over."

In an attempt to calm his friend and appearing relaxed, Seth patted Juba's arm. "You and me, both." He glanced at his dwelling. "I never should've allowed Neb to take my home as he did. It showed weakness."

Jubal peered at the simple dwelling. "Perhaps not. It might've been wisdom to be so accommodating. Perhaps Neb is not what he seems…"

Accad scowled at his brother.

Seth lifted one eyebrow, surprised. He glanced at Jubal's twitching hands. "Jubal, go tell Ashkenazi that his presence is required immediately. Don't let him put you off for any reason. Tell him that his brother's life might well depend upon his quick and courteous response." Seth paused as he saw the hesitation in Jubal's eyes. "What's the matter? Your brother will be here at my side. Nothing will happen while you're away."

Jubal swallowed and peered at his brother, holding his gaze for a moment.

Accad nodded through a grin. "Go on! We'll be fine."

Jubal stomped into the darkness.

Seth whispered just within Accad's hearing. "It's when Ashkenazi meets Neb that we'll face our trial." Exhaling a long breath, Seth strolled the perimeter of his village while the final dishes were set in place. He glanced at his home as he passed. What was Neb doing in there?

All remained quiet and dark.

Seth sent a man to tell Hezeki that the festival was

ready.

The messenger sprinted to the weaver's house and plunged through the doorway.

Seth waited with Accad at his side.

The messenger returned, his face downcast. "He's sound asleep. I could not rouse him."

With a grunt, Seth shook his head. "This will never do. He must get up and greet his son and brother. It was he who came for assistance. I will give it now or not at all." He gestured to Accad. "Rouse the old man. I don't care if he is exhausted with worry; he must face his own kin and resolve the issues he brought before me. I will not have Neb and his warriors stay one day longer than necessary."

Accad nodded and sprang forward, stepping lightly into the weaver's dwelling.

Seth paced around to the front of his own dwelling, a flush of fury burning his face. He stepped determinedly toward the entrance.

Suddenly, Neb stood on the threshold, apparently waiting for him. He smiled and lifted his arm in welcome.

Confusion froze Seth in place.

Neb seemed to delight in the moment. "I'm glad to see you, Seth, son of Seth. Your dwelling has charmed me, and I'm grateful for your generosity. I'm sure that you wish to sleep in your own bed tonight, so I've directed my men to make ready to leave as soon as the feast is over. I find night travel exhilarating. Besides, once this business is over, I have no more reason to stay, do I?"

Seth stared in speechless wonder.

Neb rested his hand on Seth's shoulder, speaking just above a whisper. "You have pleased me much, my young leader, and I will count you among my friends."

He lifted his hand off Seth's shoulder and strode past him toward the fire where now only one hog turned on a spit. The other two lay carved upon platters.

Seth, stunned, felt relief seeping through his body. Dizzy with light-headedness, he started back toward the assembly.

A loud yell stopped him. Voices rose as Jubal, with pounding feet, sprinted to him with another man in his wake.

Seth lifted his hand in warning. He didn't want trouble just when it looked like things might work out peacefully after all.

Jubal thrust his way through the crowd to Neb. "You treacherous liar! You did it! No one else could have! No one from this clan would have harmed a hair upon his revered head. How could you? After all, you said about being misunderstood. You devil from hell!" Jubal sprang at Neb.

Had Puti not been standing between them, Neb might have been injured. Neb, however, lifted his arms, his hands cupping the air as if calling upon spirits. He grinned through a knowing smile.

Sweat dripping down his back, Seth ran forward and pulled Jubal's arm, dragging him away from Neb before any real harm was done.

Neb, clearly in no immediate danger, relaxed and stared at Jubal through wide eyes, as if wondering if the man before him had lost his wits.

Seth grunted with the effort of jerking his formidable friend, a head taller than himself, away from the scene. "What's gotten into you? I sent you to do a simple task, and you return acting like a madman!"

Jubal spun around and flung away Seth's clasping hand. "Ashkenazi is dead! His body lies in his cave. And that man"—he pointed at Neb—"is the one who did it!"

Icy prickles shivered over Seth's body. "Ashkenazi? Dead? You're certain?"

Jubal flung his arms wide, shouting in exasperation. "I

wasn't alone! I brought two men. They saw what I saw. Ask them if you don't believe me!"

Seth turned to the two men who stood with Jubal. The taller of the two, his face flushed and his arms crossed, jutted his chin toward Seth. "Speared. His body was quite stiff. It can only have been—" His gaze shifted to Neb standing in the background.

Another confused babble broke out.

Accad dashed forward, circled around Neb with a look of disgust on his face, and then stopped in front of Seth. He bowed low. "Seth, I'm sorry to report that Hezeki has been killed in the weaver's dwelling. The body was still warm but growing stiff." He sneered at Neb and Puti. "I think we know who did this."

Neb stepped from the shadows into the firelight.

The flickering flames danced across his face, causing him to appear not altogether human.

Seth's stomach clenched into painful knots.

Like a father disappointed by his children, Neb shook his head. "Once again, I'm judged not by what is known but by what is feared. I had hoped this clan was advanced enough to discern truth from lie, but I see that is not so."

Jubal sprang forward. "You lie too well, like you lied earlier today!" He snorted. "Let your father live out his last years in peace with his brother, you said, while all along, you knew they were both dead!"

Neb shrugged. An innocent victim. "How could I? I've been inside Seth's dwelling the whole day. My men were hunting with your own warriors." His eyes narrowed as he locked his gaze with Jubal's. "And you and I spent some time in serious discussion." He turned to Seth, tilting his head in appraisal. "Did he did not share our conversation with you? No loyal servant would keep such a secret. He came to kill me this afternoon."

Jubal spat an oath and leaped forward.

Seth stepped in his way and lifted his hands. "No! I will discern the truth in my own way."

Neb wandered to the laden table and lifted a thick slab of meat, letting it dangle before his face, as if to consider its worth. His voice slowed to emphasize each word. "My father and my uncle have been killed while in your care, under the protection of your warriors. I think it is I who should be angry."

Accad spun away. "You didn't care for them!"

After taking a bite and chewing with slow deliberate motions, Neb turned and focused a penetrating stare on Seth. "And what do their deaths mean to you? Two men have died, and you have no idea how they were killed." He took another bite and chewed. One thing is certain: you cannot blame my men or me." He signaled to his men to come to the table. "We're leaving after we enjoy this repast you so kindly arranged. Though my men did as much as any to provide for the feast."

His mind numb, Seth took a step but then stopped. "I will not eat until I know who killed Ashkenazi and Hezeki. Though you are their kin, I have more feeling, for I am too grieved to make merry at this time."

Neb continued to eat, helping himself to bread and pouring a cup of wine. "As you wish, but fasting won't help me grieve any more…or less."

Accad and Jubal flanked Seth as the three stood in stupefied silence.

The order *Get out!* rang in Seth's ears, as if he actually said the words. But he could not bring them to his lips. A strange habit of propriety stood in his way. How could he prove that Neb had killed his uncle and father? A dense cloud of confusion and Neb's extraordinary behavior upset his wrath. He glanced at the men and women standing around, clutching their children as if to protect those they could.

He took one more step toward Neb. "You must leave now. There will be no feasting this night. Though you may not feel the weight of it, evil deeds have been done. The mind that did this will destroy us all. My men should kill you, but I have no bloodlust in me—only grief. Go now before you kindle—"

Neb waved a piece of flatbread in the air, chuckling, his eyes glinting in the firelight. "Kindle what? Your wrath?" He laughed outright.

With swaggering steps, Neb's men stuffed their bags with food.

Tossing a carafe of wine to Puti, Neb nodded at Jubal. "If you want to find the cause of your grief, I suggest you speak to the man at your elbow. If he would strike me down to rid his clan of uncertain danger, would he not kill my father and uncle to make me look like a guilty man?" Neb gestured for his men to follow him. Their satchels hung bulging and heavy over their shoulders.

Before he passed, Neb stopped and smiled at Seth. "If you're going to rule by your heart, you should watch that one there." He nodded toward Jubal. "He is not what he seems."

Fury raged as doubt flickered inside Seth's mind.

He stepped to the center of the village and raised his arms in salute. "Bury Ashkenazi and Hezeki with all honor as is your custom. But do not grieve. They died as they lived—in obscurity and doubt. Farewell. For now."

His shoulders squared and his head high, Neb strode into the night with his men trailing after him.

The moon shone gloriously through a faint haze of torn, grey clouds. A breeze swept over the village. Men shuffled in place, not daring to partake of the feast. Women tugged their whining children home.

Dread seeped through Seth's bones. Evil had touched him too personally to be denied. He would bury the bodies of Ashkenaziand Hezeki with all the honors he could muster. Yet no matter what tradition he preserved, emptiness remained. It was the duty of a firstborn son to bury the body of his father. The murder of two innocent men was only the culmination of a series of crimes. Seth peered into the darkness and shivered.

CHAPTER NINETEEN

—WILDERNESS—

WHAT DEFINES A MAN?

Hul trotted behind Neb, who jogged at a comfortable pace beside Puti. Though Hul's arms and legs performed their accustomed duties, his mind roamed far from the land he trod over. His eyes saw nothing of the sloping green hills in all their natural beauty. He cared not a bit for the majestic green boughs they passed under, the blue skies overhead, or even the men who ran beside and behind him. His mind returned to the village of Seth and the look upon the inhabitants' faces as Neb and his company departed. Furrowed brows etched by anxiety and hate-filled glares followed their every move as he and Neb's men stuffed their packs with meat and provisions and then departed.

Neb grunted a remark to Puti.

Hul glanced up. He saw their sly smiles, and his stomach clenched.

He dropped his gaze again and reviewed the past two days' events in his mind. Yes, Neb had ordered the murder of Ashkenazi, but Hul had assumed that Neb had some secret knowledge that compelled such drastic action. But even as he mulled this idea over in his mind, his stomach churned. He had heard snatches of conversations about Ashkenazi and soon realized that the man had been loved for his kindness. If truly the case, then Neb had murdered an innocent man.

A bird cawed in dismay at their approach, setting off a chorus of squawks as a flock of ravens rose into the morning sky. A cool breeze replaced the heavy warmth of the night, and Hul's skin prickled.

But who killed Hezeki?

The question haunted Hul, breaking through both memories and observations. A first son would never kill his father. It was unheard of. Yet doubt lingered like an unwelcome guest.

Hul stumbled. He reached out and clasped Neb's shoulder, saving himself from a fall. But as Neb turned, the rage in his face clarified everything. Hul squeezed his eyes shut.

Yes, what Seth had said was true; he should have killed Neb and all his followers before they left the village.

Hul halted in his tracks, stunned by his thoughts.

Riphath, following just behind, ran into his back with a guttural retort.

Neb and Puti also stopped.

Puti, lean and in good health, appeared calm and cool.

Riphath, irritated by his own exhaustion, bent over and sucked in long slow breaths.

The rage in Neb's eyes dissipated like a summer storm. A masking gleam entered his eyes. "You need rest, Hul, and it will do none of us any harm. We are far away now and can slow our pace. Let's sit and eat a bit."

As each man found a place and sat or reclined, Hul walked further on and pulled out his drinking bag. He gulped the last of the contents then glanced around for a stream.

Riphath pointed to an embankment some distance off. "I need a refill too." He shook his limp water skin as if to emphasize his point.

Hul exhaled. He reached out, but Neb snatched Hul's water skin and tossed it at Riphath. With a grin, he tossed his own water bag into Riphath's arms as well. "Fill mine too."

Smothering a flash of irritation, Riphath rose and bounded away.

Neb sauntered in the opposite direction, leaned against a majestic pine tree, and peered at the glorious valley below. "You are disturbed by something, Hul?"

Hul shivered. He stared at Neb's back and, like a vision from the nether world, he could see Hezeki's frail form rise from the valley and sway above Neb's head. It did not speak but only pointed at his son in mute agony.

Hul heard a groan and realized it came from within himself. The words he dreaded dropped from his lips without permission or fear. "You killed your father, the leader of our people."

Neb shook his head, a look of wonder suffusing his features. "You don't see the truth, do you, Hul? How could I be responsible for killing our leader when our leader ceased to exist when his leg grew to disgusting size, he grew frightened, and ran away? I killed no man. I merely denied a phantom, a memory. What defines a man, Hul? Is it his position as a warrior, a cook, a weaver…a spy?

Peering at his scarred hands, Hul remembered Hezeki's mournful eyes. "You murdered your own father."

"A father supports his family. I merely faced the truth of Hezeki's death before you did. Do not think that you have been betrayed by the death of an old man. No murder took place because no man was killed. He was rotting, deformed flesh. No man is valuable unless he is useful."

Neb's words hammered Hul's heart. His every sinew cringed as the truth settled in. He couldn't move.

Neb laughed. "You think too much, Hul. Or you feel too much! By the gods, do you think I would harm our clan? I want to save our people from death and disgrace!"

"Meshullemeth might agree. Many men think as you do. But the People of Seth do not live by your vision. They loved Ashkenazi. They cared about Hezeki despite his weakness." Hul lifted his head and met Neb's gaze. "If others value what we do not, whose judgment holds sway?"

In the gleaming sunlight, Neb's muscles appeared golden as he flexed his arms. With surprising gentleness, he plucked a green stem with a fragile purple blossom. Sniffing in the sweet fragrance, a smile broke over his face. Then he turned and tossed the flower to the ground.

"Hul, you surprise me. There is order in our world, and certain things are ordained. Animals sustain us with their bodies. Do we ask permission to take their flesh? We do what we must, or we die. Preservation is the highest law. As the leader, I must preserve my clan. I must be obeyed. Seth is the leader of his community, and his own people must obey him. But between the two of us, I have more wit and wisdom. I will rule everyone I encounter because it is so ordained."

Tears pressed against Hul's eyes, and a massive ache pounded in his head. He pictured his wife and children, his village, and neighbors. "I would like to go home, Neb. I miss my family."

Exhaling a sigh, Neb's expression clouded. "We still have a mission to complete. I have not yet found my brothers."

As all hope fled, Hul tried one last time. "Nonetheless, I think I will serve you better at home."

"You serve me best when you serve me first."

Neb locked his gaze on Hul and held him.

Riphath plodded into view. Seeing the silent engagement, he stood apart.

The company of men sat tense and silent.

Neb turned and pointed south. "My father wanted me to believe that my brothers had gone north, but all evidence proves they went south. There are few groups of men traveling with a single girl. The signs are obvious. They probably think that we'll give up the search, but once I'm after my quarry, I'll not rest until I achieve my aim." He peered once again at Hul and enunciated his words carefully. "I need you for now, but—"

Hul tossed his weapons to the ground. He unslung his bag and let it fall. "I am lost to you."

Rage filled Neb's eyes. He thrashed his arms in the air. "Not until *I* say! Not until *I* decide!" Neb clasped his spear and pointed it at Hul. "I should kill you!"

The surrounding men jumped to their feet. Riphath and Puti closed in next to Neb.

Hul remained silent and still, his arms hanging at his sides. Hopeless dread blinded him to everything but the dirt at his feet.

Neb paced a few steps away, then came back and leaned toward Hul. His words slithered like winter ice slipping off an incline. "I am your master. You do as I say."

Hul remained motionless.

Neb screamed, "Will no one rid me of this impudence?"

The pain of the spear's impact in his back obliterated all clear thought as Hul fell. He did not feel surprise, only immense disappointment. He had followed the wrong man. But it was too late to change direction now.

Chapter Twenty

-Ishtar's Home-

Ingots Have A Lot to Learn

Teal shivered. He had taken the form of a spotted lizard sheltering under the lip of a large boulder near the base of a natural spring. Water trickled in a rivulet from a rocky basin to a curving stream that flowed between natural hedgerows. He blinked in the blackness. Only distant flickering flames gave shape to the night.

A crowd of family and clansmen, women young and old, and a few sleepy children encircled the village center, where a great fire burned, sending orange embers into the air like swirling fireflies.

Ishtar's story burned into Teal's mind. How could a man murder his own father? How could Neb attack his innocent uncle and pursue his brothers as if they were prey to be slaughtered in a hunt?

Teal flicked his long colorful tail and stretched a stiff back leg. He was getting too old for this. Next time he'd take the form of a hawk and land in the bough of a tree where he could see and hear better. And rest secure.

A shuffling at his right stiffened every molecule in his body. Good thing he wasn't a rock. Rolling away would not be an option. But he'd prefer not to get stepped on. Or eaten. He scuttled backwards.

Long fingers snatched him by the tail and dangled him before vicious black eyes.

The good thing about lizards is that—when stressed—they can detach their tails.

Teal dropped to the ground and scuttled forward.

Pinched hard in the middle, he was pinned to the

ground, sending his irritation level to the boiling point.

Morphing into human shape, he prepared to lunge at the shadowed figure before him, expecting a shriek at the very least.

A burst of happy laughter stabbed the night air.

Teal clapped his hand over Tcesni's mouthpart, felt the sharp outline of a breathing mask, and dragged her under the ledge. He wondered if blood could actually boil. "What're you doing here?" He tried to keep his voice low, but it resembled a boar's angry snort.

Tcesni's grin, pouring from her eyes, practically glowed in the dark. Wrapping her long prickly hand around Teal's arm, the insect queen dragged him from the safe enclosure toward the wooded stream.

Once they were away from the crowd, Tcesni chuckled and patted Teal's hand. "You're a nervous sort, aren't you?" She dropped his hand, bent low, pulled the mask aside, and lapped at the water, barely breaking the surface tension. "Changing forms so often must make you delicate."

Teal rubbed the prickly feeling off his arm. He glanced at the tiny spark in the distance. He didn't want to miss the story. Facing the insect woman as she readjusted her breathing mask, he crossed his arms.

"It's considered rude to scowl at the queen."

Teal narrowed his gaze and glowered. "We're on Earth now. You're not the queen here." He stared at the mask, one eyebrow rising.

Lighthearted laughter ran riot over Teal's nerves as Tcesni started back toward the flickering fire. She scampered faster than Teal imagined possible. He hustled to get in front of her and pointed emphatically toward the clan still absorbed in Ishtar's story. "You want to be discovered?"

"I want to discover what holds you so spellbound that I could practically eat you before you noticed."

"I'll send IANI reports to Sectine. Read those!"

"I prefer to find out for myself."

"This isn't your planet!"

Tcesni tapped a long-nailed finger along Teal's arm. "Not yet."

Teal intensified his glare, morphing into an enormous bird of prey.

Tcesni's grin vanished and she instinctively jerked backwards.

An owl hooted in the distance, answered by owls on their right and left.

Swallowing a nervous gulp, Tcesni lifted her chin. Her eyes glowed in the dark. "How about you show me around? Give me a chance to assess this planet for myself. It's only fair since you've asked for my help." She successfully suppressed the quiver in her voice.

Unimpressed but satisfied, Teal reverted to his human shape. "You *could* help save the human race from annihilation."

"Perhaps." Her bravado back in place, Tcesni started toward the firelight. "But someone would have to convince me that I want to."

—Planet Helm—

Ark quivered in indignation. "How dare she! What an idiotic thing to do! Blast!"

"Are you done yet?"

Ark swung his gaze to his friend and pursed his lips. "No. I'd like to rant a bit more if you don't mind."

Zuri lifted a vegetable-protein pita-pocket to his mouth and chomped down. He chewed slowly, his jaw working in neat circles, and stared at Ark.

"That brainless, prickly, evil insectoid queen scuttled off to Earth! After Teal, I'm sure."

Zuri's jaw froze. He swallowed a thick chunk, his throat bulging with the effort. "You don't know that she's evil. That's just your opinion."

Shivering away the bulging throat image, Ark twirled one appendage like a cowboy doing rodeo tricks. "My opinion is based on facts…verifiable knowledge. More than you can say for—"

"I sent a message to Sienna."

Ark's tentacle flopped to his side. A blur of images ran through his mind: Sienna's lovely Luxonian form, Sterling's covert lust, Teal's fingers squeezing Zuri's neck when he found out. "What? Why?"

Zuri masticated the last of his pita pocket and stretched—a delaying tactic most certainly. "Teal's never been happy since she left. I think he's been trying to fill that intimacy void; you know what I mean?"

Could it be true? Could an Ingot, sloughing off his rightful mechanical armature, be so besotted by emotion that he turned his gaze from logic and reason to see everything through—dare he say it—love-lenses? Ark's voice rose to a squeaky pitch. "You think Teal's hankering after the insectoid because he's longing for a romantic interlude?"

A buzzer snapped Zuri's attention to his data-pad. He read the message, clapped his hands over his heart, and exhaled a long slow breath.

He can't be praying! "What?"

"Kelesta is awake. The surgeon says she had a small blockage in the brain, but she'll be fine now." Zuri started forward at a fast clip.

Flummoxed at the relief that surged over his body, Ark toddled after his friend. He wrapped his tentacles around his middle to keep them from dancing. "That's good. Glad to hear it. Now back to—"

Zuri lumbered forward, a grin spreading over his face. "I never thought I'd get another chance. You know how it is—" He stopped at a door marked Recovery Room and pulled it open. "Bad things happen, and you just have to accept them. It is what it is."

Ark followed Zuri's footsteps though he wasn't following his logic. He peered across the room as they entered.

Kelesta laid on a narrow bed, covered by a thin blanket, her datapad in hand, and her brows furrowed.

Zuri bounded forward with his arms out.

Furious at himself, Ark swiped tears blinding his vision. After waiting through the delicate emotions of reunited lovers, Ark lumbered forward with unobtrusive throat clearing and a rush of bubbles bursting from his breather helm.

Zuri held Kelesta's hand, smiling into her eyes.

He tapped Zuri's shoulder, only glancing at the Bhuac. "You want to tell me about Sienna?"

Kelesta's gaze whipped from Zuri to Ark. Her brows arched.

Zuri rushed in for the save. "I sent Sienna a message that Teal is in trouble. A dangerous Uanyi—also known as the Insect Queen—plans to interfere with his work on Earth and will destroy him if she can."

Prepared for outrage, Ark blew bubbles until he could think of a more appropriate response.

A nurse stepped in. Cute with large eyes, a slightly upturned nose, cherub cheeks, and a dainty figure, she slipped between Ark and Zuri and read Kelesta's vitals off the electronic monitor. She grinned. "Glad to see you're doing so well, my dear."

Kelesta grinned and squeezed Zuri's hand as she nodded at the nurse. "This is my aunt, Shwen. She works here. Been a nurse as long as I can remember."

Shwen waved her hand. "I helped to bring you into the world!" The glow in her eyes dimmed. "As I did many who will not live to see the light of another day." She glanced at Zuri, and her jaw clenched.

Ark swung a protective tentacle over Zuri's shoulder. "He wasn't responsible."

With a professional nod, Shwen flashed a silent goodbye to her niece and stepped away.

Zuri slumped to the chair, plopped down, and dropped his head into his hands.

Kelesta frowned and turned her gaze on Ark. "He's not responsible? Explain that."

Feeling as if he had just landed in a drained pool, Ark shuffled next to Zuri. He met Kelesta's gaze. "Ingilium leadership attacked Helm in the supposition that if the Ingoti Rebels could see what they were risking with their whole 'back-to-nature' scheme, they would forsake their foolish cause and put their armor back on." He patted Zuri's shoulder. "Sorry."

Zuri shrugged. "I can't blame you for being succinct."

Kelesta's eyes filled with tears. "Ingots did this? To us?"

Zuri lifted his gaze, met her eyes, and nodded.

With a quick swipe of her hand, she brushed tears away and then jerked her covers off. She swayed a moment as she landed on her feet but recovered quickly and started forward.

Zuri jumped to his feet and gripped her arms as she nearly fell crossing the room. "What are you doing? You can't—"

Kelesta glared at him. "Damn you! What are you doing here? Go home and deal with your own people."

Shock spreading over his face, Zuri gripped her arms tighter. "But I can't leave. You need—"

"No! I don't. I have my people, and we haven't attacked anyone—ever! We aren't like that. Even if we get blasted out of the universe, we are better off than you. Go home and teach your people what it means to be civilized."

Zuri stared at the furious, pink-cheeked Bhuaci, his face blanched to dead white.

Ark hustled over and peered at Kelesta. "You are right. Ingots do have a lot to learn." He leaned in. "But so do you, my dear." Slipping his tentacle around Zuri's forearm, he tugged. "Come on, you besotted fool. You can earn her love by daring deeds. But all in good time. We need to go now."

Ramrod straight, Zuri kept his gaze on Kelesta. "Do you really want me to go?"

Kelesta pointed to the door. "Now."

Once in the hallways, Ark tugged Zuri along like a good citizen helping a blind beggar. "Don't be so despondent."

"She told me to leave."

"Not forever. And in the meantime, we must save Teal from two females and Earth from four alien races. We have our work cut out for us. I only hope Tcesni hasn't eaten anyone yet."

CHAPTER TWENTY-ONE

—VILLAGE OF HAVILAH—

BE PREPARED

Enosh dropped his gaze from the heavy clouds as drizzle, like a fine mist, sprayed his face. His sister, brother, and the rest of the clan stayed in the background as he strode into the neat, well-organized village. Clusters of men, women, and children huddled in doorways and watched his approach through wary eyes.

Two swarthy clansmen jogged forward and stopped him in the center of the village with their arms crossed over thick spears, their eyes flashing between him and his men. "Who are you?"

"Enosh, son of Hezeki." He pointed back to his clansmen. "We're traveling through and mean no harm."

The two warriors exchanged glances and then, without a word of explanation, gestured him forward.

After mouthing silently to his companions, *Wait there!* Enosh trotted after the retreating figures. They stopped outside a solid hut and pointed to a bench under an awning. "He'll call you when he's ready."

Confusion swarmed over Enosh as he tried to make sense of the situation. "But I just arrived. Does he even know I'm here?"

The taller man merely shrugged. "He knows. Just wait."

With little option, considering the lateness of the day and the exhaustion of his people, Enosh dropped onto the bench and leaned back against the hut wall. At least it was firm and held his weight. He closed his eyes.

When he opened them again, the moon was high, and it

was pitch black. The entire village rested in late-night slumber. A crick in his neck made him wince as he sat up. How long had it been? He looked around, but he couldn't see anyone.

"By the gods! What is this? To leave a guest outdoors all night?" He stood, stretched, and felt the full weight of the long days of marching he and his people had made since they left the Village of Seth. The news of his father's and his uncle's murder weighed like a rock on his chest.

Cursing under his breath, he fumbled toward where he thought he had left his clan. A ring of rocks surrounding an open fire pit tripped him, and he nearly sprawled in the dirt. Biting back a furious oath, he retreated to the bench and plopped down, his shoulders drooping, and his heart cringing at the thought of failure. Once again, he leaned back and rested his head against the wall. He stared at the stars until sleep took him again.

A slap on his arm woke Enosh from a nightmarish series of images, all involving Neb and a hunt where he was the prey. He shielded his eyes from the rising sun and peered at the figure before him.

A gray-haired man with sinewy arms and a broad chest glared down at him. With shoulders squared and a stout cudgel in his hands, he grunted a greeting.

"I am Uzal, the leader of this clan. I have heard from my scouts of your approach, and I know your story. Rumor has reached me that you are running from your brother, a man named Neb who has killed both his father and uncle."

A flush of shame and fury burned through Enosh. He wanted to correct the story, or at the very least, the snide way Uzal related their history, but the truth could not be altered. He merely nodded and met Uzal's unblinking gaze.

"You can stay. I've told your people to make camp on the outskirts." He started to turn away but stopped and grinned mischievously. "We are about to start our seasonal contests for sport and amusement. You may join us if you wish."

Startled by this sudden act of generosity, relief seeped through Enosh's body. "We'd be honored. Thank you."

"Wait until after you meet me in a contest. You may not feel so grateful then."

~~~

Enosh strolled toward the center of the village as a new day dawned bright and sunny. Good humor enveloped him at the thought of being entertained by games all morning. A mingling crowd encircled a wide-open space. Men slathered oil on their arms and legs in tense concentration, their weapons ready at their sides. Various women chatted in groups; a few carried babies on their hips and wiped their brows with cloths tucked in their belts.

Kenan followed his brother, staying close.

Uzal glanced up and met Enosh's gaze. He waved him over.

The first sensation of light-hearted happiness in months quickened Enosh's steps. He grinned as he drew near.

His eyes flashing amusement, Uzal held out a short spear.

Faces in the crowd turned in their direction. Sober. Alert. Watching.

Enosh's feet faltered. He slowed to a stop as he gripped the spear. "For me?"

Uzal's smile widened. "You said you would participate. Try your strength against an old man, won't you?"

A flash of concern sped over Kenan's face.

A slight catch in his chest, forced Enosh to pause, but Uzal's grin turned wicked and teased him.
~~~

Enosh stepped into the clear circle and faced his opponent.

Dressed in a short tunic, his muscled arms and legs glistening in the morning sun, Uzal's grin continued to taunt. Gray hair and wrinkles at the corners of his eyes bespoke a man twice Enosh's age, but Uzal moved like a wary cat, his knees bent, his shoulders arched, and his demeanor relaxed. As he circled, he watched and seemed to wait for Enosh to make the first move.

Enosh cut the air with his knife, more for show than from a desire to do harm.

As the crowd drew back and watched, a few commenting audibly, some grunting, a woman gasped at a close swipe Uzal inflicted on Enosh.

Enosh discovered that he had to fight hard just to stay on his feet. At the first moment of their contest, Uzal thrust his spear between Enosh's feet and knocked him to the ground.

As Enosh rose, the sun glared in his eyes and sweat poured down his back. His early joy was overrun by the necessity of staying upright and not being pierced by the old man's spear.

Kenan leaned forward, his hands clenched, his face taut.

Rotating around his opponent, Uzal swung his spear again. This time, it landed a stinging blow to the side of Enosh's head.

Falling backward and in searing pain, Enosh realized that he was meant to fight in earnest. He jumped to his feet, determined to show the old man what he could do.

Uzal slipped a blade from his belt and thrust quickly, slicing Enosh's arm. While not deep, the cut bled freely.

Rage nearly blinded Enosh. Even Neb, in all his cruel taunting, had never attacked like this. He pulled his knife with one hand and twirled his spear with the other. Plunging forward with his head down like a mad bull, he thrust like an angry child.

Uzal stood stone still, giving Enosh a clear target and then stepped aside at the last moment.

Enosh plunged headfirst into the watching crowd.

A couple of women screamed, and the crowd parted, the men cheered, intoxicated by the scene.

Fury heated Enosh's face as he struggled to maintain his composure, while losing all hope of ending this day with a warrior's well-earned respect.

Uzal stood back and chuckled.

To Enosh's embarrassment, he panted, breathless, one hand clutching the wound on his arm.

"Enosh, you're dead! I could send one of my daughters to fight you, and she'd win!"

Uproarious laughter burst from the crowd.

Enosh wiped sweat from his brow and tried to shake the sting from his arm.

Through narrowed eyes, Kenan watched his brother. He pursed his lips, disgust marring his handsome face.

Eva was nowhere in sight.

Holding his burning face high, Enosh could not help noticing the disappointed stares of his men. He had paid a dear price in the hopes of gaining an ally in the coming battle against Neb. Clearly, Uzal held him and his men in little regard. Now, as he stood before the crowd of bystanders as the source of their amusement, he regretted accepting this challenge. Worse still, he regretted his unpreparedness to face such a formidable opponent as this unassuming old man. "I regret my foolishness. I didn't realize the seriousness of your games."

Uzal sneered. "No man should be unprepared for combat. It is your duty to win!" Uzal looked around, and he spied Kenan looking at him through hate-filled eyes. He grinned and swung his spear directly at the younger brother. "I would like to challenge this one. He looks ready for battle."

Enosh glanced at Kenan, whose gaze stayed locked on the old man. Enosh knew that his younger brother was no better prepared than himself, for he was the boy's own teacher, but when he tried to catch Kenan's eye, the boy refused to acknowledge him. Enosh shrugged and stepped aside.

Kenan hefted his spear, clutched his knife in one hand, and stepped into the ring of watchers.

Uzal circled slowly, his grin replaced with a determined expression, cold and serious. After four failed attempts to knock Kenan off his feet, he switched tactics and darted forward, jabbing at Kenan's gut.

In a surprise move, Kenan swung a mighty blow to Uzal's head. Uzal darted back, but as he tried to counter the move with a thrust, Kenan blocked the move with his own and thrust with his knife.

Blood trickled down Uzal's forearm. His jaw set, and with a series of quick moves, Uzal knocked Kenan backward. With his spear, he pinned the boy's tunic to the ground, grazing his side.

Shouts from the crowd showered Uzal with praise from his clan, while Enosh and his men watched stiff and tight-lipped.

In a final move, Uzal bent forward and held a sharp blade against Kenan's throat.

All commentary stopped.

Kenan stared hard at Uzal.

Uzal's grin returned.

With a last unexpected move, Kenan thrust his knife from the side and aimed at Uzal's chest.

But Uzal nicked Kenan's throat, halting Kenan's move.

Enosh stepped forward, his hands lifted. "Enough!"

Uzal leaped to his feet, dragging Kenan with him. His grin widened into a full-blown smile. He thrust his arm around the young man's shoulder and lifted his arm high. "The winner!"

The crowd burst into applause. Then cheerful commentary took over the scene as the circle broke into small groups and returned to other duties.

Uzal wiped sweat from his face and met Kenan's angry stare. He shrugged. "You fought well and regained the honor of your family, but you still have much to learn. If I was not so kind, you might have gotten hurt. As it is, you have a few nicks to remember me. You should take over leadership of your clan for the sake of those who still follow you." With a call to another clansman, Uzal departed from their company.

Stunned beyond all thought, Enosh started to walk away.

Kenan strode beside him, seething fury. "He doesn't know what he's talking about. Everything I've learned, I have learned from you and Father. He doesn't speak for me or the men!"

Enosh and Kenan stopped when they rejoined their men.

Thubal clipped his words, his face a frozen mask. "We followed Hezeki because he was the leader, but when he ordered us to follow you, it was in expectation that he would soon follow. We have made no determination as to what we would do if Hezeki does not come."

Enosh glared. "You'd go back to Neb?"

Kenan pushed himself in Thubal's face. "You'll not betray us! Uzal took unfair advantage. Hezeki sent Enosh as our leader. That is what Neb fears! Don't let your judgment be clouded by a few words from a man who knows no better."

Thubal thrust Kenan back. "None of us knows what we'll face in the future, and if Enosh is to lead anyone, he'd better be able to stay alive!" Thubal stomped away.

Kenan started forward, spitting an oath in fury.

Enosh gripped his shoulder and held him back.

Kenan thrust Enosh's hand off his shoulder. "I'm loyal to you because I have set my heart on it, but you'll have to fight for the loyalty of every other man who follows you."

Enosh stood solidly upon his feet and looked his brother in the eyes. The burn of embarrassment had faded, though his shame clutched his innards. "What you say is true, and what Thubal said is true also. Even what Uzal said is true. I have learned a bitter lesson today. I now see how Neb succeeds. Neb believes he is the leader because he is the most ruthless and determined, and for that reason, he could not let father live out his time in peace. He had to take over. Warrior strength is leadership. Tradition and family ties have little to do with the matter."

Enosh sighed and squared his shoulders. "I know now what I must do to lead our men and raise a new community, but I am loath to do it. I must become like Neb."

"You will never be like him!"

"Let's hope not."

~~~

Enosh returned to camp several months later, flushed with victory. The sun shone, and his heart swelled in pride when he saw Eva outside. He ran to his dwelling, grabbed his little sister by the waist, and swung her in a circle, shouting in unleashed exuberance. "I beat Kryce today! I outmaneuvered him, and he's the one going home with a sting to mend!"

Eva met the beaming face of her brother and grinned. "I'm happy for you, brother, though" —her smile faded— "it will take more than a sting to stop Neb."
~~~

His joy draining away like water through a net, Enosh felt a sneer worm its way through his body. "Neb! The way you talk, one would think he's a god who can't be beaten. He's a man. Looks like a man, bleeds like a man, and can be stopped like any other man. Kryce is an excellent warrior—one of the best—and when I struck him today, I proved that I'm stronger and better than I've ever been before. Can't you be glad? Can I never prove myself even to you?"

Eva dropped her gaze but quickly turned at the sound of pounding feet.

Kenan raced toward them and came to a halt, practically colliding with Enosh.

Several men sat outside a storage hut, attending to their weapons. They looked up, their eyebrows rising.

"Enosh! Uzal wants you. You remember Hul? He served father faithfully but then decided to stay with Neb. He and Accad and his brother Jubal from the People of Seth have come, and they spent the morning speaking with Uzal. No one looks happy. Hurry!" Kenan turned and sped up the steep incline toward Uzal's home.

Holding back, Enosh nodded. His staunchest warrior, Thubal, could make or break his leadership position. "Tell Thubal where we've gone and that I want him to join us. He has as much of a right as anyone." With this, Enosh nodded to his sister and started after his brother.

~~~

Uzal ignored the press of too many bodies in the confined space, stifling the air in his dwelling.

Dark clouds swept across the sky, promising rain.
~~~

Uzal nodded at Kenan, but when his older brother, Enosh, arrived, he gestured for Hul to step forward.

A slight gasp escaped from both Enosh and Kenan.

Hul's once robust figure had shrunk to a shadow of its former self. His skin hung in baggy looseness, and he peered through grief-stricken eyes.

Uzal opened his hands, bidding everyone to sit. "I believe you know each other. This man was brought into my presence by these two." Uzal gestured to Accad and Jubal, who sat side-by-side and as still as stone carvings. "Serious tidings indeed. I'll let Hul repeat his story, so that you can judge for yourselves." Uzal nodded to Hul.

Hul lifted his head, though his back remained hunched. His words, vibrating with painful intensity, rose slowly. "Enosh, you must not blame me too severely for my lack of loyalty toward Hezeki. If ever you are able to rejoin our people, please be merciful to my family, for they, like me, thought it best to follow the young, healthy leader rather than cling to the old and lame."

Enosh winced. "Your family has nothing to fear from me."

With a meek nod, Hul went on to tell the story of what happened in the Village of Seth after they left, including how both Ashkenazi and Hezeki were murdered and how he was left for dead. He described his torturous trek back to the Village of Seth and how the people there nursed him, despite his history with Neb.

After he healed, Accad, Jubal, and Hul found Neb's trail and followed him back home. They stayed hidden and learned that Neb had turned to marauding and enslaving other clans.

"Neb attacked clans, showing no mercy. He follows a strange god and has powers no man should have. Clans far and wide are terrified of his approach. Some even offered to pay him tribute if he would promise not to attack. Neb killed the messengers but kept the gifts." Hul shuddered. "I didn't see him for what he was until too late. My family still lives, but I can do nothing for them. My only hope rests with Meshullemeth, that she might oppose her son, but—"

Enosh sucked in his breath. "She never will."

Kenan leaned, glaring at Hul. "Where is Neb now?"

Accad shifted and met Kenan's furious gaze. "He's heading this way. He knows you're settled here, and he has heard enough of the People of Havilah to come well prepared. He comes to steal and destroy, but most of all, to kill what remains of his family. He will not let you live to challenge him."

Leaping to his feet, Enosh paced to the open doorway. "Challenge for what? Brutal leadership? I know the men who follow him—Puti and Riphath, Torgama and Kittam—they have no honor, no decency. They follow Neb for their own gain. If Neb were to weaken, they would leave him too. I would never lead such a people!"

A girl's voice rose. Eva emerged from a dark corner. "They are not all evil. Many have helped strangers or assisted those in need. They were not beasts, though beasts they may have become under the influence of our all-too-evil-brother."

Kenan spat his words. "Neb didn't work alone. Remember, Mother encouraged him."

Uzal stood and gestured for everyone to follow him outside. Once in the open air, he called his warriors to assemble.

Arriving after a successful hunt, a fat stag slung over his shoulders, Thubal hustled forward.

"My people!" Uzal raised his voice, catching every villager's attention.

Men, women, even children halted and stared at Uzal.

"A warrior clan comes to enslave our women and

children. Prepare yourselves. There will be no second chance if you fail. Set guards and send out scouts. Gather your weapons; sharpen your tools. I want every blade at my service. We will meet Neb and teach him to bow before us as he wishes us to bow before him. Prepare well!"

Accad, Jubal, and Hul stood to the side, frowns etching their brows.

Uzal strode to them and lowered his voice. "This is not your fight. You have done well in warning us, but" —he took a long appraising look at Hul— "this man has seen enough horror. Take him home and assure Seth that we will stop this menace here. Neb, eldest son of Hezeki, will go no further."

Accad and Jubal glanced at each other and then back at Uzal. Accad spoke for them both. "We thank you for your kind intentions, but this is our battle as well as yours. Neb came into our village and deceived us, murdered a friend of ours, an innocent man. We must regain our honor. Seth has promised to send men as soon as the time and place of battle is known. My brother and I will take Hul back to our village, but we will return with warriors to destroy Neb and all who follow him."

Uzal rubbed his chin, considering the men before him. "I'm not averse to capable warriors, but I've heard about your clan, and they're not known for their fighting skills. Still, you may come with trained warriors. Fools only get in the way. I'll not risk my people's lives to spare feelings when battle comes."

Accad nodded. "We'll return with the best we have to offer."

Uzal watched Accad and Jubal pace away with Hul's emaciated figure hustling just behind. He shook his head and then refocused his attention. His men needed him now.

~~~

Tamar, Uzal's adult daughter, stood by Eva and gently rested her hand on the girl's shoulder. "Don't worry, Eva. Our men know how to fight. You're safe here."

Eva lifted her gaze to the square-jawed, dark-haired woman and muttered, "If only they were fighting mere men."

Tamar jerked her hand back. "Why, for goodness sake, who else are we fighting?"

"You shall see." Eva peered into the crimson horizon. "Something invisible creeps into a man, and he becomes the creature of an unseen power."

Tamar's voice rose, incredulous. "Can no man fight with honor then?"

"Not for long. When the passion takes him, reason flees and bloodlust rushes in."

Tamar bent down, peering into the young girl's face. "You're younger than my little sister Sari, and she has lived in a warrior clan all her life. How do you know such things when I am certain she does not?"

"I know Neb, and one man can teach a girl terrible things."

The first drops of rain splattered onto the ground.

Tamar watched the forlorn figure walk away, blending into the village throng, and fear shivered down her spine.
~~~

CHAPTER TWENTY-TWO

—VILLAGE OF HAVILAH—

SATISFY THE VICTOR

Neb's chest swelled in exultation. He had come upon the People of Havilah far swifter than they had anticipated. Surprise and unremitting brutality would lead to a glorious victory.

Despite his initial advantage, Uzal's warriors managed to push Neb's men to the edge of the woodlands.

The fighting grew fierce as the two matched combatants battled, each claiming advantage one moment and then just as quickly losing it.

Neb trusted that his killing instincts had been sharpened to a keener edge than his opponents.

Despite their losses, Uzal's warriors fought manfully to protect their own throughout the long, bloody day. However, no one is immune to strange misfortune.

Uzal, despite all his honorable intentions and valiant skill, was capable of a costly mistake.

As he pushed further into the village, Neb happily took advantage of even the smallest weakness. In one hut, Neb peered through the doorway and noticed women assisting the injured and attending bewildered children.

During a momentary lull, a beautiful young woman called from the doorway. Her perfectly oval face framed keen black eyes, while her lithe figure rounded in womanly promise. "Father? Where are you?"

An older, harsher figure hustled forward and pulled the girl's arm. "Leave be, child. Uzal has better things to do than come to the aid of his spoiled daughter!"

The girl jerked away and ran outside. “Faaaaather!”

The woman screamed. “Leah! Come back!”

Neb stepped behind a tree.

Pacing forward with determined steps, Leah scanned the area, her hand shading her eyes from the bright sun. Screams and calls drew closer.

Uzal’s voice rang out. “Press forward!” Demanding absolute obedience, a chorus rose in reply, but Neb’s warriors countered with a volley of spear throws.

Leah’s mouth dropped open as she watched her kinsmen falling around her, pieced by enemy spears. Her horror escaped in a scream. “Faaather!”

Splattered with blood, his eyes open unnaturally wide, Uzal raced into the small clearing like a man possessed and spied his daughter.

Leah stood with her hand before her mouth, trembling and bent over.

Neb grinned and circled around to the back of the hut.

Uzal grabbed his child and held her a moment before he glanced at the carnage around them.

Screaming a war cry, Neb called from behind the hut. “Uzal! Meet your enemy!”

Leah clutched her father’s arm, but Uzal wrenched free and tore past the hut.

Neb sped from his hiding place, barreled into the girl, and lifted her over his shoulder. With bounding steps, he fled into the woods, his grin growing wider as branches struck the stunned girl into breathless silence.

When surrounded by his own men some distance away, Neb unceremoniously dropped the girl to the ground.

Leah rose, gasping for breath, her terror replaced by child-like fury. “What have you to do with me, you terrorizing demon?”

Neb chuckled and considered his men in a surveying glance.

Various nods and satisfied expressions told him that the battle had gone well.

Neb returned his gaze to the girl. "I've saved you from a cruel fate."

"But I'm innocent!"

"I doubt that. A companion to power, perhaps."

Leah scowled, her contempt obvious. "A compan—"

Like an eagle diving for the kill, Uzal jumped at Neb, tumbling them both to the ground.

Leah shrieked and threw herself on Neb, beating his back.

A warrior grabbed her by the waist and dragged her away, screaming.

After giving Neb a slice to the face, Uzal glanced over to his daughter.

In Uzal's unguarded moment, Neb plunged his knife into the older man's throat.

Uzal toppled to the ground, one hand clutching his throat.

Neb reared up for a final thrust.

Against all hope, Uzal staggered to his feet.

Surprised appreciation stayed Neb's hand.

Uzal swayed, staring through haunted eyes first at Neb and then at his child.

Leah bent double, straining against the arms that held her back. Her voice fell into a ragged whisper. "Father."

Uzal groaned, his head dropping to his chest as his gaze scraped by Neb.

Neb gripped the old man by the arm and helped him fall to his knees. "A worthy opponent. I would've let you live so that I might test my skill against you another day."

A guttural sound bubbled from Uzal. He glared through eyes red-rimmed and glimmering with unshed tears. "I curse you. Till—stars—fall."

Neb shook his head. "Not even till the sun falls, old man."

Uzal fell face forward onto the ground.

Breaking free, Leah scrambled to her father and lifted his head onto her lap, tears streaming down her face, sobs choking her. She rocked her dead father like a mother cradling her child.

Neb turned to his warriors. "Gather our men. We will regroup in the hills and return well-rested. Without a leader, they won't last much longer. " He rubbed the ragged cut that ran down his face.

Leah peered up. "Murderer! You know nothing of my people. Our strength leads us!"

Exhaustion mixed with relief flooded Neb as he considered the last stages of battle. He grabbed Leah and dragged her away from Uzal's body. "I know more than you think, and you'll listen, for I'm your leader now!" Using his foot, he pushed Uzal over so that the dead man's lifeless eyes stared into the blank sky. Neb sneered as he shook Leah's arm. "I'll take your daughter as my wife. She's mine now. If you curse me, you curse her as well."

Leah covered her face with her hands.

Men called from the distance. "Uzal—Uzal?"

Neb wrenched Leah away, dragging her along as he and his men sped into the hills.

~~~

Eva sighed as she surveyed the destruction of the village and the bodies of so many innocent villagers. Everyone was at odds without Uzal to unify them.

Dodan, Uzal's eldest son, discovered the body of his father, and despite his best efforts, he could not keep his father's warriors from spending their exhausted resources in useless fury. They raced after Neb into the hills as
~~~

darkness fell and accomplished nothing.

Kryce ranted in fatigued distress as he dragged the bodies of the dead onto a funeral pyre.

Enosh marched away with scouts to see if they could pick up Neb's trail.

Tamar, Uzal's eldest daughter, directed the women to care for the injured and to prepare food for those who could eat.

The youngest of the family, Sari hid in a corner, angry and frightened by the loss of her father and sister, though she complied with Tamar's demands.

Having learned much about healing herbs from the people of Seth, Eva tried to assist. With everyone else busy, she took matters into her own hands and pulled dried herbs from a bundle hanging from the rafters and seeped them in boiling water. The brews would soothe aches and relieve pain.

An expectant mother cried out as she leaned in the doorway, huffing deep breaths.

Alarmed, Eva helped the young woman lay on a mat and offered her some of the steaming brew in a wooden bowl.

Sari rushed over and knocked the bowl from the girl's hand. "Don't give her that!"

"Why not? She's suffered too; she lost her brother, and her husband is injured—"

"She'll lose more if you give her that brew, stupid girl."

"It is only a common herb!"

"For most of us, true, but it would end the life of the child that grows inside her. Too late have some women learned the bitter truth of that soothing herb!"

Eva bowed as shame flushed her cheeks. Was there no end to the evil her clan inflicted on others? Ashkenazi had been brutally slain because her father had brought Neb in his wake. Now these people were battling for survival because Enosh had hoped to find allies. Allies they proved to be, but would they be able to hold off Neb? And what about her brothers? Were they capable of escaping the clutches of one who hunted them so relentlessly? Some had said that the Clan of Seth was going to come and assist, but that hope had proven fruitless. The worst had already happened with the death of Uzal. Eva swept the curtained door aside as she stepped into the black night, despair her only companion.

~~~

Neb sliced a chunk of charred flesh from a venison haunch, ripped off a bite with his teeth, and chewed with hearty delight. Only occasionally did his glance dart aside.

Leah huddled under a large, spreading tree a few feet away. Her gaze remained fixed ahead, unseeing, while unshed tears glazed her eyes.

One of his men teased another warrior who had been forced to plunge his dagger into his victim three times before the young man would drop dead. Neb laughed with casual mirth and clapped the blushing warrior on the shoulder as if they had just come home from a successful hunt.

Riphath tended to the roasting meat, while others arranged the spoils that they had pillaged from Uzal's village.

Leah covered her face with her hands, rocking like a frightened child.

A sensation Neb could not identify plucked his nerves. He wiped his sweaty brow and turned back to his men. "Uzal was a mighty opponent—though no match for me. He even tried to curse me!"
~~~

Torgama wiped his dirty hands across his tunic and grinned.

Kittam smiled knowingly as if he had seen hauntings enough, and they only amused him.

Leah's head jerked up, her eyes awake and alert.

Neb swallowed a strange lump in his throat.

Puti strode forward and bowed before Neb. "All our men have been accounted for. The dead were left behind, and the wounded are being tended. Uzal's men have sent out scouts. One is Uzal's son. The warriors defer to him though he is still young."

A burst of joy surged through Neb. He glanced at Leah. Their eyes locked. With force, he dragged his attention back to Puti. "Ah, here is my first opportunity to show what kind of man I really am. Go and capture that son of the late father, who is brother to my soon-to-be wife."

Neb gestured for Kittam and Torgama to assist. "I want that boy unhurt if possible. And I warn you, he is of no use to me dead."

When Kittam and Torgama joined Puti, the three men bowed to Neb and then disappeared into the outer darkness.

Leah sobbed, leaning against the rough bark of the ancient tree.

Neb made himself comfortable before the fire. Success in battle he had expected. He glanced at Leah, savoring the sight of his newest challenge. He grinned.

~~~

Eva peered through the darkness and shuddered. As they approached a makeshift camp, a woman's figure lay crumpled in a heap at the foot of a tree. Neb sat silhouetted against flames, resting with his eyes closed before a fire.

The repugnant Torgama forced her to keep moving, his
~~~

dirty clenching fingers digging into her upper arm. If her hands weren't bound, she'd lash out at him or attempt to get away. The vile beast. But she had no choice except to move where directed, traipsing over an unbroken trail, her bare feet aching with each step.

Kittam dragged Kryce along behind while Puti led the way.

The sun crested the horizon, sending pink fingers into the sky.

A cool morning breeze shivered her exhausted body.

Puti halted before Neb and cleared his throat.

Neb opened his eyes and peered up.

The firelight played against shadows.

"We have brought you what you asked for and a little more. I hope you are pleased." Puti retreated a few paces and Torgama shoved Eva forward, into the firelight, where Neb could see her. Kittam shoved his captive forward too.

Neb rose to his feet, a smile breaking across his face. "Ah, yes, you have done well. This is an unexpected treat. To have the son of my enemy and, at the same time, to be reunited with my own dear sister."

Nausea roiled inside Eva at the sight of her brother.

Neb turned to the scowling young man. "So, what is your name, son of so noble a leader?"

Kryce stood with his arms pinned behind his back and stared with such a look of hatred that if his glare could have killed, Neb would have burst into cinders. He clenched his jaw.

Kittam squeezed Kryce's arms tighter.

With a gasp, Kryce's knees nearly buckled, but he stayed on his feet. "Kryce, the second son of the man you brutally murdered for what purpose I will never understand."

Tears throbbed in Eva's eyes. How could any man commit so much evil?

Neb stepped nearer. "Oh, I will explain so that when you return home, you may explain it to the others. I have no complaint against you or your men. On the contrary, I am impressed with your people. You're much better adversaries than the People of Seth. I couldn't bring myself to attack them openly, though they did deserve annihilation for allowing my brothers to flee when they knew full well that I wished to speak with them."

Neb circled around Kryce, clasping his hands behind his back like a man pondering deep matters. "I came seeking my own flesh and blood, and again, I am opposed. I killed your father against my wish. It was not his death I sought. And I do not seek your death either—though—"

Wretched fury boiled inside Eva. "You lie!"

Neb turned. "I almost forgot you." He gestured for her to come closer.

Eva braced herself and lifted her head high.

Torgama shoved her from behind.

Digging her toes into the ground, Eva fought to keep her distance.

Neb lifted his hand in a motion of futility. "It's of no matter. I have little use for you, but" —he smiled grimly— "I know someone who will be delighted with your return. Our own mother's heart was broken when you were spirited away."

Eva's hands trembled, and her stomach heaved. Only fury held her upright. "Have you no acquaintance with truth?"

Neb grinned. "Whose truth?"

Eva nodded to Kryce. "What do you intend to do to him?"

"Watch and see." Neb retreated into the shadows, and after a few moments, he led Leah into the light of the glowing fire.

Leah raised her hands against the sudden light.

Squinting, she met her brother's gaze and screamed, "Kryce!" She leaped forward.

Kittam maintained a firm grip on his prisoner despite Kryce's attempt to break free.

Neb pulled Leah close to his side and gripped her chin. He forced her to look at him. "After I have your word that you'll stay beside me, I'll order my men to release your brother so that we can discuss matters. If all goes well, he'll be released, and the fighting will end. Do you agree?"

Leah nodded as she glanced at her brother.

Kittam let go of Kryce.

Neb lifted his hand from Leah's shoulder.

Leah rushed to her brother, wrapping her arms around him.

A tear slipped down Eva's face, but she could not brush it away.

Neb smirked at Leah. "As predictable as you are beautiful." He motioned for Torgama and Puti to step aside.

Kittam hovered over Kryce.

Neb lifted both his hands and raised his voice. "I have chosen Leah. Eva will be a dutiful daughter to her mother, and Leah will be my cherished wife. But first, I must pass judgment upon my brothers. Their treachery will end here."

A memory of Enosh and Kenan leading her forward, their broad shoulders youthful yet strong but no match for Neb's cruelty twisted her stomach into knots.

Leah stared at Neb through wide, horrified eyes.

Kryce spat, "My sister will never be your wife! She'd rather die."

A puzzled expression filtered over Neb's face. "Really?" He peered deep into Leah's eyes. "Which would you rather—a quick death with your brother or a long, useful life with me?"

Leah buried her face in Kryce's shoulder.

"I'm her brother, and I speak for her. She'd rather die than live with you!"

Neb turned away. "I think you're wrong. Leah would be my first and only wife. She'd rule with me." He turned to Kryce again. "An alliance between our people—a much better offer than anything my brothers or the People of Seth can give you."

Kryce dropped his gaze.

Neb tugged Leah away from her brother.

With her gaze down and shoulders slumped, Leah followed.

Leaning in, Neb whispered in her ear.

Leah looked up and met his gaze.

Neb wiped a tear off her cheek.

Glancing at Kryce, Leah nodded.

Kryce's face flushed. He jerked forward. "Leah, no!"

Kittam gripped Kryce's shoulders.

Kryce fought, glaring from Neb to his sister. "Don't listen to him!"

"As her first marriage gift, I offer Leah your life and your peoples' freedom."

Kryce jerked against both Torgama and Kittam's restraint. "You're a liar!" He screamed at Leah, "Don't trust him. He'll betray us all!"

Leah's head snapped up, flushed and furious. "How do you know? What if—" She dropped her face into her hands and sobbed.

Sick dread filled Eva. She had to force out her words. "Have you forgotten your father? He awaits burial in the cold ground."

Neb struck Eva across the face.

Eva reeled backward, the sting bringing fresh tears to her eyes.

Neb clapped his hands then motioned to Kittam. "Kryce

may return home, but Leah stays with me. I will meet my brothers in due course. It depends on how long the People of Havilah wish their destruction to go on."

Kryce straightened. "I will give your flesh to the woodland scavengers as meat for their young, so at last, you may serve some purpose."

Neb bowed in mock honor. "How kind." He snatched Leah's hand and marched away.

Kittam shoved Kryce toward the dark woods. "Go home and await our revenge!"

Leah looked back once as Neb pulled her along. She met Eva's gaze and then turned away.

Eva didn't struggle as Torgama tied her to a tree. She could lie down, but no rest was possible. She stared at the faint sparks of light as the campfire faded to embers. Had she been taken from home, brought to the People of Seth and then to the People of Havilah for no purpose? Hate seethed through her.

She closed her eyes and tried to calm her breathing. In her mind, she saw the herb that almost killed the baby growing in the young mother's body. Her mind surveyed the many plants she had come to know as she served the People of Havilah. Some were much more dangerous than that simple, comforting herb. Some could kill a grown man. Smiling, she imagined the look of shock on Neb's face as he realized his final and fatal mistake.

CHAPTER TWENTY-THREE

—VILLAGE OF HAVILAH—

CALL ME GENEROUS

Tamar grieved over the dual loss of her father and her husband, but the warrior spirit of her people did not flow in vain.

During the night, the rains came, and the sky poured, soaking anyone who ventured out. The wounded had been retrieved from the fields and woods and tended by those with enduring strength and proper skill. Warriors beyond healing were laid ceremoniously in a cave called the House of the Dead. The night grew bitter, and few slept except in utter exhaustion, though troubled dreams haunted them all as the storm raged.

In the morning, the mountainous clouds moved off, and a cool breeze danced between the low white sky and the muddied earth.

When she awoke, Tamar pondered the need to reorganize the clan with new leadership and considered her brother Dodan as she went about her work.

During a meeting of elders and clansmen in the center of the village, Kryce stumbled, wet and disheveled, into the village. Ignoring his sister on the edge of the circle, he squared his shoulders, standing tall and defiant, and described what Neb had done.

Tamar trembled, despite her attempt to calm the rising panic in her chest.

Sari, turning from her task of grinding wheat, clasped her hand to her mouth and stifled a sob. She shook her head in mute misery.

Kryce peered at his elder brother, Dodan, and their eyes locked in understanding.

Dodan stepped into the inner circle and spoke in his usual slow, measured tone. "Long have our people valued our sacred traditions, and we will continue to follow the noble path set for us by the ancients. Though we fought valiantly, we have lost much." Dodan's voice cracked as he stared fixedly ahead. "I am my father's first son, and by right, I should lead our men into the next battle. However, I know myself. A warrior, I am not. I was made for another purpose. I am Kryce's elder by nature, but he shall be my elder by choice. I shall serve him with loyalty and bravery. I submit that Kryce shall be the leader of the People of Havilah. After our revenge, we shall prosper once again." Dodan stepped back into the folds of the circle of men amid heavy silence.

Tamar stepped forward, her hands clasped, and her head bowed. "I agree with Dodan, though I do not believe that the size of a man measures the greatness of his spirit."

Kryce leaped to the center. "I cursed Neb to his face. Now I vow to kill him for what he has done to my father, my sister, and all our people. I will lead every willing man in battle against him. Dodan will protect those who remain behind."

Then Enosh, who had been standing silent on the sidelines with Kenan and his men, stepped forward. His face flushed, and his eyes glittered with anxiety. "I know my brother; he is aided by a power that cannot be easily overcome in battle, no matter how skilled the warrior. But I also know that he relies on his most trusted men and that they have no such protection. Ruthless brutality is their only strength, but as they give, so they shall receive. Instead of attacking Neb, my brother and I will destroy Torgama, Kittam, and Puti. If we cut off his legs, he will fall."

Kryce nodded through a grim smile.

Tamar glanced at Dodan and saw only misery there.

~~~

Kenan gloried in the dark night, though the clammy air clutched at his skin. Few animals stirred, but cries of wild things rang out as the casualties on the recent battlefield ripened.

Kryce, with Enosh's help, surveyed the enemy's camp and determined an effective approach.

In turn, Enosh sent Kenan ahead to ascertain Torgama, Kittam, and Puti's positions.

Two were sleeping, and only Puti stood awake, strolling the camp as sentry

Kenan smiled. He smelled victory in taking these three away from Neb. Kenan turned to tell his brother what he had discovered when he dislodged a twig, and it snapped, sending a sleeping bird screeching into the air.

Puti froze and stared in Kenan's direction, gripping his knife.

On impulse, Kenan unsheathed his blade and hurled himself onto Puti, plunging the sharp edge into his opponent's middle as the two wrestled on the ground.

Puti, though strong, was no match for a furious opponent after such an injury.

Torgama and Kittam awoke to the struggle, as did other warriors. Soon the air was filled with shouts for assistance.

Kryce poured water on the campfire and sent choking smoke to engulf the campsite. His men rushed in, battle cries rising from every direction.

In the disorder, two of Neb's men attacked each other. Like enraged bulls, madness reigned.

~~~

Neb, away from the main camp, awoke suddenly. Upon seeing the melee, he rose and stood back, ascertaining how best to snatch victory from sudden chaos.

Leah, lying next to him, awoke to the noisy violence and leaped to her feet, terror in her eyes.

After ordering her to stay put, Neb crept closer to the fighting men.

Kenan and Torgama fought hand-to-hand, while Puti's body lay sprawled near the campfire's smoking embers.

Neb wasted no time grieving.

Kittam, battling Enosh, offered Neb a perfect opportunity to finish what he had long desired to do. He crept forward until he was just behind Kenan and then launched himself onto his brother. It was a dangerous move, but his little brother could never hold his weight.

The two men crashed to the ground in swirling confusion.

In red-faced fury, Torgama grasped his spear and threw with all his might at Kenan as he lay just under Neb's body.

At that same moment, Neb rose and pressed his thigh over Kenan's chest.

Torgama's spear pierced Neb's thigh to the bone. He heard himself scream. In a desperate final stroke, he threw all the force he could muster into one last thrust as Kenan struggled to get away.

Horrified, Torgama shoved Kenan aside and wrenched the spear from Neb's leg. A spurt of blood gushed forth.

Neb's world turned black. As if from a distance, he felt his body lifted from the ground and thrust over a man's shoulder. With pounding steps and his head bobbing mercilessly, he lost all thought and slipped into oblivion.

~~~
~~~

Enosh heard the scream and, in shock, his own personal battle was forgotten. He ran to his brother's side, surveying the scene in a brief glance.

Kittam raced to Leah, swung her over his shoulder, and trundled her into the woods after Torgama.

Neb's warriors, glancing between their advancing enemy and their departing leader, fled like scattered rats.

Making his choice, Enosh turned his attention to Kenan and staunched the flow of blood staining the earth red.

~~~

Kryce and his men chased after their enemy, and in due course, Dodan joined in pursuit. Though they only killed a few of the fleeing warriors, victory tasted sweet as those who had come to conquer now retreated in humiliation.

Only the thought of Leah darkened Kryce's mind as he tromped home. He found bittersweet consolation in the realization that since Neb had captured her as a prize, he would take care of her, for even a fool protected his prize.

When the new day dawned, the heavy clouds vanished, and a blue sky ruled. The air turned hot once again.

Bloody bodies lay strewn across the village. Though repulsed, Kryce knew his duty. He and his men gathered the slain and prepared them for a mass burial. He would have to fashion a custom, for nothing like this had ever happened in his lifetime. As he sweat under the hot sun, he prayed that it never would again.

~~~

Sari did all in her power to assist the wounded. Kenan, though seriously injured with a deep gash in his side and a blow to the head, had not perished like so many others, and she was grateful.

Those she could not save died in peace and goodwill, honored for their brave deeds and valiant service.

The bodies of the hated enemies were taken outside the village and buried in an unmarked grave.

After washing his wounds with cool water, Sari tried to soothe the burning pain in Kenan's side by daubing it with medicinal oil.

He winced and attempted brave humor. "A cut like this is nothing. I've heard of men who returned from battle carrying parts to be sewed back on later."

Sari grimaced, her stomach churning at the image. "I have enough to do trying to heal the wounded without managing the impossible as well."

Despite his clenched jaw, Kenan forced a grin. "Perhaps you don't know your own powers."

Bewildered, Sari frowned. The strong drink she had given him could only numb the worst of the pain. "You're never going to recover if you don't lie still and rest." She began to peel off the old bandage.

Kenan stifled a groan and gripped her wrist. "I choose not to die. You understand?"

Jerking free, Sari laid a fresh cloth over the wound. She bent forward and peered into his eyes. "Such things are not for me to decide. I do what I can, but you have to—"

Kenan hissed. "Don't say that! As if some council far from here has settled the matter. You saved my life, but I will continue to live because I must!"

For the first time in months, amusement quivered inside Sari. "If determination makes for a strong body, you will be up by tomorrow!"

At this, Kenan sighed and fell back onto the soft skins covering his pallet. "Maybe not tomorrow but soon. I will be strong again."

Sari relaxed and watched him fall into a fitful sleep. After a long backward glance, she returned to her work.

~~~

Enosh watched as Tamar washed the bodies of the slain with her customary care before they were taken to the House of the Dead.

Though he and her brother Kryce were bound by a desire for revenge, as the same man who had abducted both of their sisters had also killed both of their fathers, he was not sure what his position in this clan would be now that he had suffered the loss of so many of his men.

He did not have family or warriors enough to seed another clan, and he wondered how he would survive if he were sent away in retaliation for what Neb had done. Yet as the day wore on and Kryce said nothing, Enosh dared to hope that he could stay.

After her duty caring for the dead, Tamar returned to her children, and though grief etched her face, she remained capable and attentive to all who needed her help.

Enosh consulted with his men to offer what assistance they could and to help with the hunting and meal preparation.

By the end of the day, he wiped his sweaty brow and sat under the shade of a large oak tree.

Tamar swayed by, carrying her little girl on one hip while her young son trailed behind. In the other hand, she swung a water skin. "You must be very tired, Enosh. I've never seen you resting before."
~~~

Enosh forced a grin. "I have no excuse, for I have not worked hard today. I'm not very useful."

Cocking an eyebrow in mock severity, Tamar scolded. "You just don't know whom to ask."

Like a cool breeze over his skin, Enosh felt suddenly refreshed. "Perhaps I have been blind."

Tamar held out her dripping water skin. "Perhaps you could use a suggestion?"

Enosh accepted the water skin, moved aside, and patted the ground.

Tamar sat beside him, rocking her baby girl in her lap while Put played at her knees.

Enosh took a long drink and returned the bag. He stared at the two little ones, good humor tickling his mood. "What are their names?"

Tamar ruffled her son's hair. "This one is Put, after a father's father, and my baby is named Rachel, after a mother's mother. My husband was fond of all things ancient. Tradition was sacred to him."

Enosh's exuberance vanished as he dropped his gaze. "He was a brave warrior." He slid his gaze to Tamar, his voice growing thick with emotion. "In all truth, Tamar, I wish I had been the one killed and that he had lived. If I could make the trade, I would."

Tamar bit her lip, her eyes shining with unshed tears. "We are not the fate makers. If we were to try, we would be consumed by madness. I think that's what has taken your brother Neb."

"But what we do matters. Surely it must! Otherwise, why resist evil? Why care?"

A single tear fell, and Tamar brushed the rest away. "You're right. You have been a great help. I thank you for your generosity."

A lump rose in Enosh's throat. "Was it generous of me to share my evil brother with you? To bring rampaging warriors to your village?" His neck ached, and a pain throbbed behind his eyes. “I would hardly call me generous.”

Tamar met his gaze. “You carry too great a weight for one man. You’re responsible for your own offenses only. Not your brother’s. You’ve been a generous man since you came here.”

Put toddled toward the center of the village.

Adjusting the baby in her lap, Tamar called after her son.

In obstinate determination, the little boy continued forward.

“Oh, you naughty thing! I just barely sit down—”

Enosh jumped to his feet. “Let me.”

A stray dog ran by and jostled the child, knocking him down.

Put howled.

Enosh scooped the little boy into his arms and, laughing, soothed the child’s cries.

In embarrassment, Put thrust his shirt over his head and attempted a game of hide and seek.

Chuckling, Enosh lifted the boy high. “You want to play?” He glanced back at Tamar, who watched with wide-eyed fascination. “First, we’ll gather firewood while your mother makes dinner.”

Put nodded, his face still hidden under the tunic.

Tamar clapped her hands. “After dinner, we’ll visit Kenan. And you both can make him laugh.”

Enosh grinned. “Look who is being generous now.”

CHAPTER TWENTY-FOUR

—VILLAGE OF HAVILAH—

BROTHERS IN SUFFERING

Tamar pounded nuts in a large wooden bowl with fierce blows, her brows scrunched in determination, giving her a headache. Her baby lay in her lap, and her sister sat by her side.

While they worked, Sari plucked shells from the bowl as if she had no concern for the safety of her fingers. Her tone suggested only honest concern. "What's wrong? I thought that you'd be happy now that you and Enosh have become such good friends." A teasing smile replaced her frown as she snuck a glance at her sister.

Tamar sighed, pushing her baby's fingers away from the basket. "I am happy we've become friends, but I'd rather . . ." She hesitated, a warm blush working up her face.

Sari waved her sister's embarrassment away. "If you want to marry him, just say so. If he's willing, then have him ask Kryce."

A sour taste filled Tamar's mouth. "You don't understand. You were young when Mother died; she never explained these matters to you. I'll not have a husband who thinks he was caught like a fish on a line. He must think of it himself." Tamar pulled Rachel's hands out of the basket again and plunked her on the ground.

Sari laughed. "Enosh would love to be caught by you. As a matter of fact, I think that he feels so guilty about Neb that he doesn't dare ask you."

A painful knot formed in Tamar's stomach. "How do you—?"

"I've spent a lot of time with Kenan. The two are brothers."

Tamar's face burned as she turned her full attention to her sister. "You've become *friends* with Kenan?"

"I won't say that exactly. I'm a healer, and he needed healing. But I wonder what'll happen to Kenan and Enosh. They have no home and not nearly enough men to seed another clan. I may take pity on Kenan and save him from a dreadful fate."

Tamar poured the nut meat into a fresh sack. "And what fate would that be?"

"Having to marry you if Enosh should fail."

Embarrassment turned to fury as Tamar glared at her sister.

Sari burst into peals of laughter.

Snorting at her own annoyance, a wave of relief flooded Tamar.

Sari nudged her. "You never know. We may be double sisters before long."

Tamar wrapped the bag tightly and swung the loop over her shoulder. She stood, brushing the broken shells from her dress. Then she scooped Rachel onto her hip. "Only if I do something about it." She grimaced and wiped her hot brow. "Why do the women have to be the brave ones?"

~~~

Tamar caught up with Kryce and Dodan late in the day. The two men sat in council outside the family hut. "Kryce, may I speak with you a moment?"

Kryce stood and faced his sister. Certainly, what may I do for you?"

Dodan rose and stepped aside.

Tamar swallowed and forced out the words she had
~~~

practiced all afternoon. "We have suffered great loss, and without our father and many warriors, we are not so mighty as we used to be. And as you know, we have in our midst a man who has equally suffered. I need a husband for my children, and Enosh needs a clan and a home for his men who have fought bravely in our defense. I think I should take Enosh as husband, and after some time, we should have our revenge on Neb and take back our stolen sisters."

Kryce peered into the distance, silent and brooding.

Dodan stepped forward and pressed Kryce's shoulder. "May I speak with you a moment?"

Kryce nodded, and the two paced away.

Tamar stood very still, listening to her brothers' conversation, certain that she had every right to hear their discussion.

Dodan smiled, gripping his brother's arm. "I understand your anxiety. But Enosh is not like Neb, and though one of our sisters is lost to that family already, this is another matter entirely. In fact, you may have to accept more than even this."

Kryce scowled and spat his words. "What do you mean?"

"Nothing yet, but everything that Tamar said is true, and I agree. Enosh needs us, and we need him. He has done no wrong. To the contrary, he has displayed great bravery and skill. And Tamar needs a husband and a father for her little ones." Dodan glanced over Kryce's shoulder.

Tamar turned, following Dodan's gaze, and saw Enosh some distance away, laughing and swinging Rachel in his arms while Put attempted to climb him like a tree.

Kryce turned to see what his brother was staring at. He winced. "It appears that the matter is already settled." He strode back to where Tamar stood waiting and nodded. "I give my approval. Enosh is a good man. You may tell him I said so. You may be married when the moon is full." He paused. “As for our revenge and recovering Leah, that is best left to the men to decide. But don’t worry; revenge will be ours in good time.” Kryce nodded to Dodan, who gestured toward the woods. The two started away.

Tamar bowed as her brothers passed. She turned to rejoin Enosh and her children, a spark of joy igniting her senses.

~~~

Enosh joined the People of Havilah as Tamar’s husband, and his men joined the clan also, quickly finding suitable wives. Everyone kept busy, repairing homes, mending tools, and replacing lost food stores. Few looked for another battle.

The harvest season came and went. Rain poured from the sky for weeks, and in time, the clan contested in their annual games.

Kryce, quieter and solemn, kept his own counsel. His anger abated, and he treated Enosh with a brother’s kindness.

The two men hunted together and discussed all matters relating to the clan. They found solace in their mutual desire to discover what had happened to Neb and to bring back their stolen loved ones.

During the winter, when sunlight seeped weakly through ever-changing clouds and cold winds stirred dead leaves, they traveled into the hills together, accompanied by only a couple of men.

On the second day out, they met with a band of hunters from Seth’s clan. The two groups approached warily, uncertain if they were friend or foe.

Jubal, recognizing allies, stepped out to greet Enosh and Kryce. “Well met, my friends. What is the news?”
~~~

Kryce signaled his men to continue the hunt without him, and Jubal ordered his men to do the same.

After the four men were settled in the mouth of a wide cave, Enosh leaned forward, eager for news. "You order your men with authority, Jubal, and not as an equal among peers. Has there been a change in your clan?"

Jubal snorted, but no smile lighted his eyes. "A change of fortune leads to a change of order. Ever since Neb came, evil haunted us. Word spread throughout the territory that we were open for attack, and after Neb set the pattern of destruction and conquest, other clans began to raid and pillage. We were attacked twice in a matter of two moons, and then our people took ill. Hul soon succumbed, as did many elderly and children. My own brother, Accad, was stolen away, and I have yet to find him."

Enosh dropped his gaze, nausea rising through his body.

"Laid low with both injury and illness, Seth has not been able to lead the men for some time. He should be married, but too much evil has come upon us. He appointed me as leader in his stead, and though I am reluctant, I do as I must. One more attack, and we'll be scattered to the ends of the earth."

Kryce's voice rose softly. "I wondered why you never returned. Neb attacked us, though he was wounded in the end, and we hope he went home to die."

"We heard the rumor that he was dead, but then it turned out that he was simply injured. The injury became inflamed, and he was near death. Several times, we received reports that he would not survive the season and that he had appointed another to take his place, but later, he was seen walking about in good health. He's not a man but a demon spirit."

Enosh peered at the distant mountaintops. "You're not far wrong. A man cannot do so much evil without aligning himself with something terrible." Straightening, he shook his head as if to throw off his dark thoughts. He waved them aside. "Kryce is now the leader of the People of Havilah, and I'm his brother for I have married his sister Tamar, whose husband was killed in battle. I adopted her children. After so much grief, it feels wrong to gain a bounty, but I'm doing what I can to make amends for my brother."

Kryce nodded. "Though you could not come to our aid, we will come to yours if you call."

Jubal lifted his hand in warning. "Until I know what afflicts us, I would rather you not come. I go out for meat and provisions and to hear the news from afar, but I'll spread our bitter fate no further."

The two hunting groups approached with three slain deer.

Kryce laid his hand upon Jubal's shoulder. "We are brothers in suffering. Enosh's offer holds. If you need aid, send word, and we will come."

A brief smile flickered over Jubal's face. "Though I miss my brother, I am glad to hear your words, for if brothers of flesh are lost to us, then we must forge our own brotherhood. I commit our clan to yours in return. We have learned how to fight, and we're committed to ending Neb's rule of terror. If you learn of an opportunity, call us, and we will come. We have innocent blood to avenge."

Kryce clasped Jubal's arm, sealing their agreement.

Enosh stared at the two men, desiring, above all things, that Neb was dead.

Chapter Twenty-Five

-OldEarth-

Does She Care?

Teal gripped Tcesni's hand as they stayed out of sight.

The clan, mesmerized by the story, focused their attention on Ishtar, undisturbed by Teal's contest of wills with the insect queen.

Restraining her from leaping into the open took all of Teal's muscular strength. "You can't kill him!"

"Why not?" Tcesni's eyes protruded from her angular face as her nostrils flared, clouding the inside of her narrow breathing mask. "You heard what he said. He held those women against their will."

"That wasn't him. That was his grandfather, Neb the Great. Ishtar is just retelling his family history…sordid as it may be."

If Tcesni's eyes bulged any more, Teal feared they would pop out of her skull. "This is something they must work out for themselves."

"So why are you here? You aren't going to intervene when atrocious stories are shared as family entertainment—"

Confusion swirled through Teal's mind. *This from a creature that eats her enemies?*

Tcesni tapped her foot, standing with her arms crossed high over her round breasts.

Teal ran his fingers through his shoulder-length hair and tried to shake off a dream-like reality. *Or is this a nightmare?* He lifted his gaze and met the insect queen's hard stare. "I'm not here to protect them from each other. I'm here to protect them from us. We're the real threat.

They can only kill a few of their kind at a time. But we, meaning you, the Cresta, or the Ingots—"

The resounding slap sent frightened birds scattering into the four winds.

Teal rubbed his burning face.

Tcesni's stare turned decidedly hostile as her eyes narrowed. "How dare you compare us to the likes of them!" She scuttled in the direction of her ship camouflaged by the wide spray of a waterfall.

Teal marched after her and grabbed her prickly arm. The resulting sting made him jump back, wincing. "I didn't mean to suggest that you would act like them. Or that you're like them—really. But you must admit, you're known for depleting the natural resources of every planet you visit, and you have a habit of being rather overwhelming—"

"We love new experiences. It's our natural curiosity that has brought us so far. We're nothing like the creepy Cresta, Icy Ingots, Baby Bhuaci, or you Luminous Luxonians."

"No, and for that, I am eternally grateful." Teal perched on the edge of a rock that projected from the side of the waterfall. A cooling mist swept over his body. "That is one reason we need you. You are different. You can help maintain a balance of power in the region. And humanity can grow uninhibited by outside forces."

Tcesni tilted her head to the side, her bulging eyes blinking in unabashed admiration. "There are a great many interesting minerals right here." She slapped the wall. "Have you done a thorough study of the content?"

"You mean the landscape?"

"No. I mean the content of the soil, water, rocks, plants, animals…" She glanced around. "Even the light and air could be useful."

Teal stepped in front of her. "Remember the mystery

race? The one that attacked Crestar…and is currently putting out the lights around this planet? The universe will soon become invisible."

"Only from Earth's perspective."

"Are you sure?"

Tcesni frowned. She peered back to where Ishtar sat, resting from his story-telling labor. "He might actually taste—"

"Don't even—"

"I won't eat your precious humans. What, you think I'm a barbarian? I only eat my enemies as ceremony requires. I'm strictly vegetarian otherwise."

Teal closed his eyes.

A shout sounded in the distance.

His eyes flying open, Teal reached for Tcesni, remembered her prickly arms, and waved her forward. "Come on. We have to move before—"

The shout repeated. "Teal! Is that you?"

Teal shaded his eyes, perplexed. "Who the—"

Zuri jogged into view. A smile broke over his face as he met Teal's gaze. "Finally!" His gaze swiveled to Tcesni. "Uh, oh."

A headache pounded behind Teal's eyes. He narrowed his gaze. "Where's Ark?"

A woman strolled to Zuri's side, her lithe figure draped in a light rippling fabric. She stood glorious and clearly delighted.

Like an ant that's just gotten whiff of an outdoor picnic, a dangerous smile curled Tcesni's lips. "Who is this?"

Teal murmured the Luminous Luxonian's name while his hands and his heart clenched. "Sienna."

-Zuri's Ship-

Advantage

Sienna glanced from the insect queen to Teal, both seated on a white, curved couch. The lounge on *Advantage* appeared surprisingly comfortable. Her own chair, heavily cushioned, reminded her of a Bhuaci bedroom, where they made comfort into an art form. She winced as her eyes traveled the walls to the ceiling. Zuri had no eye for color, though. The surfaces remained the same gray-green of a Bothmal prison. Ingots had little interest in cheerful hues.

Movement caught her eye.

Tcesni leaned too close to Teal, cocking her head to the side, listening intently. A snarl twitched Sienna's nose as she watched one long insectine finger slide up Teal's leg, making slow ovals. How could he stand to be touched by that *thing*?

Teal cleared his throat and stood. One hand wiped the side of his leg while he gestured to Zuri with the other. "You have anything to eat besides standard rations?"

Zuri shrugged noncommittally. "Well, not exactly. But Ark has been picking up what he refers to as *delicacies* every time we go out. There's a noxious smell coming from his quarters—"

A door slid open, and Ark stepped into the lounge bearing a wide tray laden with a deep-dish tureen, cups, and a platter of what Sienna imagined was some kind of bread.

"It is hardly noxious. Just because something has a smell, you think it must be disgusting. Your sterile upbringing has ruined you for any kind of culinary adventure."

Zuri rolled his eyes.

Tcesni sniffed, and a whip-like tongue flickered between her lips.

Ever the gentleman, Teal cleared a space on the low table in the center of the room.

Sienna shuddered at the image of spilled Crestonian soup.

As if reading her thoughts, Zuri leaped forward and blocked Ark's final step. "Hold on. Let me get something before you make a mess."

Within a few minutes, Zuri placed a large, flat rock on the center of the table, raising every eyebrow except his own. He glanced around. "It's a mineral sample. This way, nothing gets damaged."

Ark laid the tray on the rock and passed cups and bread with a host's practiced charm. Displaying expert finesse, he ordered everyone to eat up, and then demonstrated how to fill the cup half full of the chunky soup, dip the bread just-so, and slurp the delicious offering with the proper um-hmm to please any chef.

Teal stepped forward—brave man—but Sienna maneuvered in front of him, grabbed a cup, poured the soup, and snatched a piece of bread. She turned and bowed with her offering. "Here, take these. I hate to see a grown man go hungry."

Hesitation flickered over Teal's face, his gaze hard.

Sienna locked onto his gorgeous blue eyes, her heart constricting painfully.

Teal's face softened.

Bang!

Sienna whirled around.

Teal threw a protective arm around her, glancing aside.

A scarlet flush flooded Zuri's face. One raised hand clenched as he leaned toward the insect queen. "You want to be crushed, insect?"

Tcesni, clearly amused, laughed abruptly. "The truth

pricks, does it? Well, you shouldn't attack innocent beings and expect no one will comment. The whole universe condemns the Ingoti Magisterium. As well they should."

Imagining a brawl leading to death and mayhem, Sienna gripped Zuri's arm and glared at him, lowering her voice to a whisper. "She wants a fight."

Zuri glanced from Sienna's hand on his arm to Teal's stone-faced expression.

Sienna stepped back and faced Tcesni. "I don't think we've been properly introduced."

Tcesni grinned. "I know your name. You know mine."

Sienna waved toward the front of the ship. "I should check on Ishtar. That's why I'm here."

Teal frowned.

Ark murmured in Zuri's ear, "You must eat. An Ingot hero can't save a beautiful Bhuaci—or his reputation—by withering away."

Tcesni motioned to Sienna and led the way to the front of the ship. "I'd like to see the locator. Humans fascinate me." She glanced back. "As do others."

A wide screen ran a series of images in a loop: a wilderness scene, stray animals scurrying from place to place, a quiet and thoughtful Ishtar seated in front of his home. Amin holding Gizah as she leaned back in his arms with both pairs of hands resting on her pregnant belly, villagers shuffling in subdued routine, birds streaking across the sky. An old woman stumped forward, carrying a tray of broiled fish to Ishtar. He accepted it with a smile. Amin roused his wife as she struggled to her feet…

Sienna and Tcesni peered at the images for several moments in silence. Finally, the insect queen glanced aside and cocked her head, one hand caressing the side of her face. "You intrigue me, Luxonian."

Her face growing unaccountably hot, Sienna glanced at Teal. Emptiness clawed her insides. With forced composure, she returned Tcesni's gaze. "Why is that?

"Teal obviously favors you." Running her hands down her shapely body, a ridge grew between her brows. "I'm so much more attractive—and a queen. Yet he seems…disinterested."

A sudden insight sent shock waves through Sienna's body. *Does she care? Does she feel…rejected?* She tried to shake the observation away, like knocking dirt off the soles of her boots. "He's Luxonian. I'm Luxonian. Naturally, we…" *Enough said. Let the alien figure it out for herself.*

"But he is attracted to humans. I've seen it in his eyes. So his interest is not limited." She flicked a finger to the back of the ship. "I've heard that the idiotic Ingot favors a Bhuaci female. And she returned his affection—until his people decimated her planet, that is." Tcesni leaned in. "I've even heard that Crestas like to do little experiments…" She raised her eyebrows to tremendous heights.

A sick dread filled Sienna. "Is that why you're here? To discover if crossbreeding is possible?"

"Oh, I know it's possible. I just think it's crude and distasteful. Unless, of course, it is done right." She glanced around and then retrained her gaze on Sienna, stepping as close as possible without touching her. "The mystery race has abilities I would love to acquire—"

Teal cleared his throat. "Wouldn't we all?" He stepped forward, forcing the two women to step away from each other, widening the circle.

His grin did not reach his eyes. "Certainly, we'd all like to understand the mystery race better. And I'm glad that you understand how distastefully the universe would view crossbreeding experiments. In fact, I'm quite sure that the mystery race would—"

Ark stepped forward.

Zuri brushed past, clumped to the console, and targeted the screen on Ishtar. “Ishtar is starting his story again.” He waved a hand. “Let’s hear what happens next.”

Ark swiveled his gaze from Teal to Sienna and landed squarely on the insect queen. “Yes, let’s. Shall we?”

Sienna stepped next to Teal, her arms limp at her sides, one hand near his.

With a light brush, the back of his fingers touched hers.

Lightning could not have excited her more. When he twined his fingers through hers, her heart melted with gratitude.

CHAPTER TWENTY-SIX

—NEB'S VILLAGE—

AS EVIL AS YOU WISH

Neb had never endured such suffering. After a long walk, he sat on the hard-packed earth and leaned against a great tree. He tried to calm his mind to match the quiet stillness all around him. The pain of straightening his leg made him grit his teeth. Once settled, he sighed. His strength was returning, though he needed to rest often.

Torgama bustled ahead.

The man had practically become his slave. Neb enjoyed insisting that Torgama would have died rather than hurt him and that it had been some unseen assailant who had done the treacherous deed. At first, Torgama had attempted to correct Neb, but Neb would accept no other explanation. His horrific curses upon the unknown assailant sent Torgama into squirming fits.

Kittam, without allies after the death of Puti and the isolation of Torgama's guilt, knew the truth. But as Neb graphically described the torturous death he wished upon the man who had injured him, he never dared to speak.

Drawn into a web of servitude, the bonds of which they could never break, both Torgama and Kittam became tied to him as never before. They would never again laugh behind his back or challenge his orders with a snide remark.

As Neb healed, his men's devotion grew. They admired his refusal to be conquered even by the worst of pain.

A comfortable breeze blew majestic white clouds across a blue sky, rising and falling like soft fingers over his skin.

Leah crossed his path.

Neb's pleasure deepened.

Her growing belly attested to his returning strength. Soon a son would be born and named Madai, after a long-dead grandfather who had been renowned for his strength and endurance.

Leah accepted the reality of being his wife better than he had anticipated. She remained quiet, rarely offering a word in conversation, but she had grown attentive to his needs.

He, in return, offered her the respect of a beloved wife. Her every desire was met, and every comfort attended to. She never referred to her old clan but acted as if she had forgotten her past. Her gaze remained downcast, but this Neb approved of as a sign of her increasing modesty and a better understanding of her role as wife and mother.

The brilliant sun had fallen far from its pinnacle, deepening the rosy colors on the horizon. A fresh breeze carried the scent of honey and warm bread.

Neb luxuriated in the refreshing scene while the villagers finished their daily toil. He closed his eyes and rested his mind.

Birds twittered in the treetops, and bees hummed.

A woman's complaint ripped through the peace.

Furrowing his brow, Neb turned away. He would not hear.

The whine continued, like an insect buzzing in his ear.

He opened his eyes, glancing around for Torgama, but Torgama was already responding to another call. Neb's scowl threatened a headache.

Meshullemeth's words, shrill and sharp, matched the aimless darts of her hands. "I want her moved into my place today. She will give birth to the most noble of babes, and no one else knows as much as I do in the matter. Get her things now and do as I say!"

Torgama bowed, his back humbled, but his eyes seething. "I must speak to Neb. He has not told me–"

"Do as I say!"

Though he hated to hobble before his men, Neb stood, balanced himself against the tree, and grabbed the staff on which he had engraved fierce animals. Setting his face in his accustomed stern acceptance, he faced the horrific pain of walking on his mending leg. He moved with deliberate care, forcing his muscles to stretch and strengthen. Ignoring the sweat that streamed down his face, he stopped before his mother. "Leah stays with me. She is my wife, not yours. Torgama can do nothing. When her time comes, I have chosen skilled women to assist her. I want none of your spells or interference."

Meshullemeth stepped backward as if slapped. She even lifted her hand to her face as if to cover the mark of the blow. "How can you say this, my son? Who cared for you the moment I learned of your injury? Who arranged for your every comfort and watched over your wife?"

"You almost killed me in your incompetence and nearly frightened my wife to death. You are skilled at making noise and little else. Go see to the evening meal. I need to eat well to heal."

Deflating like an emptied water skin, Meshullemeth stared at her son, one eyebrow rising. "What happened in that last battle? You have none of the gracious temper I honored you with and little of your father's bearing. While Torgama at least gives me some respect, you offer insult and odious accusations. I fear a child of yours will be little more than—"

Neb smacked his hand against his leg. "Watch your tongue, Mother, or you may see a side of me that you have yet to witness."

Meshullemeth's eyes widened. "I can do nothing more." She turned on her heel, her long, flowing garment billowing around her. She halted and returned Neb's hard gaze. “Dark powers raised you. They can take you down just as easily.”

Neb watched his mother stalk into her own hut. A low hiss escaped between his teeth.

His eyes roved over the village, and this time, rested on his sister, Eva. Still small and thin, she strolled through the village with a bundle of fresh leaves in her arms. She was forever experimenting with herbs and plants. He had allowed her a little hut of her own to make brews, for she had proven her knowledge of herbs.

Shortly after he had brought her home, she had made him a brew for his injury. Despite her apparent concern, he only pretended to accept her ministration. Later he had given the drink to a bird. The bird died in a convulsive fit.

He smiled at the memory. He was strangely proud of her daring. He knew she had no plans to kill anyone else, and he was quite able to defend himself from her artless attempts to poison him. In fact, he considered her knowledge useful. There would come a day when he would use her skills to his advantage. His eyes roved from his sister’s hut to his mother’s.

~~~

Leah sat on the bank of a clear, flowing stream and watched the reflected clouds billow past in the small side pools.

The rushing flow bubbled and twinkled in the failing sunlight.

Her nausea rose and fell. Only the silent, still pools calmed her. She had relived her father’s death uncountable times and heard her brother’s defiant words repeated in her mind. Should she have chosen death?
~~~

She laid her hand on her belly, caressing her skin in slow, meditative circles.

As Meshullemeth scurried in the background, Leah shook her head. *Always in a hurry but never doing anything.*

Neb appeared, limping toward her, and a blush crept up her cheeks. *He looks like a boy, an earnest child, with his heart pulsing through his eyes.* A shiver ran over her arms.

Neb stood a moment, watching her. Pain etched a furrow across his brows.

With her hand resting comfortably on her belly, Leah met his gaze. "Are you all right?"

Neb jerked his head and attempted a smile. "I'm quite well. I came to check on you."

Leah accepted this kindness. "I'm better. The baby is moving. He'll be very strong."

As he gentled himself onto the creek bank beside her, Neb's smile grew genuine. "He'll be the strongest baby under the sun." He winced as he adjusted his leg.

Leah glanced aside until he was comfortably settled.

Neb turned his face to the setting sun, staring at the long shadows, and shivered.

Leah felt the child inside her body and knew that when this baby found his way into the world, Neb would lose himself. She smiled sweetly, though it tasted bitter.

"My mother has not been bothering you?"

Leah faced him. "Your mother?"

A flock of birds settled in a nearby tree, arranging themselves for a night of rest.

"No, why would she? I told her that all the decisions are yours, not mine."

Neb nodded, his gaze downcast. "I do not mean that she would be unkind. I mean, rather, she wants the baby for herself."

Her skin crawling, Leah wrapped her arms around her

middle. “What do you mean? This child is ours, flesh of our flesh.”

Neb grunted. “She failed to mold me into the serving vessel she imagined, so now she wants to try with my son.” Neb gripped Leah’s arm, staring into her eyes. “She uses dark powers, and she’d stop at nothing to gain a new tool.”

Nausea rose from Leah’s middle. She tried to stand but crumpled on her attempt.

Using each other for leverage, Neb and Leah leaned on each other and rose to their feet. Neb clasped her arms, supportive and yet supported. “I didn’t want to upset you but rather warn you. My mother is not what she seems.”

Tears sprang to Leah’s eyes. “Is anyone?”

As if he had not heard, Neb wrapped his arm around her shoulder, hugging her close, and led her home.

The quiet bustle of families settling in for their evening meal, bees returning to their hives, birds warbling their goodnight songs, and a soft pink glow on the horizon mellowed Leah’s mood and reminded her of the still pools.

Neb’s voice, gentle but insistent, broke the peace. “Do you believe in me?”

Heavy, suffocating weariness enveloped Leah. “You are neither as good as you claim nor as evil as you wish.” Letting go of his grasp, Leah hobbled ahead, one hand rubbing her aching back while the other caressed the jerking kicks of her baby.

~~~

Neb watched his wife as if she were part of a soothing dream he did not want to disturb.

His mother’s voice rent the air. *Again!*
~~~

With a scowl blackening his features, Torgama strode directly to Neb. "Your mother wishes to eat now, and she has sent me to tell you that if you do not come, there will be nothing left." His fingers wrapped around the hilt of the knife tucked in his belt. "You must do something about her. She acts as if I am little more than—"

Neb lifted his hand in command, fury seething through his whole body. "Say no more. You need a better reason than that to dispense with my mother."

Baffled, Torgama waved toward Hezeki's hut. "You had no such—" He caught himself and blushed in confusion.

Neb straightened to his full height. A desire to see someone die surged through him even as his leg ached in fresh agony.

Torgama stuttered an apology. "I—I'm sorry. Of course. You have every right to do as you please. She is your mother." He glanced back to where Meshullemeth harangued a serving girl. "It's just" —a new light entered his eye— "once I heard her tell Hul to keep an eye on you. She seems to believe that she rules with greater authority than her son."

Ice settled into Neb's bones. He dismissed Torgama with a curt wave and watched the clan gather for their evening meal.

Torgama hurried off, blending into the clan like a dog among its pack.

Meshullemeth gestured and huffed, her shrill comments stabbing the deepening darkness.

Neb rolled his gaze to his hut, where his wife leaned against a post in the doorway as she ate her evening meal. Her rounded belly rose like a mountain from the hills.

CHAPTER TWENTY-SEVEN

—NEB'S VILLAGE—

UNTOLD BATTLES

Eva tilted her head as she concentrated on her stew. One of the men had given her a fat rabbit in gratitude for helping his ailing son. She pondered the strangeness of fortune, for she was not at all certain how she had cured the child. She had made a strong brew from chamomile leaves and added honey for sweetening. Had it been the chamomile or the honey? Or both?

How could such a simple remedy help a child recover when he had been plagued with headaches ever since his mother had given birth weeks earlier?

Eva straightened and peered north to where the child lived with his family. Yes, there he was, running outside his dwelling while his mother looked on. Though his mother had had a simple delivery, she had been exhausted by her exertions. Eva had recommended rest, and the father had sent the older children to a sister. Eva had offered her the usual poultices, salves, and nourishing meals of hot stew and warm drinks.

As Eva watched the family, the small crease that arched her eyebrows relaxed. The little boy begged his mother to watch him as he committed another act of agility with daring jumps over a pile of sticks. The mother grinned and applauded his efforts. Perhaps it had not been her ministrations to the boy that had cured him as much as her ministrations to the mother?

A flush worked over Eva's face. Someone was watching her. She dipped a long, wooden-handled spoon into the pot and tasted the stew. Approving, she turned and looked around.

Leah stood behind her.

Eva nodded.

Leah opened her mouth, but no words formed.

Alarmed, Eva took Leah's hand and led her to a bench built into the outside wall. "Are you ill?"

Leah shook her head, swaying on her feet. "I don't know. I feel pain and am so tired. I can't eat anything."

Eva helped her sit down. "How long has this been going on?"

"A few days…getting worse each day. At times it stops, but then it starts up again." Leah gripped Eva's arm, her eyes wide with fear. "Don't let anything happen to my baby!"

Eva could feel her chest tighten as she clenched her jaw. "You want this baby to live?"

Leah jerked away, stifling a sob. She struggled to her feet.

Instantly repentant, Eva reached out. "Stay. I'm sorry. I just thought—I mean, if I were carrying Neb's baby, I'd—"

A strangled scream burst from Leah. "You would be its mother! If you had a heart, you'd love your baby."

Eva stroked Leah's arm. "I didn't mean it. How can I help?"

Leah wiped her eyes. "Forget Neb and think about the baby."

A flush of heat washed over Eva. "Yes, I deserve that. All right, I'll forget the father and save the baby."

A spasm sent Leah into a shivering fit.

Sitting on the bench, Eva wrapped her arm around Leah.

Leah stared straight ahead. "Neb might say or do something stupid. Just remember, I'm the mother. And I'm nothing like Neb."

Eva chewed her lip. "I hated you for becoming Neb's wife. I thought you were a coward. Worse even."

A single blackbird flew in an arch far overhead.

Leah sighed.

"But really, you're braver than I." Eva brought her gaze to earth again and glanced at Leah. "I tried to poison him."

Leah nodded, her attention fixed on the ground. "He told me. I was amazed."

"I have every reason to want him dead."

"No, I mean, I was amazed he told me. After we were married and spent time together, he began to speak to me about things— things he never told anyone else. He was a different man."

"Can a man be two people?"

Leah nodded. "I think that is often the case."

Eva stood, offering her hand to Leah. "What can I do for you?"

Leah struggled to her feet using Eva's strength to aid her. "I want to stay strong, and I want this baby to live."

Eva stared across the village at the little boy, who now sat nestled under his mother's arm while she nursed her baby. "I don't know what powers I have, for they do not come from me. All I know is that I intend to do good. Things generally work out."

Leah snorted. "Well, at least you won't poison me."

Eva shrugged good-naturedly. "I'm still not sure why my attempt failed. The drink I gave him should've killed him."

"He never drank the brew. He gave it to a bird."

Eva swallowed. "So, he has known all this time?" A shiver ran over her spine. "Why hasn't he killed me?"

"He was proud of your daring. It took an uncommonly strong spirit to attempt such a thing. He made Meshullemeth leave you in peace, and he then gave you this hut. He says that your skills will be useful someday."

"He is not kind."

"There are untold battles inside each man."

Eva darted inside her dwelling and returned with a carved wooden bowl and a skin of spiced drink. "Hunger and thirst can set in labor early, so we must see to it that you're well-fed and have plenty of good drink on hand. I'll bring some each day, and we'll talk. If anything alarms you, send word, and I'll come."

"You won't be afraid of Neb?"

"He is not afraid of me. I can return the favor."

Eva dished out the stew and gave the steaming bowl to Leah.

Like a storm, Meshullemeth raged across the village, her voice screeching. "Leah!" She stopped dead in her tracks. "Don't eat anything that witch gives you! She'll kill you and the baby! Get up and come with me. I'll take care of you." Meshullemeth slapped the bowl from the girl's hands.

Horrified, Eva froze.

Leah swayed, bent over, and retched what she had eaten.

Shaken from her stupor, Eva called for help as she stepped between the mountain of fury and the cringing young woman. Many faces turned, but no one dared to interfere with Neb's mother.

With an oath, Eva ran panting to the place she knew that Neb liked to go for peace and quiet. She leaped over a large rock, heard a voice call, and stumbled. She landed in a heap at Neb's feet.

Neb peered down at her. "Why are you running like a frightened rabbit? It's not like you, Eva."

"Mother—you must stop her, Neb, or you could lose both Leah and the baby."

Though his limp still hindered him, Eva marveled at the speed Neb climbed the hill and hobbled to intercept his wife and mother.

Meshullemeth had dragged Leah as far as the door of her dwelling, though Leah looked as though she could hardly walk another step.

Eva rushed to her side, gripped her arm, and braced her.

Neb's eyes glowed with fury as he glared at his mother. He raised his hand.

Eva shook her head as Leah sank to her knees. "Not now! Help me!"

With surprising gentleness, Neb lifted Leah into his arms and carried her back to Eva's dwelling. He laid her on Eva's bed. Then he called to one of his men who stood in the doorway wary and concerned. "Get my blankets and pillows. Bring them here."

As the man rushed off and Meshullemeth bustled in the background wringing her hands, Neb comforted his wife, caressing her arm, laying a pillow under her head, and wrapping a blanket over her shivering body. He spoke no words, except through his imploring eyes.

Eva watched his ministrations, amazed. *Neb loves his wife?*

Clearly terrified that Leah might die, he ministered to her as if his life were in question.

Leah accepted Neb's kindness and closed her eyes; sleep offering the best medicine.

Neb stood back and took hold of Eva's arm. He led her to the doorway. One glowering stare sent Meshullemeth back several steps. "You will do everything possible to save her and the life of the child."

Eva looked intently at Neb, her heart pounding. "And if I must choose between the two?"

Neb squeezed her arm painfully. "You will not choose. It's not for you to decide."

Forcing herself not to look at her throbbing arm, Eva nodded. "I'll do everything in my power, but I make no promises. Unlike you, I can't control the forces I serve."

"I don't want a promise. I want her safe." He glanced from his wife lying quietly to his mother, pacing a few feet away. "This will never happen again."

A thrill of fear shot through Eva, but when Leah moaned, she darted to Leah's side.

Neb paced to the back wall, where Eva kept her herbs and vials of soothing brews. He ran his fingers along the shelf line.

Eva stared at him, swallowing a lump rising in her throat. "What are you looking for?"

"You know perfectly well."

"You can't kill her!"

Neb turned and stared straight into her eyes. "You tried to kill me."

"That was before I met your wife! She changed—perhaps ruined me."

Neb pulled Eva across the room and gripped her shoulders, making her face the wall of potions. "Give me what I want."

"I can't help you kill anyone."

"Why?"

"Don't you see? The same reason I can't help to kill her is the same reason I can never kill you."

Baffled, his anger mounting, Neb glared.

"I want to be like your wife, the one who draws love from the darkest place imaginable. Not like you."

"You are not helping me solve my problem."

"Send Mother away. Let her go—"

Neb pounded to the doorway and stepped outside. He soon returned, leading the boy Eva had cured of the headaches. He shook the child's arm. "Either give me the potion, or I'll have this boy drink everything in this room until I find what I am looking for."

Horror gripped Eva. A retching sensation surged from

her stomach. “How could you?”

“My wife and child are important to me.”

Leah groaned and thrashed in the bed, shoving the blanket off to one side.

Eva felt around the top shelf and dragged a small, clay vial forward. She handed it to Neb, sneering. “You always have a good reason for your murders.”

Neb snatched the container from her hand and pushed the boy out the door. “I don’t have to justify my actions. I’m the leader of this clan.” He turned and hobbled through the doorway.

Eva went back to her patient, shook off the dusty blanket, and placed it around Leah’s shoulders. “Only you could love the unlovable.” Heaving a sigh, Eva perched on the edge of the bed and watched over her friend.

CHAPTER TWENTY-EIGHT

—NEB'S VILLAGE—

YET ANOTHER CURSE

Meshullemeth felt old to the bone. She dropped down on her pallet and sighed heavily. Only one thin window slit near the ceiling allowed light into her small dwelling. A broad sunbeam sliced the air, exposing dust particles and oppressing her heart.

Her breakfast bowl sat unwashed on a shelf, and her blanket lay tangled on the floor. Loneliness squeezed her heart.

An image of Hezeki rose in her mind. What happened to him? Neb refused to speak of the matter, and his men avoided her whenever she asked questions. Hul would have told her the truth—even against his better judgment. But his fate also lay shrouded in mystery.

She shivered. Hezeki once teased her, saying that she should have married a god, as only a god could make her happy. Deep down, she agreed with him. Life had cheated her. She should have been married to a much greater man. But after Neb was born, her vision cleared, and she began to see that her purpose was not to marry a great man but to form one—to raise a god from mankind itself.

An ache throbbed behind her eyes. Neb never accepted her counsel willingly. Of late, he sneered at her advice. Had her whole life been a miserable lie?

A shadow eclipsed the light from the open doorway. Neb's shadow spoke, his voice even and calm. "I have a present for you, Mother."

A heavy weight pulled Meshullemeth's head to the ground. She wanted to rest in peace. It took a great force of will to mumble a response. "A present for me? How unlike you."

Neb stepped into the room, his hand clasping a small vial.

Meshullemeth raised her head and looked her son in the eye. "What happened to your father? Despite everything, I was fond of him."

A snort cut the air like a blunt knife.

Neb stepped closer and offered the vial. "Mix it with whatever you like, and you will sleep well tonight."

Meshullemeth stared at the long, brown arm extended toward her and bile rose. The pounding in her head beat a throbbing tune. "Did you kill him?"

"Kill whom?"

"Your father." She waved the vial away. "Don't deny it." She clasped her head in her hands as if she could keep it from bursting. "I raised you to be strong and brave beyond the lot of mortal men, yet you were afraid of the weakest man we knew. Why did you have to snatch leadership before your time?"

Neb straightened and spoke, his voice cold. "What I learned, I learned from you." He hobbled across the room and snatched her water skin hanging from a peg on the wall. He opened it, poured the contents of the vial into the bag, and dropped it beside her.

Meshullemeth nodded in oppressed silence. As he limped past, she caught the end of his garment. "And Hul? What happened to him?"

Neb shrugged. "He died." He started forward, but her fingers clutched his garment.

"And my other sons? What about them?"

Neb wrenched free and limped to the doorway. "Nothing! They are living with a clan to the southwest. Very happy, no doubt." His jaw clenched, emphasizing the angular lines in his face.

A gust of wind blew gray strands of hair into her face.

"You'll not leave them be, will you?"

Neb hobbled as he stepped to the doorway. "Rest, Mother. Take that draught and go to sleep."

Thirst scratched her dry throat. With trembling hands, she lifted the bag and opened it. The water skin was not heavy. She eyed her son. "Will I ever see him again?"

Neb halted just outside the doorway, his back to his mother. "Who?"

"Your father."

"Perhaps." Neb stepped into the deepening darkness.

Tears streamed down Meshullemeth's face. A sob bubbled up and choked her. She threw the bag on the ground.

The contents spilled, leaving a black stain.

Hot and exhausted, the pain in her head suddenly leaped to her chest. She pressed her hands against her breasts, the same breasts that once fed the man who walked away from her questions and her counsel.

Hezeki rose before her. Calm. Reasoning. A small man.

She lifted her aching arms.

His voice murmured, soft and mournful, "Now, do you see?"

With a shriek, she waved the apparition away.

The room fell into blackness. She could see nothing.

Weakness enveloped her. The water skin. She reached for it, her fingers scrambling over the dusty ground. A crushing weight took her breath. She fell back on her pallet.

Fear writhed around her like a snake coiling about her neck.

"Neb!"

No response.

Neb would think he had done the deed. He would live with a curse. But she had cursed herself. If only she had breath enough to laugh. Darkness swallowed her whole.

~~~

Neb said nothing, though Leah gasped in surprise at the news of Meshullemeth's death.

Torgama stood just inside Neb's dwelling and lifted the water skin. He opened his mouth, but no other words came.

Neb snatched the water skin from his grasp and turned it upside down. It was empty. He handed it back to Torgama. "Burn it. I don't want anyone else getting sick with whatever she had." He paused and then met the man's unwavering stare. "Burn her hut down to the ground and throw her god into the fire as well."

"Your mother?"

Neb glared.

Torgama nodded. "I'll see to it." He stepped outside.

Neb turned to his wife. "I'll be gone for a few days, so I want you to stay under Eva's care. She'll make sure you eat properly, and my men will protect you from harm."

Leah's eyes widened. "What harm could come to me here?"

Neb shrugged. "None that I know of, but it is always best to be prepared for the unknown."

A pout formed on Leah's lips.

Neb gently ran his fingers across her lips. "Do as I ask and rest. I must check the boundaries. The time is right for raiding, and I'm not fool enough to think that no one would like to conquer me."

Leah nodded.

Neb rose and started for the doorway.

Leah lifted her head and met Neb's parting smile. "I'm sorry about your mother."

Neb nodded and stepped away.
~~~

The morning sun shone bright in a glorious blue sky. Not a cloud in sight. The entire village bustled with industrious activity. Children played around boiling stew pots and slinking dogs.

Neb stopped before Eva's dwelling.

Eva sat on a bench in the sun, sewing a garment.

Neb stared down at her bent head. "You'll help Leah and keep the baby safe."

Eva nodded, not looking up. "I will be kinder to your wife than you were to our mother."

"She was never kind to you."

Eva lifted her eyes. "But she was our mother."

"What difference does that make?"

Eva stood, rolled her garment under her arm, and stepped to the doorway. "You'll know the answer to that when your son is born."

A mighty eagle soared overhead and screeched.

Neb watched the majestic form fly away. When he dropped his gaze, Eva was gone, but his mission remained.

CHAPTER TWENTY-NINE

—WILDERNESS—

MY OWN DARKNESS

(TEN YEARS LATER)

Accad chopped tangled vines from his path with ruthless strokes. He snapped at his wife, who trailed behind him. "Stay close, Obal!"

"I'm doing the best I can. Can't we rest? We're getting lost."

"We're not lost! Just delayed."

"Delayed? You said we'd reach the grasslands in a few days. It's long past a few days."

Accad slapped the leaves, shouting. "I know what—"

A wail rose as Accad's youngest rubbed his eyes with his fists.

Obal comforted the child on her hip even as she struggled to wrap her arms around the two girls who sniffled and clung to her skirts.

"All right, we'll stop, though it'll be dark soon."

A rustling sound froze the family in place.

Dangling vines and bushes parted.

Three men and a tall youth climbed through the foliage.

Accad glared at the men, his weapons ready and his arms spread wide in front of his wife and children.

The strangers stared back at him.

Accad swung his spear and sliced the nearest vine.

The tallest man snorted. Enosh stepped forward and raised his hands in mock surrender. "Please don't kill me, oh mighty warrior!"

Accad's jaw dropped. He turned his head to the side,

peering out his good eye. “I know you?”

Enosh dropped his hands to his side. “You crush me! I thought that when we came to your village bringing Neb in our wake, you’d never forgive us, much less forget us. I’m Enosh, here with my brother Kenan.” He drew the youth forward. “And I have a son now.”

Accad relaxed, his shoulders drooping. “I—I’m sorry. Yes, I see you now. It’s been so long.” He stepped back and gestured to his wife and children. “My wife, Obal, and my children. We’re…traveling.”

Kenan bowed at the introduction and then returned his gaze to Accad. “Through this trackless wilderness?” He drew Accad aside and lowered his voice. “Where have you been? We’ve visited the People of Seth many times, but they speak as if you’re dead.”

His face flushing, Accad stared at the ground. “I was.” He glanced around, anguish wringing his insides. “Can you lead us out of here?”

Kryce stepped forward and gestured ahead. “We’re not far from a tableland. Once there, I can show you the surroundings so you can get your bearings. Where are you heading?”

Accad met his wife’s gaze, exhaled a long breath, and the first peace he had known in years filled him. “We’re going home.”

~~~

Accad leaned against a warm rock and stretched his legs. With a full stomach and a little rest, his mood had improved drastically. He stole a glance at Enosh. “What happened to Neb?”

Sprawled on the ground, with his head propped on his
~~~

hand, Enosh chewed the last of his dried meat. "He attacked the People of Havilah, killed Uzal, and took his daughter for his wife. He was injured and returned home. Though he continues to raid, he has not ventured our way since. He has a family now, I hear, and he keeps to himself. When he does go out, he stays far from us. I think his wife keeps him distant."

If he had seen a fish fly into the clouds, Accad would not be more amazed. "Neb lives at home, directed by a woman?"

Kryce spoke up. "She is my sister and a more beautiful woman you'll never meet."

Accad pursed his lips. "No doubt, but Neb cannot be tamed. After what he did…"

Sitting to the side, Kenan leaned forward. "What did he do? To you, I mean."

Obal squeezed her husband's hand.

Accad sighed. "By his own hand? Nothing. But by example, he made raiding profitable. We resisted every attack, but eventually, I was caught and enslaved, tied like an animal and marched far from home. Because I was uncooperative, I was traded uncountable times. In the end, I was sold to a clan deep in the mountains. It was there that I met Obal. She was a slave, too, but we were married and soon blessed with children."

Both Obal and Accad's gazes fixed on the children sleeping near the fire. Accad turned his head to the side. "But last season, we learned that they planned to trade our children to another clan."

Kenan frowned.

"We made an escape, but…as you see, I got lost."

Astonished, Enosh's eyebrows climbed his forehead. "What an adventure!"

"Not one any sane man would want to share."

Kenan leaned forward, his brow puckering into a deep

frown. “Why do you turn your head when you speak?”

Accad tipped his head back. “It’s the price one pays for making a master angry.” He turned again so Kenan could see his full face. A thin scar ran through one eye.

A flush filled Kenan’s face. He glanced away.

Enosh stood and stretched. “Enough discussion. There is still light to travel by. Home is several days away, and we need to find food along the way.”

Kryce stood. “We will take them to the Village of Seth first, and then go home.” He looked at Accad’s young family and smiled. “We can carry the little ones and hunt as we go.”

Kenan nodded. “We’ll bring enough food for a banquet.”

Tears welled in Accad’s eyes. “I feel alive again.”

~~~

Seth wandered along the flowing river, his back to the sun.

Sparkling water reflected blowing grasses in still pools trapped between boulders. Contentment filled every crevice of his heart. He pictured his wife nursing their newest baby. Four sons! He was blessed beyond the lot of mortal men.

As he crested the hill leading into his village, he heard a shout.

Jubal sped toward him, his head bent with exertion.

Seth raised his hand to stall the coming excitement.

Jubal panted, coming to a sudden halt.

Seth’s heart clenched as fear rose. “What’s happened?”

“Men are coming from the west!”

Seth exhaled, hope turning his anxiety into humor.
~~~

"That alarms you?"

Jubal frowned. "We can never be off guard."

Seth nodded respectfully. "How many men?"

A darting glance spoke more than words. "Five men with children and a woman."

Seth pursed his lips, drawing his brows into a concentrated frown. "This could be serious. Warn our best warriors."

Jubal's shoulders drooped. He cut his eyes toward Seth, searchingly. "I wanted to prepare you. We've not always had the best luck with visitors."

The comment bit deep. "Yes. True. Always wise to be careful. How far away?"

Jubal fingered the knife tucked inside his tunic. "They'll be here before noon."

His peace scattered, Seth nodded decisively. "I'll check Debora then meet you and wait for them. If they are harmless and only looking for a night's shelter, we will offer what we can. If trouble follows them, we'll send them on their way."

~~~

Seth met with Accad after a visit with his wife and children. Laughter bubbled up inside him.

With his jaw clenched, Jubal clearly tried to control his annoyance. "What are you smiling about? You look as if you swallowed—"

Choked laughter broke free. Seth leaned in as if sharing a secret. "While I was speaking with Debora, Chus was jumping about. She asked him what was the matter. He said that he decided to become a grasshopper. Debora told him that it wasn't possible. He was a boy and must grow into be a man. But he kept jumping, so I scolded him,
~~~

saying, 'Can't you hear? You aren't a grasshopper. You're a boy.' He looked at me and, in all seriousness, said, "'So, I'll be a boy-hopper then.'"

Seth struggled to keep a straight face.

Jubal pursed his lips. He nodded soberly as if he simply refused to admit that his leader was acting like an idiot. Clearly, Jubal wondered if Seth were fit to rule the clan.

Seth sighed and wiped the mirth off his face.

Villagers murmured as they slowed their work and gathered into small groups.

Seth turned and faced the arriving visitors.

Kryce led the way, with Enosh and his son on his right and Kenan directly behind. A few others straggled along, but they hardly appeared intimidating. Forlorn really.

Jubal's serious expression broke into a wide grin, and he stepped in front of Seth with his arms extended. "Welcome, friends! It has been a long time since we saw you. How have you and your families fared these past years?"

Kryce quickened his pace, the smile on his face growing enormous.

Joy at this happy sight brought a fresh smile to Seth's lips.

The two friends met and embraced.

Seth stepped forward, and greetings were exchanged as Enosh and Kenan joined in.

After vigorous backslapping, Jubal shouted gleefully to Enosh's son, "How you've grown, Boy!" He turned to Enosh. "What are you feeding him?"

Put grinned, his gaze dropping modestly.

Enosh laughed whole-heartedly. "Ask his mother. She's always sending me out for more food. 'More food, Husband, and fix the roof while you're at it!"

The nearby villagers laughed.

Seth waved toward his hut. "Come, rest awhile."

Kryce raised hand. "Wait, I have a surprise."

Disquiet fell on the assembly.

"I have someone here that you'll want to meet." Kryce glanced at Jubal, his grin matching the joy in his eyes.

The strange man stayed in the background while the woman and children appeared to be rooted to the ground.

Kryce stepped over, took the stranger's arm, and led him forward. He stopped in front of Jubal and placed a hand on each of the man's shoulders. "I return your brother to you."

Accad lifted his head, and his whole face became visible. The two men stared at each other in silence.

Finally, Jubal choked back emotion and clasped his brother. "Long have I dreamed of this day!"

Tears of joy rolled down Seth's face unhindered.

~~~

Jubal walked beside his brother, watching his every move, fearing that the man might suddenly vanish into thin air. The two hardly had a chance to speak in private, so great was the clan's desire to hear all about Accad's adventures.

Obal and her children rested with Debora. She assisted the new mother, clearly comforted by the kindness of her husband's clan.

Most of the villagers had retired, but Seth, Enosh, Kenan, Jubal, and Accad sat close to the dying fire and spoke in hushed voices.

Seth yawned repeatedly, fatherhood being a heavy though happy burden. He glanced at his friend, an anxious look in his eyes.

Annoyed, Jubal arched his brows.
~~~

"You appear as grim as ever, my friend, despite your brother being returned to us." Seth flicked a stick to the side.

Irritation sizzled over Jubal as he fought an angry retort. Warring emotions gnawed his insides. "Joy has never been my friend."

Seth shook his head and turned the conversation to a lighter topic. He shifted and focused his gaze across the circle. "I am curious, Enosh, how you grew such a large son. Are there many men of such stature in the People of Havilah?"

An evening chill descended, and Enosh rubbed his hands near the fire. He grinned as he glanced from the youth sleeping near the fire to his friend. "He is the wonder of the clan. And I'm grateful he is a well-behaved boy, for I'd hardly like to discipline him. He contested in the games a few years ago and beat nearly every grown man. He is not simply big; the boy is unnaturally strong."

Seth yawned even as he spoke. "It must be your wife then or her first husband who gave him the advantage."

Enosh shook his head. "No." He rubbed his chin thoughtfully. "There is no explanation other than God wanted him strong. He must have a battle to fight someday that will match his greatness."

Accad glanced sharply at Enosh. "I didn't know your people believed in God."

Enosh shrugged. "The People of Neb do not, but when I married Tamar and accepted her child as my own, I also accepted the God of the People of Havilah as my own."

His stomach tightening, Jubal swallowed back bile. He bit off each word. "And what do the People of Havilah believe about God?"

Enosh hesitated, a scowl forming between his brows. "We—"

Kryce spoke up. "We believe there is one God who

rules the world, a Creator of all things, benevolent and good. He hates injustice and suffering. We want to become like Him."

Anger shattered Jubal's composure. "As if such a thing were possible! The People of Seth believe in God, too. We know the stories—Creation, the Great Flood, Noah. We're descendants of Japheth, but we do not aspire to become God!"

Stiffening like a startled wolf, Kryce eyed his friend. "The People of Havilah do not claim to become God, only to imitate His kindness through strength. We are stewards of His trust. Why do you act surprised?"

Jubal stood and kicked a fallen ember back into the glowing mound. "So, does the Almighty bend down and speak into your ear?" He spat to the side, the taste too bitter to endure. "Innocent men, women, and children suffered death and destruction, but God offered only silence to our people."

Shaking himself, Seth appeared to wake from slumber. He rose and clasped Jubal's shoulder. "I do not agree, Jubal. God does speak to us, though not in words. He speaks in every life…the breaking of each new day…in the quiet of our thoughts. We have survived so much grief for a purpose."

Long suppressed fury exploded from Jubal. He waved a shaking finger at the black sky. "Did God have a purpose for the years of suffering my brother endured? For the loss of his eye?"

Slowly, Accad stood and faced Jubal. "Is it not strange, brother, that you are angry, while I have suffered the greater loss? When I was far from home and traded like a goat, tied and beaten, still, I believed that I would return home one day—even when I ceased to look for that day. After I married and had children, I realized that my home lived in my heart. Now we're all here. Together. And my joy is only clouded by your anger. It was the hand of God that led me to Kryce." He tilted his head and stared hard in the dim light. "Are you angry with me for returning?"

Jubal groaned, a vaporous cloak shrouding his reason. "No, you are most welcome. I'm happy that you found joy in your wife and children. It's just—" He rubbed his face, his head aching and his eyes burning.

Accad rested his hands on his brother's shoulders. "What ails you?"

Tears streamed down Jubal's face. "I believed you dead for all these years. I have lived too long without hope to accept it now. Though you are returned, what about those who will never return? The wives who will never see their husbands, the children who will never know their fathers, the slaves who will never know freedom. What about them?"

Pained silence filled the air.

A woman's voice broke through. Debora swayed as she rocked her infant in her arms, strolling toward the circle of men. "Suffering brought our babes into the world, Jubal. You agonize but must not despair. The God who made us will receive our spirits, and we shall know peace." Stepping closer, she whispered into Seth's ear.

Seth looked up. "Your wife asks for you, Accad. Debora will show you the way."

Turning to follow, Accad stopped and patted Jubal's shoulder. "Grief does not have to become a life-long companion." Accad followed Deborah into the night.

Seth nodded goodnight and turned toward home.

The night stillness shattered as an owl hooted a long wailing call, and another, in the distance, answered in kind.

Shaking off the disturbance, Enosh spread a pallet on the ground beside Kenan, near where Put lay sleeping.

Kryce sat with his arms wrapped around his knees, staring into the fire. He spoke in a whisper. "My father died at Neb's hands. My sister is imprisoned as his wife. You are not the only one who has suffered."

Sleep threatened to overwhelm him. Jubal closed his eyes. "I'm sorry."

Enosh spoke up, "Perhaps a wife would do you good."

Forcing his eyes open, Jubal rubbed his arms. He couldn't think about this now. Exhaustion disabled a reasonable response.

Speaking up for the first time, Kenan shifted in his seat. "Sari and I have helped each other to accept our loss and grief. We have no children, but we still hope."

Jubal nodded in the dark.

Kryce lay down and stretched out, pillowing his head on his hands. "When the dark comes, the stars appear, and we see without an earthly light."

A lump rose in Jubal's throat. He picked up a stick and gently laid it on the dying coals. A bright flame illuminated the night. "I have become my own darkness."

An owl hooted deep in the woods. Another answered.

Jubal turned aside. "I'll see you in the morning." He stopped. "If you don't mind, I'd like to visit the People of Havilah. I'll see my brother safely settled and then go with you."

Flickering firelight highlighted Kryce's smile. "We'd be honored."

Jubal walked home, alone as ever.

Chapter Thirty

–OldEarth–

The Best Armor

Teal leaned back against an ancient tree trunk, his legs splayed wide with Sienna nestled between them, the back of her head resting on his chest. He absorbed through every possible sense the comfort of his arms wrapped around her, protective desire pulsing through his body.

She slept calmly, breathing evenly. Her hands rested on his. She had crossed her legs, and her light slippered feet pointed towards one another, like friends never to be parted. Her tan dress folded gently over her body, undulating in a soft breeze and accenting her soft curves, hills, and valleys.

What would Sterling say if he could see them now? Or Ark, for that matter. Zuri wouldn't notice…too much on his mind.

She shifted, a whimper of…pleasure? Discomfort?

Sienna opened her eyes, and her hands slid from his hands to his thighs.

Definitely not discomfort.

Fighting a storm of personal protests, Teal sat up. Every cell in his human body and more synapsis in his Luxonian brain than he could count screamed. *Stay still! Enjoy this…*

As if sensing the end of the moment, Sienna yawned and stretched, ready to face the dawning day.

Zuri clumped into view on the brow of the hill before them. Bright pink rays lit the earth. If his somber face was anything to go by, all was not well in the Ingot world.

A disgruntled sigh escaped as Teal rose. He held out his hand and assisted Sienna to his side. It felt surprisingly natural to slip his arm around her waist. She didn't seem to mind.

Ark scuttled behind Zuri like a child tagging after his mother, his tentacles waggling every which way. Trying to keep balance on the downslope, undoubtedly.

Sienna pressed the flat of her hand to his stomach, giving a light finger caress as if to say, "It was nice while it lasted, but I must act like a professional now."

He pulled his arm free and let her wander a few steps away. *Or is she giving Zuri privacy? A thoughtful move... One I wouldn't have thought of...*

On close inspection, Zuri's expression darkened, looking more depressing than at first glance. The Ingot came to a full stop in front of Teal, his gaze flickering to Sienna's retreating figure and then to the Luxonian.

Teal's stomach tightened, and his heart fell from dizzying heights. "What's the news?"

"I should be asking you that."

Ark waddled closer, his shoulders heaving and his breather helm well beyond normal bubble capacity. "Slo-slow-down, Zu—"

Zuri's lids dropped to half-mast. He glanced over. "I told you to wait. There's no discussion. I'm going home. You and Teal can do whatever you want."

Teal turned to Ark, his eyebrows raised. If he wanted a succinct and impartial account of recent events, Ark was clearly the better option.

A deep breath, followed by a vaporous exhale, and Ark was ready to tell all. "The Ingilium are holding a hearing for those accused of traitorous activity. Zuri has been called as a witness. He plans on telling the powers that be a thing or two about naughty Ingot responses to even the most innocent challenge to technological supremacy."

Teal swiveled his gaze to Zuri. "If you want to be killed, there are easier methods."

Zuri's hands clenched, his jaw tightened, and his eyes narrowed. He was well and truly annoyed. "Kelesta was nearly killed, and a part of her homeworld was destroyed by Ingoti belligerence. You think I should let that pass?"

"Certainly not. Neither do I think it's advisable that you face down the entire Ingilium by your lonesome."

When his shoulders relaxed and his face softened, Zuri looked like a boy-child wavering on hope, as he peered through wary eyes.

Ark threw up his tentacles. "Of course, we're going. We can't let you have all the fun. This is the stuff Bhuaci poems are made of. A valiant hero going against heartless—"

Teal cleared his throat. "I need to talk with Sienna before we leave… Alone."

It took several awkward moments for Zuri to catch on.

Ark rolled his eyes. "Just remember, she's entrusted with our…ahem…trust."

Teal nodded. "I'll make that very clear." He waved in the direction of Zuri's ship. I'll get there on my own."

Zuri turned and plodded away.

Ark followed with a wave. "Just make sure that Sterling knows who's where, so he doesn't blame me if there's a mixup."

Teal shooed the Crestonian away and searched the horizon for Sienna. She stood on the hilltop, offering a smile as Zuri and Ark passed.

Once he reached her, he took her hand and lifted it, staring at her fingers. "The hands of a healer."

Sienna's eyes filled with tears. "That was always my dream. I would cure every wounded Luxonian and end suffering in our world."

"There are many methods of healing."

She nodded and stared at her feet. "I heard what they said. You need to go, and I need to stay."

"If you're willing."

"To be entrusted with your trust?"

"Not just mine."

Sienna lifted her face and wiped away the trace of a tear. "It's an honor. One I never thought I'd be blessed with."

"Consider yourself blessed then." A spark of joy enlivened Teal's whole body.

Sienna leaned forward and placed a kiss on Teal's cheek. "I'll keep an eye on Ishtar's family and record the story so you won't miss anything." She peered into the distance. "He's probably about ready to start. The clan gathers each evening after sunset, and Ishtar is a master storyteller. I should go."

Teal nodded.

Sienna blinked away.

An ache of loneness welled inside Teal, like a river running backward, choking his thoughts and feelings. "I'll be back."

He winked away.

-Ingilium Home World-

Zuri couldn't believe his ears. The Ingilium Council wasn't holding an inquiry but rather a trial. He searched the crowd.

Teal and Ark stood on the left, sorrow chasing horror across their faces.

The Ingilium Director raised his fist—and his voice—above the clamoring assembly. "Will the New-Born traitors now state their position?"

Zuri stared at the group of near-naked Ingots who had been taken from their homes, handcuffed, and now stood on trial for their chosen way of life. His heart twisted even as a part of him revolted at the sight of so much bare flesh. Surely, they had taken a good idea too far.

One tremulous female Ingot, her hands manacled behind her back, and her flat breasts making no discernable impression on the thin fabric wrapped around her body, stood in front of the others. Her long pale legs peeked through the slit in a long skirt, which did nothing to hide the scrapes and sores marring her otherwise perfect skin. Though manacled, she kept her shoulders back, her head high, and her bare feet firmly placed on the platform. A short tuft of dark hair sprang from the top of her head, offsetting her oval eyes and giving her naturally somber expression a jaunty twist.

"We have done nothing to incur your wrath, Director. Nor have we threatened our world in any way. All we ask is to be able to choose for ourselves how much technology we attach to our bodies. Some of us" —she waved to the stricken group—"have kept much of the armor given to us. While others…" She pulled the wrap tighter. "Well, I and a few have chosen a complete release from technology."

A collective gasp broke the stern silence. Then a loud babble ascended to the metal beams overhead. Second story observers leaned over the railing, eyes wide, arguments ensuing.

The Director pressed a buzzer, and an ear-splitting siren blasted for three seconds, dropping Ark to his knees. Teal wavered, clasping his hands to his ears. Winces and grimaces rippled through the crowd.

The Director raised his hand. "I will have order!"

Zuri stepped forward; his head bare except for a short mop of white-blond hair. "As an Ingoti diplomat, I must be allowed to speak."

The Director glared, a disappointed teacher facing down an unruly truant. "I know all about you, Zuri. Through you, we were able to discover this traitorous plot and bring these misguided fools into the light." He stepped forward and leaned toward the smaller Ingot, his huge armored physique bearing down on Zuri's lightly armored body. "Did you think we were blind?"

"Not blind. But not this stupid either."

The crowd gasped again, louder.

Zuri lifted his hand. "Even if I do not get a fair hearing, I will be heard. You will be forced to listen."

"Your actions speak loud enough! You were the instigator of this Born-Again cult. These pathetic followers planned to overthrow Ingoti Tradition in a weak attempt to level the playing field for aliens. Did your Cresta and Luxonian *friends* suggest that your armor was a sign of emotional weakness? Did they taunt you with a lack of spiritual awareness? What could have turned you from the truth? You know better than anyone: an impenetrable shield keeps the universe safe."

Ark waddled forward. "Except when it doesn't. You know that Cresta was attacked not long ago, and we had thought we were invincible as well. The Mystery Race didn't take kindly to simple inquiries, and they let us know just where our vulnerabilities lie in no uncertain terms." He waved his tentacles, encompassing the entire watching crowd, and even nodded to the holoscreens perched at every corner of the octagonal room.

"I certainly did not encourage Zuri to pursue this…private passion. But I did respect his desire to discover his own unique strength."

The Director shouted. "Words…words…words! Crestas are known for manipulating more than scientific instruments."

Teal winked away from the perimeter and, with a flash of brilliant light, appeared nearly twice his normal size on the center stage, wearing the bulkiest armor seen this side of Bothmal. He flexed his arms and roared like a caged lion.

Stunned silence.

Teal's voice took on a decidedly mechanical tone. "I've seen powers beyond your reckoning. Powers that can transform a man, no matter how well armored, into a monster. It hides in the folds of a mind and sneaks into the warmest heart, turning it to ice. Reason covers it from head to toe, but madness rules every act."

Teal strode in a wide circle, eyeing various faces in the room. His gaze landed on the Director, over whom he now towered.

"Zuri knows about destructive power…and he knows of another power too. Stronger, more resilient. A power you have yet to discover, but one that can resist all opposition and take life into a whole new realm. A universe yet undreamed of by Ingots, Luxonians and even…" He smiled at Ark's wide bulbous eyes. "Crestas."

Zuri squared his shoulders, listening, his gaze fixed on the enhanced Teal.

The assembly held their collective breath.

Teal continued his circular march, his sharp-toed boots pounding the floor with each step. "The Born-Again venture into dangerous territory, but they do it by their courage to become more than their armor, by facing their true vulnerability, so they discover strength as yet unknown on this planet."

The Director tilted his head as if listening to a whisper. "An *invisible* shield?"

Teal's abrupt laughter broke the tension.

Everyone smiled.

Ark's face lit up with a grin.

Zuri's eyes shined.

Still chuckling, Teal returned to his former shape. "Yes. That is how it must seem to you. An invisible shield."

Zuri stepped next to the thin, proud female Ingot, and wrapped his arm around her shoulder.

The Director wagged his finger, his voice incredulous "She has this shield?"

The Ingot woman met his gaze, her eyes steady and bright.

Teal stepped to Zuri's right. Ark hobbled to the woman's left.

Zuri nodded. "She's discovering it. Just give her time. Give us all time."

~~~

Ark dragged himself from the water, dripping but refreshed. He plopped down on a boulder by the shore and watched the evening light play over the sea, twinkling like midnight stars in the sky.

He sighed in utter contentment.

A buzz whirred by. He smacked at the enormous flying insect but missed. Another buzz flipped his serene disposition on end. He swore. "By all the powers of Cresta—"

The buzz tickled somewhere in his upper left quadrant. An "Ah-ha!" moment.

Shaking the last drips off his top right tentacle, he pulled a datapad from a tight pocket. A light tap and a message played before his eyes.

Contentment fled, and irritation barged into his conscious mind. A bully ready to get rough. "That insectoid thinks she can just scuttle off to Helm without getting proper clearance on the flimsy excuse that she wants to see the damage for herself…well… Assessing planetary resources, more like. This will hardly do!"

Standing abruptly, Ark stared at his terrestrial boots sprawled beside the boulder. "Where's that Ingot gotten
~~~

to? I don't care if he's instructing the Born-Agains on how to make a healthy dinner, he must pay attention to larger matters." He glanced around. "Teal?" He listened.

Nothing.

"Oh, that Luxonian! Always blinking off to who knows where. And I've got news!"

The female Ingot, freed now on a paid fine, wandered near. She peered at Ark and hesitated.

Ark beckoned. "Come. I'm no one to be afraid of."

"I wanted to thank you…for supporting Zuri…who supports our cause."

Ark nodded. "He's a silly fool most of the time, but I like his determination. An Ingot who dares to be more than an Ingot, if you know what I mean."

She continued to stare.

"What's your name?"

"I was named Yester." She shrugged. "But I call myself Tomor."

"Well, in case you're interested, Tomor, my name is Ark, and I am helpless without my boots." He blinked winningly, a beseeching child.

Tomor knelt at his side and pulled the boots forward. "I have spent the last year tugging every article off my body that I could. But I see; you do need help."

"Armor isn't wrong, Tomor. It's just that no one should be left naked and helpless without it." Ark winced as he forced his swollen three-toed foot into the stiff boot. "Sometimes, the best armor is a good friend."

CHAPTER THIRTY-ONE

—NEB'S VILLAGE—

WE ARE NOT ALONE

Neb observed his two young sons carefully. Despite being strong, Madai never used his body to his best advantage. Sadly, the child had a soft, delicate touch. He usually stayed near his mother, complying with her every wish.

Neb tapped his side impatiently.

Serug, the younger boy, bellowed at his brother like an angry bull, demanding an early supper.

Madai appeared dismayed but did nothing.

Leah stepped forward, but Neb raised his hand. "Let the boys handle it."

Leah's face clouded, though she obeyed.

Neb motioned for Leah to step away.

Serug's temper mounted into full-blown fury. The little boy kicked his older brother and screamed. "I want honey bread. Go get it."

Madai, as was his custom, tried to explain matters in a calm, patient manner. "The honey bread is for later, when you're really hungry, so stop crying and go play."

Serug threw himself down on the ground and sprawled in the dirt, kicking and screaming.

Leah wrung her hands.

Neb dismissed his eldest son with a wave. He told Leah to get some honey bread and bring it to him.

Leah trotted away.

Neb stood over his youngest son, considering the wild beast-boy. He glanced back as Madai sauntered away, and his flesh crawled. He would trade that son if he could.

Leah returned and handed him the honey bread.

Serug sat sprawled, panting in the dust, sweat beaded on his round, red face.

Neb broke off a small piece and held it up. "You want this?" He took a bite and made a pleased noise as he swallowed.

Serug's eyes followed his father's every move. He motioned for his father to bend down and give him the bread.

Neb grinned. "No, you come to me."

Serug began to kick and scream again.

Neb ate another piece of bread. "Only one piece left."

Serug scrambled to his feet and snatched the bread from Neb's hand and stuffed it in his mouth.

Neb laughed. He opened his other hand, revealing a larger piece of bread.

Serug looked to the ground, clearly contemplating a repeat of his maneuvers in the dust. Instead, he tried to snatch the bread.

Neb was too quick. He drew his hand back.

Serug grabbed his arm and tried to bite him.

Neb shoved the child away roughly and dropped half the bread on the ground, grinding it into the dust.

Serug screamed.

Neb lifted his right hand to strike, dangling the bread in the other.

The child flinched, his eyes narrowing.

"Ask politely."

Frowning, Serug thrust out his hand. "Please."

After ripping off a small piece, Neb ate the larger and handed the smaller to the child. He grinned and patted his son on the head. "You'll learn.

—YEARS LATER—

Madai hated the hunt. But hunter or hunted—his life was defined by those he had no desire to emulate.

Neb had seen bear tracks the day before, so he decided to let his sons take the bear together.

Serug exalted in the challenge. Tall and thin but sinewy like a cat, his green eyes sparkled.

Though a bear would bring home a lot of meat, Madai marveled at a bear's natural strength and beauty and had no desire to kill one. He felt foreign, as if he never belonged to his clan.

Once they had found the bear's fresh tracks, Neb had left them. He said he would see them after they made the kill, skinned her, and packed the meat in fresh leaves to be carried home in woven baskets—which they were expected to make themselves out of hanging vines.

Neb made light of the situation. Only one son could rule, and as leader, he had to decide which son would be trained to inherit all. Clearly, he wanted to see which boy would master the hunt and reign supreme.

Keeping his face slack, Madai simply stared at his father. Questions or any sign of uncertainty infuriated Neb. A she-bear, many times the strength of a full-grown man, could kill either of them with a swipe of her massive paw.

Even if they did manage to kill her, how would they skin her in a single, complete piece, as was the practice of those who knew how? Skinning a bear was well beyond his skill. On top of that, the meat would weigh more than the two of them put together.

Madai shrugged. He was used to being asked to do difficult, even painful tasks, but he had never been asked to do the impossible before.

Serug beamed in anticipation. Apparently, neither hesitation nor fear entered his mind. "Madai, we have a formidable task ahead. Let's get ready."

Madai peered at his brother. "What do you suggest we do?"

His smile ingratiating and his voice high, Serug yanked vines from the trees. "We'll make the baskets first and then get a space ready for skinning."

Madai shook his head. "She is liable to run when she sees us."

"Not at all. She likes this place. You can see she has come here often. When she turns to fight, we'll kill her."

"You make it sound like a simple matter."

Serug rolled his eyes. "You act like a girl."

Burning irritation seeped through Madai. He stepped back and waved in surrender.

"I'll make a basket and clear a space. You can circle around and make noise so that she runs this direction. We'll make the kill together."

Irritation turned to panic as Madai considered all the things that could go wrong. "What if she turns to pursue me? Or if she gets ahead of me, how will you take her down by yourself?"

Serug snorted as if he had to explain simple matters to a slow child. "I'll be close at hand and draw her to me. When you've caught up, I will throw my spear right into her heart. Then you'll help me finish her off."

Madai swallowed hard. In unusual generosity, Serug seemed to be attempting to share the glory of the kill. Yet, Serug would never have a chance to kill the bear before she mangled him beyond recognition. "I'll stay, and you go around. When she charges, I'll wound her, and you finish her off."

Serug stomped his foot, his childish temper unleashed. "I'm a better thrower, and you'll run away!" He slammed down his spear, screaming in a fit of temper.

Madai held his breath.

A rustling sound brushed against his ears. His skin prickled.

Serug thrashed a bush with a stick.

A huge, muscled bear broke through the brush only a few paces away, stood on her hind legs, and bellowed.

Serug fell backward.

A jolt like lightning heightened every sense in Madai. He gripped his spear.

The bear dropped on all fours and tromped noisily toward Serug.

Panic seized Madai. “Run! Serug, run!”

Rising in a stupor, Serug looked around for his spear.

Madai circled to get between the furious bear and his brother.

Serug unsheathed his knife and lifted it high into the air with both hands.

The bear stood up again, her claws extended.

Just as the bear lurched for Serug, Madai swung in and braced his spear underneath. Her weight drove the spearhead into her chest, snapping the shaft.

She howled and reared up.

Madai snatched Serug’s spear from the ground, stepped back and threw with all his might. It pierced her in the side.

In furious pain, she clawed at her side and then at Serug, tearing his face and body.

Serug screamed.

Madai unsheathed his knife, jumped into the bear’s back, and slashed its neck repeatedly, grunting and whimpering with his extreme effort.

The bear thrashed, trying to get Madai off her back, but the spear dug deeper into her insides until the point struck home. With a mighty shiver, she dropped to the ground.

Kicked and scraped by her thrashing, Madai managed one more powerful thrust before she finally lay still.

The world misted before his eyes, the trees swayed, and darkness took him.

~~~

Madai awoke on his own bed.

His mother sat beside him with her hands clasped, and her face lined with tormented anguish.

His head ached, and his leg and side burned. He forced himself to sit up.

"Where's Serug?"

"He's in his hut, healing. He'll have scars for the rest of his life, but Neb says that they're wounds of glory."

Madai fell back onto his pallet. "Glory?" He shook his head and closed his eyes, the nightmarish scenes playing before him. "Did he tell you?"

"He said he took the bear all by himself."

Madai groaned and opened his eyes. "He would lie."

"Serug looks to emulate his father in all things." Leah patted her son's hands. "But you're alive, and that is what matters." She took a deep breath. "This cannot happen again."

"As long as I am Neb's son, this is my life. He'll send me on a raid next."

"That must not happen."

Surprised, Madai glanced up and met his mother's unwavering gaze.

"I'll let you rest now."

Neb entered, nodded to his wife, and then peered down at his son. "I heard voices as I went past." He paused. "I'm glad to see your eyes are clear and steady." He turned to his wife.

Leah took the hint and passed through the doorway with
~~~

a single backward glance.

Madai watched her leave and then faced his father.

Neb sat on the edge of the pallet and cleared his throat. “Tell me what happened from the time I left you.”

Madai told the sorry tale, uncertain of what his father would believe but determined to tell the honest truth.

Neb listened without comment.

Madai’s body burned, and thirst tormented him, but he did not want to mention his suffering to his father.

Neb seemed to sense his need. “I am glad you lived.” He stood. “Your meals will be brought, and I’ll send someone to care for your wounds.”

Confused, Madai glanced at the doorway. “Mother takes care of me.”

Neb pursed his lips. “You will be trained to rule. We’ll expand our claim and make ourselves great throughout the land.”

Swirling in a mist of doubt and uncertainty, Madai hesitated but then forced himself to speak. “I thought you favored Serug.”

Neb shrugged. “He won’t learn discipline. Besides, his injuries are severe. He may never be whole again.”

Grief battled pride and gladness when Madai realized that his father had chosen him over Serug. But then his eyes shifted to the doorway. *What about Mother?* His stomach churned. He felt light-headed.

Neb turned. “I’ll go now, but you’ll be well cared for. I’ll take over your training, and once you are healed, we’ll go on our first raid. I have an old matter that must be attended to.” An odd glint entered his eye. “I see no more fitting companion than my son when I go to settle matters with my brothers.” He smiled grimly and walked through the open doorway.

Madai lay back and stared at the rafters, every breath a painful stab. He closed his eyes.

A hand clasped his.

"Mother?" His eyes snapped open.

"You'll not be trained to become like Neb." Her jaw hardened, and her eyes held his gaze in a vice grip. "I was afraid to die before, but not now. For you, I will lay down my life." Her whisper grew husky. "We'll steal away when you are well enough and do the one thing that Neb does not expect."

Leah patted her son's hand and kissed him on the cheek. "In this, I will have my way. We are not alone." She smiled and slipped outside.

A quiet confidence seeped into Madai's heart. He wondered at this strange sense of peace. The sensation comforted him, and he fell into a deep, dreamless sleep.

CHAPTER THIRTY-TWO

—VILLAGE OF HAVILAH—

YOU CHOOSE

Enosh pushed away troubled thoughts about the future and smiled as he watched his sons play with long sticks.

Though his son, Gomer, at three years of age, used every ounce of his childish strength to swing his staff, his aim was wildly inaccurate, so he rarely struck a true blow. His older brother, Put, as a young man, allowed him to make his mark every now and again, dramatically grimacing and grunting to the delight of his sibling.

Put was not his flesh and blood, still the youth was his son in every sense Enosh could imagine. The baby he had inherited had grown into a man under his guidance. There had never been a more receptive, good-natured young man put upon the earth.

Gomer was late in coming, with two sisters between the boys, but the brothers were inseparable. While Put stood massive, towering overgrown men, his thick black hair and rich brown eyes attracting every available woman, Gomer appeared tiny, almost doll-like.

Gomer wanted so much to be like his brother that he would try to eat mouthful for mouthful what Put ate, making himself sick in the attempt. But his valiant spirit showed itself no less than his brother's as they sported together.

Each wielded a stick, though Gomer's was quite a bit longer. Their deft moves sent a surge of pride through Enosh.

Put offered a quick thrust at his little brother, who

managed a surprisingly able defense, whapping Put in the thigh. Put, unwilling to let his little brother win so quickly, returned the thrust, but Gomer sensed the coming retribution and attempted a run-away maneuver.

Put caught the little boy and swung him high in the air and then gently lowered him to the ground.

Gomer surprised them all by whacking his big brother over the head with his stick.

Using every bit of his dramatic skill, Put fell slowly to the ground, uttering horrible, groaning sounds.

Gomer smiled broadly at his grand success, ready to finish off his opponent when Put suddenly grabbed his brother. Gomer squeaked and howled for assistance.

Enosh stood by, transfixed by the engagement, one hand on his hip the other dangling a long rope.

Kenan strolled by, stopped, then without warning, dropped his tools, and rushed to Gomer's rescue. He fought to take the child out of Put's mighty grasp and ran off with him.

In hot pursuit, Put chased him around the village center. Soon a fierce battle ensued between Put and Kenan, with Gomer either slapping Kenan onto success or grabbing him heartily around the neck, choking him.

Enosh had never laughed so hard in his life.

When Gomer hurled an invisible spear, Put reeled and pretended to die dramatically on the grassy plain.

Kenan slid Gomer to the earth to pay his worthy opponent a final farewell.

Gomer bounced over, all fear and apprehension gone, and plunked down on Put's chest. The game over, Gomer sat on the throne of victory.

Enjoying the game as much as his sons, Enosh walked over and laid his hand on Put.

Gomer jumped off to watch this impressive ritual. Always after these splendid battles, his father would awaken the fallen.

Put brushed himself off and smiled at his brother, who grinned back in sly relief. Then he faced Enosh, the game forgotten. "So, what is your plan, Father?"

Enosh blinked, forcing himself back to reality. "Yes, the plan. The usual harvest is not enough for our growing clan. I talked with Kryce, and he agrees that we need a larger store of lentils. So we've been put in charge of making a central garden."

Put grinned. "I'll be glad to help, and I can find a few more volunteers." He patted his brother's head.

As Enosh watched his sons meander away, the larger holding the hand of the smaller, like best of friends, his heart rejoiced in his family as it never had before.

~~~

Kryce made plans for battle. Word of Neb's coming had reached his ears, and this time, he would not wait for Neb to advance upon them. They would destroy the rising evil like attacking hornets.

In council with Jubal, they decided to organize war parties.

Though still early in the planting season, he could see Enosh busy with his sons in the newly prepared field. He strode forward, studying his friend. As he neared, doubts rose in his mind.

Enosh rested upon a rock on the edge of the field and waved in greeting. "See what industrious workers we've become? We shall feed the whole village!" His face was bright with sweat, his smile broad.

Kryce merely nodded toward the field and then looked his friend in the eye. "Neb is preparing to raid again. This
~~~

time he brings his grown sons."

A red blush spread over Enosh's face as if someone had slapped him. "Neb…is coming? Here?"

Kryce clenched his jaw. No one expected Enosh to be happy at this turn of events, but he had never considered the idea that the man would be afraid.

"I realize this is ill news, but I thought you'd want to know." Kryce waited.

Enosh stared at his sons working in the field.

"After much consultation, Jubal, Seth, and I decided to form war parties. We will surprise Neb and defeat him and his sons before they have a chance to attack us."

"N-no one forewarned me. I heard nothing from Seth or Jubal."

Kryce shrugged. "They didn't want to worry you."

Exchanging his fear with fury, Enosh frowned and straightened, his shoulders squared. His voice dropped dangerously low. "Worry me? So intimate a matter discussed and decided without me? And Kenan? When was he going to be told?"

Kryce lifted his hand in defense. "I informed you. You can inform your brother."

"Do you doubt our loyalty? You think we have forgotten—"

Seething with anger, Kryce raised his voice. "I'm the leader, and I make the decisions. Don't let fears divide us. That only gives Neb the edge he wants. We need your strength to defeat your brother, for his power is like no other. If that is not trust, then I do not know the meaning of the word."

Enosh glared at the broad horizon.

Kryce waited.

"You are the leader and my wife's brother. Kenan and I will fight by your side. Together we will end Neb's threat forever."

Kryce nodded, satisfied.

Looking beyond the grassy plain, Enosh crossed his arms. "Whatever happened to Eva…"

Kryce, too, stared toward the limitless sky. "I've wished to see Leah's face, to know my sister's fate, yet I have only been tormented by her loss. Destroying her sons will only add to her grief, but if they fight for Neb, they are evil. It's either their destruction or ours."

Enosh sighed, his gaze dropping.

Kryce pressed Enosh's shoulder. "Call your sons from the field. We have much to do. I'll be off within three days. Seth and Jubal and their men will join us the day after tomorrow."

"And Accad? Surely, he has as much cause to fight as any man."

"Seth wants someone he trusts to watch over those left behind." He paused. "Accad is no longer strong. His years of suffering weigh heavily upon him. Seth is wise in keeping him at home."

The sun hung low over the horizon, the sky turning blood red. Birds chirped evening songs while a breeze blew from the west.

Put, face flushed and eyes sparkling, jogged to his father's side. "Are we really going into battle?"

"Yes, as soon as Seth and his men arrive."

Put's smile broadened. "I'm old enough and strong."

Enosh stared at his son. He swallowed, face contorted. "Yes. We need your help." He glanced toward the village where women prepared family meals, and small children ran in playful abandon. "Let your mother hear it from me."

"Of course." Put sped off, his excitement quivering in the air.

Kryce frowned. "What's the matter? Your son wants to fight. How could that displease you?"

"He does not displease me." A strangled groan escaped Enosh. "He'll fight his uncle and relations…men from my clan."

A surge of bile rose inside Kryce. “Who is your clan? Those you are born with or those you choose?”

Enosh muttered as he ran his fingers through his disheveled hair. “Both.”

Kryce remembered his father’s bloody body, his sister’s despairing face, and he hardened his heart.

CHAPTER THIRTY-THREE

—WILDERNESS—

INGENUITY

Adam knew he was completely ordinary in every visible way. Bequeathed by his parents with light brown hair, auburn eyes, tan skin, and a medium build. There was nothing unusual in his manner, style, or occupation. He traveled at his leisure, trading, and doing as he pleased. Most often, he spoke with few words, his voice naturally soft and low, but listened intently and enjoyed gaining knowledge as well as goods.

Though few could explain why they liked and trusted him, almost everyone did.

Adam crossed paths with distant traders, and, having just come from a village rich in wine and ready stock, he shared his good fortune liberally. Acting the generous friend, he showed his goodwill through kind donations of food and wine.

The acquaintances grew generous in return. One elder became almost fatherly, offering advice to the younger man.

"Listen, I will share with you a great secret." With a furtive glance to each side, the old trader slung his heavy bag from his shoulder.

Adam scooted closer, sensing the importance of this secret.

"I discovered something that will change the fortunes of war." The old man fidgeted with the straps of his bag and then glanced up, his eyes holding a serious look. "A new weapon from distant lands."

Barely able to contain his curiosity, Adam held his breath as the old man stuffed his hand into the bag. Then he drew out a curved piece of wood with a strong, thin string of sinew tied from end to end. Then he pulled out several sharpened sticks. He fitted the blunt end against the sinew and pulled the stick back, stretching the sinew to tautness. Aiming in the direction of a cluster of trees, he lets the stick loose. It sailed through the air, flying a considerable distance.

Without speaking a word, Adam acquired a prize.

The next day, after groggy, good-mornings were exchanged, the traders continued on their way, promising to meet again in this life or the next.

Adam continued his travels alone, deep in thought. Deciding that he could improve on what he'd seen, he soon crafted a better version of the bow and arrow.

His new invention worked, though not nearly as well as his imagination had told him it could. After days of thought and practice, he rejoiced in a weapon that could either save or destroy an entire village.

As his food supply dwindled, he decided to approach a new village and considered his options. He had heard that the leader of the village of Havilah, a man named Kryce, was a fair man. If he liked him, they might make a pleasant deal.

But fate had other plans.

Near evening, two strangers intercepted him.

The taller man folded his arms across his chest and planted himself in the way. "What is such noble a youth doing so far from home?"

The shorter companion didn't waste time with nice words. "Speak, fool."

Though his heart beat like a war drum, Adam considered his interrogators with a steady smile. "My name is Adam, and I'm a trader of goods and news. If your leader is near, I would be happy to speak with him."

The taller man aimed his gaze and narrowed his eyes. "Well, Adam, Neb the Great is our leader, but he does not indulge in chatter, and he has little need for trade goods."

The illogic of certain men stood out like a sharp stone. He must watch his step. Neb was not the man he looked for, but that made little difference. One leader was much like the next. In an attempt at clear thinking, Adam offered his opinion, grinning good-naturedly all the while. "You don't know what I carry, so how do you know that your leader won't want it?"

"Show us, boy, and we'll decide."

Adam straightened and met the tall man's gaze. Tall fools were no different from any other fool. Amusement banished his fear. "I have goods meant only for the bravest and the wisest. I can show them to no one but the leader—on pain of death."

The shorter man snorted. "On pain of death? We can arrange that neatly enough! Come show us what you have, and we'll decide whether you should visit Neb or die here." The smoldering hate in his eyes hinted at his preference.

A flicker of anxiety knocked Adam's mood from the heights. He repositioned his bundle. "You wouldn't see its value."

"Show us!"

With a rough jerk, the short one grabbed the bag and dumped the contents on the ground. The assorted goods fell in a sprawled heap on the bent grass: a few sticks—one thick and curved, several sharpened stones, a ball of twine, a pile of ordinary knives, one broken spear, and a set of decorated cups, bowls, and spoons.

The tall one shook his head, and the short one sneered. "Your insolence tests our patience. We should kill you now."

At the sight of another man approaching with quick determined steps, Adam's spirits rekindled. "Unless you plan on telling your leader that you killed an innocent man who only wished to do him a good turn, you had better—"

The new, younger man stepped forward and waved the other two aside with an authoritative gesture.

They stepped back.

The young man pointed across the grassy plain. "He's waiting."

With curt nods, the two turned and traipsed away.

The young man's eyes followed the men some distance. He sighed and faced Adam. "So how do you feel being accosted by the two most unworthy warriors of Neb the Great?"

Adam rubbed the strained grin off his face. "Weary of their games." In a sudden, inexplicable attraction to the newcomer, he leaned forward. "I'm Adam. A trader and traveler. And you?"

"I'm long past weary." Exchanging his serious expression for one more comical, the young man bowed and gestured dramatically. "My name is Madai, the firstborn son of the firstborn son of . . . Well, it goes on."

Sensing a spirit-kin, Adam exhaled, relaxed, and allowed a real smile to spread over his face. "I am also a firstborn, though my lineage is not so noble. My father was the son of a mad man."

Madai arched his brows, clearly interested. "A mad man?"

Adam grinned, picked his bag off the ground, slapped the dirt and grass away, and replaced his goods. "So I'm told."

Madai led the way to the edge of a wooded glen. They strolled together shoulder-to-shoulder until Madai perched on the edge of a boulder jutting from a stream. "Do you think your grandfather was truly mad?"

Adam stopped at a fallen tree trunk and plunked down with a sigh. "I don't think so, or if it be the case, then most men of adventure are mad. My grandfather liked to have his own way. He would eat things never eaten before, go places never gone before, and say things never said before." Adam chewed his lip. "He often got in trouble with my grandmother for that."

The heat of the day cooled in a gentle breeze.

Madai searched Adam's face. "Are you sure you want to offer your wares to my father?"

Adam scratched an insect bite, surprised at the sharp sting and the question. "Why not? I have something that could change the fortune of a leader—and his whole clan."

Madai clenched his jaw and glanced around fugitively. "You may be offering it to the wrong man." He peered hard at Adam. "Do you even know who my father is?"

Adam shrugged. "I've heard of Neb the Great. It's said that he cannot be killed, though his men die like mortals. I know that he suffered a great injury but refused to be defeated. His sons are—"

Despair peered from Madai's eyes.

Confused, Adam's words failed.

Snorting bitterly, Madai urged him on. "Tell me, what about his sons?"

Hot embarrassment flooded Adam's face. He could not fathom why he had become so talkative. "It's said they are as different as night and day. One is strong and brave while the other is—"

"Is what?" This demand came from another man coming around from behind Adam. He swept before them and propped his hands on his hips, blinking furiously.

Madai stifled a low groan and gestured. "Adam, meet my brother, Serug."

His feet planted wide, Serug reminded Adam of a child about to throw a fit.

His voice high, Serug snapped each word. "Come, come! Don't be scared. Tell me!"

Adam passed his gaze over Madai and focused on the brat. "It's said that the other son is brilliant with insight not given to ordinary mortals."

Madai ducked his head.

Was the man choking or laughing? Adam wasn't sure. He fixed his gaze on the tyrant, unwaveringly.

Appeased, Serug lifted his chin. "In that case, my father will want to speak with you."

A mask resettled on Adam's face. "Of course. You want to report the news to your father, loyal son that you are." He stood and stretched in exaggerated exhaustion. "I've been traveling for a long stretch of days. Would your father be kind enough to allow me a night's rest within your camp tonight? I'll gladly share the goods, which" —he tapped his bag with his toe—"I still have in my possession."

Shading his face with his hand, Serug scanned the horizon. "If I speak with my father, he will welcome you, though we do not have much time to spare. We're preparing for battle."

A gut twist shook Adam's composure. "Oh?" He darted a glance at Madai. "I didn't know." Slinging his bag over his shoulder, he pointed his feet away from where the other men had gone. "If this isn't a good time, I'll move—"

"You'll meet my father!" Serug turned on his heel and strode away.

With a laconic wave, Madai started after his brother. "You have little choice now but to follow."

Like a rock, the stream must go around. Adam squared his shoulders. "I always have a choice. In my family, we do what we like."

Only a hint of sarcasm tinged the air. "You and my father shall get along splendidly."

Contrary to previous experience, those words offered not a bit of comfort. Adam wondered at the knot tightening in his stomach.

Madai's steps plodded with steady, unhurried rhythm. "You're right. This isn't a good time."

Despite his bafflement, Adam trudged forward. "But, really, I can help your father win the next battle."

Madai's face contorted in deadly earnest. He dropped his voice low. "That's the last thing I want."

Tripping over his feet, Adam stumbled but quickly regained his balance. He wondered if he would do as well after meeting Neb the Great.

—NEB'S CAMP—

Madai sat before the evening fire, his stomach full of roasted meat, bread, and wine, his heart empty of everything but despair.

Orange and red flames danced in the black night.

Neb had not been around all evening. Madai canvassed the various possibilities of where his father might've gone when suddenly Neb appeared in their midst. With a stern expression, he strode into the light and sat by his eldest son. "I have news that might interest you."

Madai stared at his father's sharp profile against the flickering flames, ignoring Adam's watching eyes.

"You have a choice to make."

Nauseous confusion swirled through Madai. He had learned the art of playing the mouse to his father's cat-paw, but shame flooded him as Adam sat by, seeing all. "Yes, Father?"

"Your mother is dying. She wants you, but we draw near to the greatest battle of our lives. You have a choice. You can either leave us to see your mother, or you can stay by my side and conquer our enemy."

Dreadful silence hung heavy in the night air.

Serug opened his mouth, but his father gestured for his silence.

Madai now knew how it felt to be stabbed in the dark. "I will stay with you, Father, for it is not only my duty but my honor."

A twisted grin spread over Neb's face. "I knew you would."

Serug huffed, leaning into the firelight. "Why trust him, Father, when he means you no good? He is a liar and a thief. He hates you, though he will not say the words."

Neb looked from one son to the other. Then his eyes fell on the stranger. He pointed at Adam. "Who is this?"

Madai started to speak, "A friend—"

Serug drowned him out. "A *stranger* who says—"

Neb held up his hand. "The man will speak for himself."

Adam stood and clasped his hands, making a formal show of his introduction. "I am Adam, the son of a trader and maker of things. I come from a clan far to the east, near the mountains. We are a valley people, and many travelers cross our lands. We live in a vast territory, moving south each winter, while in the summer, we climb into the hills. It is a beautiful land, rich in gardens and alive with young animals. Our women are beautiful, and our children are strong and healthy. I travel and share what I learn with others."

Neb nodded. "And why does a man wish to leave such a perfect land and wonderful people?"

Adam offered one of his disarming smiles, though Neb appeared not to see it. "I like to see new things. My father was much the same, though my mother did not like it so much. Eventually, my father turned to creating things instead of aimless traveling or warmongering—" Suddenly Adam frowned, clearly confused.

Neb's brows knit together as he stared at the youth

through the dim light. He ordered that another log be added to the fire.

Several men rose to obey.

"Have you much skill with invention?"

Adam cleared his throat. "I like to try my hand at fashioning new things, though I'm no match for my father. He could carve wonderful figures in wood, making handles for blades he fashioned strong and enduring."

Neb's gaze fell to his sons. He focused on Madai.

Deflecting his father's stare, Madai watched the flickering flames. *Please, let me be.*

"So what have you to say about our new friend, Madai? Shall we keep him with us for a time?"

Another test? Madai peered over the flames at Adam, and though only silence passed between them, an understanding formed.

Neb cleared his throat.

Serug smiled.

Neb rose and stretched in the fashion of a man tired after a long hard day. "I'll take my rest." He looked over at the young trader. "Adam will stay with us. I'll learn about you and your people." With a sweeping glance, he ordered them all to bed.

Warriors, young and old, stood and started for their beds.

Serug appeared to be planted in place for the duration of eternity.

Neb stopped by his son's side, his hand near Serug's shoulder, a silent command.

Serug stiffened. After a long moment, he rose with a whine. "But why do they get to stay?"

Neb clenched his jaw.

Serug's shoulders sagged as he stomped away, pouting in fury, as he had countless times before.

Madai stood, but Neb waved him back. "No, stay and

keep our friend company. You can sleep near the fire. Nothing bothers the young."

Madai did not raise his head. He did not need to see his father's face to read the bitter irony. Neb counted on Madai to make him young in war, but this was a dream fast slipping away. They both knew that Serug saw too much and spoke too truly.

Neb hobbled away.

Adam tapped a stick against the log on which he sat on of several that had been rolled near the fire.

Adam had chosen a particularly tall log and then taken an ax and chopped down one side just to the middle. Then, using the edge of the blade, he smoothed the center, making a comfortable perch.

Peering at the newcomer, Madai marveled at this ingenuity. "You have many talents."

Adam shook his head. "But do I have wisdom?"

Madai remembered his mother, and tears welled in his eyes.

CHAPTER THIRTY-FOUR

—NEB'S VILLAGE—

ENTRUST HER MISSION

Leah stood on the brink of a precipice, her cloak wrapped over her shoulders against the morning chill.

Neb had traveled west, inflicting indignities on the surrounding clans as he went. It seemed he wanted to send word ahead to the People of Havilah that he was coming, without actually burdening himself with too many trophies as of yet. He was holding his men back for the big battle.

Her sudden illness had laid her low, but even as her body healed, her mind shadowed Madai's every move. She sent scouts out so that she could keep abreast of what was happening. She learned that a trader, a creative youth whom Neb accepted into the clan, had befriended Madai. Her spirits lifted at the news. At the first light of dawn, she sent for Eva.

Eva arrived promptly. When she saw Leah standing near the window, she sighed with chagrin. "What is so important? The sun hasn't even shown its face."

Leah paced like a tethered dog. "I must free Madai from Neb before it's too late."

Eva threw her hands up into the air and stepped forward. "Wonderful idea! Why don't you free us all?" She shrugged. "I wish I had escaped when I'd had the chance."

Leah stopped her pacing and searched her friend's face. "I will free everyone. Mostly myself."

Eva plunked down on a pillow. "Are you running away? To your old home? Where Neb is heading…to be slaughtered with the rest? Will that free you?"

Leah knelt before Eva and clasped her hands. "I tried to love Neb enough, but it didn't work. Even when Neb loved me back, I was not free. I sacrificed my honor for my life. Madai was all the justification I needed. But if he is corrupted, my sacrifice will have been in vain. He must live to undo Neb's evil."

Eva pulled away. "Madai is not Neb's keeper. He's not responsible for his father's deeds."

"Every son bears the sins of his father; he must accept or reject them. Madai wants to reject them, but he's afraid." Exhaustion swept over Leah. She couldn't manage without Eva's support.

Eva climbed to her feet and plodded to the other side of the room. The scent of fresh herbs, hanging by the open window, invigorated her limbs. "So where will he find courage? From you?" She gripped the frame and sucked in a deep breath of air

Leah stepped to the doorway and watched the village awakening. A group of women hefted basketfuls of clothes toward the river, one man replaced the thatch on his roof, while two men cleaned a pile of fish at an outdoor table. "I've lived intimately with a man bound to darkness. He does not rest easy. He is more tormented than his worst enemy."

Eva stood behind her friend. "If only that were true."

Leah turned around, a stream of grief and fear cascading into fury. "Don't you see? We lose every time one man gives up his soul. All of us—family, clansmen, all of us—become weaker by the loss!" She grabbed her water skin, flinging the strap over her shoulder, and stepped outside. "I must save my son. He's my only hope."

Clearly alarmed, Eva trotted ahead and intercepted Leah. "*Now*? You just got out of bed! You need time and preparations."

Leah increased her pace, winding through the village and following the path Neb had taken. Urgency directed her steps, the realization that without her healing presence, Madai would be lost to her forever.

Eva ran in front of Leah and blocked the path. "I'll come with you! Just wait a day, and I'll get everything ready."

Unwilling to delay another moment, Leah stepped around Eva.

Eva called after her friend. "What about Serug?"

Leah's step faltered, but she recovered and continued her march. "I've already lost him."

Before she reached the first hill, the sun glowed in white brilliance. Birds flew across the bright blue sky, unheeding the steps of those below.

Eva, like an abandoned home, remained behind, left but not forgotten.

For two days, Leah marched with nothing more than sips of water to ease her thirst and her thin cloak to protect her against the night chill. Constant hunger and weariness dampened her resolve.

Wildcats, smelling fear, dogged her steps.

On the second evening, she found a stream meandering from the rocky crags near the mountainside, and she sat, refilled her water skin, and drank her fill.

As she rested on a rocky ledge, doubts wormed into her mind. *Am I mad? Did the fever make me think I could find Neb's war party—alone—in the wild?*

The sun settled behind the mountain. She pulled her wrap tighter over her shoulders. Was she too far north…or south? She closed her eyes, the sound of flowing water echoing in her ears.

A moment later, the thrashing sound of men's progress sent chills over her body. The sun had long gone, and only a sliver of the moon shone bright in the night sky. Leah pictured her mother and her father and pleaded like a child for their help, but no words would come. She curled up into a ball and squeezed her eyes shut.

"What is this?" A scornful tone. She knew that voice. Torgama at his best.

A foot nudged her in the side. A laugh. "I know who it is! The mouse who plucks weeds and roots."

Kittam's voice rose soft and sibilant. "No, Eva is small, and her bones are like a bird's."

A hand grabbed Leah by the shoulder and pulled her upward.

Staring into Kittam's eyes, she spat her words. "Get your hands off me! I'm looking for my husband. I have important news."

As if bitten, Kittam jumped back.

Torgama laughed. "You shouldn't lay hands on Neb's woman.

Kittam turned toward Torgama. "Shut up, slave! Or I'll ask Neb how his leg feels today!"

Fighting dizziness, Leah climbed to her feet. "If you value your lives, you will take me to Neb quickly."

The two men exchanged wary looks. Torgama pointed east, across the small stream. "He's a few hours march from here, if we go directly. That is not how Neb likes to travel, but you may do as you wish."

Leah wiped her hands on her filthy dress and peered across the murky stream into the darkness. "I've had nothing to eat."

Torgama bowed in mock kindness. "Permit me to share my meager provisions." He unslung his bag from his shoulder, reached inside, and pulled out a dirty piece of dried meat.

Leah took the offering, her hand accidentally brushing against his. She jerked away.

Kittam choked back a laugh.

Leah chewed the meat, swallowed, and spoke in forced calm. "Once I am satisfied, we will go to meet my husband."

Their eyes glinted liked predators.

Sweat beaded on her forehead. She tried to out-stare Torgama as she finished her disgusting meal, but exhaustion seeped into the fiber of her being.

Kittam jostled ahead. "Follow us."

Torgama allowed her to step ahead.

Strong guides who would lead her to Neb surrounded her, but her soul felt no comfort, only a mountain of grief.

~~~

Neb waited until the scout caught his breath. He tapped his fingers against his aching thigh.

"Kittam and Torgama have returned, bringing your wife."

Neb looked to the west and saw the scout's words realized.

Leah appeared, exhausted, pale, and trembling with cold.

Torgama and Kittam marched on either side of her, their faces perfect masks of complete indifference.

Alarm sprang from deep within Neb, and he wondered at it. He started forward. Her mud-splattered dress with its ragged hem contrasted sharply with how well she normally dressed. Stray locks of matted hair flew into her face. She stared like a hunted animal.

Neb's eyes roved over his two warriors. Would they have attempted to disgrace his wife? They would've liked to. Neb swallowed, squared his shoulders, and intercepted his wife.
~~~

"Leah? Explain yourself."

Swaying on her feet, Leah halted, her shoulders drooping, and her head low as if it were too great a weight to carry. "I've come to warn you of danger."

"Torgama, you and Kittam go and see to the sentries around the camp. Check every man; see that everyone is alert and watchful. I will speak with my wife, and then we'll meet in counsel."

Torgama and Kittam turned away in silent compliance.

Neb noticed the lack of a respectful bow. He called out. "Have you forgotten something?"

The two men exchanged a brief glance. They bowed in unison, with the slightest mockery that did not deceive Neb. He faced his wife and gestured for her to follow him into his tent.

Leah stood stock-still. "I'll see my sons first."

Neb glared, fury seething through him. What was this, some new defiance? He gestured to indicate a tent next to his own.

Like a sleepwalker, Leah paced to the opening and called, "Madai? Serug?"

Serug's face peered through the opening. "Mother?" A flicker of joy passed over his face, chased away by a dark frown.

"Yes. I've come to see you and your brother. Is he inside?"

Serug's face pinched into displeasure. "Madai? He's never here. Always with that stupid trader, the son of an idiot."

Irritation boiled over as Neb pushed forward. "That's enough. Your mother wanted to see you and know you are well. Tell her the news. I will bring Madai."

Neb beckoned one of his men and ordered him to bring Madai.

Serug stepped forward and stood in front of his mother.

Leah reached out, but Serug leaned back. "I'm too old

for your caresses now, Mother. You shouldn't have come."

Dark lines under her eyes emphasized her exhaustion. "Why not?"

Serug offered a knowing smile. "The men will laugh and say that Neb cannot control his wife."

Leah looked around as if searching for something. She faced her strong, stubborn son. "May I sit down?"

Serug led her to an open space before a smoldering fire.

They sat.

Neb stood by, impatience warring with concern.

"Tell me about this trader, the stupid one you spoke of," she kept her voice low, unemotional, too drained to suffer for her youngest son's foolishness.

"I didn't say he was stupid, but rather that his father was stupid. He is proud of his father, though he hardly knows how to fight. I could kill him in a moment."

"Why would you want to do that?"

"I don't need a reason. It's just knowing that I can."

"If he is a trader, he must be years your elder."

"He doesn't have the warrior's spirit in him."

"But you do?"

"Certainly."

"But he might not let you kill him. He might fight back, and then where would you be?"

Serug grinned. "No man can watch his back all the time, Mother."

"Would you stab a man in the back, Serug?"

"If I needed to."

A growl rose from deep within Neb. Serug's commentary did nothing to enhance the family. His hand twitched to smack the boy's arrogant head.

Madai strode forward with Adam. As his gaze fell on his mother, his eyes widened. He sucked in a breath.

Serug rose. "I'll leave you now." He began to turn away. "You know that we are set for battle tomorrow?"

Leah nodded.

Serug glanced at Torgama and Kittam, who stood conversing with two other warriors. "You are lucky you weren't left with Torgama or Kittam."

"Why?"

Serug walked away as he flung back his last words. "They hate Neb." He strode past his father, grinning.

Heated in fury, Neb wanted to slap him. But now was not the time. He must make plans to meet his brothers in battle and not lose control of his wife and sons in the meantime.

~~~

Madai's heart fluttered as he lifted his hands in greeting. "Mother, I'm surprised to see you here." He nudged Adam forward. "This is Adam, a trader from the east. His father is an inventor."

Leah dragged her eyes from her son, bowed in formal courtesy, and leaned in, speaking low to Adam, "Save my son."

Adam nodded as if he had just accepted a quaint compliment. "I'm happy to meet you as well. Your son has told me so much about your people."

Dead silence.

With a blush, Leah turned and stepped up to her husband. "I have seen them. I am very tired and must rest before I speak any further."

Neb gestured to indicate his tent.

Serug frowned as he watched his mother and father stride away.

Madai's heart ached. As he had secretly confided to Adam, in order to survive Neb's rule, he had to thrust aside his mother's words and moods, her gentle speech, and the
~~~

life she envisioned beyond Neb's ambition. Even when he had told Adam about her and her brothers' clan, he had spoken as if recounting an ancient past. Perhaps it was merely an illusion, but he wanted so much to live in her world, not his father's.

Adam stared at him with a strange glint in his eye.

Serug watched, still frowning.

Adam laughed as if Madai had made a joke. He slapped him on the back and shouted in mirth. "You always tell a good tale!" Gripping Madai's arm, he led him away from camp and dropped his voice. "We're leaving. Pretend we are going to the spring. I know what to do."

Madai swallowed a lump in his throat and covered his face with a mask of amusement. "You'd better know how to fight as well as laugh!"

Adam threw his hands up in mock irritation. "You want to see who's the better man? I'll race you!"

Madai puffed out his chest. "You're challenging me?"

In a moment, the two young men sped off, leaving Serug wide-eyed and open-mouthed.

Madai ran as if the mother bear of his nightmares were at his heels. Sweat trickled down his face, and his side ached, but he would not stop.

Adam loped along, appearing calm and cool, without fury or fear taking its toll.

As soon as the sun touched the horizon, Madai motioned for rest. With gasping breaths, they sprawled in the grass, heedless of snakes slithering away and birds cawing overhead.

Madai struggled to form his words. "So where—are we—running to?"

Adam chuckled. "Don't you know?"

Anxiety tightened Madai's stomach into a painful knot, his mind dizzy and confused. "I know Mother, and I saw that look in your eyes, so when you ran…"

Adam rested on his side and propped his head on his hand. “You’re going to meet your uncles.”

As if he had touched fire, alarm rippled over Madai’s skin. “The ones Neb is about to attack?”

“The very same.”

“But we’ll be killed! Surely my mother wanted me to go somewhere safe.”

“You and your uncles will be safe when they learn what I carry.”

Madai sat up and stared, his eyes searching. Adam carried nothing in his arms or on his back. “What do you carry?”

“Something that will give strength to the weak and make the frightened brave.”

Nausea bubbled in Madai’s gut. “Neb will want to kill more than my uncles if we don’t return soon.” He stood and peered from where they had come. “My mother? What will happen to her?”

Exhaling a forced breath, Adam leaped to his feet, his expression grave. “Your mother loves you. Do not waste her sacrifice.” He jogged forward.

Madai clenched his hands, pictured his mother’s face, and sprinted head.

Chapter Thirty-five

-OldEarth-

Survived So Long

Sienna held her datapad in front of her face and enunciated every word clearly.

Dear Sir… No, that won't do. *My friend Teal…* oh, that makes me sound like his classmate. *Darling?*" She blushed. "Not yet…not for a long while yet." She bit her lip and stared at the sun setting behind Ishtar's bustling village.

A baby squalled.

Sienna closed her eyes, dropped her chin to her chest, and exhaled. She lifted her head, drew in fresh air, and puffed a breath. *Ready?*

She opened her eyes and whispered. "Courage!" She turned her back on the village, clutched the datapad, and plastered on her most charming smile. "Teal, a great deal has happened in Ishtar's story, so get yourself a cup of Ingoti brew and settle down for a long listen. I have a lot to tell."

Taking it slow, she paced before the purpling world and recounted Ishtar's tale. She only stopped once. Tears threatened at the retelling of Leah's willing sacrifice for her son.

In the end, it didn't matter which way Sienna faced, the whole world was covered in darkness. She had lost Teal's love, and no one could see the agony of emptiness inside her.

-Planet Ingilium-

Teal leaned back on an extremely uncomfortable gray couch, crushing a thin pillow under his neck to soften the ache in his head. He twisted and turned. "What kind of people make a couch out of metal?" He tossed the pillow aside and sat up, rubbing his temple.

A buzz ripped through the last of his nerves. He shouted. "Come!"

The door slid open, and Ark slipped into the bare rectangular space.

Without any adornment, the room resembled the inside of a confinement cell. Only the couch and a single table offered any support.

Ark stroked the side of his face. "It's helpful to spend time on a person's planet of origin. I understand Zuri so much better now."

Teal shook his head, a thousand bees buzzing in his ears. "You've been to Ingilium before."

"Always as a welcomed guest. Never like this. Never treated to an inside look of the hardcore reality of Ingot existence. The other times, everything was set for show." He sighed. "I think I actually respect the idiot now."

Teal glared at the Cresta, no words forthcoming.

"I've always loved him, of course. As do you. But this…" Ark shook his head. "Such a cold world. Even our deepest oceans have more warmth."

Using every ounce of strength he could muster, Teal climbed to his feet. "I just listened to Sienna's report."

"Yes?"

"All is well…though I respect humans more. Some humans anyway."

Ark plodded closer, his gaze fixed on Teal. "But…?"

"But they are not ready for the larger universe. If there

is one thing I am absolutely sure of—human beings must never get too powerful."

With a snort, Ark waved toward the door. "I could've told you that the first day we met. Come on. There's a park not far from here with a fountain. I think they built it for visitors—probably afraid they'd get too sensitive if they took pleasure in natural beauty, but they don't mind if they corrupt us aliens." Ark waggled his eyebrows. "Let's get corrupted, shall we?"

~~~

Teal sauntered at Ark's side along a broad city walkway. Cubicle buildings branched at right angles from the road, with maze-like symmetry. The sound of splashing water and a colorful array of flowering trees planted in a perfect circle around the fountain alerted him to the designated park area.

The fountain stood, like all things Ingoti, in perfect alignment to the rest of the city. Dead center. Towering above the populous, it rose to a pointed peak in the green-hued clouds that permanently hung from the orange sky.

Ark attempted a whistle.

Teal grinned at him. "You finally found something on Ingilium that you like?"

With a well-aimed splash directed at the Luxonian, Ark smiled. "Say, rather, I found something on Ingilium that I don't hate."

A Bhuaci elder strolled near, his gaze fixed ahead. He stepped in front of Ark, and the two collided.

The elder fell, crumpling like a dispirited child.

Teal took the old one by the arm and helped him to his feet, darting an annoyed expression at Ark. "So sorry. We didn't see..."
~~~

Ark harrumphed. “I saw him perfectly. I just didn’t expect him to walk into me broadside.”

The elder clasped his hands and bowed in abject apology. “It was my fault. I wasn’t looking…” He blinked at Teal. “You’re a Luxonian?”

With a nod, Teal bowed back. “I’m Teal, and this is Ark. We’re here with an interested Ingoti friend, Zuri. He has taken the crime against the Bhuaci to heart, and—”

The Bhuac shook his head. “It’s no use.” He sighed and sat on the edge of a low wall enclosing a flower arrangement. “My name is Mire. I was here on diplomatic business when the attack came. The Ingots won’t let me leave until I promise to plead their case before the Inter-Alien council.” His eyes drifted to the horizon. “I’ll never plead for them, so I’ll never see my home again.” He met Teal’s gaze. “Or my family.”

Ark slapped one tentacle into the pool of water. “Does Ingot treachery have no limits?”

His glance swerving from the elder to Ark, Teal frowned. “Apparently, I need to return home and make a formal complaint to the Luxonian council. After all, if Ingots treat friends like this, then how can any of us sleep safe in our beds?”

Mire’s eyes lit up. “Would you do that? For us?”

Not to be outdone, Ark raised three tentacles like a pod making allegiance to Cresta. “And I’ll make a formal report to the Ingal. I’ll certainly mention Ingot’s complete disregard for water-based life forms who would see this miserable pool as little more than a taunt.”

Appreciative tears glistened in Mire’s eyes.

Teal rubbed his aching temple in thought. “But I need to check in on Earth first. I can’t abandon Sienna.”

Ark chewed his lip. “And we mustn’t forget that insect queen. She’d as soon dissect a human or a Bhuaci as help them.”

Teal grimaced, his headache pounding.

Ark swiveled his tentacles in wide arches. "What to do? We have only two bodies and four planets to cover?"

Mire leaned in and dropped his voice to a conspiratorial whisper. "In our world, when the Regent of Song needs help, she gathers her friends. First, they sing, then they pray, and finally, they make a plan."

Teal peered at Ark. "There is a reason that the Bhuaci have survived so long."

Ark lunged forward. "In that case…let's go."

Teal gripped a tentacle. "Where?"

Ark slapped his hand off and swept ahead. "To get Zuri, of course."

~~~

Zuri stared at the manacles wrapped tight around his wrists. He clenched his jaw and lifted his gaze to the judge on the platform.

The judge, a hulking Ingot with glowing orange eyes, slapped a round black button, ripping the air with a shrill blast.

The courtroom shuffled to order.

Teal and Ark hurried through a side door, their eyes wide with confusion.

Zuri tried to motion for them to wait, but the soldier at his side smacked his arm when he lifted his hands.

Teal jogged forward, waving frantically. "Wait! As a Luxonian representative in charge of a vital Inter-Alien Coalition, I insist on knowing what you are doing with this Ingot Representative."

The judge smirked. "This"—he grunted—"representative is about to be stripped of his armor and every shred of covering on his body and sent to Hungr for
~~~

his crimes."

A collective gasp filled the air.

Splintering icicles prickled Zuri's skin. Hungr—a frozen wasteland. A torturous death in exile. Though he'd not be entirely alone. Low flying monitors would record his every shivering moment as he struggled to stay alive—even when life ceased to have meaning. At the northern peak, the far distant sun didn't set for months, but no one ever lived long enough to find shelter. He had seen clips in instructional videos—the result of a traitor's actions.

Zuri glanced up and met Teal's shocked eyes.

Then a familiar voice rang out with furious authority. His heart thumped at the sight of Ark charging forward.

"He is no traitor, and I can prove it! Though stripped of honor and armor, this Ingot still has friends."

Zuri grinned.

CHAPTER THIRTY-SIX

—VILLAGE OF HAVILAH—

THE WAY OF MEN

Kenan wondered if his wife had gone mad. "You don't know my brother! If you did, you wouldn't be so complacent now."

Sari slapped a wet rag upon the windowsill and peered into the wide expanse, her chest heaving. "I was there when Neb attacked, and I washed the bodies for burial. I can still hear the wailing of women who lost husbands, brothers, and sons." She flung herself around and faced her husband. "I lost my father and sister, if you've forgotten." She hesitated as if searching for the right words. "But Neb is older now and has had the influence of Leah all these years. He has sons, and that will make a man reconsider waging war. Perhaps Leah's sons will—"

Like a bull ready to charge, Kenan hunched his shoulders. "You think his sons will be like Leah? Not possible! They must be like Neb, or he'd have cast them out. He would've killed them at birth if he thought for a moment that they wouldn't be true to his command." A hot flush burned Kenan's cheeks. "We must kill Neb, all his men, and every male child that sprang from his clan. Only then will we be safe."

Sari's eyes welled with tears. "Is there no other way? You sound so much like—"

Kenan's voice rose as he marched to the doorway. "Neb *wants* to kill. I kill because I have to!"

Dropping her voice, Sari stopped him. "If we had sons…would you take them into battle? To kill your brother, their uncle?"

His back to his wife, Kenan stood on the threshold. "They'd do what they must."

A tear slid down Sari's face. "Then—oh, God—I'm glad I have no sons."

In fury, Kenan swept out of his house and pounded into the blinding sunlight.

~~~

Tamar watched her son prepare for battle. She nodded. "Yes, you may take the whole bag of nuts. Of course, there will be fresh provisions in time." Her heart alternately swelled with pride and then clenched with terror.

Enosh slipped into the room. After glancing at his son, he focused on his wife. "Ready?"

She nodded.

He motioned outside, and they stepped into the blazing day, though mountainous clouds loomed on the horizon.

Tamar followed Enosh to a stream on the edge of the village.

Leaning against a tree with its roots sunk in the water, Enosh watched her.

Tamar stepped into the cool bubbling flow and soaked her worn feet. She did not often get a moment's rest during the day.

Enosh peered at the gathering storm clouds.

"My days are so busy; I no longer see the trees. Only the outline, the great shapes, but never the details." Tamar shrugged, sadness weighed her down, and tears formed in her eyes.

Enosh held out his arms and beckoned his wife closer.

She stepped over and snuggled into his embrace.

With a sigh, he tucked her head under his chin. "I wish I were as clever as you."
~~~

Tamar laughed into his chest. "Oh, I'm not clever. I wish I were. Perhaps then, my heart would not be so divided."

Enosh nuzzled the top of her head. "Perhaps it's not your heart that's divided but rather our world." He straightened. "We go into battle to reconcile an old injustice. Yet, nothing will fix the past. Neb's death won't bring back my father or his brother. Will killing Leah's sons return her innocence?"

Tamar shrugged. "Neb's death will free us from his threat forever. We fight to keep our families safe from slavery and death."

Her husband's body tensed, his muscles clenching into hard knots. "I don't want to act like Neb to save us from Neb." He exhaled a long breath. "Kenan plans to kill his whole family."

Horror swept over Tamar. "Not Leah, surely!"

"He'll kill her sons, which to a mother means much the same. He says that they are merely Neb repeated twice. Bloodlust."

Tamar squeezed her eyes shut against memories of death and gore. "Seth and Jubal thirst for battle as well. I've heard them speaking with Kryce about it."

"Doesn't this trouble you?"

A picture of Uzal's face filled Tamar's mind. "There are hunters like Neb, and there are defenders like Kryce and Seth. Men must fight. It is how they live out their existence."

Enosh exhaled, his shoulders drooping. "I have no wish to fight. I hate Neb, but still, I don't look forward to the day of battle." He pulled away. "What's wrong with me?"

Tamar caressed his clenched jaw. "You'd rather build in peace than destroy an enemy."

"Am I not a man?"

"You are a man among men but not *of* men."

Movement in the corner of her eye caught Tamar's

attention.

Two slim men sprinted toward them. Gulping breaths, exhausted, and stumbling, one lifted his hands in a gesture of defenselessness.

She touched Kryce's shoulder to draw his attention.

Enosh glanced over, still preoccupied.

Fear and excitement rippled over Tamar. The younger one resembled Leah! She started running, her arms outstretched.

Enosh followed more sedately.

When the four met, the two strangers halted, and the younger man fell upon his knees.

Tamar searched his face.

Enosh crossed his arms over his chest. "My name is Enosh of the People of Havilah. Who are you, and why have you come?"

The young man rose and bowed formally. "I am Madai, son of Neb the Great, and I've come to save you."

CHAPTER THIRTY-SEVEN

—VILLAGE OF HAVILAH—

SON OF MY ENEMY

Enosh brought Adam forward, introducing him as a man who wanted to help their people, but as soon as Kenan learned of Madai's identity, he summoned Kryce, Seth, and Jubal.

The men gathered quickly, for on the eve of battle, everyone was ready for anything—anything other than the sudden appearance of the son of their enemy.

Enosh stood at a distance as the four men studied Madai through cold, narrowed eyes.

Adam had been told to stand back, for he was nothing more than a trader who had become mixed up in the affairs of warriors. Their interest focused on the son of Neb alone.

"We have Neb in our hands now!" Kenan exulted. "Send a runner, Kryce, and tell Neb that we've captured his son."

Kryce's eyes darted aside, his skepticism obvious. "I doubt that Neb—"

Madai swept his hand through the air. "My father would not walk across the village to save my life if it meant a blow to his pride." He stood tall and defiant. "He hates me now as much as he ever hated you. I have refused him, and as you must realize, Neb cannot tolerate dissension. He will kill me himself if given the opportunity."

"So why have you come? Why aid his enemy?" Seth's voice remained calm and low.

Madai searched the faces as if looking for someone familiar. "I am my mother's son."

Jubal shook his head, gazing at his friends, turning his back on Madai. "He has his father's blood flowing through his veins, whether he accepts it or not. We can never trust him."

Madai clenched his hands, his face flushed, and his tone rising. "Trust me or not, you won't defeat Neb on your own. His clan has grown in recent years. They like the taste of victory, and men from all over flock to him for the spoils of war. His men trust him implicitly...though some he trusts which he should not." Madai stared at Kryce, their eyes locking. "I want to end his threat so that I can live in peace. My mother is still in his care, and I want her freed at any cost."

Sarcasm rippled over Jubal's face. "And how do you propose to assist us? You are none too large, and I don't see a weapon in your hand."

Madai glanced at Adam. "I offer my hands and heart willingly, but I have brought someone who can do more. He comes bearing gifts, though at the moment, you can't see them."

Jubal spat. "Stop speaking in riddles and tell us what you have to offer. If anything."

Adam stepped forward, calm, and resolute. "I have the skill and knowledge to make new weapons that will give you a great advantage." He surveyed the gathering, and his proud expression dissolved into a pouting scowl. "But at the moment, I'm not sure I want to reveal my secrets to you."

Madai turned on his friend wide-eyed. "But that's why we came! You said this was the answer to all my problems. We'd be free and could save my mother—"

Adam gripped his friend's shoulder like a sorrowful father breaking bad news. "I believed that the enemies of Neb would be enemies of his hate, but instead, I see only anger hidden under the guise of justice. What would I save you or your mother from? They are conquerors all."

Seth's face contorted, fury glowing in his eyes. "How dare you compare us to Neb! We are nothing like him. My clan was set upon, and my men enslaved for years of suffering untold. Ask Jubal! His brother has only lately returned. The Men of Havilah battle not for conquest but for peace, protecting those who needed protection. And Enosh and Kenan have suffered at Neb's unworthy hands. Neb killed their father in cold blood. Yet you dare suggest we are like him?"

Adam focused his gaze on Seth. "Once I let this knowledge out, there will be no calling it back."

Kenan snorted. "You think too well of yourself!" He brushed Adam as he strutted past. "You couldn't teach a child to fight."

Adam stiffened, his head high.

Running his fingers through his hair, practically pulling it out by the roots, Madai fought to keep from screaming, his voice high and tight. "I brought you a mighty gift, but in your arrogance and stubborn anger, you see nothing but the son of your enemy." He glared at Kenan. "Who are you but the brother of your enemy?"

He beckoned Adam. "We're leaving. My mother couldn't save Neb. She can't save these people either. At least I can still save myself."

Kryce stepped in Madai's path. "We'll decide your fate at the proper time. Our men are prepared for battle, and I will not disappoint them. Neb will meet justice with or without your help." He gestured to warriors standing near.

Two men stepped forward and led Adam and Madai to a storage shed, shoving them inside. Then they stood just outside the doorway.

Kryce gathered Seth, Kenan, and Jubal closer. "Let's get an early rest. I want to start out before the light of day tomorrow."

Enosh continued to stand off to the side, unnoticed and clearly unwanted.

Clouds swept overhead with a chill wind.

Jubal gestured toward the hut. "What about them?"

Kryce grimaced. "They might be spies."

Seth cleared his throat, shooting a brief glance at Enosh. "I don't see treachery in their eyes. They truly believe they can help us defeat Neb."

Kenan shrugged. "We have our appointed task to attend to first. We don't need them."

In agreement, Kryce, Seth, and Jubal strode away with not one backward look.

Enosh watched his brother and friends walk away. His head swirled in confusion, and his heart ached.

With an oath, Seth stopped and smacked his hands together. Separating from the others, he turned and headed to the opposite side of the village.

On impulse, Enosh hurried after him. "Seth, stay a moment, I have a question."

With an irritated scowl, Seth stopped. "I'm in a hurry. What?"

"Who is this Adam? The name sounds familiar somehow."

A flash of lightning and then thunder rolled overhead. Large pelting raindrops began to fall upon their heads.

Seth lifted his hand above his head as if to protect it from the rising storm. "There is a story about an Adam of old, the firstborn who ate fruit from the tree of knowledge of good and evil...an ancient story." He snorted. "But this is hardly the time to give a history lesson."

Ignoring the downpour, Enosh crossed his arms and thrust out his chest, almost in challenge. "So? What happened to him?"

Clearly impatient, Seth turned and started to jog away. "He brought death into our world."

Enosh watched his friend scurry into a nearby hut. A bitter chuckle rose as the irony struck him.

CHAPTER THIRTY-EIGHT

—VILLAGE OF HAVILAH—

DARING TO HOPE

Enosh sat alone in the dark, listening as the storm passed overhead. The room was quiet. A damp cloth hung on the windowsill, a stack of pots leaned against the wall. His ax hung by its strap near the doorway.

Tamar had finally fallen asleep, and Put breathed deeply in expectation of the morrow's adventure.

Childhood memories rose in Enosh's mind. His mother, father, and his family as they had once been. If only Neb had chosen a different path and not forced his father to abdicate as leader before the rightful time. If only they had not tried to find his uncle and settle with the Clan of Seth. If only he had never met the People of Havilah. Yet, he could not truly wish to change that. Though Uzal had been killed and Leah taken away, still *his* fortune had changed for the better.

The People of Havilah were more like family than his own clan had ever been. He loved his wife more than his own life, and Put was a son any man might wish for. The antics of little Gomer lightened his heart in ways no one else ever could. He sighed.

Neb was coming, and if the reports were true, the People of Havilah might cease to exist very soon. A lump rose in his throat. He should be more like Kenan, thirsting for the blood of his enemy—no matter who that enemy might be. Or he should be like Kryce, who knew the art of warfare. Or at very least, like Seth, who took command and saw to the protection of his people.

But darkness held him, alone and miserable.

He rose and walked to the doorway, where a cool breeze caressed his face.

The storm had passed, leaving the foliage dripping slow drops upon the wet earth. What was he afraid of? Death? No, he had faced pain often enough to know that the nameless doom was not his master. He knew Tamar and Put were capable and would see to every need.

But Neb coming...killing and conquering...the People of Havilah destroyed. His wife being taken. His sons sold into slavery like dogs with ropes around their necks. He could feel the burning lash, the spears whizzing past his head, his turning and finding Neb at his heels. He and Neb—alone. He would grab Neb about the neck, squeeze with all his might—with more strength than he ever knew he had—and he would rejoice in ending the life of his tormentor.

He would *become* Neb…relishing hate.

Enosh fell to his knees, sobbing.

Unexpectedly, like a swim on a hot day, quiet comfort settled over him. He could stop Neb without *wanting* to destroy Neb.

Released, Enosh wiped away the last vestige of tears and stepped inside his dwelling. He woke his son.

Put slipped from the comfort of his bed.

Enosh grabbed his provisions bag and draped it over his shoulder as the two left the dwelling. Speaking in a low whisper, he led his son in the direction of the storage shed. "I know how much you want to experience your first battle, but I have another task for you."

Put followed in silence.

When they arrived at the hut, Enosh faced the guards. "I must speak to the son of Neb."

The guard scowled. "Does Kryce approve?"

"He will."

The guard looked dubious but nodded and stepped aside.

Madai and Adam slept on either side of the door.

Enosh shook Madai's shoulder.

Madai and Adam jerked upright. Madai rubbed his face. "Has the battle come already?"

Crouching, Enosh kept his voice low. "Soon enough. Tell me, what is the secret Adam carries that will help us defeat Neb?"

Madai peered into the darkness. "Why do you ask?"

"You were speaking to men on the eve of battle who have the bloodlust upon them. They are not interested in a change of plans. They are only interested in slaying their enemy."

Adam shook his head. "And what are you interested in?"

Enosh exhaled, almost choking with the force of his thumping heart. I do not want to become Neb to defeat him."

Adam and Madai glanced at one another.

Adam rose to his feet. "In that case, I have a surprise for you." He stepped over to a dark corner and pulled into the moonlight a long, pliable stick and a bit of long twine.

Madai reached behind his pallet and pulled out several long sticks with slit shafts on one end and blunt ends on the other.

Adam grinned.

"We asked for these to amuse ourselves, and your men, seeing no harm in them, gave us what we asked for. We do not have the final weapon, of course, but if we can go outside, I will show you how this works. I think you will see its usefulness."

Puzzled, Enosh shoved disappointment aside and followed the two men outside.

The guards stared, puzzled frowns on their faces.

They walked into the still night air.

Put and Enosh followed and then waited.

With great care, Adam fit the string to the bowed wood, tied it securely, and then pulled tight, bowing the thin wood even more. He placed the shaft end against the string and pulled back as far as it would go. He eyed the point. "Imagine that I've secured a sharp point to the end."

He let the arrow fly. It sailed high into the black sky and then fell to the ground.

Adam straightened. "These are weak examples. But imagine if I made this bow from strong wood and tied a wiry sinew from end to end and attached a fine, sharp flint tip to the shaft. Then I aimed it at a beast or a man."

Silence hung in the air as the images were securely placed into each man's mind.

The guards glanced at each other, comprehension dawning.

"I've practiced with various materials, and at times, an arrow tip bit deep into the trunk of a tree. With practice, I could take a bird from the sky." He looked at each man in turn. "I no longer have to stand near enough to touch my enemy. I can stand back at a safe distance and let my weapon fly into his heart."

Enosh's eyes widened. "With this, we will outnumber Neb—no matter how many warriors he brings into battle. Each arrow is like a warrior flying from heaven to earth."

Put looked at his father. "What do you want me to do, Father? Learn this new skill?"

"Yes, and more. You have been to the Village of Seth many times. Take Madai and Adam. Show the villagers what you've learned and tell them to make such weapons and come to our aid." Enosh clapped his son on the shoulder. "Do this, and you will be worth all the warriors standing upon the battlefield."

Put glanced at Madai and Adam. "Are they still prisoners or . . ."

Enosh grinned. "They are giving us the gift of a

lifetime. I would call them friends." He bowed. "You've saved us from a fate worse than death."

Adam nodded. "It was given to me freely. I pass it along freely."

As they moved off, Madai stopped. "If you meet my father, do what you must…but if you find my mother—"

"I know." Enosh returned to his dwelling and lay down next to his wife. He wanted to sleep, but his dreams would take him to places that he did not want to go. He lay in quiet repose, remembering and daring to hope.

CHAPTER THIRTY-NINE

—NEB'S CAMP—

GRAVES OF THE INNOCENT

Neb waited for Torgama and slapped his thigh in frustration. When he learned that Madai had fled with Adam, it hit him like a blow to the chest. Stunned, he refused to think about it. He ignored Serug's request to send men to kill the deserters, and he would not meet Leah's eyes when she asked what he planned to do. He did not even listen to Kittam's report but merely asked Torgama to stand guard while he slept.

As the clouds gathered, Neb retired. He fell asleep to the drumbeat of pounding rain. In the middle of the night after the rain stopped and the air had cooled in a soft breeze, he stepped outside. Torgama's shadow loomed on the right side of the entrance.

Neb inhaled a breath of fresh air. "Where's my wife?"

Still as a statue, Torgama's deep voice rumbled like distant thunder. "By the fire, peering into the flames."

Neb started for the fire where Leah sat slump-shouldered. *Has she fallen asleep?* He stopped by her side and cleared his throat.

Leah didn't move a muscle.

"You should sleep. Our warriors might need a healer's skill tomorrow. Since you are here—"

She blinked. "I will do nothing."

Neb peered at his wife. He wanted to hate her. He had good reason to hate her. If she had been different, then Madai would have been different. She didn't admire Neb; she admired only Madai. She didn't trust Neb; she trusted only Madai. Nor did she love Neb. Madai alone held her heart.

Her words, heavy and slow, made no attempt to convince; they only conveyed a statement of truth. "I wish only for the life of my son, and this you cannot give me."

Prowling like a cat, Neb circled and stopped between his wife and the flames. "I might save Madai. It is within my power."

Leah's gaze meandered over her husband. She shook her head. "He betrayed you." She stared ahead as if she could see through him to the flames. Her voice dropped into a bottomless pit. "You can't allow his challenge to stand. The clan would follow him."

"There is no challenge, only treachery. My wife conspired with my son to abandon me on the eve of battle. I would have given—"

Leah's temper flared, her eyes blazing in the reflected light. "You would have given what? A hunger to rule at all cost? The terrors of war so he can conquer?" A cry choked her words.

Neb stepped away and faced the flames. "You could've chosen another fate; death was an option if life with me displeased you. I make no apologies. I unite men—bring them together in strength and wealth."

"You fill men with hate."

Neb snorted. "Men have hated since the dawn of creation."

"Madai does not hate. He could rule with kindness—"

"I lived under the rule of a kind man, and it was like drowning in a swamp! No progress, strength, or greatness."

Leah stood. "There is another path, though you cannot see it. A man can be strong and yet remain kind." Leah brushed past her husband. "You have such a son, but he will have to face one terrible truth before he can rule."

Neb grabbed his wife's arm. "He will not rule in my stead—not without killing me first."

Leah met his furious gaze. "I know."

~~~

Kryce led his men across the grasslands with their weapons swinging at their hips.

Seth strode on his right, and Kenan marched on his left.

Enosh followed behind with Jubal next to him.

The advancing warriors, masked by the darkness, moved stealthily. Battles were rarely attempted after a hard rain, for the ground was slick on hills and near creeks, but Kryce insisted that nothing would stop their advance. When Enosh told him of the new weapon he had seen and how he had freed Madai and Adam, he had merely shrugged in impatience. He did not believe that the two young men would find Accad, even with Put's direction, and return with anything useful. There would be no miracle.

Neb must be killed with whatever weapons they had at hand. Nothing short of that end would satisfy him or his men. They hurried their pace as dawn lightened the horizon.

~~~

Neb rose to the dawning of a new day, stepped outside his tent, and stood transfixed. The late-night mist had cleared and there, in front of him, behind him, circling his camp as far as the eye could see, stood the Men of Havilah.

His posted guards lay sprawled on the ground, dead.

Impossible!

Yet there they stood, grim-faced victors ready to take

captives.

Neb called out, “Awake! See what the day has brought!”

Startled, his men woke from slumber, blinking, disheveled, and confused. They rose and gathered mumbling and scowling.

One of the enemies stepped forward. His large body, silhouetted against the rising sun, seemed to glow with heavenly light. Not a good omen for Neb’s men. They would think a god had come against them.

Heat rose in Neb’s face. He stared at the encircling enemy.

There stood Kryce, the son of Uzal, whom Neb had once captured and freed in a moment of clemency. Not gods! These were only men, and among them, somewhere, were his little brothers whom he had sought through the long years, as well as the boy-leader named Seth, who always looked like he might cry. Neb sneered in silent relief.

Enosh stood before the others, tall, grim, and determined.

His sneer contorted. He would enjoy killing this brother more than the other, for it was this face that haunted him. Today he would end that private torment.

Neb glanced around. *Where’s Madai?*

Silence covered the land. The sun enlightened the day, even as bloodlust darkened his mind.

Neb turned his back on the enemy and faced his men.

His assembled warriors squared their shoulders in supreme confidence. As he opened his mouth to shout his accustomed war call, someone called his name. He swung around, furious. “What do carrion have to say to me?”

Kryce stepped forward. “Send Leah to us, and we will spare your lives.”

Neb spat. “Leah is mine. We will spare no one. The

birds will feast on your flesh today!"

His warriors roared approval and began chanting. "Neb! Neb! Neb!"

The sun rose higher. Sweat beaded on every forehead.

Kryce no longer stood in the glow of a new day.

Neb grinned. Bloodlust swelled with the vaporous heat.

He raised his hands and bellowed. "Kill them!"

Kryce raised a fiery spear, arched back, and then threw with all his might.

Warriors lunged forward, slashing. Some fell. Others rushed into the chaos of hand-to-hand battle.

Blind rage thrust Kryce into the midst of the fighting.

An injured warrior grabbed his arm, pulling him down. Kryce tried to shake free, but the dying man would not let go. Kryce stumbled and tried to right himself, but he slipped. A spear flew harmlessly over his head.

Neb fixed his gaze on his enemy. Yes, Kryce, son of Uzal, had slipped in a pool of blood. Too easy. Neb fought his way forward, yelling orders, and slaying those foolish enough to have their backs to him.

After a quick thrust between a warrior's shoulder blades, he realized with chagrin that he had killed one of his own men. He shook his head at the blunder. Gasping, he surveyed the scene.

Torgama fought hand-to-hand with Enosh.

Momentary confusion stopped Neb in his tracks. Who should he kill first? His brother who betrayed him or Torgama who had injured him?

With careful aim, he threw his spear.

Attempting to assist Torgama, Kittam rushed forward and stepped in the spear's path.

Torgama's eyes widened at Kittam's fall. His eyes followed the direction of the spear.

Neb stood still bent in the posture of the thrower.

Torgama bellowed like a mad bull.

Hit by a heavy blow from behind, Enosh fell, sprawling on the ground.

Torgama met Neb's fixed gaze. His right arm rose, swirling a slingshot over his head while gripping a knife in his left hand. He crept forward.

Neb crouched, preparing for Torgama's assault, but suddenly a man's weight dropped on Neb's back, a voice from the long past hissed in his ear.

"Murderer!"

Neb glanced aside.

A ray of sunlight glinted off Kenan's knife.

Torgama released his slingshot, knocking Kenan off Neb's back.

Enosh scrambled to his feet and faced Riphath, who had darted forward and sliced his arm. Enosh stumbled, though his eyes stayed fixed on Neb.

Blood dripping from his head, Kenan lay motionless.

Neb rushed forward, gripping his knife with both hands.

Enosh jumped over two bodies and blocked Neb. "Your rule is over!"

Exultant laughter tore through Neb. "You see the future now? Tell me—as you die—who will rule in my stead?"

Hate filling him, Enosh suddenly shifted his gaze. Shock replaced rage.

Uneasiness forced Neb to glance over his shoulder. Laughter died on his lips.

A thick, black, swift-moving cloud undulated across the land.

Neb slashed his brother, cutting his hand, forcing Enosh backward.

Warriors across the battlefield shouted. Then suddenly, they stopped and stared. Panic ensued as they rushed in all directions, scrambling to get out of the way.

The Men of Havilah stood their ground, watching as if a vision of Heaven descended.

The strange cloud landed, a fabric made entirely of locusts, clawing, chomping, spitting in numbers uncountable.

No man could stand as the scaly creatures pelted their bodies, crawling and jumping. Even as men slapped and hopped, masses fell from the sky.

Neb stood with his hands limp, stupefied. His plans awry, he rallied his men, waving and running. They followed him south, away from the cloud.

After hours of running, Neb fell to the ground, a nauseating headache swarmed over him, blinding him, and draining away what endurance the locusts had left.

~~~

Enosh thrust his bleeding hand under his arm as he rushed to his brother.

Kenan called out, “I’m all right. Help Kryce!” The two gathered their strength, Enosh using only one arm, and they pulled Kryce clear of the rampaging men.

Jubal appeared from the murky haze and thrust Kryce over his shoulder.

Together, they outran the flying horror.

~~~

Serug found his mother first, for he had stayed on the outskirts of the battle the whole time. Neb had positioned him well within the thick of the battle, but when the first screams and yells thundered in his ears, he ran back and watched. When the cloud came, he grew terrified beyond words and ran to his mother, announcing their doom.

She merely asked, "Where is Madai?"

Peering into her blank face, he knew he would find no safety with her.

—VILLAGE OF HAVILAH—

Seth watched as Kryce lay in a dreamless sleep, sweating out a fever that would not abate. He could not lead his men to victory.

Where had the evil cloud come from?

Seth reached back in his mind to various stories, and he remembered hearing of strange events in nature that changed the lives of men. Always he had been told that the God above who renewed the race of men through the honor of Noah had done all these things to assist the just and afflict the wicked. Yet this scourge had come upon them all. It had fallen upon the just and the unjust alike.

Neb was the wicked one. He followed the ways of false gods, called upon powers of darkness, violated the innocent, killed the valiant, and enslaved the defenseless. The Men of Havilah had followed the precepts of goodness and generosity. The People of Seth were followers of the true God. So why had the cloud fallen on them? Had Enosh and Kenan carried the unclean spirits into their midst? Was God cleansing them all for the sins of the few?

Seth propped his exhausted head upon his hands as he sat next to his friend, pondering events, his heart confused and divided.

Leah's body had been discovered, stabbed in the heart on a routine boundary check. Kenan had carried her into the village, and the People of Havilah mourned, for they had the bitter misfortune of losing her twice. Dodan, the eldest son of Uzal, buried her, while Tamar sobbed, and

Sari mourned in wretched grief.

Kenan slipped into the room and crouched by Seth. "I would've killed him. I almost did, but then fate intervened. Why was I denied my glory?"

Seth rubbed his temple. "Perhaps this happened because we were not ready for victory. Maybe we don't want the victory that God has in mind."

"To kill one's enemy in battle is victory."

"Perhaps we are becoming the enemy."

Kenan raised himself up, furious. "You sound like Enosh! He says that God spared Neb to purge us of some malady. We fight to end terror. We need no purging. It's Neb and his men who need to be purged!"

Kryce stirred.

Seth fixed his gaze on Kenan. "When he awakens, do not speak of the battle. Allow him time to heal. Above all, do not tell him of his sister."

A few days later, Jubal called a meeting in his home.

Kryce was carried in on a stretcher.

Seth sat stoically aside, for he was not sure what to advise.

Kenan perched on a feed sack next to Enosh, though they had become divided in spirit.

His hand heavily bandaged, Enosh stood in the corner, his gaze roaming from man to man.

A distant shout turned their attention, and they filed outside. Kenan assisted Enosh so he could sit against the outside wall.

Accad led a small host of men into the village. Men, women, and children stopped what they were doing and stared, watching their approach in silence. Four men gathered near, their weapons ready.

Kryce motioned for Seth to do the honors.

Seth waited until Accad came within reach, and the two embraced. "Is there news from home?"

Accad tilted his head, a puzzled expression spreading

over his face. "Haven't you been waiting for us?"

"Waiting? The battle was fought days ago and not to our glory. We're now considering our next move."

Accad countered Enosh's gravity with a bold smile. "We bring you victory!" He motioned Adam forward from the assembly.

Adam carried a couple of pieces of wood.

Before a word was said, Accad pulled piece of fruit from his bag and flung it into the air.

Adam swung his bow up, let an arrow fly with a sharp twang, and the fruit fell to the earth pierced through the middle.

The assembly stared in dumbfounded silence.

A chuckle bubbled from deep inside Seth. "This is the answer to all the questions. Here is the reason for our delay. We were not defeated. We were held back until victory could be ours! Do you not see? God is with us!"

Relieved smiles spread through the village.

Kryce forced himself to sit up and reached out for the new weapon. "I'll heal quickly now, for I must practice. I'll be as good as our friend here before our next battle."

A large gathering crowded around, asking questions and patting Adam on the back.

With ready answers, Adam smiled and shared the story of his first adventures with the bow and arrow.

Madai stayed in the background, his gaze wandering across the village.

Enosh stepped over to him. "Do you look for anyone in particular?"

Madai exhaled. "I had hoped to visit my brother's grave."

"We would not have honored him with a grave." He rubbed his face. "But we did honor your mother."

Seth watched the two men walk to the burial mounds in a lonely glen with one ancient tree whose roots fed from a gentle stream.

~~~

Enosh peered at his brother's son, his voice low and respectful of those who made the land sacred. "What will you do now?"

Madai stared at the mound covering his mother. "I will fight, though the only person I ever really cared to fight for is gone."

"Surely, your life still has meaning."

Tears glimmered in Madai's eyes. "Didn't you suffer when your mother died?"

Sick dread filled Enosh. "Has my mother died?"

"She's been gone some years now, but of course, you would not know of it."

"How did she die?

"Eva said Neb killed her, but the poisoned vial was empty on the ground. She could've died from some other cause."

"Had Neb been with her the day she died?"

"Neb was the last one to see her alive."

Enosh squeezed his eyes shut. "Is there no evil that man will not do?"

"He has not killed his brother yet—or his son."

Enosh opened his eyes and turned to Madai. "How do you live, knowing from whence you sprung?"

"And you?"

The two men stared upon the graves in silence.
~~~

Chapter Forty

-Planet Ingilium-

What Happiness Feels Like

Ark pounded up the incline to the central platform and faced the Ingot Judge. With an appraising glance, he surveyed the usual assembly. "Not being scientists at the level of Cresta magnificence, your ignorance must be tolerated with a modicum of understanding. But this—" He jerked his tentacles in a decidedly judgmental manner and swiveled his glare hard on the judge. "This speaks of complete idiocy!"

The Ingot judge raised his hand over the buzzer, but Ark's reflexes were faster. A quick swipe and the buzzer spun across floor, skidding to a halt before Zuri's boots.

Zuri swallowed but said nothing beyond an appreciative glint in his eye as he watched Ark.

Traipsing across the platform, his tentacles crossed just so, Ark personified a determined pedagogue. "It has come to Cresta attention that Ingots will turn into mindless zombies within two generations due to the unregulated use of techno armor and their unimaginative acceptance of synaptic connectors that repeat worn-out patterns. In other words—fools—you are devolving."

The judge raised his hand, his jaw bulging. "If you weren't a Cresta representative, I'd have you dismembered for—"

With a jerk, Zuri strained against his fetters. "You'd lose the insight and advice of one of the best minds in the universe."

Ark stared at Zuri, his mouth dropping open.

Zuri threw back his shoulders. “You allowed the Born-Agains their freedom under the council of Teal and the Luxonian High Council. Have the intelligence to listen to what this Cresta has to say. We have real enemies to face—but we won’t survive for long fighting our friends.”

His hands clenched, the Judge faced the assembly. “We will listen and deliberate a verdict in private at another time.” He nodded to Ark. “Say your piece only if it has a bearing on this traitor’s case.”

A prima donna before a packed audience could not have staged her presence more forcefully. His bulbous eyes glowing, tentacles at the ready, and Cresta boots firmly placed, Ark launched his case. “Not that Crestonians have any interest in seeing a potential competitor and universal threat to the inter-alien balance of power flourish beyond their natural levels. Still, it might rise to your awareness that mindless robots intent on mere survival without any interior development will eventually succumb to their lowest elements. In other words, as attached as you are to tools, you will, in time, become the tool of another and not even realize you’ve lost your identity.”

The silence in the hall permeated the air, stifling even hushed conversations. The Judge dropped his gaze from a high browed glare to a direct stare, instigating a battle of wills between the large Ingot and the rotund Crestonian.

No one appeared to breathe.

Sweating under the tension, Zuri wiped his brow and shuffled one foot forward. He unexpectedly kicked the buzzer. A short blast startled everyone.

Titters rippled through the crowd.

The judge broke away, faced the assembly, and ordered everyone out.

Once the room was cleared, he faced Zuri. “You are free to go.”

Zuri closed his eyes, his shoulders relaxing.

Ark laid a tentacle on Zuri’s shoulder, his gaze still on

the judge. "What's the price? Surely freedom has a cost."

The judge rubbed his shoulder and then unbuckled a conduit that lead from his ear to his chest. He pulled it free and exhaled. "How you knew is beyond me. But your insight stands on the edge of our abyss. Our leadership discovered a traitorous link to the Mystery Race—where minds meet as one and few discern the danger."

Zuri swallowed. "We've been infiltrated?"

"It was not the desire of true Ingots to attack Helm. That idea came from another source and held sway when stronger minds should have prevailed." He focused on Ark. "You are right—without interior development, we will succumb to slavery, all the while calling it freedom and a defense from that which already holds us in bondage."

Tears filled Zuri's eyes. "I am once again proud of my Ingoti Heritage. Thank you."

The judge nodded in solemn acceptance and waved them toward the open door.

Out under the bright sun, Zuri paced at Ark's side, glancing at his friend. "How did you know?"

Ark smirked. "I didn't. But I figured they wouldn't be trying so hard to destroy you if there wasn't a real threat. I just knew—you weren't it."

–Helm–

Teal would've liked to dress to impress when meeting with Kelesta's Aunt Swen, but knowing the Bhuaci preference for pixie and elfin figures, he could not bring himself to change from his accustomed masculine form into something so dainty. He smoothed down his brown tunic and ran his fingers through his long unruly hair. No one would look at his stained strapped sandals. Surely.

The wooded glen with smooth, curved benches in shaded niches highlighted the best in Bhuaci land development. They never wholly transformed a place but simply adapted the environment to meet personal desires. In this case, a place to sit, shade from the heat of the day, grass and flowers mowed not by a machine but by a herd of small herbivores which nibbled the sweet morsels in meandering complacency, returning to low thatched huts just outside the city each evening.

A variety of animals wandered through the park, neither alarming nor being alarmed by the presence of Bhuacs or other life forms. Few animals were ever hunted, though traditional roundups occurred twice a year to maintain their food supply. Being ever gentle, the animals suffered less than the processors, who bustled and sweated with effort to keep the animal life unalarmed, but their families and neighbors fed.

Swen didn't walk so much as float into the glen, her long trailing skirt and silky blouse billowing in a gentle breeze. She met Teal's gaze as she neared the center of the park.

Teal bowed. "Swen. I'm glad—"

With unexpected gravity, Swen tapped her finger to her lips in a quick motion. "I'm being followed. Act surprised. Our insect queen thinks she has me cornered."

Teal glanced around. Yep. Sure enough. Tcesni lurked on the perimeter. He frowned. "I'll play no games with her." He called, "Tcesni, come and meet one of the finest healers in the universe." He winked at Swen. "You might teach her to value unique life forms."

"If she was willing to learn, she'd know already."

Tcesni, her head high and her eyes narrowed, practically whiplashed her way over the short grass and stopped with the most unconvincing smile Teal had ever seen.

"So glad to have run into you both. I've heard such wonders of Helm and the Bhuaci people, despite your recent tragic losses, that I simply had to see this place for myself. Uanyi are not insensible to the trials of persecution. We, as much as any race in the universe, wish for peace and justice."

Teal wondered if his head might implode.

Swen bowed in recognition of formal curtsies.

And lies. Teal coughed into his hand. "Did you have a nice look around then?"

A sharp glance from both Tcesni and Swen thrust Teal back into his diplomatic role.

Tcesni pointed to a steep mountain in the distance with a dainty castle perched at the top. "I was impressed with Song's picturesque abode. Surprising that it survived the attack. Almost beyond belief that it was spared by chance. One wonders if perhaps your regent has friends in Ingoti chambers."

Swen's intake of breath blended with the hum of a small bird that flew into their midst. The sparrow circled, twittering pointedly in Swen's direction.

Utterly fascinated, Teal watched the conversation. Though Swen said nothing with words, she used her body language, motioning with her fingers and tapping her foot.

Tcesni, annoyed by the interruption, tried to brush the bird away.

With an impertinent flutter, the bird flew off, heading directly toward the distant castle.

Teal folded his hands and waited.

Flustered, Swen redirected her attention to Tcesni. "I'm sorry, but your observation is far off the mark. Though it is true that the Regent of Song's home was not destroyed, many members of her family were killed. She mourns in the lower levels of their burial chambers, where she will stay for a full moon cycle. After that, her advisors and”—Swen glanced aside at Teal—“Friends will assist in planetary reconstruction and Bhuaci justice. We are aware that the Ingots did not work alone, and that other beings have plans to take advantage of our present weakness.” She tilted her head. “Simple, yes. But we are not blind. Nor are we without resources.”

Tcesni’s bony chin hardened into a firm line. “I hope you count the Uanyi among your friends.”

Swen pointed to the castle and started along the path toward the city. “So much depends.”

Teal kept pace at Swen’s right side but refused to ask the obvious question.

Tapping her prickly thigh and high stepping along on Swen’s left, Tcesni clipped her words. “Depends upon—what?”

“Where the bodies lead.”

~~~

Kelesta grabbed Teal’s arms, and though she had to tilt her head back to meet his lowered gaze, she felt his equal, in this matter at least. “I must go with you!”

Teal sighed and tried to pull away, but her grip held strong. “You’ve been seriously injured, your planet could use every able body to heal its wounds, and the Regent needs someone—”

Stomping her foot, Kelesta swiveled away and shouted. “Aunt Swen is the best advisor any regent could ask for, my body has healed, and I don’t know a thing about planet reconstruction!” She turned and faced Teal. “Zuri almost died because I ordered him home when he should have stayed on Earth. He has a valuable place at your side, and
~~~

what Bhuaci need more than anything is a stable universe. We won't get that if we abandon our friends."

Teal's gaze raked the gorgeous array of hues as the sun bled over the horizon. "What would you do on Earth?"

"I'll help Zuri." She pounded in front of Teal, demanding his attention. "He has been faithful to me and his own people. He's been a friend to humans and aliens alike. We all face threats and dangers, but the worst dangers pull us apart from the inside."

"Us? Meaning…"

"Me and Zuri…you and Sienna. Ark…and…" She wrinkled her nose. "Who does Ark care about?"

Teal chuckled. "Everyone. But don't tell him that!" He peered at the diminutive powerhouse. "I don't know what Sienna and I—"

"Oh! Stop lying, protecting yourself behind a façade of indifference and perfect strength. You care just as much as Ark and Zuri." Her heart pounded as if she stood facing a cliff and her toes gripped the slippery edge. "I don't know who betrayed you—mother, sister, friend, or lover, but you can't define your future by past failure. Old hurts either deform or inform us. If you hold back from ever trusting and loving again—then the traitor wins. And what good does that offer the world?"

Teal frowned. "I could be giving you the same lecture."

"You could. I'd deserve as much. But I'm on my feet, willing to fight once again. I'll find Zuri and discover the best in him—not huddle at home, fearing the worst."

Teal threw back his head and stared at the shadowed sky. "Was it the illness? Or has Swen brought about this change of heart?"

Kelesta laughed. "Hope, you idiot." She grabbed his arm and tugged. "Let's get going. Zuri and Ark are heading back to Earth soon, and if Tcesni gets there first, she might set Sienna up for mischief. I don't trust that insectoid. Even a queen shouldn't be so sure of herself."

"I told Ark to wait for me…and I'm sure that Zuri will be glad to see you. I'm just not sure what to say to Sienna or to Tcesni, for that matter."

Kelesta shrugged. "You're a Luxonian and a brilliant diplomat, so you'll make friends and enemies. Just know the difference between the two."

A buzz vibrated in Teal's ear. He tapped the tiny receiver.

Ark's disembodied voice echoed in his head. "Are you coming? Our Ingot friend is wearing new sandals, ready to leap into the next mission. I'm hoping to tackle the insect queen—maybe we can have some fun together, eh?"

Teal grinned. *So this is what happiness feels like.*

CHAPTER FORTY-ONE

—VILLAGE OF HAVILAH—

I BELIEVE SO

Neb gathered his men and decreed a night of worship to bind all powers to them. Animals large and small were slaughtered, and a great fire kindled. While feasting and drinking, the warriors called upon the forces of darkness and demanded the strength of the blood poured out for them.

Throughout the ceremony, Neb hid his illness and pretended that the loss of his wife did not bother him. Once she had learned of the mysterious cloud, she'd gone off alone, Serug had told Neb. He looked for her and questioned his men, but Torgama returned his questions with a bold stare. Too unwell to challenge anyone, Neb merely regarded him with grave suspicion. That night while he lay alone in his tent, he remembered Torgama's eyes and their proud glint, and he knew what had happened to his wife.

Neb allowed his men all manner of wildness that night and planned to strike while the moon was high, and the Men of Havilah slept. Illness would not hinder his plans, for revenge burned hot as flames in his heart.

~~~

Madai headed for the village center to speak with Enosh, skirting around men that attended to their evening duties.

Distant flames glowed against the evening sky.
~~~

Scouts reported a wild commotion in Neb's camp, tightening every nerve in his body. Madai squared his shoulders and declared his position. "You have not seen my father for many years, but if you knew him at all, you must realize that he serves a dark power. Though he claims to have bound all to himself, I am convinced that it is their will he serves, not his own. When facing a fearful challenge, he whips his men into frenzy. Madness rules." Madai glanced at distant sparking flames. "We must strike now before they come for us."

Enosh listened and said nothing but turned and marched to Seth's dwelling. He brought Madai forward to explain his concern.

After listening to Madai, Seth led them to Kryce's dwelling.

Kryce made a quick decision. "Gather the men and our new weapons. We will move tonight and wreak havoc on Neb's plans before his warriors recover from their feasting."

While the men prepared for battle, Madai stood alone with his thoughts.

Accad found him and turned his one good eye fixedly on the youth. "You do not have to go into this battle, for you were the one to bring us the weapons of victory. You have done enough."

Madai watched his uncles prepare. "They will fight. Shall I refuse to do as much?"

"They do not have the bond of father and son between them."

"Is the bond of brothers any less?"

Accad propped his bow against his side. "You suffer a burden, not of your own making. I understand your grief. When I was captured, I was forced to endure humiliations I thought would kill me. I was beaten for the pleasure of those who were no longer men. They had become beasts.

When I beheld my wife's suffering…it nearly crushed me for she was always a gentle person. But in her, I found unexpected strength. She maintained her innocence by remaining honest in the sight of God. Through her example, my spirit was calmed, and I found I could live as a man. I'll never be a slave again—of this, I am sure. But more importantly, I have accepted the most important truth of my life. God's plans are better than mine."

Madai looked across the vast darkness into the glimmer of a great fire. "Does he have a plan on how to save us from ourselves?"

Accad peered at the stars above and clasped the young man's shoulder. "I believe so."

CHAPTER FORTY-TWO

—BATTLEFIELD—

AS THINGS NOW STOOD

Serug arched his neck as he watched a burning stick fly high into the air, and then he brought his head down as that same flaming arrow landed amidst his men. He should have known! But it was too late now for second thoughts. The son of an idiot was not so stupid, after all. Serug shook his head. The enemy was near at hand, and Serug knew—better than anyone—the hopelessness of this battle.

His father's yellow pallor and weak spells as he fought to stay on his feet proved that he was no longer the man he had been.

Burning arrows set fire to the field. Smoke and flames everywhere. The men, even in their bewildered, intoxicated fury, became unnerved.

Serug approached Father, who watched the arrows as if they were falling stars. "Come, Father. The men will follow, and we will attack at another place and time that they do not expect."

Neb looked at his young son, his eyes expressionless. "Did I ever have the blessing of Uz? I never became a god... The spirits have abandoned me."

Serug closed his eyes. His doom was entwined too closely with his father's. He could not allow Neb to accept imminent death.

Shouts rang out as the Men of Havilah encircled them. Burning arrows landed all around, and Neb's men became further disorientated, like wolves tormented by wasps. Insults and curses flew along with the arrows, and Neb's men, in their stupor, returned every insult and curse, though they could not return the arrows.

Serug opened his eyes, rubbed his face, and surveyed the madness around him. In blind fury, Neb's men tried to engage the distant, deadly enemy but to no avail. Soon they fell flat on their faces, as if admitting defeat.

He called Riphath and Torgama, directing them and a chosen few to stay and fight. Then he ordered everyone else to flee from camp. He grabbed his father's arm and led him through a break into the trees. "Our men can hold them off while we gather our strength at a more opportune time and place. We will slaughter them all—but not right now."

Neb frowned as the warriors all around him stumbled in awkward attempts to organize themselves. "But they will face the enemy alone."

Serug nodded. "Yes, of course. That's your plan. We'll find a better vantage point and annihilate them—later."

Neb stood silent for a long moment and then slipped into the darkness, away from the fire.

Confused warriors called out, "Neb, where are you?"

Deaf to the calls, Serug pushed ahead.

Neb followed, stumbling frequently.

Torgama pushed past Neb and almost knocked him down.

Riphath reached out a helping hand.

Neb panted in sweaty exertion but refused the offer.

Screams echoed from the camp. "Neb? Neb!"

Riphath halted and listened, his head cocked, his eyes wide in anguish.

Serug pressed forward.

Torgama did not halt.

Neb lumbered ahead, but then he stopped and looked at Riphath.

They both turned and glanced back.

Riphath spat his words. "I've got nothing to lose. I'll go back and defend what I once had."

Neb tottered, his eyes unfocused, confused. “What…did you…have?”

“Loyalty.” Riphath jogged back to camp.

In no mood for reflection, Serug tugged his father’s arm, and they thrashed their way into the dark woods.

~~~

Serug counted the survivors and grinned. After three days, more warriors than he dared hope had found them and gathered their strength. Not everyone had been killed or captured, as his worst fears predicted. A grim image of what Kryce and his men would do with the wounded or captured filled his mind, but then he shoved the uncomfortable thought away. He needed to make plans.

Neb burned with fever, and they could not rest. They needed to move deep into the woodlands and bury themselves there for as long as it would take to be forgotten or given up for dead.

He approached his father, who lay under a large spread of trees as rays of light played with leafy shadows. “The men will carry you to a safer location since you are not yet fit to travel.”

Neb peered through bloodshot, unfocused eyes. He nodded, his hands falling to the side in helpless acceptance.

Serug smiled. Apparently, defeat was not always a tragedy, for suddenly he was no longer a younger son in the shadow of an elder brother. Neither would he have to endure the long years of waiting for Neb to die as an old man.

As things stood now, Serug would lead the clan, and no one would wonder why.
~~~

CHAPTER FORTY-THREE

—ISHTAR'S VILLAGE—

IN THOSE REMEMBRANCES

Ishtar, Amin, and Gizah sat in a circle around the communal fire in the evenings, while clansmen gathered to listen. Once it was known that Ishtar was telling the history of Neb the Great, many stopped to hear the tales, and those that had missed parts were filled in during the work of the day.

The dead came to life, and the village listeners saw in their minds events that had happened more than three generations ago. The forces that had formed Neb the Great reached through time and history and touched them.

Ishtar wondered anew that he had ever managed to break free of the invisible ties holding his family in bondage for so long.

Gizah often arrived late or left early to manage family affairs, but Amin always stayed and learned all he could. During the quiet of the nights as they snuggled together, he would share with Gizah what she had missed.

Weariness enveloped Ishtar. His bones ached with it.

Out of the quiet night, Gizah padded forward and placed a tray laden with food and drinks between Ishtar and Amin. Then she crouched at her husband's side. "When you didn't come to eat, I took matters into my own hands." She grinned as she waved at her offering. "What's happened?"

Amin smiled and tugged his wife into an embrace so she could lean against him. "Ishtar described how the Men of Havilah brought burning arrows against Neb's men and how Neb then abandoned his men to a hopeless defeat. I'll tell you more later, but" —he glanced aside and dropped his voice—"I'm afraid Father is very tired."

Hushed expectancy filled the air. The clan shuffled, eagerness to hear the tale warring with a respectful desire to let Ishtar get a well-earned rest.

Ishtar attempted to stifle a yawn. "I'm not sleepy but perhaps a little weary." He shrugged and peered into the black surroundings. "The spirits of the past seem to edge closer as we review their mortal lives."

Amin glanced around uneasily as did many others, but Gizah motioned for him to eat. "Perhaps it's time I told what I know from my father, for Aram liked to tell stories while we worked."

A spark of interest rekindled Ishtar's enthusiasm. "Do you know about Madai's rule? He and Serug never met again after Neb left the last battle. Enosh and Kenan fall out of my story, for they stayed with the people of Havilah. Though I did hear that during a severe drought, they moved further south and entered a new land, leaving only their law engraved upon a stone to tell the tale of who had occupied that land."

Amin spluttered, incredulous. "So that's all we know of Neb's brothers? We never heard from them again?"

Ishtar shrugged. "My grandfather never ventured south. He went north into the great forest, and when my father was born after Neb the Great died, Serug moved east for a time and then north into the low hill lands. It was my father who traveled to the Great River, and there, my adventure began."

Her hands fluttering like birds ready for flight, Gizah leaned forward. "In that case, let me tell you what I know of Madai. He was the Grandfather of Aram, and his story is no less interesting than Serug's."

Excited commotion stirred through the village as men, women, and children settled down for the next tale.

Gizah grinned. "Madai recovered the remnant of Neb's warriors and kept in contact with both Enosh and Kenan, though Enosh was his favorite, I was told."

Ishtar smiled in pleased relief, for he dearly wanted to learn the history that brought into a desperate world his beloved friend Aram.

CHAPTER FORTY-FOUR

—BATTLEFIELD—

I MUST FINISH THIS TASK

Madai stepped forward. He had stayed in the thick of the battle and acquitted himself valiantly; no one could deny his right to speak. If he had not left his clan and accomplished his mission, Neb's men would not be standing at their mercy.

Though covered in blood, he wasn't seriously injured. He was most certainly the son of Neb, for it showed in his features, yet he was not Neb. He had declared—and they believed it to be truth—that he was also the son of Leah, Havilah's daughter.

As he looked around at Neb's men penned in by angry warriors, he threw his hands up in a gesture of defiance, not unlike something Neb would have done. "They are mine! I am Neb's eldest, and these men belong to me by right. I have conquered by force of arms, and I will not see them slain."

Clearly astounded, Kryce glared at Madai. "What gives you the right to take our prisoners?"

"I claim the right to reclaim the inheritance of Hezeki, which was lost to us during Neb's rule." He pointed to the defeated warriors as they hung their heads in stoic silence, his eyes flashing in fury between Kryce and Jubal. "Do you condemn their families—women and children—to death, too? Surely, they will perish if they have no men to help them. Are you going to march to their village and dispatch them for justice's sake?"

Despairing groans rose from the prisoners.

Jubal lifted his hand. "We are not without mercy. We

will allow you to tend to the women and children. Those that wish to may join our clan."

Thubal, one of Hezeki's most loyal warriors, stepped forward. He had married into the clan, had several children, and was trusted by many. "We have forgotten Hul and others who wished to go with Hezeki but were unwilling to leave their families behind? They had wives and young children, aged parents, and crops to tend, and they could not do what my men and I were able to do. These men were led into their deeds by a force beyond reckoning. Neb demanded obedience and loyalty. Would you admire them for blind defiance?"

Kryce stepped back, and Jubal nodded, cold acceptance in his eyes.

Thubal and those who had followed Hezeki stepped forward. "With you to lead us, we'll return home."

Madai swallowed in relief for this second victory was no less great than the first.

~~~

Riphath stayed in the background. In his mind, he saw the years he had dedicated to Neb; yet Neb had abandoned him. He had tried to save a friend's life, but now he faced only a deep hole in which to bury the body. He thought of his wife and daughters, and relief washed over him. He had survived and could still see to their needs. Then he remembered the men lost in the last battle and the families left to perish for want of care. He wept.

~~~

Madai paced the length of the village. His plans were made, and he knew what he had to do, but he was not sure he was equal to the task. Neb had prepared him to lead proud warriors into battle, not a defeated clan into reunion with those who had left in defiance.

Adam jogged forward and caught him by the arm. "All set?"

Madai shrugged. "Where will you go from here?"

A twinkle glittered in Adam's eyes. "Since meeting you, my life has taken on a whole new perspective. I'm not ready to return home just yet."

"Won't your family be worried about you?"

"My father will look for me, but he will wait for many moons to fill and empty before he becomes anxious." Adam grinned. "Perhaps we should share meetings. I meet your clan…and you meet mine."

Hope sparked life into Madai's sagging spirits. "I'd like that."

"Then it is agreed. I will go to your home and help you settle in, and then you will come to my home and help me."

Madai had started to look away, but his eyes swiveled back to Adam's face. "Help you?"

Adam spoke over his shoulder as he sauntered away. "Oh, didn't I tell you? I have five sisters."

~~~

Madai stood ready to depart at the break of a fine, sunny day, when a man strode forward.

"I am Dodan, Kryce's elder brother. When Kryce and his men are off on a hunt or in battle, I usually remain at home to tend to the matters of the clan and guard the
~~~

village. I saw you when you came to us first. We met briefly, but I doubt you remember me."

Madai considered the diminutive figure, and though he had not remembered the name, he did remember the man. "Yes, I remember you." He glanced aside. He wanted to be off soon.

Dodan cleared his throat. "I have come to offer you my services. I spoke with Kryce, and he agreed that the more successful you are at home, the better things will go for all of us. I can act as a liaison between you and the people of Havilah. If ever Neb should try to come back or there is any serious trouble, then you will have the firm assurance of our clan's assistance."

The fear of disgrace and longing for pleasure warred inside Madai.

Dodan dropped his voice and leaned forward. "I am not a warrior, and I have not fought in the battles between our men. I don't think they will know who I am unless you tell them. Only Thubal and his men would know, and they are men of discretion."

Madai rubbed his chin, a flush of embarrassment and confusion heating his face. "Word might get out. Someone would know, and they'd tell the whole clan."

"And say what? That I'm not a warrior? That I remained at home to heal and protect the innocent?"

Madai shrugged. His bold leadership evaporated. "Do you have a family that will join you?"

Dodan peered into the distance. "No, I am a man set apart."

Madai wanted to laugh.

~~~

Madai's face flushed with rage when he saw his village;
~~~

he wanted to find his father and strangle him with his bare hands.

It had been a tedious march, and their arrival anything but joyful.

The men who were supposed to watch over the women and children had gone off to find Neb and bring him home. A drought in the southern region dried the creeks to muddy sludge, and few fish or animals could be found.

Women and children plagued with fever and hunger stumbled in misery through the village.

Thubal held Madai back, his hand firmly clasping his shoulder. "Remember why you came. It was not so you could chase after Neb." He glanced around. "These people need you here. Now."

Stuffing his fury deep, Madai agreed.

With the help of Adam, Thubal, Dodan, Eva, and the men left in the clan, Madai formed hunting parties, arranged for the collection of medicinal herbs, and assisted the women to gather what harvest they could.

Despite his efforts, the drought continued, and four children died. On a stupefying hot day, he wandered to the river's muddy edge. The stench of rot and sludge filled his nose. His shoulders slumped from exhaustion.

Out of the corner of his eye, he saw the form of a man moving along the bank, bending and rising, throwing something into the murky water.

Dodan had thrown a stranded fish back into the water.

Madai shook his head. "It won't make any difference."

Dodan stood to his full diminutive height, his slight form contrasted with the greatness of the earthen embankment behind him. He held another dying fish. Swinging his arm up into a great arch, the fish flew unnaturally and then plopped into the stream. "To that one, it makes all the difference in the world."

Dodan smiled and wandered to Madai's side. "I am

small in stature but not in imagination. I must be content to change the fortune of a fish or a man in small ways. Is a single life worth less than the whole?"

"You speak like a man of faith."

Dodan shaded his eyes from the brightness of the sun. "My people believe in the One, but I'm no prophet."

Madai chewed his lip. "You are a better man than me. I fear the return of my brother and despair of my people's future."

Dodan tipped his head. "I will be glad to be of assistance, for that is why I came."

With a snort, Madai started back to his village. "Perhaps you don't save fish but men."

~~~

Madai's heart softened like soil under autumn rains.

The time of trial ended.

With Adam's ingenuity, Thubal's loyalty, and Dodan's wisdom, the clan of Madai grew prosperous.

Madai's only wish was that his mother had lived to see it. He dreamed of her with him again, but always she seemed to yearn for another place. He awoke certain that she lived on in some form he could not see.

He strolled across the village to where Dodan worked the soil, assisting a young family with their garden. He perched on a smooth rock and described his dreams.

After wiping his brow, Dodan laid the spade aside and sat on the ground next to his friend. He shared a story about a woman named Ophir, explaining how she had been stolen from her clan and how tragedy took her life. "Despite the horror she lived through, I believe that she now lives in a world where she finally knows joy."
~~~

The sun had lowered considerably, and a cool breeze picked up. Madai listened in absorbed concentration. He wanted to believe that another world existed, for this life seemed cruel and unjust. “My mother is dead, and I fear it is a childish wish to believe in a world where those that suffer in this life are rewarded in the next.”

Dodan rubbed his jaw with his grimy hand. “I too wonder… Why does God hold His hand back from a man like Neb?” He shrugged. “But really, who are we to tell God how to reason or arrange life in this world or the next?” Dodan grinned.

Madai blanched. “Do you think I’ll ever see Him?”

“One day. Perhaps.” Dodan clasped his spade and climbed to his feet. “But I must finish this task. The family here needs help. The father is sick, and though Eva has done everything in her power, she has not been able to cure him.”

Madai glanced at the quiet hut. “I have duties to tend to also.” He took a few steps away and then stopped. “Thank you.”

Though Dodan did not raise his head, his gentle voice echoed the beauty of the setting sun. “You’re welcome.”

Chapter Forty-Five

-OldEarth-

Two Different Realities

Teal listened as Sienna recounted the story. With a shiver, he tried to process the mixed horror and joy involved, but it was too much to integrate into his mind at one time.

"You feeling alright?"

Teal met her gaze. "Do *you* believe in God?"

Sienna swiveled her glance from Teal, across the grassy expanse, over Kelesta wandering along the edge of a copse of trees, to the brilliant blue sky.

A falcon soared high above.

Smiling, she nodded. "I do."

Teal rubbed his face. "I do too. Just, I can't understand—"

"Belief and understanding are two different realities."

As if on impulse, Kelesta marched across the grassy plain and stopped before them. "I hate to interrupt, but Ark has been trying to reach you. He said that you're either deaf or in love."

Alarm surging through him, Teal slipped his datapad from his pocket and then tapped his earpiece. "What's wrong with—"

Sienna nudged his arm. "Were you with Tcesni recently?"

A memory played in Teal's mind. "She wiped a bug off my neck."

Laughing, Sienna nudged Kelesta. "That's not all she wiped!"

Embarrassment heating his face, Teal motioned to Sienna's datapad. "I'll use yours."

Sienna handed it over and clasped Kelesta's shoulder. "So, tell me all. What happened on Helm? And—" Her eyebrows wiggled in mischievous delight. "How are things going with Zuri?"

With a groan, Teal stepped back. "I'll find Ark and see what he needs. You two catch up."

~~~

Ark stood on a wide grassy plain and wanted to scream. If Zuri described one more back-to-nature plan and how Ingoti civilization would soon discover a whole new "balanced approach" to life, he would strangle the idiot. Besides, there wasn't a drop of water in sight. Terrifying really.

At the sight of Teal blinking into view, relief bubbled over his whole body. "Thank God!"

Teal chuckled. "Have things been that bad?"

Zuri tripped over himself in his excitement to tell the news. "We've discovered signs of alien intervention!"

All humor vanished.

Teal stomped over to Ark and glared. "You want to tell me what's going on?"

Bouncing his best I'm-really-annoyed-at-you glare off Zuri, Ark smacked his tentacles together, ready to explain. "We just discovered signs of architectural development impossible on a human level. If you look over there"—he pointed to a circle of enormous upright stones—"you'll see that a solar and lunar calendar appear to have been developed using the—"

Zuri wagged his finger, like an overeager student who needed two points to graduate. "But there's no way humans could get those stones lined up just right. It's
~~~

clearly beyond—"

Teal waved Zuri down. "I can see. You don't need to explain." He frowned. "Are you sure humans were involved at all?"

"We saw them working on it…well, on part of it. But how they got the skills and intelligence when they're still in their infancy—"

Ark intercepted Zuri's rant. "The Mystery Race is having fun."

Teal clenched his hands. "No Crestonian amusement?"

Scandalized, Ark jerked back and patted his chest to keep his pulmonary circulation in proper form. "No! We experiment to gain insight and understanding. We don't give information away for free."

Zuri nodded in solemn agreement.

Teal sighed. "In that case, we have more work to do."

Ark sucked in a deep draught from his breather helm. "If only our friends outnumbered our enemies."

-Docking Bay Seven-
-Planet Crestar-

Tcesni sidled up to a tall Cresta in a long lab coat and slipped a data-chip into his waiting hand. "Getting paid to make a new scientific breakthrough. A Cresta's dream come true."

The Cresta peered down his breathing helm at the Ingot Queen. "We've known about sterilization for eons—just never applied that knowledge to Luxonian women."

Tcesni's eyes widened. "They won't be sterilized forever, surely? It'll just be a bump in their population road."

The Cresta shrugged, his tentacles waving. "Since it has never been done before…"

Tcesni turned to her waiting ship, a snippet of gossip appropriate now. "I heard that Ingots are considering less invasive armor technology."

A head wag and dutiful Cresta grief. "A pity. Their dependence made them so easy to infiltrate."

Tcesni smirked. "Can't have it all your own way."

Three Crestas loped forward. Lab Coat toddled off with a brief wave. "Safe trip home!"

Tcesni rubbed her empty stomach as she watched the four rotund figures gather for a quick consult. "Edible. Definitely edible."

CHAPTER FORTY-SIX

—ADAM'S VILLAGE—

SOME MEASURE OF HAPPINESS

Madai enjoyed meeting Adam's father, mother, and his five sisters. He stayed quiet for the most part, but soon one of the sisters caught his eye, and he looked on her with favor. Ester was quite beautiful, with large, shy eyes and long, thick, dark brown hair. She was soft-spoken, more so than her sisters, and Madai felt drawn to her. Her generous, careful manners made him feel stronger and braver than he had ever felt in his life.

Adam and Dodan clearly noticed the budding attraction, but to his gratitude, they kept their own counsel. It was a man's own business whom he chose for a wife.

Near the change of the season, Madai realized it was time to return home, but first, he had to speak to Adam and his father about his intentions.

Adam's father smiled his approval, for he had heard about Madai's goodness and honor from both Adam and Dodan. His answer was direct and sincerely expressed. "My daughter's wishes show through her eyes when she looks at you. I am glad that she has found a worthy man and will have a good home soon."

For the first time in his life, Madai felt assured of some measure of happiness. Powerful as he may be, Neb did not set his eldest son's fate.

CHAPTER FORTY-SEVEN

—MADAI'S VILLAGE—

UNITE THEIR LOVE

Eva stood off to the side when Madai brought Ester home to his people, watching the introductions with wary interest. Leah's death had devastated her, and even though Neb was exiled far away, her heart had not recovered. Though Neb had not killed her friend and rumors told that he was seriously ill, still she could never forgive him.

Leah had been more than innocent. She had shown strength in her innocence, a quality that tugged at Eva's heart. Leah had not lived in vain—her strength had meant something. She had watched Madai grow up with apprehension, for inevitably, Neb would become jealous of his son's closeness to his wife. Yet Madai was formed in his mother's image, not his father's. Though an extraordinary young man, still, Madai could not comfort Eva's aching heart. He was not even aware of it.

After Leah's death, the defeat of their clan at the last battle, and Neb's abdication, Eva's heart was wrung so tightly that she ceased to feel anything. When Madai told her about his desire to meet Adam's clan, Eva assented without comment. Only when Dodan—the eldest son of Uzal—asked to travel with Madai, did Eva's soul stir.

When Madai returned with Adam and Dodan and his new bride, a dull ache developed.

Ester, she soon learned, was the cherished daughter of Adam's parents, and besides being quite beautiful, she was wonderfully skilled in weaving.

The whole clan seemed to have forgotten the losses they

had suffered, and the lessons of the past were abandoned. Neb could yet return, and he would find them completely unprepared.

When Eva attempted to speak of her fears, Madai turned the conversation to other things.

Eva retreated into her injured soul.

In time, Eva's grief turned to anger, and she began to show her disdain openly. When Ester became pregnant, she avoided the woman, and when she went into labor, Eva ignored the news.

Soon, it was apparent that the mother and baby were in trouble. Madai asked for help, but Eva ignored him too. In desperation

Madai begged Dodan to convince Eva to help. "You've spent some time with her discussing herbs and the qualities of various brews. She respects you and knows your intelligence. She will listen to you."

When Eva heard Dodan calling for her, she stopped her work and remained as still as a mouse being sought by a cat. When she heard the call again, she realized that Dodan was right outside her dwelling and knew she was home. She laid the garment she had been sewing aside and stepped outside.

"Dodan? It is not often you travel out this way. How are you?"

Only a responsive smile sped over Dodan's face before he stared in earnest supplication. "I've come to beg for your help. Ester is near death, and Madai fears for her and the child. We need you to see what can be done, or both are lost."

Eva stared at Dodan for an awkward moment. "Why come to me now, when there is little hope? So that I can be blamed for their deaths?"

Dodan's eyes widened, and he shook his head. "There is no such thought in anyone's head. We did not ask sooner for the simple reason that everyone knows that you don't like the girl."

"I don't like her? Is that how it stands? I am a cruel, unjust woman who dislikes a girl for no reason!"

A woman in the distance beckoned to Dodan. He returned his attention on Eva. "A woman and her baby are dying, and if you ever considered yourself a healer, do something! Your mission is to heal—not to give in to anger and hate."

A bolt of shock sizzled through Eva. She saw her father as he stood in their last moments together, and she remembered her vow. She remembered why she had made that vow. Without a word, Eva brushed past Dodan, sped up the incline to Madai's dwelling, and pushed her way through all the men, women, and children crowding around. "Go away and leave me to do my work." Eva reached for Ester and clasped the young woman's hand.

Sweat poured off the girl's face, and Eva cursed herself inside for her obstinacy. She gave orders like birds flying from the nest.

Ester tried to speak, but she was too weak. Her eyes, however, pleaded with unspoken humility.

Eva worked in a fury to do all that she could for both mother and child, while Madai and Dodan were sent to care for the rest of the clan and tend to the duties of the day.

Throughout the cold, drizzly night, Eva stayed by Ester's side. She nearly despaired at times, but by the next day, it was clear that all was not lost.

Using every skill she had—and inventing a few she had never thought of before—she saved the lives of both mother and baby.

Madai, in his joy, did everything he could to make up to Eva for his earlier negligence, and Ester, in her gratitude, treated Eva as her foster mother.

As Eva rocked Neb's grandbaby in her arms, new life flourished in her soul.

~~~

Dodan stood by and watched Eva's resentment melt and her hurt heal, and he decided it was time to return to his own people.

But as he watched Eva, something burned in his chest. He had accepted the fact that he was not born to be a great hunter or a great warrior. Though he could furnish game for the clan, it was not something he would ever be renowned for. Yet he yearned to be renowned.

It had been Eva's grace to heal what he could not heal. He watched her, and before he knew what he was doing, he found himself standing before her. When she looked up and met his gaze, a wide smile replaced the sullen pout that he had seen formerly.

"Good day, Dodan. See our newest family member? You will have to help Madai build a bigger house."

Dodan shrugged. "He doesn't need me anymore. Perhaps it's time for me to return home."

The sparkle in Eva's eyes dimmed. "Surely not! Madai would not know what to do without you and—"

His stomach twisted even as a spark ignited in his heart. "And?"

"I suppose men must define themselves by a trait or two rather than by that which makes them truly human."

Dodan frowned.

Eva shifted the baby, smiling into the little one's face. She smoothed his wispy black hair. "You don't realize your value. Just because you are not a warrior, it's as if you do not think of yourself as a man."
~~~

“I’m a small man.”

Eva smiled. “I think you are every bit as large as any man I have ever lo—” Eva closed her eyes and rocked a moment. A tear slipped down her cheek.

Nudging her aside, Dodan sat beside her and wrapped his arm around her shoulder.

Still clasping the baby, Eva laid her head on his shoulder. “I’ve been so sad for so terribly long.”

Dodan understood. “Only when we have nothing left to give but our grief, do two people really unite in their love.” He stroked Eva’s hair and then checked her tears. He peered at the sleeping baby and smiled. “I’d like a child of my own.”

Eva nodded.

With a chuckle, Dodan patted the baby’s head. “We best not drown Madai’s baby then. I have a favor to ask of him, and it would be good to keep his son peaceful.”

Eva relaxed in Dodan’s embrace. “It takes a man among men to father a whole clan, and you have done so. I have no fear of your fathering a child.”

Dodan sighed deeply and let his chin rest gently on his soon-to-be wife’s soft head.

CHAPTER FORTY-EIGHT

—ISHTAR'S VILLAGE—

LOST YEARS

Gizah glanced at her husband, and though he was still listening, his eyes drooped in weariness. Everyone in the clan had fallen into drowsiness. Eyes were open, but no one was moved. The fire had burned low, and even the surrounding lands remained quiet.

Ishtar's head dropped to his chest, and his eyes closed.

Gizah motioned for her husband to stand as she nodded toward home.

Ishtar jerked up. "I was resting. Heard every word you said."

Gizah smiled. "It's late, and perhaps we should start again another time."

Amin rose to his feet. "It's been a long day, and I don't want you overtired."

Ishtar stalled his son. "I am tired, but I really want to hear about Aram." With beseeching eyes, he focused on Gizah. "Perhaps you could just—"

With a giggle, Gizah repositioned herself more comfortably. "Yes, if you want. I will speak more briskly, for, in truth, there is not much left to tell. But there is one event that occurred later and changed everything. Do you want me to tell of that?"

After a long drink from a skin bag, Ishtar wiped his mouth and sat up straighter. "Yes, that would be good."

Amin threw more wood on the fire, fueling the flames back to life. Everyone stretched and settled into comfortable positions.

Gizah leaned her head against her husband, with his arms nestled gently around her, and continued.

~~~

Keram grew up strong and healthy, and it was not until much later that his little brother was born. But this babe was not as lucky as the first, and he died in his first year. Others followed, but Keram was raised to be the inheritor of all that Madai had established from the clan of Neb, son of Hezeki. It was as if all memory of Neb had been blotted out of his people's memories.

Eva warned Madai that their people might forget the lessons of the past, but Madai assured her that Neb would never return, and so he was proved right. Neb did not return, and the clan lived on in peaceful security.

Blessed with several children, Eva fulfilled her vow to be of service to others and became famous for her healing powers. Clansmen from all over sought her advice. Dodan continued as mentor and father figure to Madai, and the two of them brought peace to the land.

Adam visited often, always bringing new ideas that he had gleaned from clans near and far.

And so it went year after year, with only births and deaths to change the pattern of their days. But then as Madai grew into old age and his son Keram was nearing the age to become leader, an event occurred that drastically changed the fortunes of all.

A new people traveled through, and though they were friendly, they brought disaster to the whole clan. A terrible sickness invaded, and though both Eva and Dodan did everything they could, there was no known remedy for this silent stalker, which claimed lives with horrible speed.
~~~

Several of Madai's children were taken, as well as Eva's infant daughter. Old people succumbed in a matter of days, and even those who had lived through years of drought and poor crops and other hardships now failed in the face of this new illness.

After nearly a third of the clan had been laid to rest, Madai called together all those still able to make a clear choice, and he stated the matter in definite terms.

"Whatever is killing our people will claim us all if we stay here. We must move on and make a new home away from these southern hills. The strangers came from the south and headed east. I think it would be best if we head west, into the wilderness."

Keram supported his father's plan, and Dodan and Eva agreed.

A heartbroken assembly thrashed a trail through the dense woodlands, heading they knew not where. But as they hacked and broke all barriers, new terrors haunted them. Wild animals they had never encountered before attacked in the night and killed those unaware and unprepared. One enormous creature—with hard bumpy skin, stubby legs, enormous claws, and a mouth that opened wider than anyone believed possible—crawled out of the western river and devoured men.

In terror, Madai turned northeast, away from the river, desperately trying to hold his people together. But as time went on, it seemed as if they would be taken one by one to their ultimate demise.

Keram, as eldest son, believed that if the clan split in two and each tried to make its way, at least some might survive. After a furious argument between Keram and his father, a final decision was accepted, and Keram moved on with a few who were brave or foolish enough to follow him.

One of those who followed him was Miriam, the youngest daughter and last surviving member of a once-large family. She believed that she had nothing to lose and everything to gain by going off with the only man in the clan she trusted. Neither of them ever saw or heard from their clan again.

Certain knowledge and skills that had been accumulated from recent generations were lost in that departure.

Keram knew the stories of his father and his grandfather, and he knew much about healing herbs from his mother, but he had not studied weapons or how to grow crops or the tools of an established clan. He reinvented his people, and so they were remade as a woodland clan that wandered from place to place, living off the resources of a dark, dank forest.

Keram and Miriam gave birth to a son soon after their joining. The son born to them was great in size and very strong, and he soon showed signs of being very much like his great-grandfather, Neb, for he wanted to rule the clan before it was his time to do so. This first son was named Elath, and he became Keram's bane.

But after the loss of three sisters, a second son was born, and he was named Aram. Aram loved his father and did not desire leadership.

Keram had to choose between his sons. But this time, Elath claimed the right to separate rather than overthrow his father, and Keram was left with his wife and his second son, Aram, and half his clan.

And so began the life of Aram and his rise as a leader of men.

~~~

Gizah met Ishtar's steady gaze, relieved to have finished the tale.
~~~

Clan members stretched. Mother's bundled sleeping children into their arms, and fathers led their family's home. Soon nearly everyone had slipped away to bed.

Sadness etched deep lines in Ishtar's face. "You've explained much."

Gizah nodded as she and her husband rose.

Amin reached down to assist his father, but Ishtar waved his hand away. "I can sleep here as well as anywhere." He looked at the dying embers. "There is not much more to tell, but I will share the rest of Neb's history tomorrow. Thank you, Gizah, for what you have kept in your memory. I never understood why Aram's people acted so primitive when it was clear that Aram himself came from a developed heritage. Now I see the lost years. Much the same occurred in my grandfather Serug's clan."

Ishtar rubbed his face. "Men may move forward only to step backward time and again." He sighed. "Get your rest, children. We will see what tomorrow brings us."

CHAPTER FORTY-NINE

—ISHTAR'S VILLAGE—

RECOUNTED BEFORE ALL

Ishtar completed a full day's work and strolled to a stream that meandered near their village. Resting his feet in the cool water, he saw Amin and Gizah heading toward him and grinned. "Come and refresh yourselves."

Amin laughed and galloped into the stream, splashing his wife. "You used to do this every morning, Father, saying that it helped you think."

Ishtar nodded. "Ever since living in the desert lands beyond the mountains, I never cease to be grateful for the refreshing beauty of abundant water. Pity those who have never known it."

"Tonight you'll tell us about Neb the Great's last days and explain how it was that Serug brought another Neb into the world?"

Ishtar peered into the bright sky, soaring from one memory to another. Grief awaited him in those memories. Straightening up, he argued within himself. *The story did not end there.* "Yes, we'll gather again in the evening, and I will tell the final tale of Neb the Great." He sucked in a deep breath, stretching his arms, his feet stirring the cool water. "But for the moment, I will live in the present and rejoice that the past is no more."

~~~
~~~

Amin sat with his wife leaning against him, and though he was wide awake, he felt as if he were already drawn into another world, for he felt the hidden presence of more than those clan members gathered around. The retelling of these tales seemed to bring the spirits of the dead to life for the judgment they had not received during their lifetimes. There were no secrets now, and all knew the truth that many had sought in vain to conceal.

He shuddered, for he realized with shock, that someday it would be his turn to hear his life recounted by those who lived to judge his actions in the light of reason and through revealed history.

His own child would consider his actions of supreme importance. He could never again think that what he did in the course of a day, secret or not, was of no importance, for there would be a record somewhere, in someone's mind, and it would be recounted out loud before all.

—WILDERNESS—

Serug laid his father in a quiet cave and tended to him himself. Serug was not concerned that his father might die but rather that the men might pick another leader before Neb formally appointed him.

With great care, Serug managed their daily affairs, his men watching while he tended to his father's needs and hunted with the warriors in the woodlands, feeding everyone better than they had dared hope. They made suitable shelters, and after a time, they no longer regretted leaving their former homeland.

When Neb felt well enough, he called for Serug to arrange a council meeting. At the meeting, Neb clutched at the thin skin blanket that covered him, his face contorted with disgust. “Of all my men, only Puti died as a noble warrior should, fighting the enemy.” He glanced around, his gaze chasing the air as if phantoms appeared with the long evening shadows.

Seeing bewilderment and uncertainty on Neb’s face, Serug took charge. “My father wants to thank you all for your faithfulness.”

A snide grunt turned everyone’s attention.

Impatient, Serug took the bait. “Torgama, was that you? Do you doubt your master’s gratitude?”

His face deeply scarred, Torgama crept forward, his gaze taking in the whole assembly. “Neb is grateful, but it has little to do with us.” His gravelly voice rose, a tone of authority giving strength to his words. “He cares for nothing and no one. Weak now, he is lost and cannot find his past glory.”

Fire burned in Serug. “Worthless traitor! You ought to be speared through the heart. No one wants a man like—”

Torgama lifted his hand, a bemused expression spreading across his face. “I’d like a word with you alone.”

Confused but also intrigued, Serug stopped short. He stepped to the side.

Torgama followed.

Neb watched them go through narrowed eyes.

When Serug returned with Torgama and faced the men, an idiotic grin stretched across Neb’s face, as if he knew the news but no longer cared about the outcome.

“I have been informed of the clan’s wishes.” He glanced furtively at Neb. “Though I will always honor Neb, I see the importance of making a quick and firm decision.”

Serug tapped his fingers against his thigh and faced Neb. “Father, the men have chosen me as the new leader. You will always be very important to us, but I will make the decisions from now on.”

Neb stared ahead. “Hezeki is watching you.” He broke

into a loud cackling laugh.

Serug's eyes grew wider with every burst of mad merriment. "Father, what ails you? I thought this would be a relief. You deserve rest and peace."

Neb practically choked with uncontrolled amusement. "You offer me what I denied my father, yet you condemn me even more surely than I condemned him."

As he continued to laugh, the men shook their heads and walked away one by one.

Serug maintained his position, taking a deep breath. He owed a great deal to Torgama, for it was clearly through Torgama's maneuvering that the men had been united. Yet he was fairly certain that Torgama had killed his mother and would like very much to kill his father.

Neb stopped laughing, staring sightlessly ahead, alone in a world of his own mind.

Serug tipped his head and studied his father. He had no desire to end his father's life. Neb the Great was now subject to his son—a second son at that. If he had been the laughing sort, Serug might have laughed, but he only smiled as he walked away. He could finally plan his future.

Chapter Fifty

-Planet Lux-

Power Isn't Everything

Teal sat back on an oval, plush couch, silently watching his friend and mentor, and wondered if he had been wrong his whole life. "I don't think I understand you, Sir."

Sterling, dressed casually in an orange tunic and loose-fitting white pants, added three red drops to a half-filled glass of amber liquid and swirled the concoction in a gentle rhythm. "Here, try this. I made it up. But that doesn't mean it isn't any good."

Trying hard not to hesitate, Teal, in his usual OldEarth clothes, leaned forward and accepted the drink.

Sterling watched, his eyebrows arched in enthralled interest.

With battle-hardened courage, Teal tossed the beverage down his throat. It burned like hell.

Apparently in expectation of the coughing, eye-watering, throat-tightening second step, Sterling held out a glass of what Teal hoped to God was water.

It was.

After wiping his eyes and clearing the vestiges of his raw throat, he plunked the glass on the round table and glared at the man he now wanted to hate. "You're trying to kill me?"

"If I was, you'd be dead."

Teal rubbed his hands along his pant legs and stood. "Not necessarily."

Sterling followed Teal to the balcony overlooking the bustling city.

Twenty stories high, it offered a long-range view of the

business district, three surrounding residential neighborhoods, and the purple mountains in the distance. Two crescent moons rose in the west.

"I just wanted to see how you handle a traitor."

Teal gripped the handrail, his already frail mood spiraling into the abyss. "You're a traitor now? How convenient for someone aiming to join the Supreme Council!"

Sterling laughed. A long, loud belly laugh. He practically danced with giggles.

"Not me, you idiot! The insect queen." He waved a finger like an administrator chastising a clumsy employee. "She'd like to kill you and find a puppet to make nice with while stealing Earth from under our nose."

Teal sighed. *He finally caught on.*

Sterling leaned against the railing and eyed his friend. "You don't agree?"

Still facing forward, Teal rested his arms on the railing. The luminous sky enchanted him, his mood rising. "You're right as far as Tcesni goes."

"Is there someone else?"

"A lot of someone elses. The Mystery Race bothers me."

With a hearty snort, Sterling apparently agreed. "No surprise there. The Mystery Race bothers everyone. Ask anyone on Crestar, Helm, or Ingilium."

Teal turned and locked his gaze with Sterling. "They won't leave Earth alone."

Sterling nodded. He nudged Teal in the shoulder. "Are you feeling better? A little more hopeful maybe?"

Teal clasped his hands and stopped for a moment of introspection. Golly, he did feel good. Mellow, peaceful, yet energetic and refreshed. "What in h—heaven did you put in that drink?"

Sterling grinned. "It's my secret. But just so you know,

nothing that will kill you."

"Ever so thankful."

Sterling waved the deadpan gratitude away by shooing a fly off his shirt. "As for Tcesni, be sure that you have plenty of evidence before we confront her. Though Uanyi are vastly inferior, they are developing at a remarkable rate. I believe that with the right queen, they may surprise us with inherently decent, likeable qualities."

"In other words, keep pleasant planetary relations but never trust her with my back?"

"It would be nice if she didn't devour our friends. At some point, her own people will realize that personal power isn't everything. Eating up the neighborhood just won't do.

Teal glanced at the empty glass on the table. "I might need another before I go."

-Planet Sectine-

Zuri bent low and whispered in Ark's ear. "I think Teal got here late last night and wants to meet Tcesni early this morning."

Ark hunched his shoulders and slapped Zuri's face away. "Would you stop that!"

A smidge offended, Zuri glared. "I'm just filling you in."

"I don't need to be filled in. I checked Teal's public itinerary first thing." He glared at the Ingot. "What were you doing all night?"

"I sent Kelesta a message."

Ark rolled his orbs. "By the stars above, you two can't be separated for a few days without going into starvation mode."

"She's taking on an important mission on behalf of Helm and needs all the advice she can get."

"Sienna is there and will tell her what to do, so don't worry your head about it. Concentrate on Teal and the fact that Tcesni wants to eat him for breakfast."

While strolling down a long, narrow avenue, the two pulled up short. A crowd of Uanyi surrounded two combatants in a fistfight.

An average-sized male Uanyi, flushed and furious, faced a large female who had balled her hands into fists, her eyes blazing and her breathing helm hissing. "If you don't believe me, then investigate for yourself!"

The crowd's gaze swiveled to the male combatant.

"She's our queen! You oughtn't be talking like that. You owe her your loyalty!"

"Loyalty? She's blown up places of business, homes, and even laboratories. All in her grand plot to sow suspicion and fear among our people. She's not a queen. She's a traitor."

A collective gasp.

Ark wanted to plunge forward and chat with this interesting Uanyi, but discretion held him in place.

A siren sounded.

Heads swiveled toward the approaching Interventionists flying in on hover scooters.

The male Uanyi puckered his lips and lifted his hands in protest. "Wasn't me. I'd have beaten you with my own two hands." He glanced around, his eyes flickering nervously. "Let's call it even. You said your piece, and I've said mine."

The female nodded, her wide eyes filling with fear.

The crowd broke up, and the two combatants sprinted off in opposite directions.

Ark looked at Zuri, their gazes connecting. "We'd better get out of here."

Zuri nodded as he marched across the street. “Funny. Instead of getting eaten…we get to feed Teal some delicious news.”

Ark loped at his friend’s side, his tentacles swaying easily. “He’s always been lucky to have us around.”

Zuri grinned.

CHAPTER FIFTY-ONE

—NEB'S VILLAGE—

A SON JUST LIKE ME

Neb endured each day exiled in the remnant of his clan and his mind.

The days had grown mild, except at night when a bitter chill descended, and he'd wrap himself in his worn blankets, shivering, despite his best efforts to stay warm.

Serug kept distant, watching through narrowed eyes.

Neb meandered along a gurgling stream, observing small changes each day. He had no plans, not hopes, no dreams. At first, he pondered overthrowing his son the way he had overthrown his father years before, but the idea held no appeal. Even the slightest physical exertion sent him to his bed for days.

Of course, there were many ways to rule. Leah had ruled him more than anyone had suspected—more than she had imagined.

One warm, sunny day, he wandered through the woods to an ancient tree that drank directly from the stream through enormous roots dipped in the water. The sun stood at its peak. He rested his head against the broad, gnarly trunk and let his shoulders slump in relaxation. He was not sure how much time had passed when he awoke to the sensation of being shoved in the side.

Long shadows stretched around him.

A wet spot on his arm and the scent of a large, furry animal caught his attention. He jerked forward and glanced around. On his right towered the largest bears he'd ever seen. A matriarch of the forest. Quite likely she had cubs near, though she seemed uninterested in him as a threat or a meal.

Neb scanned his environment then returned his gaze to the great she-bear. He remembered his first great hunt and his ignominious defeat.

A slow grin crept across his face—he had turned defeat into revenge and became renowned throughout the clan when he brought home his dead enemy. It did not matter that it was not the same bear. What mattered to him and everyone who heard the tale was how he had conquered himself and had accomplished what few would have attempted at his young age.

He knew full well that he was not in shape to kill this bear, and she had not been particularly threatening. In fact, she ignored him. Neb remembered his thin blankets and knew for the first time since his sickness and exile that he wanted something. He wanted her skin.

He fingered the ornate knife in his belt. He would need more than one blade. But she was near, and that was all that mattered. He could accomplish this task in his own time.

Her fur changed sheen, from tawny to dark brown, as broken sunbeams filtered through the branches and leaves.

He imagined himself wrapped up in the thick fur, its softness against his skin. Grinning, he slipped away, edging out of the sight, smell, and imagination of the great beast.

~~~

Neb awoke to the sound of howling, a cold wind, and a full moon. He sat up, his heart pounding. The great fur he had won for himself had slipped to his knees, and he
~~~

clutched at it wildly but could not escape the chill that pinched his nerves. He had seen the face of Uzal in his dream and felt the old man's grip on his shoulder.

Neb wrapped the blanket around his shoulders and shook his head. Why now? Who was Uzal that he should haunt him? Uzal was dust in the ground. Like Leah—dead and gone. All the battles that ever mattered were over. Neb lived in obscure wilderness.

A screaming wail of wind tore through his dwelling. What had Uzal promised? To haunt him? A grim laugh filtered from his chest to his throat. He was neither fully alive nor definitely dead. The warm fur rubbed against his bare shoulders. He would not succumb to terror and madness.

The future still existed, and he could still affect the outcome of another's fate. Suddenly, he understood for a moment how his own mother must have felt when she tried so desperately to control him. But Neb was not Meshullemeth. One thought led to the next, and Neb nodded as he imagined the son that Serug would one day have. He still had one great victory to accomplish. Uzal would wait. Neb was not afraid of man, beast, or the spirits of hell.

~~~

Serug watched his men with a jealous eye. Though the leader, he was never secure that he would stay the leader. One man that did not belong had come with them during the final battle. He was of the family of Torgama, but never were there two so different mortals walking the earth.

Eymard was as silent and thoughtful as his kinsman, but his eyes betrayed a different mind. Eymard had followed the wishes of his father and served Neb faithfully, but he
~~~

had seen little in the way of battle. He had worked among the men more as healer than warrior.

Apparently, Neb had never taken notice of Eymard, and when illness came, he called upon Eva, as was his habit. But now, Serug found himself forced to notice this medium-built, brown-eyed, nondescript man.

Eymard spoke seldom, never calling attention to himself.

As Serug watched his men work and his father rest, he became obsessed with Eymard's quiet ability. Something about his nature disturbed his peace of mind.

During the big hunt, when the men brought in fresh meat for the dark days ahead, Serug noticed Eymard managing things differently in the village. He directed the building of more permanent structures, and he instructed the men to bring young animals to raise separately, especially pigs and goats.

Eymard had ideas of his own! Perhaps he remembered the ways of Hezeki and the stories of the settled clans, and he wanted to try his own invention. Plans for stability and peace kindled little ambition in a warrior. Serug traipsed to where his father rested on the edge of the stream.

Neb sat up and listened to his son's complaints, his eyes glittering. "Keep the clan moving. Do not let them rest too long in one place. They will look to you for direction, and Eymard will find his plans come to nothing. Don't approach him directly. Just say you have knowledge the clan does not have, and they must move on. Make it imperative, and they will follow you."

Serug knew his father was right, but he didn't understand why it was true. Without recollection, he spoke under his breath, "But why will they believe me?"

Neb smiled a secretive smile and leaned forward. "Men want to be led. A few think they'd like to lead and could do better than anyone else, but the truth is—few want the role." Neb glanced around. Only the stream bubbled, and a gentle wind stirred the surrounding leaves. He spoke more openly, his chest rising and falling in easy rhythm. "Men want to do what they like, but nothing turns out as planned. Even in the dullest man, there is some realization of this. So, men like to complain about the evils that we all must endure without bearing the weight of their part to play. Give them time to wear themselves out. Leaders are always despised. Such is fate. Never care for others' opinions. That's the only way to rule."

Serug looked blankly ahead. He did not care whom he had to conquer or kill, so long as he would be obeyed. He considered his father. "Don't you still want to lead, Father?"

Neb peered into the distance. "I am leading."

Serug pursed his lips and thought about those simple words for a long moment. He decided that he could accept them. It did not matter if he sought advice from his father. He made the final decision. His father had accepted his own position with apparent indifference, and it suited them both for the time being.

As for Eymard, Serug would rid his clan of this dangerous influence. Men who thought for themselves were dangerous. He needed men who did not want to lead but merely complained in their sterile effort to relieve themselves of responsibility.

Serug stood up and looked down upon his father. "I will give the order today, and it will be a matter of life and death for every man to obey me."

Neb stroked his chin, his gaze turning north. "Head toward the mountains. I've heard stories about small clans in the valleys. You'll find a wife—a woman untainted by the blood of the Men of Havilah."

"What about the Men of Seth? Do they not come from the north?"

"Not this far west. They live higher in the hills. We'll stay in the lowlands."

Serug considered his life from a new perspective. "A wife?"

Neb closed his eyes and leaned against the wide tree trunk, resting comfortably. "A wife and a son—a son just like me."

A thrill surged through Serug, as if he had just been handed a mighty weapon. A son who would do his bidding. A son to bring power and glory to his name. A son who—

Serug paused. What if he had a daughter first? He had been told such things happened.

Neb seemed to read his mind. "Don't worry. Girls are fragile things. If born first, she'd not live to matter. Eva taught me many things, even when she did not mean to. I know how to dispose of a mistake. Besides, I am a first son of a first son going back for generations."

Perplexed, Serug felt his euphoria fade. "But I'm a second son."

Opening his eyes, Neb seemed pulled out of his reverie. "I have no other son, so therefore you must be my first son."

Serug nodded decisively. He would lead his clan toward the mountains, find a wife, and have a son—all as his father directed. As the recognized leader, his future glowed brightly.

CHAPTER FIFTY-TWO

—NEB'S VILLAGE—

LIFE IS SURE TO FOLLOW

Neb stroked his thick fur blanket in relief as the weather had turned cold, and the nights grew bitter. He leaned against a rock face as his son organized the men for the night.

The group huddled under an overhanging cliff. Nothing had gone according to plan. Their journey had been longer and more difficult than they had imagined. Men began to grumble, and Torgama openly questioned the direction they were taking.

As the evening meal was prepared, Serug asked where he wanted to go, and Torgama responded that he would go somewhere warm.

Amused grunts approved his wit.

In defense, Serug argued that weak men complained the most.

Bitter silence met this charge.

Exhausted and hungry, Serug and his men had followed Neb's direction and now faced a cliff that went straight up into the sky as far as the eye could see. The western hills loomed dark and forbidding with massive trees growing from rocky ledges.

To the east, a swampy muck reeked.

Neb doubted that anyone could navigate through it safely.

His face set in grim defiance, Torgama faced Serug and folded his arms across his chest. "We're captured by stones and water. If an enemy approached, we'd have no escape."

Irritation flooding his face in a hot rage, Serug clipped

his words like a man lobbing limbs off a tree. “I need no escape. The enemy fears me. I fear no one.”

A belligerent smile crept across Torgama’s face. “In our last battle, when fire fell from the sky, you were quick enough to flee.”

Serug clenched his hands into fists. “You will see who flees when we attack next.”

“Who will we attack? Rocks?”

“Enough!” Neb raised a stick and pointed east.

Forcing himself into calmness with deep breaths, Serug faced the rest of the men. “We will head east and conquer the first clan we come across.”

Torgama shook his head, his eyes wide in mock wonder. “I suppose you will lead us through the marshlands?”

Serug smiled as a sudden light came into his eye. “No, you and Eymard will lead the way. You are brave, and he is smart. Head out tonight, come back tomorrow, and show us the best path to take.”

Torgama’s mouth dropped open in an unspoken retort.

Serug shrugged and lifted his hands in acceptance of an unpleasant truth. “Unless, of course, you’re afraid.”

Torgama slowly turned to Neb.

Neb twirled his stick between his fingers. The fading horizon had captured his attention.

~~~

Eymard threw his bag over his shoulder, his mood quiet and thoughtful. Neb was possessed by an evil that he could not control, and Serug was clearly possessed by his father. Though Eymard had lived as a man set apart amid beasts, up until now, he had survived and had even helped a few
~~~

men to think for themselves. But the swamp ahead led to certain death. Apparently, Neb and Serug no longer needed their services, and no one would halt the hand of fate.

He studied his companion as they made their way into the dark wetlands beyond the light of the campfire. No farewell. No expressions of regret or grief. They had been told to go, and no one would look at them as they picked up their bags and headed into the night.

Even when Torgama stopped in front of Neb on his way into the darkness, Neb had refused to meet his eyes.

Torgama waited.

Neb ignored him.

"Leah was not surprised when I followed her. She seemed to know I was coming."

Neb remained as still as the rock.

Torgama shrugged. "She died quickly. I don't think she felt much. Once her son was gone... It was a mercy."

Firelight glinted in Neb's eyes, but he said not a word.

His arm swinging, Torgama screamed. "It was never about her!"

—THE SWAMP—

Eymard gripped Torgama's shoulder. "Let's go."

Torgama swung at Neb. "I've always hated you. Everyone who has ever known you hates you!"

Eymard dragged Torgama away as Serug hustled forward.

Sullenly, Torgama shook Eymard's grip off, though he plodded along at his side. "He wanted us dead all along, didn't he?"

Eymard had no answer to give Torgama, so he stayed quiet, as he led the way into the darkness. Instinctively, they grasped each other's shoulders to keep their balance. Eymard would never go back to Neb, and Torgama was a dead man if he ever returned. Their fates were entwined as they stepped into the swamp.

They traveled slowly, tugging each foot out of the sucking mud for time uncounted. They wanted to rest. They needed rest. But they came across no solid surface on which to sit or recline. Even standing still was not an option, as their feet sank deeper into the ground if they stopped even for a moment.

Horror grew in them, but exhaustion and despair gained the upper hand.

Grunting and groaning, Eymard broke the silence, his throat raw, and his voice a mere whisper. "If I slip and fall, do not save me. Use your strength to get out."

Torgama faltered. "What?"

With a weak wave, his strength nearly gone, Eymard struggled to say his piece. "Keep moving!"

"Why do you care?"

Eymard slapped at a mosquito but missed. Not that he cared. The sting was nothing in comparison to their mutual suffering. "I want you to survive."

Torgama shook his head, his eyes wide with wonder. "Why?"

"Hul spoke of a God who lives, and I wonder what kind of greeting I'll receive when I enter His land."

Torgama rubbed a muddy finger under his nose. "I only know of the gods of the dead. What has your God to do with me?"

Eymard shook his fist. "I will not die a beast like Neb!"

Torgama stopped beside Eymard and squeezed his shoulder. "As we sink into hell, I wish I had known better."

Tears filled Eymard's eyes. "Don't stand still."

Torgama shook his head. "I killed the only good person I've ever known, not because she deserved to die or because I hated her, but because I hated *him*."

A scent tickled Eymard's nose. He lifted his head and sniffed. "Fire?

Torgama dragged himself forward, clasping Eymard's arm. "You're dreaming. There is nothing to burn. We'll walk until—"

A thrill greater than any he had ever known surged through Eymard. He pointed, his muddy hand shaking. "Smoke! Our fate is not sealed."

A choked sob rose from Torgama. "I do not deserve to live."

Arms clasped around each other's waists, Eymard and Torgama trudged ahead toward the gray smoke ascending into the sky.

"If God gives me another chance, I'll not hesitate to try again."

Like swimmers at high tide moving in slow motion against a force that would have overwhelmed lesser men, the two crept to shore and soon fell on their faces in exhaustion and relief.

Eymard heard Torgama's sobs between his own.

—THE SHORE—

Aaron, an old man by anyone's standards, watched in amazement as two figures stepped out of the misty murk known by all as the Forbidden Lands. It was a death trap, while just paces away lay sound land that supported numerous animals and a clear, healthy stream. He never wondered at the contradiction of good land and life-giving water so near a terror that swallowed men whole without mercy. He had lived near this reality for all his life, and never in all his born days had he seen anyone walk forth from this land.

When two men alighted, one tall and the other thickset, both exhausted and covered with muck, he stood before them speechless with both wonder and horror. Were these men alive, or were they spirits of the dead?

Raising his head from where he had fallen, the taller man panted his words. "We've come from across the swamp and barely lived to see the day."

His head turned to the side, the thickset man seemed to speak to the air. "Oh, God! I'm still alive."

Aaron knelt between the two men. "You're blessed indeed."

The large man tapped his chest, "Eymard." He pointed to his companion, "Torgama."

Torgama groaned.

The old man grinned and patted Torgama's filthy shoulder. "My name is Aaron, and you'd better come with me, rest a bit, or your spirit may yet decide to depart for another land."

After struggling to their feet, Eymard and Torgama staggered forward.

Aaron grasped their hands and led them to his village—a father leading his lost sons.

—THE VILLAGE—

Eymard and Torgama sat together in peace, watching the sun set on another day.

They had come to know these simple people and their quiet existence as if discovering a new kind of human being.

Torgama had fallen sick with fever the first days he had been among them, but with gentle care, he had grown strong enough to sit and then stand again. Today he'd wandered with Eymard through the village. Though they had spoken little about it, the moment of their parting drew near.

Eymard stopped on the edge of the stream leading to the swampland. “I must move on. These people have been good to me, and I have learned much, but I want to find our people—the ones we left behind at the last battle.”

Torgama nodded. “I wanted to go back too. To find Neb and kill him. But now,” —he took a long breath—“it doesn’t seem important anymore. “Neb will die. Serug will see to that. And those who follow Serug will eventually follow his son—and so it goes. But I will stay here and learn about freedom. I will make a hut and watch for weary travelers who cross over.”

Eymard smiled. “So far, we are the only ones to make such a journey.”

Torgama set his jaw. “Still, I will be here.”

Eymard clasped Torgama’s shoulder. “I’m very glad we traveled together…and we both survived.”

Torgama blinked in the strong light, looking over the water toward the horizon. “You broke through my darkness.”

Eymard swallowed hard and dropped his hand to his side. “Keep your vigil, Torgama. Where there is hope, life is sure to follow.”

CHAPTER FIFTY-THREE

—HILL LANDS—

YOUNG NEB

Serug stood tall with his bloody hand limp at his hips, heaving deep breaths. Victory! His men had surprised the small clan and overwhelmed them quickly. Every man, woman, and child now cowered before him. He had no desire to kill anyone else. He just wanted provisions and a few slaves.

Now he looked for his father, but Neb had wandered out of sight. Disappointment crushed euphoria. Certainly, Neb knew and would be quite gratified at their success.

Serug strode along the line of forlorn folks and stared hard at each of them.

Neb had said *she* would be among the captives, so it was only a matter of searching through the throng to find his mate. But as he walked along and came to the end of the assembly, he saw no one to spark his interest. No beauty or intelligence to be seen in the whole crowd. Surely his father did not mean for him to align himself with a dog? Serug sucked in a deep breath and choked, wrinkling his nose at an unpleasant stink.

A shrunken old man quavered a step nearer. "We are rendering fat for preserving our food."

Serug spat on the ground. "Is this all your clan?"

The old man shrugged. "A few you have not seen, but we are all the same to you. So, what does it matter?"

Serug merely spat again and glanced around.

A few children clustered together. One young woman tended an enormous pot over a large fire. Serug sauntered over to the timid gathering. He peered into the pot, disgust turning his stomach.

The young woman remained stiff, her eyes turned away.

"You, girl, why didn't you come with the others when I called for the village to gather?"

"My name is Athaliah."

Startled by her boldness, Serug stared at her.

Unconcerned, she shrugged and waved to the pot. "Father told me to keep stirring no matter what, and Mother told me to watch over the younger children."

"You listen to your parents above me?" He grabbed her arm and dragged her closer. "I am your master now. Your parents have no authority. Do as I say from now on. You understand me?"

Athaliah's gaze swiveled from the pot, and she stared Serug in the face. Impenetrable but composed.

"What's wrong with you, girl?"

Athaliah bit her lip. "It is hard to have both parents and a master. My parents want me to work for them. I have always done so."

"You will work for me from now on." Serug glanced around. "Where are your parents?"

Athaliah pointed to a couple standing not far off. "If I do not stir this, it'll burn. Then we'll lose a whole season's work."

Serug clutched Athaliah's chin and tilted her head toward him. "Look at me! You see the blood on me? I have just killed men from your village who opposed me. My will is all that matters. And yet you stand there worrying about a pot of rendering? Now come with me!"

Serug tugged Athaliah across the village until they stood directly in front of a middle-aged couple. "Is this your daughter?"

The man bobbed his head. His hand flew up as if making an oath. "You have conquered us, to be sure, but you can't take that one. There are plenty to choose from if you look around."

"By the gods! Who are you to give orders? I choose whom I take and whom I leave. I have decided to take this one, and so I shall."

The woman grunted, a strange, twisted chuckle. "To your peril."

Serug snorted. "You're animals. I could slaughter you for our next meal." He looked at the girl and shrugged. "Besides, why should she be so important? She is nothing to look at and stupid as a post. Why offer me another?"

"She knows the gods, and they know her." She fixed her gaze on Serug. "Besides, she is very obedient. Yes, you will find that out. She is very obedient."

The man sniffed, wiping a filthy hand across his face, a glint in his eye.

"That is exactly what I want. Come, girl. I want you to meet someone before we go."

Neb appraised the young woman in front of him with a slow gaze. He tilted his head and stared, while she kept her face downcast, sweeping her eyes side to side almost as if she were looking for something. "You sure you want this one?"

Serug pursed his lips in annoyance. It had been Neb who had suggested he attack this clan in the first place. He said he'd find a wife. Now he had done so, and Neb questioned his choice. Hot irritation churned his stomach. "Yes, I am certain. Her parents vow that she is very obedient."

Neb looked her over one last time. "I wonder who she obeys."

Serug squeezed his eyes shut. He had done everything his father had wanted and had even obtained the prize of the village, and Neb still questioned his choice. "She will obey me, and we will have many sons."

A rustling sound turned his attention. Several men ran toward Serug. "We've been followed. Scouts say that there are enough men to overwhelm us. We must flee!"

Another runner called out. "The enemy comes!"

Neb gripped Serug's shoulder. "I thought you won your last battle."

"I did. It must be another clan from the hills. Others have heard of us and want revenge or to take prizes." Serug squared his shoulders. "I'll gather my men and put them to flight."

"Are you sure that's wise?"

The runners, along with several warriors, jogged forward.

"Begging your forgiveness, Serug, but you haven't seen what's coming. They're too many. We must flee."

To his amazement, Athaliah took a step nearer and whispered into Serug's ear. He stepped back and looked at the frail girl with appraising eyes. "Yes, I meant what I said. You'll be my wife and the mother of my sons."

Athaliah peered at the horizon, which lay dull in the afternoon light, overcast by a blanket of gray clouds. "The land has been dry of late, and we stand on the crest of a hill. Set fire to the bushes, and no one will be able to pass through. When the wind rises, it will carry the fire away. When the rain comes, there will be no enemy left."

In shock, Serug swiveled his gaze from the girl to his father.

Neb's eyes gleamed, and a smile played upon his lips.

As if in a dream, Serug nodded and gave the order.

The men ran to fulfill the command.

The enemy fled from the flames, and that night, Serug took Athaliah for his wife.

~~~
~~~

Neb accepted Athaliah as his daughter. In this mysterious child, he found a kindred spirit. She knew the gods, and the gods knew her, but she was not like the sorceress or even like his frantically driven mother. No one knew her thoughts, and though she appeared to be completely subservient, her obedience came at a price, for she knew how to threaten without appearing to do so.

Serug was clearly pleased with Athaliah, for she did his every bidding, but he, too, learned that she wanted to be left alone at times. He learned to respect those times, for she held sway over the whole clan.

When she presented him with the news that she was carrying a child, Serug grew proud beyond words and announced to Neb that he would have a grandson.

Neb stared at his second son with a bitter grin. "How do you know it will be a boy? Or more to the point, that it will be the boy that you want?"

Serug appeared positively bewildered. "I know the mother."

At this, Neb's laughter burst like floodwaters over swollen banks. "Yes, true. You know the mother. May the gods save you!"

Serug avoided his father after this and saw to the comfort of his wife.

Athaliah would no longer do menial labor, and her decision was accepted without comment. Other women saw to their daily care.

When the birthing time came, Athaliah called for two old women whom she had befriended, and they alone cared for her.

Every time Serug came to see what was happening, he was told he could not cross the threshold. For three days, he paced and waited, mumbling impotently.

By the third day, Neb became impatient too. He

marched to the hut, but as he approached, three women stepped from the dwelling.

In the middle, Athaliah held a small bundle and strode purposefully to the center of the village. She stopped in front of the communal fire pit, which glowed with smoldering embers. She spoke aside to one of the women, and soon there was a great haste and bustling throughout the village.

Athaliah stood tall and spoke in a commanding tone, demanding obedience. "No one shall touch this child until he has been consecrated to the gods."

Bewildered, Serug's face flushed red and his fury mounted. "I'll see my child first!" He pounded forward.

Athaliah shook her head. "One step nearer, and you'll die before the sun sets!"

Serug froze. His glare rotated from his wife to the surrounding villagers who had gathered to see the spectacle. He dropped his voice low, almost to a whine. "Why? Is it wrong for the father to look upon his own child?"

"There is no doubt whom this child belongs to. I will make sure of that."

Young men and children threw kindling on the fire, which grew in proportion to their exertions. Embers were fanned into flames, and the children backed away while the men continued to feed the orange glow.

Athaliah lifted her hand and murmured in a strange voice.

A distant rumble answered.

Villagers glanced around, eyes wide, faces twitching with nervous fear.

Finally, the fire grew so hot and bright that it lit up the evening as if the sun had never set.

Neb approached Athaliah and laid his hand on her shoulder.

Serug frowned but did not move.

Cradling the baby, Athaliah swayed like a dancer around the flames—first in one direction, then in another.

Neb watched her in silence.

Serug's mouth fell open, but he said nothing.

The villagers closed in, watching, wary and nervous.

Finally, Athaliah halted and carefully unwrapped the child, letting the ornamented blanket drop to the ground. She took ahold of the infant and held him high for all to see and called out, "He belongs to the gods and will bring many to serve."

Serug reached for his son, but Neb was closer, and he took the babe in his arms. Serug's arms fell to his sides.

Athaliah's eyes roved from Serug to Neb. "What shall his name be?"

In a flash of insight, Serug knew the truth. The word fell from his mouth like a flaming arrow from the sky. "Neb."

Athaliah nodded in acceptance, took the baby from Neb's arms, and wrapped the little one in a blanket. "So it will be." She carried the baby back to her hut.

As the villagers dispersed to their evening duties, Serug stared at his father. It was only too obvious whom the child resembled.

Standing alone before the flames, Neb grinned.

~~~

Serug watched Young Neb grow with mixed pride, for though the child neither looked nor acted like him, he could not find fault with the boy. Whenever he attempted to challenge his son as his father had challenged him, Young Neb would astonish him with his quick wit and curious agility.
~~~

Neb, though weaker with age, was still strong enough to carry his thick bearskin in both his arms and place it on the boy one chilly evening. He arranged the enormous fur about the child's shoulders and took a step back to survey the effect.

The boy sat dwarfed in the great fur, but he clasped the edges with his two hands and pulled it around him as if in a tight embrace. His fingers slid over the soft fur in a happy caress.

Neb watched the child, surveyed the gathered clansmen, and then spoke loud and clear. "Listen, my people, I declare that all gifts bestowed on me shall be given to Young Neb and that when it is his time to serve, you will follow him faithfully. I have seen a new land in a vision. You will depart from these woodlands to live by a mighty river. Your greatness will not be measured."

He reached down and clasped Young Neb's shoulder. "I bestow the mighty spirit of the bear on you. Worship the gods, especially the god of horns, which Athaliah has made known to you. If you obey, you shall prosper. If you do not, a curse will fall—"

Suddenly, a great crack sounded, and a tree limb broke free and began its weighty decent from the upper boughs, crashing and tumbling.

Like a message from the night sky, it landed in front of the gaping crowd. It was so large that villagers scampered out of the way lest they be crushed by the fall.

Neb stood silenced.

Serug stared wide-eyed and in shock.

But Young Neb strode up to the massive limb and tugged at it while the clan watched and wondered.

Using his sinewy strength, the boy angled the broken branch until it lay inside the ring of fire. The cracked wood caught quickly, and the fire flared to new life.

Neb grinned. He had forgotten what he was going to

say, but it did not matter now. He motioned for his people to commence their evening meal. The future was set. Neb could pass away, and his spirit would live on. He would never really die.

~~~

Serug watched the clan turn to their evening food and drink. His father had undoubtedly prophesied correctly. In time, he would lead his people to a Great River. But he also wondered how long he would rule before Young Neb felt the need to take over. He had heard the whispered stories of how his own grandfather Hezeki had been relieved of his rule. As he stood staring into the flames, Serug pondered just how much like his grandfather Young Neb would be.
~~~

CHAPTER FIFTY-FOUR

—NEB'S VILLAGE—

I WILL DO AS YOU DID

Neb labored to breathe. He did not want to die—not like this. He looked wildly about for anything that might end his torment. He tried to call out, but no one could hear his whispered voice. It was late at night, and Serug slept deeply in his own dwelling some distance away.

Athaliah lived in another dwelling, near her god.

He looked wildly around for Young Neb, knowing that the boy would see to his needs. Then, Neb remembered that he had ordered the young man to kill the largest animal he could find and to bring home its skin. Young Neb had dutifully sharpened his blade and set off. Now Neb regretted his command—for it might have been his last.

~~~

Young Neb lay exhausted and sweating from his prolonged exertions. He had awoken in the dead of night with the yowl of a cat in his ears. He raised himself just enough to place his blade and his spear into a good position for the expected fight.

As she circled nearer, he watched until she came just close enough for him to get proper aim. He threw his spear with all his might into her side and then pounced, stabbing her repeatedly.

Even wounded, she was a fierce opponent. She whirled around and scratched and bit, but Young Neb, almost as
~~~

quick as a cat, fought just as fiercely. In glowing pride, he knew he would have scars to remember this adventure. But when the glorious animal finally fell, and he watched the light from her angry, tormented eyes slowly fade away; he choked in bitterness. In grief and pity, Young Neb cried.

~~~

Neb tried to sit up, but the effort sent stabs of pain through his chest. In desperation, he yelled for help, but only a croaking sound met his ears.

He leaned back. Panic would only make the situation worse. He took long, shallow breaths to settle his confused brain. As he lay in the dark, images of his life swirled before him.

His mother carefully covering him with a blanket on a cold night and kissing his forehead with her determined, proud stare as she told him that he must rule. The injured expression when she realized that Neb no longer needed her. Her contorted face on the night she died. He saw her toss the poisoned water skin away. With surprise, Neb realized that he had not killed his mother.

Neb blinked away the visions. He shifted his weight, but his action was arrested for now his father floated before him…his contemptuous expression when he cornered the old man in the weaver's dwelling. He felt the knife plunge and the blood seep. He saw his father's fury—and grief—deep behind the old man's eyes.

Neb jerked himself higher to breathe better.

Now Uzal cursed him.

Neb choked as he laughed at this image. "You can do me no harm, you forsaken ghost! I have accomplished my ends. I have a son's son—exactly like me, and I will live
~~~

into eternity."

But the boast was cut short by the image of Leah at his side. Together in a gentle embrace, with Leah's head resting on her father's shoulder.

Neb stared. He reached out.

Leah met his gaze. "Repent."

Nauseating confusion swept over Neb. Repent? He was Neb the Great, and he would live forever.

The vision melted into the night air.

He lay back and tried to breathe. He had lived as he wished.

He would die as he wished.

~~~

Serug stepped into his father's hut as the sun crested the horizon and peeked between the trees.

Sweat beaded Neb's forehead as he panted for each labored breath.

Crouching beside the old man, Serug reached for his father's hands. They were thin and cold. "What can I do for you, Father?"

Neb rested his eyes on his son. "Get me the black vial from my shelf." His hand shook as he pointed to the only shelf in the dismal dwelling. A water skin and braided basket with a few dried viands lay on one side. Alone by itself, stood a small black vial.

Serug grabbed the vial and pulled out the stopper. He wrinkled his nose. He looked upon his father's contorted face and shook his head. No, he would not ease the old man's passage.

Serug put the vial back, knelt by his father, and clasped the shaking hands. "I cannot see any vial, Father."
~~~

Neb's eyes widened, in comprehension or disbelief, Serug could not say. It did not matter.

"I'll get fresh water."

Serug knew it was only a matter of a few moments more. He would not call for help, nor would he get water. As if it were any ordinary day, he strode away from his father's dwelling as fast as he could.

~~~

Young Neb returned to the village early with the cat skin over his shoulders. He rushed into Neb's dwelling and heard the labored breathing. Crouching beside Neb, he pulled the skin close.

"Grandfather, I've brought the greatest cat skin ever seen by man."

Neb struggled to sit up.

Young Neb eased his grandfather into a sitting position.

Neb looked the boy over, but his face stayed hidden in shadows. "Come closer and let me feel the skin."

The boy placed it in his grandfather's shaking hands.

Neb caressed the fur, stroking it in a gentle rhythm. He leaned forward. "Bury me in this."

Irritation and indignation plucked Young Neb's nerves. Bury a dead body in this treasure? One he had risked his life to earn? He scowled at the sweating, shriveled old man. "How did you bury your father?" His question amused him, as he knew the answer. "I will do just as you did."

Neb clutched his chest. "I must be buried with honor so that everyone knows—" He clutched the boy's tunic. "Save me!"

The youth reached down and peeled Neb's hand off
~~~

him, prying one finger loose at a time. "Save you from yourself? Too late, I think."

Neb gurgled a single word. "Vial."

Young Neb followed the old man's gaze. He took the vial from the shelf, looked it over curiously, and then crouched near the dying man. "You don't want to die like a poisoned dog or an unwanted baby, do you?" He shook his head in disbelief, not feeling a bit of grief. "No, that's not right. You should die like your father or like a man in battle. Bravely enduring all."

Slowly he reached inside his tunic and withdrew his blade.

Horror filled Neb's eyes. He squirmed as his gaze connected with Young Neb's.

A shaft of light slanted across the room.

With the last of his strength, Neb clasped Young Neb's hands in his, and, as he plunged the knife into his own heart, he whispered, "We will be together—forever."

Young Neb felt the blood seep over his fingers. He had not intended to kill the old man, but in some strange way, it made sense. He dropped his head onto Neb's lap, and for the last time in his life, he wept.

Chapter Fifty-Five

-Planet Sectine-

Get Your Orders In Order

Teal nearly collapsed under the weight of fresh insight. Evil was not an idea. It was alive. A living presence that inhabited a soul in much the way he took on the face and form of the race he studied. Except, he only pretended to be something he was not, while evil absorbed its host with absolute destruction.

Tcesni's eyes twinkled in sly mockery, her long shimmering dress molded to the shape of her dangerous body. "Humans annihilate their own family members. Doesn't say much for their self-preservation, does it?"

Teal refused to be baited into a debate on human merits and demerits. "Considering the fact that your citizens fear you to the point of rebellion, I'd say, you have a lot to learn as well."

Tcesni swiveled and slapped the wall next to her plush, oval bed. "I brought you to my inner sanctum with the understanding that you were open to new experiences. I didn't realize that you only care—"

Teal morphed into a Uanyi version of himself—soft, rubbery exoskeleton; huge eyes; long neck; and a striking pattern of green and orange stripes running over his body, though he still wore, incongruously, the human-styled tunic and leggings.

The riotous result forced Tcesni back a step, one hand covering her laughter.

Teal advanced. "You were saying something about new experiences?"

One arm above her head, Tcesni curved her body in languid repose. She beckoned the Luxonian forward. "Discover what I have to offer before you waste your life on a race that can never satisfy your desires."

Teal closed in, his Uanyi breathing helm humming. "What desires would those be?"

Once within touching range, Tcesni slid her hand down Teal's chest and then withdrew her hand, smirked, and ripped her dress at the shoulder. She faced the door, screamed, and sprawled to the floor in a dramatic heap.

The door slid aside.

Teal whirled around to face five well-armed Uanyi pointing their Dustbusters directly at him. He chuckled.

~~~

Ark plodded the last paces to the largest Uanyi prison on the planet and couldn't believe his luck. He always wanted to be a thief, and now he had the chance to steal the biggest prize this side of the Divide.

Zuri tapped his arm. "You'll have to brace yourself. This could get tricky."

Ark frowned. "You know how to open the cell door, don't you?"

"I know how to blow a hole through it, but that doesn't—"

With a harrumph, Ark shoved Zuri aside. "Let me go ahead. Intelligence, not explosives, is what we need now."

Zuri shook his head. "Why can't we use both?"

"Because your explosives would likely—" He waved a tentacle. "Never mind. Just watch. And learn."

~~~

Zuri sneered at the five Uanyi guards standing outside cell 36475B, two on each side of the main door, one pacing in front.

Ark waddled up, thrust out a datapad, and snorted through his breathing helm. “Cresta Representative acting as Diplomatic Interventionist in the case of the Luxonian named—”

The front guard lowered his Dustbuster and aimed at Ark’s middle. “Tcesni allows no visitors or representatives.”

His voice taking on a pleading tone, Ark wiggled the datapad in the guard’s face. “Just take a look. Please?”

The guard lowered his weapon, snatched the datapad, scrolled through, frowned…and then glanced aside at the other guards. With matching scowls, they crowded closer and peered at the datapad. After scrolling through several times, the main guard shook his head. “Could be a fake.”

Ark shrugged. “Except you know it isn’t.” He hummed low. “Quite a queen you have, an actress with definite histrionic talent. Too bad she plays her own people.” With a nod at Zuri, he made formal introductions. “Zuri, our Ingot Representative, has been kind enough to make this information available to Universal News—*Queen attempts to frame Luxonian representative so as to steal Earth’s rights.* Should be making headlines about…”

The main guard stepped forward and met his gaze. “Due process of law. That’s our job.”

Zuri nodded with a grin. “That’s what I was hoping.” He slapped a wad of goo on the door and jumped back.

Ark skedaddled behind him while the guards leaped to the sidelines.

A thunderous boom spewed rock and metal.

Teal, in his human form, stepped through the resulting hole in the door. “Good thing I knew your plan would involve explosives, or I'd be dead right now."

Ark heaved a ragged sigh. "We'd better make haste before this entire planet explodes."

The guards rose to their feet dusting themselves off.

Zuri nodded in their direction. "Don't feel too bad. My planet is going through a revolution too. Seems to be the fashion these days." He pointed down the hall. "My ship is parked at a local docking bay. Not far. We're all set, and Tcesni's plans are quite upset. A good day's work, I'd say."

Teal stepped between Ark and Zuri as they sped through the main doorway into the light of day. Sirens blared and bustling interventionists swirled through the sky.

With a decisive nod, Zuri squared his shoulders. "Now, let's find out what humanity has been up to."

–OldEarth–

Zuri kissed Kelesta with more passion than he knew he had. His arms embraced her, his whole body aching to—

Six meters away, Ark cleared his throat, sending frothy bubbles to the surface of his breathing helm.

Kelesta pulled back, tossed an eye grenade at Ark, and then met Zuri's silent plea. "I will come back. As soon as possible."

Zuri gently caressed her face. "I don't want you torn in two—I know how close you are to your mother."

With a shrug, Kelesta broke from his embrace, her hand still holding his, and strolled toward Ark. "And my sisters…but that doesn't mean that I should stay at home. It only means that I have something to carry with me when I travel into the wider universe."

Zuri's gaze rose to the horizon. "The universe needs Bhuaci wisdom."

Ark snorted. "Bhuaci need Bhuaci wisdom. Just like Crestas need science, Ingots need technology, and Luxonians need—"

A flash of light and Teal stepped forward. "We need what?"

Ark sniffed. "To stop appearing out of thin air!"

Frowning, Zuri waved between himself and Kelesta. "Mind if we have a moment?"

"You're over your limit." Ark plodded forward, stopped in front of Kelesta, took her soft hand in two of his tentacles, and patted it like a father sending off his first pod. "Be good and get your orders in order. Helm has always needed a strong representative who's not afraid to venture beyond the horizon." He glanced aside. "Don't worry. Zuri will behave himself, and Earth isn't going anywhere."

Teal stepped forward and peered into her eyes. "We'll all be waiting."

Kelesta met each gaze, finally landing on Zuri. Staring into the sky, she lifted her hands above her head, morphed into a huge bluebird, and soared toward the horizon.

Ark huffed. "I wish I could do that." He turned and faced Zuri. "Though, why you didn't just meet at the ship—"

Brushing around Ark, Zuri marched to Teal, his hands clenched. "Are you sure Earth isn't going anywhere?"

Teal sighed. "It may go dark, but it won't actually move."

Ark tapped Zuri's shoulder. "No…it's you and I that are going somewhere."

Teal frowned, and Zuri scowled at Ark.

"I just received new instructions. Our work here is almost done. You've been made Conduit to the Board of

Directors, and Cresta's leading scientists—the Ingal, no less—have made me the official diplomat…to Ingilium."

CHAPTER FIFTY-SIX

—GRASS LANDS—

I KEEP WHAT IS MINE

Serug trailed along behind, watching Young Neb move swiftly and confidently through the tall grasses. Apparently, the man knew exactly where he was going—heading directly east. They had reached the edge of the woodlands several days ago. Now they were pushing their way through a forest of tall grasses, and because it was such an open land, Serug felt exposed. He wanted to move closer to the woodlands, but Neb disagreed.

The sky grew overcast, and a misty rain fell.

Serug plodded along silently for some time, his heart heavy, and his mind almost numb, but suddenly he stopped.

Athaliah, walking behind, ran into him. "Chaaa!"

Serug wrinkled his brows. Why were they making this trip? Why was Neb leading the way? Why did he allow everyone to direct his life? Was he not the leader? Had he given over control of his clan? No!

He had done no such thing, and yet it had been assumed that Neb had some special right to set their direction after Old Neb had died.

Serug told his wife to step back. He would not allow anyone to usurp his role or go to an open land where they knew nothing of the people that occupied it. The vision of a great lake was just one more of his father's devious maneuvers to get others to do his will. But Old Neb was dead and buried. Serug had made a big ceremony of the final burial so that all could see the cold, still body being swallowed by the still earth.

There could be no doubt in anyone's mind that Neb the Great was dead and gone. He would never rule the living again. Still, he had to give some recognition to the passing of such a man, so he had allowed Athaliah to pronounce that the old man had become one with her gods. Everyone seemed pleased.

But now Neb marched ahead at a quick pace, assuming leadership.

Rage filled Serug. He stomped to the head of the line.

With a nod to his father, Neb waited, tapping his hand against his thigh.

Serug stalked forward. "I will lead my people into the low hills." He pointed northward. "There are caves and shelters, trees, and plenty of animals. We do not know what we will find out here, other than snakes, tall grass, and strong winds."

Neb tilted his head to the side, a light shade of green sparkled in his eyes. His lips parted, and his tongue circled around as if he could taste a decision. His eyebrows rose, and he lifted his hand. "We will head toward the north hills. It is your wish, therefore, it is my wish."

Serug grunted. Things were not quite right. Placing his hand on Neb's shoulder, he led him aside. "It's best that all commands come from me so that people will not get confused. I know your grandfather led you to expect leadership in his lifetime, but I'm still here." He forced a laugh, lifting his arms. "You see? I will have wit and strength for many years to come."

Neb said nothing. He strode to the head of the line and made a forward motion.

The entire clan looked between the two men and stayed in place. Neb marched forward.

Serug called out. "Come, we head to the hills." When he came alongside, he looked at the young man from the corner of his eye.

Neb stared straight ahead.

Not for the first time, Serug wondered who ruled.

—WESTERN LANDS—

Neb felt distinctly displeased. Of the many differences between Serug and himself, Neb would never accept a woman influenced by anyone else. Only on a long expedition far from home might he find someone of value.

Serug, secure now in his role, teased the young man. "Go on. Take some men and have a good hunt. I'll be here waiting for you. Come back with more men than you take, and I'll be impressed!"

Neb found a cave-dwelling clan high in the western hills, and he circled around for a day until he could spy out the perfect advantage. His men were skilled, and Neb the Great had taught him well.

The battle ended quickly, and Neb was very pleased. He considered his new slaves and decided his next move.

In the months ahead, Neb traveled from one small clan to another, taking what slaves he wished. Everyone who heard reports of him feared his approach, and battles ended almost before they began.

After he and his men had taken their rest in a forest at the foot of the mountain, Neb decided that he would wait no longer for a wife.

Stories of an ancient western community described the most beautiful women in the world, also thought to be the most intelligent.

He traveled west, leaving most of his men to make their way back to Serug's village with the new slaves.

The western lands undulated in verdant slopes near an enormous river, and everywhere farms and villages flourished, but Neb was not interested in their agriculture.

He marched into the middle of the largest town and found a marketplace. Men, women, and children carrying large wicker baskets crowded around stalls piled with foodstuff, spices, ornate decorations, and tools. His men strolled about idly, eyeing the foreign foodstuffs and ornate weapons.

In the central avenue, a chattering crowd gathered.

Neb elbowed his way forward.

A tall stone structure with steps leading steeply up the side dominated the square. Carvings of men and beasts guarded the walls and doorways. Paintings etched into the walls portrayed figures telling amazing stories for those who had time to stay and decipher them.

A procession of beautiful women and girls carrying food baskets strolled forward. They wore clothes of rich, varied colors and were covered from shoulders to ankles, the material swaying and billowing with every movement. Exotic, with their eyes outlined in black, they appeared glorious and modest.

Neb stood transfixed.

The last girl in line stepped on the garment of the girl in front of her and tripped. She fell forward, tipping her basket. The rich food spilled to the ground.

A large, burly man rushed over as the food splattered, and he struck the girl across the face.

She cringed and cried out.

Neb leaped forward and blocked the man from striking again.

The guard snarled and raised his hand to Neb.

Neb didn't pause. Instead, he bore down on the shorter man. "If you don't want her, I'll take her."

The guard gaped, confusion replacing fury. He hesitated in the face of Neb's calm, authoritative assurance. "Who are you to give orders to a man of the royal house?"

The crowd jostled nearer, eager to watch this interesting exchange.

"I am Son of Serug of the mountains and Grandson of Neb the Great, spirit of the nether world."

Fear rippled over the servant's face. He stepped back. "Do not lay your wrath on my shoulders. I only do what I'm ordered. Speak to my master about this worthless one." He smacked the young woman's arm.

Shifting her glance from Neb to the servant, the girl lifted her chin in defiance. "It is forbidden to strike a maiden. Let me go. The procession is late, and if you leave the gods to wait any longer, another sacrifice will be demanded."

The servant's eyes widened in fearful comprehension. With a dismissive thrust, he shoved the girl in Neb's direction. "Take her and go, or I'll pronounce this ill-fated delay as the doing of your foreign god!"

After the servant shouted a series of commands, the line of maidens moved on, and the crowd jostled forward.

Satisfied, Neb retreated with the girl across the mountain pass, toward home.

Settling down in the evening in a peaceful grove of olive trees, Neb considered his newest prize. The girl with black hair, large almond-shaped eyes, a generous figure, and a humble demeanor pleased Neb's sensibilities. "What are you called?"

"My name is Hagia."

"You don't struggle against your fate, Hagia. You never look back. Do you hope for a new future or simply hate your past?"

Hagia wrapped her mantle tighter around her shoulders. "Both."

Neb started a fire and then stood next to her. He reached out and stroked her long, thick hair. "Tell me about your people and your life at the temple."

Bowed by the weight of Neb's hand, Hagia leaned forward. "I know little about my people, for I was given to the gods as a child. Most of my life was spent in the compound around the temple. Only recently, I was moved into the house of the maidens, and there I was taught to cook and serve meals."

Hagia peered at her hands, and a frown puckered between her eyebrows. "I am not very graceful, though I did my best." She shrugged in resignation. "I did not please those who oversaw my work, however. My cooking was good, but I didn't move quickly or gracefully, and I . . ." She faltered. "I was told that if I was not equal to the tasks assigned, I could offer myself to the gods in a way that would not fail." She peered up at Neb as darkness fell. "After my last mistake, I would've been moved to another house, and though it is not difficult to live there, no one stays for long."

Neb offered one of his silent nods. Then he walked toward the fire, quiet and thoughtful. "I will never offer you to the gods. You are mine. I keep what is mine."

Hagia stifled a sniffle. "I will serve you well." A hint of a smile appeared on her face. "Perhaps I will give you many sons."

At this, Neb quailed with the first true horror he had ever felt. "The one thing you must never do is give me a son!"

CHAPTER FIFTY-SEVEN

—ISHTAR'S VILLAGE—

I SURPRISED EVERYONE

Ishtar's shoulders slumped as he exhaled a deep breath. He looked over at Amin and Gizah and lifted his hands in surrender. "That is the fertile soil from which I sprang."

The sun radiated pink and yellow from the eastern horizon, heralding the beginning of a new day.

Amin stretched and peered intently at his father. "I feel as if I have seen the youth of my ancestors before they became aged and the stuff of burial mounds. When you speak, I realize how relentless is the passing of time."

Gizah laughed as she attempted to stand up. "Dreams of the future—not the past—are what I need right now." She raised her hand in a silent plea.

Amin pulled her to standing, and the two met Ishtar's gaze.

Ishtar returned their smiles. "I, too, am in need of dreams, for in reviewing history, my heart has grown heavy with forgotten grief." He stepped toward his hut, then stopped and looked over his shoulder. "I'm not the man my father feared, nor am I the man my grandfather hoped for." He chuckled as he shuffled to bed. "I surprised everyone."

CHAPTER FIFTY-EIGHT

—OBED'S VILLAGE—

THE WISE AND THE FOOLISH

Eoban stopped on the edge of the village and blocked the sun with his hand for a good view. Even though it was a clear day, it felt cold—colder than he had ever known.

Obed sat hunched and wrapped in blankets outside his hut. It was odd that Obed had ended up being the infirm one. With his brilliant mind, he was the last one Eoban would have thought would end up helpless. Yet here he was, an old man spending his last days on his pallet.

Eoban rubbed his chin.

Jonas stepped outside her hut, as beautiful as ever.

A lump rose to Eoban's throat.

Obed was not Onias, but he had managed to be a good husband and father despite his abundant failings. He had raised Tobia and Onia into manhood, and they were both strong, well able to care for the clan. Onia had become the traveler, while Tobia took care of all their domestic concerns. It had worked out well.

Eoban chewed his lip and considered Obed again.

Obed's hair, nearly white, framed his sharp-featured face, and his body, though never robust, had shrunk. Time would not stop even for a moment to let a man catch his breath.

Eoban attempted to saunter to Obed's pallet in the sun, but his uneven gate would not deceive even the youngest member of the clan. He would never saunter again. Still, he could tease. "You have enough blankets to make a bear jealous, my friend."

Obed lifted his head and worked his jaw in an

exaggerated fashion as if preparing for a truly devastating response. He beckoned Eoban closer.

Eoban crouched on his haunches and peered at Obed's face.

Obed tapped Eoban's arm. "No creature alive could be jealous of an old man like me. But you now . . . that's another story!"

Eoban blinked, trying to discern Obed's meaning. He dismissed his confusion with a wave. "Speaking of stories, have you heard about Ishtar's great tale? I heard so many reports that I had to go myself. I learned things I'd never known. "He grinned. "And I thought I knew everything."

Obed nodded, eager, with a glint of fire in his eyes. "Yes, Tobia went too, and he gave me many reports. Even Jonas was eager to hear all. In the evening, everyone shared their memories."

Eoban grinned. "I'd like to see everyone gathered together again. We should invite Ishtar—not to tell of Neb the Great—but to talk about how things were, how they are, and what the future might hold."

Eager joy grew in Obed's eyes. "Yes! Ask Barak and Lud…" He looked at the sky and pointed. "See those clouds sweeping across the sky? Aram once said that life is like a cloud, vaporous and changing—here today and gone tomorrow." He dropped his gaze and wrapped his blanket tighter around his shoulders. "It's when faced with our end that a man really thinks. Then he rejoices—or regrets—much."

Eoban sat and stretched his legs. "I suppose we all do."

Two men strode toward Obed.

Eoban nudged Obed. "Grow young again, for great minds think alike. Here comes our past to visit with us a while."

Ishtar and Barak chatted as they walked together.

Ishtar glanced up and met Eoban's gaze. "I thought I'd find you two together. Word has it that Obed has decided to travel again, and he is putting you in charge while he's gone."

Eoban laughed. "By the sky above, I will not let him go anywhere without me for fear of that very thing. If he wants to wander, he'll find me at his heels!"

Obed managed to straighten, though the effort had cost him. Sweat beaded on his forehead "Where I go next, you must not follow too soon. Ishtar spoke truly. I'm leaving the clan in your hands, though my sons will see to the clan's daily cares. All I ask is that you guide them with your wisdom."

Stricken, Eoban felt his heart clench.

Ishtar knelt at Obed's side. "I'm sorry, I was only—"

Obed waved Ishtar's apology away. "Word has reached us of your epic story, Ishtar, and we want to celebrate. Let all three clans gather with a feast the like of which we've never had before."

Eoban slapped Barak on the back. "Like old times, eh? We'll sing! You can retell your tale about the great cat hunt and how your clan migrated to the Great Lake, for those who've not heard the stories of Aram's courage and your bold adventure." He winked. "We can teach the younger generation about the wise and the foolish."

Ishtar nodded as Tobia joined the group. "Yes, we have many stories that the young people have not heard—about Onias and Jael, Pele and her heroic journey, and the Sky Warrior who led her. The young must share our legacies of honesty and courage."

Eoban rose to his feet, lifted his arms, and shouted in proclamation, "And so it shall be. A great feast of merriment and memories…and lots of food!"

CHAPTER FIFTY-NINE

—ISHTAR'S VILLAGE—

UNTIL THE END

Ishtar rejoiced as the moon sailed across the sky, and the entire clan enjoyed good wine, red meat, and plenty of stories. By dawn, everyone had laughed and cried to their hearts' content.

Jonas retold episodes of Onias' life, and tears filled many eyes. Young men discovered new fortitude as Barak described Aram and his journey from the forest into the lake land. Milkan described how Eymard, though ancient in years, had brought hope and faith into their world. Tobia shared stories about Jael and his valiant heart. Amin described his little brother and the gentle love of a child who would not forget his father or abandon his brother. Lud shared stories of Pele and the Warrior Spirit so clearly that there were many who glanced about in wonderment. Eoban spoke of the friends he had met on his many adventures, while Obed related his journey from doubt to faith.

As the sun crested the horizon, hearts and minds were filled, and many wandered off for a short rest before the new day began in earnest.

Obed stretched, peering at Eoban out of the corner of his eye. "So, was the night what you hoped for?"

Eoban nodded. "More than I expected. I'm so tired; I won't tell another story for a long time."

Obed snorted.

Shades of pink and blue stretched over the horizon.

Eoban nudged Obed as he pointed toward the rising sun. "Remember how Aram wished he'd had more time? Well, we have today—and it is a good day."

Obed staggered to his feet.

Ishtar stood aside, frowning.

"What's the matter? You look worried."

"Nothing. I just haven't seen Amin for some time. I hope he's all right. It may have been hard—remembering Caleb."

Shrugging off Ishtar's concern, Eoban scanned the village. "Probably just exhausted. Half the clan has gone to bed."

Ishtar smiled. "It was like living many lifetimes in one night."

Nudging Obed, Eoban grinned. "You should've seen Rula's face when I described Gimesh. She liked that story very much!"

A distant yell turned their attention.

Amin ran across the village, waving. "Father! I have a son!"

Heart-throbbing joy filled Ishtar. He blinked back tears. "Gizah—"

"She delivered a son—your grandson."

Eoban clapped Ishtar on the shoulder. "Good news, indeed! Another warrior for our people."

Ishtar raised his hand in an oath. "Not a warrior! He'll be—"

Rising commotion arrested their attention. The four men turned.

Barak jogged into the village.

Eoban ran toward him, and they met, talking and gesturing excitedly.

Ishtar waited with Amin, but when Eoban and Barak turned and jogged away, he pointed toward Amin's hut. "Let's see the new babe."

Once outside the doorway, Milkan intercepted them. "Jonas says that Gizah needs rest, and the baby is sleeping.

Come back at noon." She grinned and patted Amin's shoulder. "You'll have many years to enjoy your son, give them a little time now."

Amin glanced at his father, his face drawn with disappointment.

Ishtar patted his shoulder in sympathy. "When it comes to birth, the women rule."

In a spirit of bravado, Amin called to Obed. "Come, join Father and me. Let's find something to eat and get some rest."

Obed shuffled forward, pointing to the horizon. "Eoban and Barak don't need rest. They run about like little boys!"

Amin grinned sheepishly. "If I know Jonas, she'll have jobs enough for us all. Don't worry. They won't escape. Let's go while we still can."

His back aching, Ishtar envisioned a soft bed, but the sight of Eoban and Barak hurrying back into the village and grinning like fools, threw his thoughts into confusion. "What? More stories to tell?"

Skidding to an abrupt halt before his friends, Eoban huffed his words. "You'll—never—guess."

Ishtar and Amin stared while Obed snorted. "Probably not."

Eoban threw back his shoulders like a flustered hen. "Ishtar, Amin, call your best men." He glanced around. "We need Tobia and Onia too. We must have a council meeting as soon as possible."

Ishtar glanced toward Amin's hut, anxiety replacing his exhaustion. "Why? What's happened?"

A baby squalled.

Jonas stepped outside and smiled at the men. She strolled toward them, her smile fading with each step. "I just wanted to assure you that mother and baby are fine, but you look—"

Amin lifted his hand. "Eoban says there is news." He stared at Barak. "Hurry and tell us what's happened!"

Jonas eyed Eoban, her frown deepening.

Eoban hesitated.

Barak stepped forward. "A new clan has arrived!"

Jonas gasped, her eyes wide with fear.

Amin started toward his hut, but Ishtar gripped his arm. "Wait."

Barak crossed his arms. "A few of the men and I went over the lake early and watched as a large clan emerged from the forest. We signaled them, but they use a different dialect, so I brought Eoban, and they explained that warriors are pursuing them. They need our help." He glanced around. "So, what are we going to do?"

Perching his hands on his hips, Eoban scowled. "We'll assist those in need, of course! Come on, Barak. We'll get Lud, Onia, and Tobia and meet with Aram's son, Bararam, and the new clan. Ishtar, are you coming?"

Ishtar nodded. "Amin and I will follow. Just give us a chance to see the baby."

With a nod, Barak started away.

Eoban chuckled. "Like old times, eh?"

Wincing, Obed followed the others. "Just don't start singing!"

Eoban laughed as he paced at his friend's side.

After watching them stride away, Ishtar faced Jonas. "We'll leave Gizah and the babe in your care for a while longer."

Jonas smiled, though her eyes followed Barak and Eoban before they traveled back to Ishtar's face. "Yes, of course."

Ishtar glanced aside as he strode toward Amin's hut. "Have you chosen a name?"

"My son will be named Thare, for he shall know his history yet be his own man with a bright future."

Once at the hut, Ishtar sucked in a deep breath, ready to take a plunge. He stepped over the threshold. "Let's meet the next generation."

When Ishtar emerged from his son's hut, Obed stood chuckling. "And so it begins...again."

Ishtar nodded, and they joined the clan members assembling in the center of the village.

~~~

Gizah rocked her baby. She knew she should be worried, but peace filled her. Men and women gathered in council to assist the new clan, planning a proper defense, should it come to open battle.

The rest of her family and friends bustled about their evening duties, trusting the wisdom of those who had proven themselves worthy.

Resting on her bed, Gizah brushed her hair from her face and gazed at her newborn son. She could see Aram's furrowed brow and her husband's strong features in the baby's face. Sleepy now, he would one day lead the clan.

A tear slipped down her cheek in a surge of protective love and joyful triumph. Like all of humanity, this child would have to travel a steep and treacherous path. But no matter the power of evil that might assail him, goodness and strength forged by those who had come before would light the way. Aram and Ishtar proved that men could overcome their worst selves and become greater than their forebearers.

Gizah hugged her baby, remembering the daughters, sisters, wives, and mothers who had cared for their men with undying love, making the improbable possible.

Ever so gently, she rose and strolled to the open doorway.

The last rays of light lingered in a melody of hues.

She felt herself surrounded by those whose love lived
~~~

on in new generations: Aram with his protective strength, forever supporting her, Enosh, Kenan, Madai, Ishtar, Amin, Eoban, Barak, Obed, Lud, Eymard, Hul, Leah, Eva, Tamar, Hagia, Namah, Jonas, Pele…everyone who had chosen light and hope when the world had grown dark and dangerous.

She lifted her son high into the pure light and offered him—and all who came after—to the same God who had loved her into being.

God would be with her people until the end of time.

Chapter Sixty

-OldEarth-

We'll Be Here

Teal slipped a simple golden band on Sienna's finger and stared deep into her eyes.

Sienna held his gaze and smiled.

"I take it that's a yes."

"I don't normally wear jewelry—"

Holding up his own ring-clad finger, Teal shrugged. "The circle is complete without ever being finished. The matching bands announce our unbreakable bond. Besides, gold complements both blue and red."

A snort startled birds from a ground nest.

Sienna glanced aside.

Sterling paced in front of Ark on a low hill, his sharp hand-gestures signaling a depleted patience.

Before a wide-mouth cave, Zuri strolled shoulder-to-shoulder with Kelesta.

Teal sighed as he released Kelesta's hand. "We'd better let Sterling have his moment before he spontaneously combusts."

They picked their way over the uneven ground and met Sterling at the base of the hill.

Sterling faced them and stared, his mouth working in exaggerated bafflement. "What on Earth took you so long? I could've proposed marriage to half the known universe by the time you two got things settled."

Sienna laughed, clasped Sterling's arms, and kissed his cheek. "Congratulations are so common. Good of you to think of an original response."

Like an exuberant pod ready for a day at the beach, Ark skedaddled down the incline and nearly tumbled into Teal.

With far greater composure, Zuri and Kelesta ambled closer.

Using every available tentacle, Ark shook every hand. Congratulations to us! We're practically a family now. With Teal and Sienna, Zuri, and Kelesta, all Sterling and I have to do is celebrate the grandkids' birthdays!"

Choking, Teal waved spasmodically. "All in good time." He glanced at Sterling. "*You* have an announcement?"

Sterling pointed north, where Amin and Ishtar gathered with more than a hundred others on the shore of the great lake.

"There's trouble ahead, though I'm confident that Ishtar and friends can handle whatever comes." Sterling swiveled around and waved to the sky. "But that's not our real concern."

Ark mumbled. "The Mystery Race is back."

Sterling faced Ark and stared through penetrating eyes. "You know, I didn't like you at first. I believed, rather stupidly, that you weren't very perceptive." He glanced at Zuri. "And I figured that Ingots would never advance beyond their latest techno-gadget." He shrugged. "But I've been proven wrong."

Kelesta sniffed. "You didn't like me either."

Teal chewed his lip. He was grateful beyond words that Sienna maintained her dignity and didn't join in.

With a wave, Sterling beckoned to the brow of the hill overlooking the great lake.

Like chicks following a mother hen, the troop filed after Sterling and lined up on the brow of the hill.

Teal shied away. "They might see us."

Sterling jerked his thumb. "The sun is behind us. They'll wonder, but they can't see us clearly. We'll remain a mystery."

Zuri jutted his jaw forward. "What about the—?"

"They've disappeared…but before they went, they left word that this Universe has gone dark and no one but a few Luxonian Guardians may visit every ten years. They want to give humanity a chance to grow up before they turn the lights back on."

Ark snorted through his breathing helm, bubbles frothing in indignation. "Do Crestas have nothing to say about this? Or Ingots, Bhuaci, or Uanyi?"

Teal sighed. "They can say what they want, but—"

Sienna wrapped her arm around Teal's. "It's not a choice. It's fate."

Ark blubbered. "Though I'm being sent to Ingilium as a Crestonian Diplomat, I still plan on visiting Lux. Frequently! By all means, visit Earth every ten years, but you must report every detail to me as well."

Zuri frowned.

Ark slapped his friend's broad shoulder. "And Zuri, of course."

New boats floated over the lake, strong men paddling toward Ishtar, Amin, and their assembly, who turned as one to face the new challenge.

Sterling raised his hands as if in benediction. "War comes, but it also passes away. Humanity may grow stronger than the evil that plagues it." He glanced at his friends. "You know where I live. Visit often."

In a flash, he disappeared.

Tugging Kelesta's hand, Zuri nodded toward the cave where the tip of a spacecraft appeared from the rocky mouth. "We'd better go. There have been rumors about a secret alliance between Cresta and Uanyi against Ingots."

Her face pale, Kelesta whispered. "What about Helm?"

Sienna shook her head, grief in her eyes. "You'll be caught in the middle again…like always."

Ark stared at Zuri. "Helm won't be alone." With a gentle touch, he stroked Sienna's chin. "Be a brave wife and bear a son worthy of remembrance. Humanity—and Teal—need all the help they can get." He swiveled and patted Teal on the shoulder. "I want to see what you two produce. It had better be good!" With a harrumph, Ark toddled to the cave.

Kelesta hugged Sienna and Teal in turn and then followed Ark.

Zuri jerked his thumb toward the cave. "They can't go anywhere. I'm the only one who can pilot the ship." He bowed in formal leave, turned, and ran after his friends.

Thunderclouds formed on the horizon.

Teal clasped Sienna's hand and faced the lake. "The universe will grow dark, but someday humanity will see the light. We'll be here when they do."

About the Author

A. K. Frailey, an author of a historical sci-fi and science fiction series, short story collections, inspirational non-fiction books, a children's book, and a poetry collection, has been writing for over ten years and has published 17 books.

Her novels expand from the OldEarth world to the Newearth universe-where deception rules but truth prevails. Her nonfiction work focuses on the intersection of motherhood, widowhood, practicing gratitude, and rediscovering joy.

As a teacher with a degree in Elementary Education, she has taught in Milwaukee, Chicago, L. A., and WoodRiver, and was a teacher trainer in the Philippines for Peace Corps. She earned a Masters of Fine Arts Degree in Creative Writing for Entertainment from Full Sail University.

Ann homeschooled all eight of her children. She manages her rural homestead with her kids and their numerous critters. In her spare time, she serves as an election judge, a literacy tutor, and secretary/treasurer of her small town's cemetery.

www.ingramcontent.com/pod-product-compliance
Lightning Source LLC
Chambersburg PA
CBHW070612310726
48982CB00001B/56

9798986180380